The Cornish
Guest House

Emma Burstall is the author of *Gym and Slimline*, *Never Close Your Eyes* and *The Darling Girls*. After reading English at Cambridge University she was a newspaper journalist in Devon and Cornwall. She now lives in South West London with her husband and three children. *Tremarnock*, the first novel in her new series set in a delightful Cornish village, was published in 2015 and became a top-10 bestseller.

Also by Emma Burstall

Gym and Slimline
Never Close Your Eyes
The Darling Girls

Tremarnock Series

Tremarnock
Tremarnock Summer (Coming soon)

Emma Burstall

The Cornish Guest House

HEAD
of ZEUS

First published in the UK in 2016 by Head of Zeus Ltd.

This paperback edition first published in the UK in 2017
by Head of Zeus Ltd.

9 7 5 3 2 4 6 8

A catalogue record for this book is available
from the British Library.

ISBN (PB): 9781784972516
ISBN (E): 9781784972486

Typesetting: Adrian McLaughlin
Map: Amber Anderson

Printed and bound in Great Britain by
CPI Group (UK) Ltd, Croydon CR0 4YY

Head of Zeus Ltd
First Floor East
5–8 Hardwick Street
London EC1R 4RG

WWW.HEADOFZEUS.COM

*For my brother, James Burstall,
with love and thanks*

Our brothers and sisters are there with us
from the dawn of our personal stories
to the inevitable dusk.

SUSAN SCARF MERRELL

Do nothing secretly; for Time sees
and hears all things, and discloses all.

SOPHOCLES, *Hipponous, Fragment 280*

KEY

1. JACK'S COTTAGE (Loveday and Jesse's Place)
2. THE VICTORY INN
3. CHILDREN'S PLAY PARK
4. EBB TIDE (Tony's Place)
5. THE NOOK (Pat's Place)
6. DOVE COTTAGE (Liz's Place)
7. SHELL COTTAGE
8. BAG END (Valerie's Place)
9. THE METHODIST CHURCH
10. COPPER COTTAGE

11. DOLLY'S PLACE
12. DYNNARGH (Jean and Tom's Place)
13. THE STABLES
14. THE HOLE IN THE WALL PUB
15. THE FISHMONGER
16. THE MARKETPLACE
17. THE BAKERY
18. GENERAL STORE
19. BOUTIQUE SHOP
20. GULL COTTAGE (Jenny and John's Place)

Chapter One

THE RADIO CAME on at seven as usual and Hazel lay in bed, eyes closed, only half listening to the random mix of news, music and jokey banter. At moments like this, she could almost fancy herself back in the family home, when her children had still been of the age when they'd bounce up the moment they woke, not yet having morphed into grumpy teenagers.

She'd hear them messing around, laughing and shouting, sometimes wailing because one or other had overstepped the mark, so that she'd have to get up herself and pad next door to sort out the argument.

She used to grumble that they never allowed her a moment's peace, but what she'd give now to be hurrying downstairs to make them breakfast. 'Chop chop,' she'd call, 'or you'll be late for school.'

Lights on, if it was still dark outside, kettle on, the rattle of knives, forks and spoons in the cutlery drawer, the smell of toast. The kids crashing in; they always made such a racket, slurping down glasses of juice or mugs of tea, racing out again to clean teeth, put on coats and pick up bags in the hall.

'See you at three thirty!' she'd say, pausing a moment to take each precious head in turn between her two hands and plant a kiss on top. Once they'd vanished, she'd go back inside to clear up the mess of cereal, spilled milk, crumbs and sticky jam, wondering what to do for tea, thinking that she'd better get her skates on or she'd be late for work herself.

Now it was just her and her four walls. If it weren't for the radio, the silence would deafen her.

She reached for her glasses on the bedside table by the clock-radio and heaved herself up to sitting. She had been useful back then. Hadn't needed to question why she was here, what for. Her purpose had been to look after Jackie and Roy, do the right thing by them, and be a good wife to Barry, of course.

But he was gone and the children had families of their own. Even the grandchildren were grown up. Nobody needed her, not really. If she stayed in bed all day it wouldn't make a difference.

She sighed. It was no good thinking like that. No good at all. Besides, Jackie might pop in on her way back from work and she'd be horrified to find Mum in her nightclothes. She'd probably threaten to call the doctor, bring up the dreaded subject of sheltered housing, care homes, even. Heaven forbid.

Swinging her legs carefully over the side of the bed, she slid her feet into the cream-coloured slippers that were exactly where she'd left them the previous night. Then she pushed herself up, using the table to help, grabbed her dressing gown from the back of the chair and shuffled to the window that overlooked Mount Pleasant Road, opening it just a couple of inches.

She always enjoyed that first glimpse of the new day. In the old house, she'd step into the garden and sort of sniff the air. It used to make Barry laugh. He'd say she was like a dog scenting food but that wasn't what she'd been after – she'd been searching for clues.

'Clues for what?' he'd ask, feigning ignorance.

'The weather,' she'd reply, topping up the birdbath with water from an empty milk bottle. 'See if I need my brolly.

Flowers smell best before rain and if my hair frizzes up, there's a storm coming.'

They'd sold the house when the children left and since then she'd had to content herself with poking her nose out of the window. Today, she caught the faint whiff of autumn, decaying leaves and damp pavement, then a sudden gust made her shiver so she closed the window again quickly. Well, it was the beginning of October. What did you expect?

The man from a few doors down left the house in his suit and opened his car. He was staring at the pavement and didn't look up once. He was an estate agent, she knew that much. His pretty young wife had told her. Neither of them were talkers, though. Too busy with their own lives for idle chit-chat.

She watched the man drive off before padding down the narrow corridor into the little kitchen. A cuppa would sort her out. She had a hand on the tap, ready to fill the kettle, when the phone rang, nearly making her jump out of her skin.

'Whoever is it?' she wondered out loud. Hardly anyone phoned these days, only Jackie or Annie. She was a good girl, Annie, thoughtful. Nice boyfriend, too. Maybe there'd be wedding bells soon.

An announcement? Hazel's tummy fluttered, then she checked herself. Annie would be teaching one of her peculiar fitness classes, Zumba, or whatever it was called, and Jackie would be on her way to work. She'd only call in an emergency.

Frightened suddenly, Hazel hurried into the front room and picked up the receiver.

'Can I speak to Mrs Clothier, please?'

It was a man's voice, quite posh. Not Jackie, then. No crisis. Hazel felt her shoulders relax and she cleared her throat, instinctively reaching up to smooth her tousled grey-white hair.

'May I help you?' she replied, in the manner she'd once

used for wealthy ladies who came into the shop to try on the expensive leather shoes and boots. He was probably after selling something, too.

'It's Detective Constable Harry Pritchard from the Metropolitan Police,' the voice came back. 'No cause for alarm. People think we only call if someone's died or they've done something wrong. Don't worry, it's nothing like that.'

He had a nice tone, easy and friendly. Quite young. Relieved, Hazel found herself nodding, even though he couldn't see her. She was remembering when her friend Doreen had got a call to say her son had been killed in a motorbike crash. Terrible business.

'It must be difficult doing your job,' she commented, almost to herself.

'Yes, but rewarding, too. I always wanted to be in the police, ever since I was a small boy. That, or a train driver.'

He chuckled and Hazel found herself joining in. 'My son, Roy, wanted to be a deep-sea diver.' She settled in her armchair and stuffed the cushion into the small of her back. 'He had one of those Action Man toys with flippers and a breathing tank. He used to play with it in the bath. Seems funny now, seeing as he repairs boilers.'

The next thing she knew, she was telling him about Jackie, too, and Barry, God rest his soul. Born and bred in Devon, just like her. Worked all his life at Malcolm's Motors. To be honest, it was nice to have someone to talk to.

'How long were you married?' DC Pritchard asked. He didn't seem in any hurry.

'Over fifty years.'

The policeman whistled. 'That's a long time.'

'"More than a life sentence," Barry used to say.'

'You must miss him.'

4

There was a pause and she was about to tell him just how much. Then she remembered that he'd called for a reason; he didn't have all day.

'Sorry, my daughter ticks me off for wittering on.'

DC Pritchard cleared his throat. 'Actually, I've got something rather important to ask you. I'd appreciate your help.'

Help? Her? For once Hazel was lost for words.

She listened in amazement as he described how there might be fraudulent activity at her bank, an inside job. It seemed that a member or members of staff had been stealing large sums from customers' accounts, though luckily hers hadn't yet been touched.

When he finished Hazel gasped: 'How dreadful!' She was constantly astounded by people nowadays, didn't know where all the decent, honest folk had gone.

'It's hard to believe, isn't it?' the policeman agreed, before explaining that he wanted her to visit her bank this very morning and draw out ten thousand pounds. She wasn't to tell anyone, though, because it could jeopardise the investigation. If a bank clerk queried the amount, she was to say it was for building work.

When she returned, she was to put the money in an unmarked envelope and a plainclothes officer would arrive to collect it. Back at the station, they'd examine the notes forensically to check if they were counterfeit and return the money to her the following day.

Hazel hesitated. It just so happened that she did have ten thousand in a savings account. Lucky, that. Barry had set it up years ago and she hadn't touched it, not one penny; as a matter of fact she'd earmarked it for her funeral and a great big knees-up afterwards.

She'd be glad to help the police. She was full of admiration for what they did but, really, he'd picked the wrong person.

'I'm eighty years old. It'd take me half the day to get to the bank and back by bus, I'm that slow. You'd be best off finding someone younger.'

But the nice constable wasn't to be dissuaded. 'You're ideal for the job, they'll never suspect.' He even promised to send a taxi to take and bring her home.

She was all set to go, already thinking that she'd dig out her special dress for the occasion. After all, it wasn't every day that the police asked you to help with an investigation, but he wasn't quite finished.

'You'll want to check my credentials, to verify who I am. You can't be too careful.'

To be honest, it hadn't occurred to Hazel to verify anything, but he waited while she shuffled off to fetch her glasses from the bedside table. Then she wrote down his name and badge number in big letters on the pad that she always kept by the phone. She couldn't believe this was happening!

After hanging up, she followed his instructions and dialled 999. The operator, with a foreign accent, didn't seem at all surprised by her request.

'DC Harry Pritchard?' Yes, I've got his name and number here. Shall I put you through?'

It was all very efficient.

'Are you sure you can do this?' DC Pritchard asked when they spoke again. 'I know it's a lot to ask.'

For some reason, Hazel was reminded at that moment of her dad. She seemed to think about him a lot these days. He had adored her, his only daughter. He'd taught her to swim and ride a bike, used to tell her she could achieve anything if she put her mind to it.

She pulled back her shoulders and took a deep breath. ''Course I can.'

'Just look at that view!'

Luke snaked an arm round his wife's shoulders and pulled her close.

'We'll buy a boat in spring,' he said happily, 'when the weather improves. I'll take Oscar fishing.'

Tabitha gazed up at the wheeling seagulls and out at the murky, tossing water, and shivered. All she could think of was the snug under-floor heating in their old house that warmed you right through, from the soles of your feet to the tips of your fingers. The tall windows that let in so much light, the trendy, L-shaped sofa in the first-floor sitting room that she and Molly used to lounge on, sipping wine and laughing till their sides hurt.

She wanted to cry.

'Just think,' Luke went on, 'no more traffic roaring past our front door, no more litter and pollution. We'll have peace and quiet here, lots of space for Oscar to play. We'll see more of each other. We can have a proper family life at last. We should have done this years ago.'

Tabitha swallowed. Her eyes were pricking and she was afraid that Luke might see.

'We should go home—' she started to say, but the familiar pressure of his hand on her shoulder, squeezing just that little bit too tight, told her that he wasn't ready, so she hung back, willing the tears away.

She watched the waves whoosh up the beach towards them then slowly recede, rattling pebbles as they went. It *would* be good for Oscar, she told herself, and in time she'd adapt; she'd have to. It was either that or go under. She must put on a brave face for her son's sake, and for Luke, of course. He'd be angry if he knew what she was really thinking…

A small dog seemed to appear from nowhere, running in circles round their feet and scattering her thoughts hither and thither. Luke turned to look for its master or mistress and Tabitha followed his gaze, but there was no one about. It was after closing time and the doors to the gaily painted shops behind were tightly shut. Only the pub, The Lobster Pot, was open for business, but there was no sign of life inside.

'D'you think it's lost?' Luke asked, frowning at the yapping animal and trying, without success, to nudge it away with his toe.

Tabitha shrugged. 'I can't see its owner.'

In truth, she was a bit nervous of dogs, though Luke disliked them more. This one, however, seemed very friendly. She found herself thinking it was a shame that they hadn't brought Oscar; he would have been enchanted.

Luke loosened his grip on her shoulder and scanned left and right once more before giving the dog another push. It was a Jack Russell, white with a tan face and ears and brown spots on its back. Undeterred, it wagged its stumpy tail.

'It's very persistent,' he muttered. 'I wonder where it lives.'

'I think it's rather sweet.'

He swung his leg, as if preparing to boot it off.

'Don't!' Tabitha pleaded, then they heard a cry.

'Sally!' And a small, blonde woman in a navy coat came flapping down the road towards them. She was in her late forties, probably, and looked terribly flustered. Luke put his leg down quickly, coughed and gave a wide smile.

'Naughty girl!' the woman scolded, stooping to grab the dog by the collar. She didn't seem to have noticed anything amiss. 'Oh, dear, my husband left the door open for one minute and she was gone.'

Luke bent down to stroke the Jack Russell while she fastened a leather lead on to the collar, then she straightened up and looked at her pet crossly.

'Bad dog!'

Sally, oblivious, was peeing on a pile of dried-out seaweed, still wagging her tail.

'I'm sorry.' The woman collected herself and extended a hand first to Luke, then Tabitha. 'I'm Jenny Lambert. I live in Gull Cottage, just round the corner.'

She gestured to her right, indicating a turning at the end of the seafront. 'My husband, John, runs Oliver's, the fishing-tackle shop. Are you the couple that bought The Stables? I heard you were moving in today.'

Luke nodded. 'Actually, I've been in the area for a few weeks, setting up my office in Plymouth, but Tabitha and our son arrived this morning.' All afternoon, he explained, they'd been humping bits of furniture around and unpacking boxes. They'd come to the beach for a spot of sea air as they were exhausted.

Jenny made a sympathetic face. 'Moving's such a to-do, isn't it? That's why we've stayed put for twenty years. Couldn't stand the thought of more upheaval!'

Luke grinned. 'I don't think we'll be moving again for a long, long time.'

He shot Tabitha a look and she forced out a small smile.

'As you know, we've done a lot of work already – new roof, new plumbing and electrics,' he went on. 'The kitchen's new, too, and all the bathrooms, and we've almost finished re-decorating, but being a listed building there were limits to what the council would let us do with the outside, of course, and we can't change any of the windows, not that we'd want to.'

The wind was whipping and he pushed the fringe of his jaw-length fair hair off his face. 'We're nearly there with it now. You and your husband must come for a drink. We'd love to show you around the place, wouldn't we, Tabby?'

The woman – Jenny – looked expectantly at Tabitha, who felt herself shrink in the spotlight.

'Oh, yes,' she replied. 'You must come for dinner – once I've managed to locate the pots and pans.'

Jenny beamed. 'That would be lovely!' Then, lowering her voice, 'I should warn you, there's been a lot of talk. People are very interested in your plans. You'll be quite the celebrities around here for a while. You'd better get used to it!'

When she'd gone, they walked slowly back in the direction from which they'd come, past what they now knew to be John Lambert's fishing-tackle shop, displaying an assortment of rods, waterproof jackets and waders, past the harbour and the big white house on the corner, and up cobbled Fore Street.

Just after the Hole in the Wall pub, currently closed and awaiting new management, they came to their property, still displaying a 'Sold' sign outside. Long and squat, the building, once an old coaching inn and stables, dated back in parts to the late fifteenth century and was white, with eight small, black, timber-framed windows on the top floor and four on the bottom that had recently been re-painted.

The heavy wooden door through which you entered was surprisingly low, so that Luke, who was over six feet tall, had to stoop. Once inside the narrow hallway, he straightened up and took a deep breath, inhaling the musty scent of wood and dust mingled with fresh paint, of a building in a state of upheaval that hadn't been occupied for some time.

'Home!' he said, hanging his coat on a peg and sighing contentedly. 'I still can't believe it's ours, can you, Tabby?'

He spun round to find his wife but she'd disappeared already, up the creaking, as-yet uncarpeted stairs, to look for her son.

Oscar was in one of the new bathrooms to the right of the building, in the section that they'd chosen as their own family quarters. It was separated from the rest of The Stables by a corridor with a peeling brown door at the end that was to stay firmly shut at all times. Tabitha intended to put a notice on it saying 'Private'. She didn't want guests wandering in by mistake.

The room was airy and minimalist, much lighter than downstairs, which lifted her spirits slightly. She'd chosen the fresh white tiles and modern chrome fittings herself, and she smiled at the sight of her two-year-old son in the bath, carefully lining up a row of yellow ducks and toy boats, unaware of her presence.

Pilar, the au pair, was kneeling beside him on the grey tiled floor, swishing warm water over his back and shoulders. She looked up at Tabitha, still in her coat by the door.

'Nice walk?' she asked, in her faltering Spanish accent. She had a round, pale face, no make-up and jet-black hair tied back in a plait.

'Bit cold.' Tabitha bent down to stroke Oscar's dark curly hair, and hearing her voice he twisted round and stretched out two pudgy arms.

'Mamma!' he said urgently, no longer interested in his ducks or boats, forgetting that he'd been perfectly happy a moment before. He stood up, splashing water on to the floor, and repeated the command, quite crossly this time. 'Ma-mma-a!'

The sight of his naked little body, pinkish and dripping, tugged at Tabitha's heartstrings.

'I'll take over now, thanks, Pilar.' She reached for a white towel on the rail behind and wrapped it round her son as she lifted him from the tub. 'Come on, little man, let's find your pyjamas, then we'll go and get your milk.'

Back downstairs, Luke was already in the kitchen, fetching a bottle of champagne from the stainless-steel fridge-freezer.

'I think this calls for a celebration, don't you?' he said, smiling at his wife and son, now dressed in soft blue and white stripy pyjamas, his curly hair still damp.

Oscar struggled out of his mother's arms and ran to his father, who scooped him up and kissed his cheek. 'You smell lovely. Nice and clean for a change!'

Still balanced on his father's hip, the little boy watched, fascinated, while Luke untwisted the cork, which flew out with a loud pop. The noise made Oscar's brown eyes widen with fright but he was reassured by Luke's chuckle and, instead of crying, clapped his hands.

'Bang!' he said excitedly. 'Bang bang bang!' Then hurried off to find the cork, which had landed a metre or two away.

'First night in our new home,' Luke said, handing Tabitha a glass and chinking his against it. 'Here's to many more!'

Tabitha, dismayed to find her eyes filling again, was careful not to meet his gaze.

She was about to say that she'd take Oscar upstairs for his bedtime story when a tentative rap stopped her in her tracks. Not even positive that someone *had* knocked, she would have ignored it but Luke cried 'Visitors!' and hurried down the hallway. Oscar was soon hot on his heels, toddling as fast as he could on short legs with a bulky nappy in between.

Hovering by the silver range cooker, shiny through lack of use, Tabitha listened, ears pricked, to see if she could make out who it was. She thought that she could detect a woman's voice but it was so soft that she wasn't sure. Then she heard another, higher and younger, and it was getting nearer. Luke was bringing them in!

Dismayed, she hung back, her hands wrapped round the

oven handle. 'Compose yourself,' she was muttering under her breath. 'Don't show him up.'

Luke pushed open the door, which had swung shut, and in walked a slight, dark-haired woman carrying a large pot plant, followed by a smaller girl of about twelve or thirteen, wearing rectangular, pale blue glasses, her fair hair cut in a chin-length bob. She had a limp – you couldn't miss it.

'Tabitha, this is Liz Hart,' Luke said, 'and her daughter, Rosie.'

The woman, who was very pretty, with round, chocolate-brown eyes that seemed to fill her face, smiled shyly.

'Her husband runs the fish restaurant in South Street, A Winkle In Time,' Luke went on. 'They've brought us a house-warming present. Isn't that kind?'

Tabitha stepped forward to shake hands, except that Liz's arms were full so they laughed awkwardly instead.

'You shouldn't have,' said Tabitha, eyeing the plant suspiciously, as if it might bite. She didn't offer to take it. 'How thoughtful of you.'

Liz looked around for a spare surface and put the gift, in a round, terracotta pot, on the island in the middle of the kitchen.

'It's only a token.' She glanced at her daughter, who smiled, revealing funny, gappy teeth. 'It's not just from us. Quite a few of the locals chipped in – Pat and Jean, Jenny and John, Tony and Felipe. And Esme, of course.'

She hesitated, reddening slightly. 'Sorry, you've got no idea who I'm talking about. We agreed it would be better if just Rosie and I came. You won't want to be bombarded with visitors when you've just arrived. Anyway,' she went on, 'everyone was so nice when Rosie and I moved here and we wanted to say welcome. We hope you'll be very happy in Tremarnock. We certainly are.'

'Thank you.' Tabitha picked up Oscar, who was tugging on

her jeans, still brandishing the cork in a fat little hand. 'That's very generous. Please thank your friends, too.'

She would have ushered them to the door, using Oscar's bedtime as an excuse, but Luke had other ideas.

'You must join us for a glass of champagne!' he announced, seizing two glasses from the cupboard before Liz had time to object. 'Rosie can have a taste too, can't she?'

Without waiting for a reply, he poured an inch into a flute before passing it to the girl. Then he filled a bigger glass for her mother and topped Tabitha up.

'So,' he went on, pulling out some stools and indicating to the visitors to sit down, 'tell us about yourselves. What's it like, living here? We can't wait to get to know everybody.'

Realising that there was no escape, Tabitha warmed some milk for her son in the microwave, then he sat contentedly on her lap while Luke prodded Liz and Rosie for information. It seemed that the pair had left London for Tremarnock about ten years ago, used to live in Dove Cottage on Humble Hill, and had recently moved just up the road to a house called Bag End.

'Robert and I only got married in July,' Liz explained, peeping through long black eyelashes at Tabitha, who glanced away quickly.

'Newly-weds. Congratulations!' boomed Luke. At times like this, when he was happy and excited, his voice got louder, but Liz and Rosie didn't seem to mind. Rosie, especially, appeared enchanted, gazing around the room every now and again to take in the carefully designed interior, a combination of old and new with its low ceilings and original oak beams, white walls and ultra-modern fixtures and fittings.

She was clearly taken with Oscar, too, playing peekaboo with him when he eyed her inquisitively between slurps of milk from his blue plastic beaker. At one point he reached out and tried to grab the silver bangles on her right arm, and for the first time Tabitha noticed that there was something wrong with the left one. It was thinner than the other, and pulled up to her chest at an unnatural, flexed angle. She lingered on it for just a moment too long then, realising that Liz had noticed, turned away, embarrassed, and touched Luke's hand.

'Shall we have some crisps?'

'Of course.' He sprang up. 'Sorry, should have thought of it.'

While he opened various packets and poured the contents into little bowls, Tabitha kept the conversation flowing.

'Do you work at the restaurant, too?' she asked Liz, who revealed that she helped out when needed but that mostly she was busy with her hair-accessories business.

'How interesting!' Tabitha had noticed the unusual silver hairpins, decorated with tiny pearl-inlaid rhinestones on either side of her visitor's head. 'Did you make those?'

They were interrupted by a shriek from Oscar. Rosie took off one of her bangles, handed it to him and he shoved it in his mouth. 'It's OK,' said his mother. 'I don't suppose it'll do any harm.'

Rosie wanted to know where the family had lived before, and Tabitha explained that they came from Manchester. 'It was very different. We had a modern town house, right in the city centre.'

Her voice trailed off and she cleared her throat again, afraid that she might give herself away.

'It had no character, none whatsoever,' Luke said quickly. 'Crime was rife and the traffic...' He pulled a face. 'Well, let's just say we were desperate to find somewhere with a bit of character and get as far away from the smoke as possible. Tabby was a Scouser originally, but I'm Manchester through and through.' He laughed. 'You can probably tell from our accents we're not from around here.'

Liz smiled. 'You'll soon get used to the Cornish voices.' She looked at his wife, whose mouth was twisting in an odd way. 'Everything's bound to feel a bit strange at first. I didn't know a soul when I arrived but everyone's so friendly you'll quickly settle in.'

Liz's voice was gentle and she had a kind, honest countenance. Tabitha reckoned that she was just a few years older than herself, in her early to mid-thirties, perhaps. They might even be friends, in other circumstances…

'You must pop in for coffee sometime, when you've unpacked,' Liz suggested.

Tabitha fiddled with the expensive diamond ring on her third finger, a gift from Luke, twisting it round and round.

'I'm going to be so busy looking after Oscar and getting everything ready for our first guests, I won't have time to socialise.'

Liz's eyes widened. She was stung, you could tell.

'Of course not.' She rose from her stool and pushed it back to its original position. 'You must have masses to do.'

She patted Rosie's shoulder and the girl rose obediently, too, trying to extract the bangle from Oscar's mouth as she did so. He was having none of it, though, and let out a shriek. 'It doesn't matter, he can keep it.'

'We must be off. Thanks for the champagne.' There was still a little left in Liz's glass. 'Nice to meet you – and good luck with the guest house.'

'*Boutique* guest house,' Tabitha corrected, immediately wishing that she could take the words back. It wasn't the woman's fault that she'd come at a bad time. Not that there'd ever be a good one.

Luke shot her a look and she wiped the palms of her sweaty hands, one by one, against her trousers.

'So good of you to call.' He grinned, ushering the visitors towards the door. 'Oscar seems to have taken quite a shine to you, Rosie. We'll give you back your bracelet next time we meet.'

'Oscar's so cute, isn't he?' said Rosie, once they were well out of earshot. She'd linked arms with her mother and was huddling into her side. This was partly from affection but also to help fend off the squally wind that had developed, whipping up their sleeves and down the collars of their coats.

'He is,' said Liz. 'Really sweet.'

'And Luke's nice. Very friendly.'

There was a pause where Liz knew exactly what Rosie was thinking. The truth was, she was thinking it, too, but she didn't want to be drawn into a conversation about Tabitha; it would be wrong to pass judgement. Give the woman a chance, she was telling herself. She'd only just arrived.

'I don't like Tabitha, do you?'

Liz flinched. Rosie never was one to mince words. 'Oh, she seemed all right. They've had a very busy day. She's probably exhausted and the last thing she wanted was visitors. Next time we see her I expect she'll be quite different.'

Rosie wasn't satisfied, Liz could tell. She would have insisted on pursuing the subject had not Jean emerged from her yellowish brick house, Dynnargh, which was situated on the corner of Fore Street and Humble Hill.

The house, built in the 1970s, was quite unlike its neighbours – mostly old fishermen's cottages painted yellow, pink, blue and white. Dynnargh wasn't as charming but it

17

was lovingly tended, with white lace curtains in the windows and a neat little garden surrounded by a picket fence.

In the middle of the garden was a miniature stone wishing well and beside it a metal statuette of a comical boy on a bike in blue dungarees, carrying a flowerpot to be filled with blooms in spring and summer. They were new additions and Jean was very proud of them. She stopped for a moment to admire them, before spotting Liz and Rosie.

'Evening, Liz, hello, chicken!' She closed the gate behind her and gave Rosie's cheek a pinch. She always called her 'chicken' even now she was twelve and a half years old. The girl smiled sheepishly.

Jean, a round, smiley woman in her mid-fifties, was a child-minder who'd helped to look after Rosie for many years while Liz went out to work.

'Where've you been, then?' Jean wanted to know. She was well wrapped up, in a green woolly hat and scarf and navy anorak. 'Last of my little 'uns has just gone. Mum was late – as usual.' She rolled her eyes. 'I'm popping into Esme's for a cuppa – or something stronger. I need it after the day I've had, I tell you.'

When Rosie informed her that they'd called in on the new inhabitants of The Stables, the older woman couldn't disguise her interest.

'Well, go on, then.' She crossed her arms, having forgotten all about the drink.

Rosie told her about Oscar first, then described Luke and the house. 'It's a bit dark and gloomy when you go in but the kitchen's amazing, with this great big island thing in the middle that you can sit round. We had champagne – I had a little bit, too!'

Jean raised her eyebrows. 'Did you now? Aren't you the lucky one?'

Hearing voices, her husband, Tom, appeared on the doorstep, but disappeared again sharpish when he saw the three of them. 'You'll be rabbiting all night by the looks of it,' he joked.

Once the door was firmly shut, Jean leaned in towards Liz and Rosie and lowered her voice. 'I hear they're not short of a few bob. How did he make his cash, I wonder?'

Liz shrugged. 'No idea.'

'Like as not in finance.' Jean sniffed. 'Or maybe he's from a rich family. That place cost a pretty penny and they must've spent thousands doing it up.' She narrowed her eyes and looked pointedly at Liz. 'What do you make of the wife, then? Is she our sort?'

Rosie's body tensed, poised to speak, and Liz nudged her in the ribs.

'She's very beautiful,' she said quickly. 'Tall and slim, with masses of black curly hair. Mixed race, I think, maybe part African or Caribbean, I'm not sure. She could be a model.'

Jean's mouth dropped open but she quickly composed herself. 'Sounds very exotic.' She was obviously hoping for more information but Liz checked her watch and declared that it was time to go.

'Robert said he'd pop home for a quick supper before the restaurant gets busy. He likes to eat with us if he can.' She frowned. 'No idea what to make, though.'

'Oh, I wouldn't worry about him,' Jean said comfortably. 'I don't think it's your cooking he's after!'

Chapter Two

You MIGHT THINK that October in Tremarnock would be a miserable month, but in some ways Liz loved autumn and winter here more than any other time of year. During the balmy summers tourists flocked into the village, charmed by the quaint, colour-washed cottages and narrow, cobbled streets, the safe little harbour, with its bobbing, brightly coloured boats, and the small, secluded beach.

Then, it seemed, every other house was either offering bed and breakfast or was let out to couples and families, complete with noisy dogs, teens and babies. The village pubs heaved so that you could scarcely reach the bar, and finding a parking space was so tricky that if you were lucky enough to succeed, you might as well hang on to it and walk or catch the bus instead.

Tills rang, businesses boomed and jobs, albeit temporary, were easy to come by, so no one liked to complain. After all, it was the tourists' money that kept the place alive. Once the holidays were over, however, a sense of calm descended and even the weekenders, with their smart second homes, tended to bolt their doors, lock their shutters and stay away until the weather improved.

Those remaining could have felt lonely, perched as they

were on an isolated peninsula, flanked on three sides by water and surrounded by empty houses, but in fact the opposite was true. Life went on and with the place to themselves, locals could once more enjoy solitary walks along the shingly beach and across the dark rocks, pitted with interesting pools, before clambering up the densely vegetated cliff to high ground.

From here, they could revel in spectacular views across the bay, undisturbed by gaggles of mums and dads, dragging reluctant children on family walks, or groups of ramblers. The only noise was the crashing waves down below, tossing and glinting in ragged confusion as they hit the rocks and flew into the air, mingled with the plaintive cries of seagulls.

Back down in the village, it was a relief to be able to find a spot in the pub and chat to the permanent staff, whose feet rarely touched the floor all summer long, and to lean against shop counters and find out how those behind them really *were*. They were more than friends or acquaintances, you see, more than people just providing a service.

The great storm of 2014, when waves whooshed over the roofs of houses, leaving behind great mounds of sand up to the windows, was still fresh in the minds of many, and some were old enough to remember the devastation of '76. Then, as always, the community had rallied, everyone helping to bale and shovel, everyone mucking in. Miraculously, most folk had been back in their homes and businesses up and running again within days. You didn't forget things like that in a hurry. It brought you together; it gave you a special bond.

So Liz always viewed October onwards as a time to draw breath, re-engage with people and catch up on some of the jobs that she put off when the sun shone and the outdoors beckoned. The buzz and gaiety of summer were all very well, but the party couldn't go on for ever.

Mitzi, the tortoiseshell cat, was sitting on the windowsill, waiting for her and Rosie to return, and the girl stopped to give her a stroke. Mitzi wasn't much more than a kitten, really, with long fluffy fur and black-tipped ears. They'd got her after moving to Bag End and Rosie adored her.

'Are you hungry?' she said in a silly, baby voice, picking the creature up. 'Poor lickle Mitzi.'

Even though they'd been in the house since April, six months now, Liz still had to pinch herself when she walked through the door. She'd grown to love her previous home, the ground-floor flat of a smaller fisherman's cottage, but looking back it had been rather a squeeze. Now, with Robert, they had three good-sized bedrooms, a proper little garden at the back, a decent kitchen and a small dining room for entertaining. But the real attraction, as far as Liz was concerned, was the original fireplace in the front room that they loved to sit around now that the weather had changed. She said it made the place a real home.

After feeding the cat, Rosie plonked herself on a chair at the old pine kitchen table, scored with marks through years of use, and watched while her mother rootled in the fridge and cupboards to see what she could find.

'I'm knackered,' the girl sighed, 'and I've still got some history to finish for tomorrow.'

Liz's pulse quickened. Her daughter had been doing so well in the year since they'd returned from Oklahoma, where she'd received proton therapy for a brain tumour. All the follow-up scans had been good and there was every reason for optimism but, still, Liz worried frequently; she couldn't help it.

'Do you want to have a lie-down?' she asked, studying her daughter's face for clues. She'd been fine earlier, but she'd been at school all day and maybe the visit to The Stables had been too much; they should have postponed it. 'History can wait. I'll write a note to the teacher, she'll understand.'

Rosie sighed. 'Mu-um, I'm just tired, that's all. I've had a really busy day. There's nothing wrong with me.'

She was accustomed to her mother's fretting, but it irritated her nonetheless.

Liz felt her body relax. She was overreacting; she must learn to control it.

'Why don't you go and finish your work now, then?' she suggested, pulling out the chopping board and starting on a red pepper that she'd discovered in the salad tray, along with an onion, a knob of ginger, some green beans and red chillies. She'd settled on a chicken stir-fry. 'You'd better get to bed in decent time.'

Rosie sloped off and Liz switched the radio on quietly while she finished preparing the vegetables. As she jigged along to Mellow Magic, she reminded herself for the umpteenth time to focus on the amazing progress that Rosie had made, rather than dwell on her own anxieties. It was true that Rosie tired easily and needed to rest, that her appetite was poor and that she was more susceptible to coughs and colds than other children.

Her short-term memory had also been affected, meaning that it took her longer to learn certain concepts at school, which she found frustrating. Sometimes her left leg shook uncontrollably because of damage to the neurological pathways, and she'd also lost her peripheral vision, though it didn't seem to bother her unduly. Overall, though, she was doing extraordinarily well and, aside from regular three-month scans and physiotherapy, she was able to lead a remarkably normal life.

No, Liz mused, fetching the wok from a drawer beneath

the cooker and tipping in some oil, she really shouldn't complain. After two years the scans would become six-monthly, dropping to once a year after five years. When that time came, they'd have a big celebration for sure, but there was already so much to be thankful for.

It wasn't long before she heard the sound of her husband's key in the lock and she quickly wiped her hands on her apron and hurried down the hallway.

His face lit up when he saw her. 'Hey, you!'

He looked terribly handsome. His hazel eyes, flecked with amber, sparkled and his brown hair was tousled from the wind. He stooped down to kiss her on the lips; he was very tall so there was a long way to go. 'Good day – since I last saw you?'

She laughed. He'd been back home briefly after the lunch-time customers had gone and had only left again around four.

She snaked her arms beneath his waxed jacket, enjoying the warmth of his body through the cotton shirt. 'We called on the new people who've moved to The Stables. The place is going to be amazing when it's finished.'

Robert buried his face in her hair and whispered in her ear, 'Not as nice as Bag End, though?'

'Never!'

They ate round the kitchen table that they'd picked up at an auction. Neither Liz nor Robert had brought much furniture with them when they'd moved, and they both liked old pieces that seemed to fit with the character of the place. Rosie chattered about school. Mandy, apparently, had been off sick for the third day in a row – 'I think she's just making it up now,' she said unsympathetically. George, meanwhile, had received a detention for swearing.

'He only said "Jesus!" under his breath when Mr Mills said

we had to learn two lots of French vocab for a test. He's ridiculously strict.'

'Well, you shouldn't swear in front of the teacher,' Liz said firmly, before smiling. 'But I agree that's pretty draconian.'

Robert's mobile phone rang when they were clearing away the dishes and he answered it in the front room where the signal was better. It seemed that one of the waitresses had called to say that she was unwell so they were a person down.

'I'm sorry,' he said to Liz, 'we're only half-full but you know what Loveday's like—'

'It's fine, honestly.' Liz enjoyed stepping in to help when needed as it gave her a chance to see the gang and catch up on the news. 'I'll run and check Pat's free.'

The old woman's cottage, The Nook, was only a few doors up, next to Liz and Rosie's former home. Liz had to rap loudly on the canary-yellow front door because Pat was rather deaf, and soon she herself appeared over the top of her china ornament display in the little window that looked directly on to the street.

On spotting Liz, her snowy head bobbed out of view and she shuffled off to let her in. Pat was well into her eighties and had a special place in Liz's heart, having been kind enough to mind Rosie almost every evening for years when Liz had worked regularly at the restaurant. She didn't know how she'd have managed without her.

''Course I'll come!' Pat said, offering a prickly cheek for Liz to kiss. 'I could do with a change of scenery. I've got some of those choccy bickies that Madam likes.' She was already hobbling down the narrow hallway to find her coat and bag. 'Tell Rosie to put the kettle on and I'll be there in two shakes of a blanket.'

*

Liz changed into a white blouse and her old black waitressing skirt, then she and Robert left the pair in front of the TV and walked quickly up Humble Hill before turning left into winding South Street. It was dark now, and the old-fashioned streetlights had come on, though they'd be switched off later as a money-saving measure. There was no one about, which was lucky because they were rather late. It was difficult to go anywhere in the village without seeing someone you knew and feeling obliged to stop for a chat.

Liz noticed that the mannequins in Seaspray Boutique had been stripped and were standing naked, bald and sad in the window. Audrey, the owner, must have done it only recently, as they'd been fully clothed at the beginning of the week. The shop wouldn't open again now until March or April when the models would be flaunting the new season's looks.

A Winkle In Time was on the right, almost at the bottom of the road, which was too narrow for cars to go up and down so you had to park elsewhere. A former sea captain's home, it stood out from the other buildings because it was larger and painted white, with bright blue wooden shutters and its name emblazoned in distinctive, swirly white letters on a matching blue board above the door.

Liz could hear noises as she entered and she hung her coat in the little cloakroom before hurrying into the kitchen, which was already humming with activity. A red-faced Alex, the head chef, was barking orders at his number two, as well as Jesse, who'd been promoted from washer-upper and jack of all trades and was training to be a chef himself.

The task of pot washer and general dogsbody now fell to Callum, who was scrubbing vegetables in the giant sink. A cheery lad of twenty-one, with two voluptuous, half-naked ladies tattooed on his forearms, he'd been unemployed before and was grateful to have found permanent work in the village.

There was no sign of the other waitress, Loveday, Robert's niece. She tended to saunter in just as the customers arrived, looking for all the world as if she was doing everyone a huge favour. She and Jesse had been going out together for a year now and, give or take the odd fracas that made nerves jangle in the kitchen, they seemed to be made for each other.

'Liz!' Jesse cried, pausing a moment from stirring the contents of a large saucepan that was simmering on the stove and giving off delicious smells. He was twenty years old, with a mass of blond, corkscrew curls and an impressive surfer's torso that he liked to show off at the slightest opportunity. 'How goes it?'

They caught up briefly, then Liz started laying the tables while Robert prepared the till and polished glasses. The restaurant was square in shape and quite small inside, with low ceilings, an uneven wooden floor and wonky tables made of stripped bare oak that were pushed quite close together due to lack of space.

Robert had talked about re-designing the interior and had asked Liz to help, but they'd been so busy with the move, followed by the wedding, that they hadn't had the chance. In any case, customers seemed to love the rough and readiness of the venue, which had a homely, welcoming feel, the sort of place where you could wear your Wellies and bring your dog if you so chose. It would be good to re-paint the walls, though, and extend the kitchen, which was rather cramped.

'Thank God it's you, not her.'

Liz looked up from folding a pile of white linen napkins to see Loveday sloping by in nothing but a low-cut, tight white T-shirt, black mini-skirt and platform heels. She was a big girl of nineteen, with a very large bust that you couldn't ignore, and hair dyed black that had recently been cut into a severe crop and shaved up both sides. The long fringe stuck out in spikes, owing to the quantities of wax she used.

Liz had been told by Robert that his niece and the new waitress weren't the best of friends. In fact, Loveday seemed to have a problem with any waitress who wasn't Liz. Demi, the girl before, had been a 'lazy cow' and 'too full of herself', although the relationship had thawed a little before she'd left. The new one, meanwhile, was a 'pernickety old boot' who should go back to where she'd come from. Somewhere in Wales, apparently.

'No coat?' asked Liz, noticing Loveday's bare legs, which had turned quite blue with the cold. She was always half-naked, that girl. It never ceased to amaze.

'Nah,' said Loveday, frowning, 'couldn't be arsed.'

She was clearly having one of her bad days so Liz thought it wise not to comment further.

Once she'd finished the tables, she checked the menu to familiarise herself with what was on offer and watched while Robert chalked the names of the specials on a blackboard to the right of the bar. There was gurnard tonight, as well as cod and grey mullet. Alex had been out at 4 a.m. this morning with the one bona-fide fisherman left in the village, and they'd come back with a sizeable catch. The fisherman, an old sea dog if ever there was one, was the only man Liz had ever met with muscly fingers. They were so thick, from handling the nets all his life, that it was a wonder he could bend them.

Anything he caught that Robert and Alex didn't want for A Winkle In Time went to Blue Ocean Seafoods, the fishmonger in Market Square, and what they couldn't source locally they'd buy from the fish markets of Looe and Plymouth.

The first customer to arrive on the dot of seven forty-five was none other than Rick Kane, accompanied by a new lady friend whom Liz hadn't seen before. Rick, who ran the village gift shop, Treasure Trove, was a fan of internet dating. Into his sixties now and sporting a bushy grey beard and sideburns, he seemed to be working his way through the county's entire population of mature women and was never without someone on his arm.

'Good evening,' he said to Liz, rather formally, she thought, and he kept a protective hand on his date's back as he ushered her solicitously to her chair. She was rather glamorous, with long red fingernails, thick blue eye shadow and a halo of white-blonde hair. She must have had a blow-dry earlier in the day.

'May I see the wine list?' Rick asked, leaning forward so that his companion had the full focus of his attention.

Liz smiled inwardly. Usually, he shunned the menu in favour of house white or red; he was obviously keen to make a good impression.

'Of course,' she said, adopting her best, professional tone. She couldn't help noticing that several of the buttons on his red and white striped shirt had been left open, revealing an impressive crop of grey chest hair. 'I'll ask the manager to advise you.'

As the restaurant filled up she darted to and fro, carrying bowls of sweet potato and ginger soup and plates of pot-roasted gurnard and spiced cod and scallop linguine. Robert popped back and forth, too, fetching wines from the store in the backyard and keeping an eye on the bar as well as Loveday, who could have done with a firm hand, though he never gave her one. He was so quiet and intent on his work that Liz didn't like to speak to him. Every now and then, though, they'd exchange glances, he'd mouth, 'OK?' and she'd smile and nod back.

It seemed hard to believe, now, that she'd once thought him awkward and antisocial. How wrong you could be! Focused, yes, unfriendly, never. In fact, the well-being of all his staff was his greatest concern.

Rick and his lady friend were deep in conversation and took ages to finish their first two courses. At one point he lifted her hand from the table and played with her fingers, interlacing them with his own. She, meanwhile, lowered her eyes frequently and gazed at him through heavily mascaraed lashes, popping off every now and again to the ladies' to refresh her pink glossy lipstick.

Liz went over a couple of times to top up their wine glasses then stopped, sensing that Rick wanted to do the honours. They were in a world of their own. The other customers were new to her and she heard one man say to his companion that he couldn't believe he'd never been here before.

'It's charming,' the woman agreed. 'And the food's delicious.'

Liz made a mental note to tell Robert and the other staff later. They worked so hard and everyone needed a pat on the back from time to time.

Towards the end of the evening her legs were aching and she marvelled at how nimble she'd once been. Amazing to think that she'd held down this job as well as cleaning offices in the mornings; she was definitely out of practice. It wasn't until most people were finishing dessert that she managed to stop for a proper chat with Jesse, who informed her in his pronounced Cornish accent that he and Loveday were shortly moving in together to a little rented flat on the top floor of Jack's Cottage, near The Victory Inn pub.

He'd previously been living with his mum, while Loveday had been paying a small amount for a room in the family home of a friend. It wasn't ideal, though, because the friend's little brother had a corn snake, called Slinky, that he liked to hide around the house to make her scream.

Liz clapped her hands at Jesse's news. 'Fantastic! I look forward to seeing it!'

Actually, she knew about the flat already because Robert had helped with Loveday's contribution towards the deposit, but she didn't want to spoil the young man's pleasure by letting on. Alex, who'd been listening in, made a joke about old married couples.

'Hope you've got your pipe and slippers ready,' he jeered, and Jesse glowered.

'How's your love life, then?' he shot back, knowing full well that Alex, who was divorced, had recently been dumped by his girlfriend. Apparently she'd grown tired of his accordion playing, and his passion for fifties pop music. The last straw had been his new, black, Elvis-style quiff. Liz rather liked it, though it had a tendency to droop in the steamy kitchen. He had a penchant for crepe-soled brothel-creepers, too.

Later, Liz and Loveday leaned against the bar for a few moments and the younger girl talked about her plans for the new home.

'I want it to be really different,' she said, eyes glittering. 'I'm going to get loads of pink cushions and throws and have candles and incense everywhere, including in the bathroom.'

'Sounds gorgeous,' said Liz, wondering how Jesse would feel about the pink theme. 'You must say exactly what you want from me, Rosie and Robert. We'd like to get you a nice housewarming present.'

She started. 'I know! Why don't we go shopping on Saturday? I'll take you out for lunch and you can choose something yourself.'

Despite Loveday's peccadilloes, Liz was very fond of the girl as well as Jesse, and was glad that they'd found some stability. Loveday hadn't had the easiest childhood, having been born to Robert's sister, Sarah, when she was just eighteen. Sarah and her husband, Andy, had rowed a lot in front of Loveday when she was little, mainly about money, which was always tight, though Robert had helped out as much as he could. Now the couple were getting divorced, which clearly upset their daughter, though she never let on.

She'd been a rebellious teenager and Sarah had been only too happy when Robert had offered her a job at A Winkle In Time, far from her home town of Penzance. It was supposed to have been temporary, just long enough for her to get some experience and decide what she really wanted to do, but she'd made friends and taken to life in Tremarnock, especially now that she'd found Jesse.

After a bottle of wine and several digestifs, Rick and his girlfriend were pink-cheeked and dreamy-looking. They left around half-ten and Liz spotted them through the window, strolling arm in arm in the direction of his flat above the shop. The evening appeared to have been an unqualified success.

The other customers lingered longer, and by the time Robert had finished cashing up it was well after midnight.

'Shall we go the long way back?' he suggested. 'I fancy a breath of air.'

Liz agreed because although she was very tired, her brain was working overtime and she needed to unwind. Working at the restaurant always had that effect on her. They walked along the deserted street, past Rick's gift shop on the corner, where a soft light was shining upstairs. There was a cold wind, and she zipped her padded jacket right up to the collar, grateful to find a pair of woolly gloves in one of the pockets, her e-cig in the other.

She'd given up smoking but still reached for the substitute every now and again. She took a couple of puffs, watching the smoke curl in front of her before floating away. Robert didn't mind, but Rosie wasn't even aware that she'd smoked real cigarettes, and Liz wanted it to stay that way.

Once they reached the seafront, they stood for a few moments gazing up at the inky sky, splattered with twinkling stars as if someone had flicked a paintbrush, spraying splashes of radiant colour as far as the eye could see. The angry ocean hissed and clattered, but Liz found its rhythmic ebb and flow strangely comforting.

All the time that she'd lived in London she'd been almost unaware of the sea; it had no relevance to her. Yet now, like the blood that flowed back and forth through her arteries and veins, it had become a part of her, as much as the sun, moon and trees; she couldn't imagine living anywhere but close by.

Robert was silent beside her and, lost in her own thoughts, she seemed to mingle with her surroundings, breathing in and out slowly in time with the waves, sensing the cares of the evening floating away like so much flotsam and jetsam on the tide.

She could have stood there for much longer, enjoying feeling her body relax and her mind empty, but she became aware that they weren't alone. Glancing round, she saw the figure of a man at the opposite end of the esplanade, huddled on a bench, a phone clamped to his ear and seemingly deep in conversation.

'He's out late,' she whispered to her husband, who had followed her gaze. 'I wonder who he's talking to.'

The spell had been broken and Robert sighed.

'Time to go?' he said, echoing her thoughts, and they made their way hand in hand along the seafront towards the figure, intending to turn left at Ashley House, which gleamed, white and eerie, in the moonlight.

As they drew closer, Liz could see that the man was well built, with wide shoulders and fair hair. He was wearing a bulky overcoat, his head was slightly bowed and he gestured occasionally, talking in a low, urgent voice. He looked strangely familiar, even from the back view, and she could just pick out the vowels and consonants of an accent that wasn't from around here.

They would have passed by, but as soon as he heard them the man stopped talking and swivelled round. By now, Liz and Robert were only a few feet away and she could see quite clearly who it was: Luke.

In an instant, he finished his call, sprang up and strode towards them, his arms wide and welcoming.

'Liz! What a surprise! And this must be your husband!' He embraced her like an old friend before vigorously shaking Robert's hand.

'I went for a nightcap.' He gestured towards the pub, The Lobster Pot, behind them. 'It's great in there, isn't it? Good atmosphere.'

He had a lovely wide smile and Liz found herself thinking that he looked very handsome in the starlight. He was tall, like Robert, maybe just an inch or so shorter, and broader, with a wide forehead, a small straight nose and a close-shaven, well-defined chin. He took quite a bit of trouble with his appearance, you could tell. His hair, though longish, was carefully cut, and the skin on his face was soft and smooth, quite unlike the rough, weather-beaten countenances of the men around here.

The most appealing thing about him, however, was his bright blue eyes that he tended to fix on whoever he was talking to, making you feel like the most interesting person in the world. He and Tabitha really were a most attractive couple.

He didn't seem in any hurry, and Liz explained that she and Robert had been at the restaurant.

'I can't wait to come. I've heard great things about it.'

Robert said Tremarnock needed a guest house and The Stables should do very well. There were plenty of cottages to rent but not everyone wanted self-catering or bed and breakfast in someone else's cramped home, and the nearest hotel was several miles away. 'But you know all that, of course.'

'We're only doing B & B ourselves,' Luke reminded him, 'but we're not cramped, that's for sure. Hopefully we'll be sending plenty of people your way for lunch and dinner once we're open.'

Robert, pleased, said that likewise he'd happily pass on the name of The Stables.

'I can see we're going to be friends!' Luke exclaimed, slapping him on the back. He paused, as if thinking of something. 'We're having a party on Saturday. Bit last minute but seems like a good way to christen the new place. Seven onwards. I hope you're free?'

Robert explained that he'd be working – 'Saturday's our busiest night' – but Luke waved a dismissive hand.

'Join us afterwards. Liz can come on ahead. We'll be going on for hours, I promise you. We were celebrated for our parties in Manchester. We have a reputation to keep up!'

He looked at Liz. 'Actually, I was hoping you might be able to help with the guest list. I'd like to invite the whole village but that's probably too many, even for our place.' He stroked his chin. 'Would you mind writing down the names and addresses of everyone you think we should ask? We want to get to know as many people here as possible.'

Liz was slightly taken aback, remembering Tabitha's look of horror when she and Rosie had turned up unexpectedly, and the way she'd declined her coffee invitation. She didn't seem nearly as keen on meeting the villagers as her husband. He'd put Liz in an awkward position, though, and she could hardly refuse.

'I'll do a list tomorrow and stick it in your letterbox,' she promised, thinking there was no way she'd knock. She couldn't help suspecting that the party was a spur-of-the-moment idea, because he hadn't mentioned it before, and, for all she knew, Tabitha might torpedo it immediately.

A dog barked in the distance and the sound echoed strangely in the blackness as the three made their way up Fore Street, their footsteps tapping on the cobbles.

They were about to say goodbye at Luke's front door when his body tensed and he turned sharply, making Liz start.

'Did you see…?' His eyes narrowed as he scanned the dimly lit road, then his face relaxed, he shook his head and laughed. 'A trick of the shadows. I'm not used to these alleyways and dark corners.'

'It's very safe around here,' Liz reassured him. 'You hardly ever even see a policeman, there's no need.'

Luke laughed again, before giving her a kiss and shaking Robert's hand. 'So pleased we've met.'

As they moved away, Liz thought that she saw a blind move in one of the windows upstairs, but there were no lights on and it seemed that the rest of the family was asleep. She decided that she must have imagined it.

Chapter Three

THE FOLLOWING MORNING at around eight, the phone rang in Hazel's little flat in South Devon and she felt a quiver of anticipation, fully expecting to hear that charming Detective Constable Harry Pritchard again with an update on her money.

She was hoping he'd say that the notes she'd handed over yesterday weren't counterfeit after all. There again, he'd told her not to worry if they were. The police would replace them with real cash, no trouble at all

She hadn't got back from the bank till mid-afternoon yesterday and by the time she'd popped the money in an envelope and handed it over, she'd been quite worn out with all the excitement. And to think she'd imagined that the most thrilling thing she'd be doing all day was going to the shops!

She'd been dying to tell Jackie about her adventure but knew not to disturb her at work, so she'd made herself a cup of tea and caught up on the soaps. Then, when she'd tried her daughter's home number later in the evening, it had been her granddaughter, Annie, who'd picked up.

'She's out, Gran,' Annie had said. 'It's her book group tonight. I drove over this afternoon 'cause I need to borrow a dress for a wedding. I have to go back first thing tomorrow. Sorry I won't have time to see you.'

Annie lived some fifty miles away; she'd been to college in Cornwall and had liked it so much that she'd decided to stay. Probably wouldn't come back ever, especially not now she'd met that nice postman, Nathan.

Hazel would have told Annie about the investigation but she'd been in a rush to meet friends. The phone buzzed again, two more rings, giving the old woman a jolt. She'd better answer quick or they'd hang up.

'Hello?' she said, clearing her throat and putting on her best phone voice. 'I'm sorry for the delay, may I help you?'

But it wasn't Detective Constable Pritchard, it was Jackie, on her way to work. The journey took about half an hour, Hazel knew, and she settled happily into her armchair.

'You'll never guess what happened!' she said, thinking that for once Jackie might pay attention. Normally she had the radio on in the background and didn't seem that interested.

This morning she was all ears, for sure, but to Hazel's surprise she didn't 'ooh' and 'ahh'. Instead, she switched off the radio and listened in silence to her mum's account and when she'd finished Jackie said, 'You gave them how much?'

Hazel repeated the figure and there was a sharp intake of breath. 'I'm going to pull in, don't go away.'

Once parked, she told Hazel to repeat the story all over again, every last detail. Hazel worried that it would make her late for work, but she said it didn't matter.

'Oh, Mum,' she sighed at last. 'I can't believe what you've done.'

The words dropped like stones into a well and Hazel felt herself shrink, her hands start to tremble.

'There's no way the police would ever ask you to do that,' Jackie added, exasperated. Hazel's bottom lip quivered, just as it used to when she was a little girl. 'You've been tricked, don't you see? You'll never set eyes on that money again.'

At the local police headquarters, Sgt Kent replaced the phone and sighed.

'Bad business,' he said, leaning back in his chair and scratching his bald head. 'Seems an old lady in Brixham's been scammed. Handed over ten thousand pounds yesterday to some fella claiming to be investigating a bank fraud.'

His colleague, PCSO Smith, frowned. She'd heard of cases like this in London. Elderly people were targeted because they were more trusting and the trouble was, the fraudsters were clever and left no trace.

'Poor old thing,' she said with feeling. 'Must have given her a right shock when she realised. Did she sound all right?'

Sgt Kent shrugged. 'It was the daughter who rang and she was beside herself. Kept saying she couldn't believe her own mum had been that stupid.'

'They're very convincing, by all accounts,' PCSO Smith replied. She'd listened to a report about it on the radio. 'All sorts of people have been taken in. Doctors, teachers…' She peeped at her colleague out of the corner of an eye. 'Even retired detective inspectors, I heard.'

Sgt Kent tugged at the collar of his shirt as if it was throttling him. He'd been in the force a long time and still had the greatest respect for his superiors, not like some of the youngsters that came in now, thinking they knew it all when they'd only just set foot in the door.

'I wouldn't know anything about that,' he growled, taking a slurp of the now cold coffee sitting on his desk and wiping his mouth with the back of a hand.

He watched as PCSO Smith removed a piece of chewing gum from her mouth and wrapped it in tissue paper before dropping it in the bin. He wished she wouldn't do that. When he was a lad, he hadn't been allowed chewing gum. His mum had said it was common.

'Well, come on, then,' he said, rising suddenly, grabbing his jacket from the back of the chair and tucking a pen behind his ear. PCSO Smith held out a hand to take his bag and he grunted in approval. She'd learned something since she'd started, then.

'We can't sit around here, watching the paint dry,' he carried on, more to himself now than her. 'Let's go and catch some criminals.'

It didn't take Liz long to compile a list of everyone she could think of who'd enjoy a party and drop it at The Stables. To her relief, there was no sign of its inhabitants, but by late afternoon, when she came out of the bakery in Market Square where she'd been buying iced buns for tea, she spotted Oscar in his stroller with a dark-haired girl.

It was almost closing time, twilight was approaching and the little boy, who was well wrapped up in a bright red jacket and pompom hat, was gazing at a ginger cat washing her fur in someone's doorway. His minder, meanwhile, was talking to the fishmonger, Ryan, who'd come out of his shop in his white, blood-streaked overall and was leaning against the window, holding something between fingers and thumb.

'Hi, Liz,' he said, breaking off his conversation with the girl, who turned to see who it was. 'This here's Pilar.' He glanced at her to check that he'd pronounced the name properly. 'She's from Spain. She's an au pair.'

He said 'au pair' in the kind of hushed tone normally reserved for royalty or pop stars, and at the same time his dense black eyebrows, which nearly met in the middle, shot up to meet his bushy hairline.

Liz smiled. 'Is she? Wow!'

Pleased with the response, Ryan went on to explain that Pilar was delivering invitations for a party at The Stables. Tabitha hadn't scotched the plan, then. Liz wasn't sure what Pilar's English was like, but she seemed content to have Ryan speak for her.

'I can give you a hand if you like, soon as I've locked up here,' he suggested, turning back to his new friend.

Pilar looked doubtful. 'I think there are not too many left,' she replied slowly, taking a tasselled brown bag off her shoulder and looking inside. 'I have nearly finished.'

Ryan was undeterred. 'I'll take you out tonight, then. Introduce you to our famous Tremarnock watering holes!'

Pilar frowned. 'Watering holes? I am sorry, I do not understand.'

Ryan grinned. 'Pubs. You know, where you go for a drink. *Una cerveza*.'

His accent wasn't the best and Liz doubted that Pilar would know what he was talking about, but she seemed to get the gist.

'OK.' She shrugged. 'I do not think there is anything else to do in this place and I am not busy.'

She didn't sound exactly thrilled, but neither had she turned him down.

'Good idea.' Liz marvelled at his quick work. Mind you, he'd probably have some competition from the lads in the village. There'd no doubt be great excitement once they heard about the new girl in town, and a Spanish senorita at that.

Half an hour or so after she reached home, her invitation arrived in an envelope marked 'Mr and Mrs R. Hart'. For a moment she thought it must have come to the wrong address; she still wasn't quite accustomed to her newly married status, having previously been on her own for so long. Handwritten on thick white card in black ink were the words 'Tabitha and Luke Mallon would be delighted if you can join them for drinks and food to celebrate their recent move', followed by the address, date and time. At the bottom it said 'No need to RSVP' and there were two small, discreet champagne glasses outlined in silver in the corner.

As she placed it on the mantelpiece, she reflected that it was perhaps surprising Pilar had been given the task of postmistress. Luke might have wanted to do it himself, or Tabitha, come to that, as it would have been an opportunity to introduce themselves and get to know the layout of the village. Still, they were both busy with the move, and maybe Luke was also working at whatever he did for a living; he'd mentioned that it was Tabitha who was to take over the main running of the guest house.

Pat called soon after, when Liz was parcelling orders for RosieCraft, wrapping hair accessories in pink, scented tissue paper sprinkled with glitter, and sticking them in envelopes ready to take them to the post. She had a steady stream of customers now, mainly from Europe and Japan, and although she didn't make enough money to live on, she enjoyed the freedom of working from home and was proud to be running her own business, however modest.

Rosie, who was artistic and keen on hair accessories herself, helped with new designs that she modelled at school, testing out the reactions of the other girls to see if they'd be likely to sell. One particular item, a tiny, flower fascinator hair clip with a draping chain, had been a particular hit, and Liz had been thrilled to spot two young women she'd never seen before wearing them in Plymouth.

It was after seven, Rosie was upstairs doing homework,

and Liz had planned to call in on Pat tomorrow, when she'd been to the supermarket and bought the items the old woman needed. Pat, however, had other ideas.

'Well, I'll be blowed!' she exclaimed, swaying in excitement on the doorstep. She was brandishing an invitation, the same one that had dropped through Liz's letterbox. 'I haven't been to a party for years.'

Fearing that she might fall over, Liz quickly took her arm and ushered her to a chair in the front room, where she threw another log on the fire before settling on the charcoal-grey sofa facing her friend.

'We can go together. It'll be fun. What are you going to wear?'

Pat huffed. 'Nobody wants to look at me. I'll just wear that green dress I bring out every Christmas.'

Liz nodded. 'Perfect.' Then she bit her lip. 'I'm not sure any of my clothes are suitable. Luke and Tabitha are awfully glamorous. She'll no doubt look stunning and put me to shame.'

'Rubbish. You're always pretty as a picture!' Liz was high on Pat's list of favourite people, though Rosie came first, of course. She shuffled to the edge of her seat and leaned forward. 'I say…'

Liz knew that expression only too well. There was gossip to come.

'Maeve from the shop called in to sell me a raffle ticket for the church.'

The Methodist church hall on Humble Hill had a leaky roof and locals had been fundraising for a new one. Countless events took place there, from Mothers' Union lunches to play mornings for toddlers, yoga and meditation classes to exercise sessions for 'mature movers'. It was an integral part of the community.

They'd been using tin cans to catch the drips for years, but recently the drips had turned into puddles and even buckets weren't big enough, so they'd had to requisition a couple of big black wheelie bins, strategically positioned in the hall with notices on saying 'Do Not Move'. Barbara, who ran The Lobster Pot and was a great organiser, had kicked off the fundraising with a charity race night, and thanks to a number of other initiatives they were now about a third of the way to achieving their target.

'Oh, yes?' said Liz, raising her voice so that Pat could hear, and wondering where this would lead.

'Well,' she went on, relishing her moment in the spotlight. 'Maeve told me that woman – Tabitha,' she corrected herself. 'She only went and bought her bread and her newspaper from Waitrose.'

It was said with such a sneer that it sounded for all the world as if she were a convicted bag-snatcher.

Liz laughed. She couldn't help herself. 'How on earth does Maeve know?'

'Saw her getting out of her flash car,' Pat sniffed. 'Carrying the *Daily Mail* and a loaf of brown bread with "Waitrose" clearly written on the packet.' She shook her head. 'Maeve wasn't impressed, I can assure you. And that couple from the bakery will be horrified if they get wind of it.'

Virtually the whole village went to Maeve's General Stores for their newspapers, and to the bakery for delicious fresh bread, hot sausage rolls and Cornish pasties. Even so, it was hard to make a decent living, especially in the winter months, and the shopkeepers needed all the help they could get.

Liz frowned. 'She probably hasn't found the bakery or the General Stores yet. I'm sure she'll go there once she knows about them. And don't forget she's invited us all to her house. It's very generous, especially so soon after they've moved in.'

Pat wasn't convinced. 'She'd best be careful, that one,' she muttered darkly. 'Party or no party, you don't want to go putting people's noses out of joint before you've hardly even arrived.'

Liz was determined not to stoke the flames. 'You should tell her about the shops at the party,' she said reasonably. 'I expect she'll be grateful for the information.'

Pat was silent for a moment, pondering her words, then her face brightened. 'I know, I can mention the church flowers, too! We're one down since my friend died.'

'Excellent,' said Liz, though secretly she didn't see Tabitha as a flower arranger. There again, she couldn't pretend to know her properly yet. She might have all sorts of hidden talents up her sleeve.

On Saturday, Liz and Rosie took Loveday to a grim, out-of-town discount store to buy things for her new flat.

'Are you absolutely sure?' Liz asked, eyeing the contents of the overflowing trolley suspiciously as they waited at the till to pay.

She had originally suggested a trip to one of the smart department stores in Plymouth, thinking that they'd have lunch afterwards in the modern restaurant on the top floor with lovely views of the city, but Loveday was having none of it.

'We need loads of stuff,' she'd reasoned, fiddling with a large silver hoop in her earlobe. 'Sheets, towels, cushions...' She'd paused, racking her brain to remember all the other items on her mental list. 'Crockery, cutlery, lampshades, curtains, ornaments. It'll be much cheaper for you at the discount place. We can get more of everything.'

Liz had taken a deep breath. The truth was that she'd

expected to buy a stylish vase for Loveday and Jesse, or a picture to hang on their wall, perhaps, not to cough up for the entire contents of their home. But neither of them had much money and, after discussing it with Robert, they'd agreed that they'd like to help. In truth, Liz was delighted to be able to do so; before marrying Robert, she'd had to watch every penny.

Loveday had taken ages to choose what she needed, spending what seemed like hours examining spotty toothbrush mugs and floral laundry baskets, and lingering over dustpans and brushes, until Liz pointed out that the flat was part-furnished so there might be one provided. Just when they thought they'd finished and nothing more could fit in the trolley, Loveday found a three-for-two section near the till.

'Which do you prefer?' she asked Rosie, picking up a set of patterned tea towels. 'These, or the plain and stripy ones? Or I could have a selection of each?'

Rosie, who was tired, hungry and losing the will to live, rolled her eyes. She'd got to know Loveday well since Robert and Liz had been going out together and enjoyed having someone older to look up to, almost like a big sister. But there were limits even to her capacity for hero-worship.

'Are you really going to do any drying up? Really? Won't you just leave things on the side to dry themselves?'

Loveday puffed out her cheeks. 'Honestly, you're no help whatsoever. Of course I won't be drying up but every house has to have tea towels. Don't you know *anything*?'

When at last they'd settled up, they loaded all their purchases into the boot of the car then made a beeline for the ground-floor café, which was bulging with other weary-looking customers and fraught children. Two other waitresses were on duty at A Winkle In Time so Loveday had the entire day off and was determined to enjoy every minute of it.

'I could eat a scabby horse!' she exclaimed, examining the menu and settling on ham, egg, chips and a Diet Coke to wash it down. Rosie chose a cheese and tomato sandwich while Liz had soup and a roll.

'Will you help me make the flat all nice and homely?' Loveday asked Liz, who was trying to ignore the little girl at the table next to theirs. She was wiggling in her seat, desperate for the loo, while her mother, deep in conversation with her friend, was deaf to all pleading. It seemed that at any moment there might be an accident.

'Sorry?' She switched her attention back to Loveday, who was swigging Coke through a straw, and the girl repeated herself, adding, 'Jesse and me want to make it really cosy so lots of people come round. His mum won't let him have more than one friend at a time but he can have however many he likes in his own place, can't he?'

Liz frowned. 'You won't be able to have endless parties and play loud music, you know. It's a terraced house, you'll upset the neighbours.'

'Oh, don't worry, we'll turn down the volume after midnight,' Loveday scoffed. 'And when you visit we'll only play old granny stuff like...' she wrinkled her nose '...like Barry Manilow.'

'But I don't like Barry Manilow!' Liz protested.

There was no room for the new purchases at Loveday's friend's house, so it all had to go in Liz's spare room. Once they'd finished unloading, and spent a while admiring their haul, it was nearly time to get ready for the party.

'You are coming, aren't you?' Liz asked Loveday. The boys from A Winkle In Time were invited, too, but, like Robert, wouldn't arrive till the restaurant closed. Rosie had chosen to spend the night with her friend, Mandy, saying that she didn't want to be the youngest person there, and they'd dropped her off on the way home from the discount store.

'I guess so,' said Loveday sulkily, 'but won't it be really boring with everyone just standing around talking?'

'You might be pleasantly surprised. I get the feeling that our new neighbours are quite an unusual pair.'

While Loveday returned home to change, declaring that she'd be back at seven thirty because there was no way she was going to turn up at the party on her own, Liz went upstairs to shower and wash her hair. It was rather a luxury to be on her own for once, and she decided to open the delicious new, orange-blossom shampoo, conditioner and body moisturiser set that her father and stepmother had given her for her birthday.

As she undressed, however, she found herself fretting about whether her daughter would be all right at Mandy's, and not just because of the brain tumour. Rosie had had an unhappy time at primary school because she'd been bullied by certain children because of her cerebral palsy. Since starting secondary school, though, things had improved and she seemed to have found a kind, close-knit circle of friends at last.

Now, instead of spending every moment of every weekend with her mother, she often arranged things with them such as cinema trips or shopping in Plymouth. This pleased Liz, but still she was super-alert to the possibility that something could go wrong. Rosie might get picked on in the street, for example, because of her limp and tricky arm. Or Mandy or one of the other girls might suggest going somewhere that involved more walking than Rosie could comfortably manage.

Of course she'd say that she could cope because she'd hate to draw attention to herself. She'd hate it even more, however, if she had to call her mother because she'd got into difficulty.

Like all children, all she ever wanted was to be exactly the same as everyone else.

Liz gave herself a mental ticking off. She was doing it again, anticipating problems that might never happen. Rosie was growing up and must be allowed to spread her wings. This felt almost as hard, though, as everything that had gone before, when every instinct screamed at her to wrap her daughter in cotton wool so that nothing could ever hurt her again.

She turned on the tap in the en suite shower by her bedroom, which was such a luxury after the shabby old bathroom at Dove Cottage. She had her back turned to the door and the noise of the water meant that she didn't hear Robert enter quietly and take off his clothes, dropping them on the floor.

'What a nice surprise!' he murmured, stepping in to join her and bending down to kiss her lightly on the back of her neck, which was dripping with shampoo.

Startled, she spun round to find him right in front of her, smiling softly and slightly shyly, as if she might just turn him away. But his eyes were burning.

'Come and stand here,' she said, moving aside so that there was room for them both under the warm water. He ran his hands up and down her body, which made her shiver, and closed her eyes, tipping back her head to rinse the shampoo out of her hair.

'I'll do that,' said Robert, his voice low and mysterious, and he massaged the foam out gently before reaching for the soap.

'What are you doing?' she asked innocently, as she watched him lather it between his two hands. 'I've been in ages. I need to get out.'

He shook his head firmly, his shyness having vanished. 'I need to make sure you've washed properly and you haven't missed anywhere. Here, let me start at the top and work my way down.'

She was still glowing, and not just from the hot shower, when the doorbell rang.

'Let's ignore it,' Robert said lazily. He had his arm round Liz, who was resting her head on his chest, and he was twisting a strand of her damp hair round his finger.

She was inclined to follow his advice until she heard Esme's unmistakable 'Coo-ee' through the letterbox.

'Quick!' She jumped out of bed and threw on the dress that she'd draped over the back of the chair. The lights were on and Esme would know she was in. She wouldn't give up; she was like that.

Liz ran downstairs, smoothing her hair and adopting her best, most guiltless smile before answering the door. Esme, who rarely missed a trick, raised one eyebrow and opened her mouth to speak, before thinking better of it and shutting it again. She was a potter, who lived on her own in the flat above Dove Cottage and she and Liz had become close, particularly after Rosie had fallen ill with her brain tumour.

A tall, thin woman of sixty-odd, Esme took off her flowing, multicoloured coat and declared that she, too, would be walking to the party with Liz, Pat and Loveday. It seemed that there was to be quite an entourage. As she was already dressed in her party frock, a batik-print, lilac and blue maxi, she clearly intended to stay until departure time.

Robert appeared to say a quick goodbye and Liz, studiously avoiding eye contact, went to put on the kettle. When she returned, Esme, who wasn't normally one to gossip, couldn't resist informing her that Nathan the postman had seen a delivery van parked on the corner of Humble Hill, transporting cartloads of groceries towards The Stables.

'There was literally mountains of food and drink,' she said dramatically. 'Enough to feed the five thousand. And the au pair told Ryan they've hired a caterer from Tavistock.' Esme sniffed, making the end of her long, thin nose twitch. 'They might have given Audrey a call. She could have done it for them.'

As well as owning Seaspray Boutique, Audrey ran a small catering business on the side that was popular with wealthier tourists in summer.

'Well, as Audrey's on the guest list, she can introduce herself tonight and mention her business,' Liz suggested. 'Anyway, she'll have more fun as she won't be stuck in the kitchen for once. Now,' she went on, changing the subject quickly, 'let's forget the tea and have some wine instead. Then I'd better put on my make-up as Pat's bound to be early.'

As she went to the kitchen to fetch a bottle and some glasses, she found herself pondering the fact that she seemed to have spent the past few days defending Tabitha to herself and others, and wasn't sure why she'd bothered. Tabitha wasn't exactly your classic landlady, she was far too glitzy and a bit stand-offish. Come to that, she wasn't the type to be living in a village like this either.

Liz couldn't help wondering what on earth had persuaded her to come here in the first place. It did seem odd. Quite frankly, the woman might have been more suited to a posh part of London than warm, friendly, down-to-earth Tremarnock. Perhaps she wouldn't stay long.

Chapter Four

'You're doing WHAT?'

A man walked past the house and Tabitha darted away from the window quickly.

'Having a party – for practically the whole village,' she said, perching on the end of her bed, the phone still cradled between shoulder and ear.

Her friend, Molly, gasped.

'But you've only just moved in, for God's sake. You must be mad.'

Tabitha examined her fingernails, which were painted an unusual shade of pebble grey. That all-too-familiar lump had started to form in her throat again and she tried to ignore it.

'It's all right,' she said in a small voice. 'I've got plenty of help. Luke says it's important to get to know everyone.' She fiddled with the thin gold chain round her neck with a tiny horseshoe on the end. 'He wants us to play an active part in the community. He says this is a good way to start.'

'Sheesh, Tabby, you hate all that community stuff. It's your worst nightmare.'

Tabitha imagined her friend sitting cross-legged on the carpet, painting her own nails, ready for an evening out in Deansgate maybe, or the Northern Quarter. Perhaps she'd be trying out one of the new bars or going to the cinema, followed by a meal at their favourite Chinese or Thai.

'He'll do most of the talking, you know what he's like,' Tabitha insisted. 'I'll just stand in the corner and smile.'

Molly sighed. 'Oh Tabby, I wish you were here. When can you and Oscar come and visit?'

Tabitha thought how tied she was going to be now, running the guest house, and the last thing Luke would want would be for her to go dashing back to Manchester every five minutes. He had been determined to get her away from there and from Molly, too, though he'd never put it exactly like that.

'Not for a while,' she replied truthfully. If ever.

She didn't suggest that her friend come and stay, she didn't need to. Molly knew the score.

'You must phone often.' She was trying to be cheerful. 'Promise me you will.'

'I promise,' said Tabitha, thinking Molly had no idea; those calls would be her lifeline. Without them, she didn't know how she'd cope.

She could hear voices outside so rose and glanced out of the window again, taking care to be far enough back not to be seen. Thanks to the yellowy glow from the streetlamp nearby, she could make out a group of women coming down the street, talking and laughing. Leading the way was a lady in late middle age, wearing a long, flowing, brightly coloured coat that reached almost to her ankles, and beside her was a young girl in nothing but a skimpy top and mini-skirt, teetering in sky-high boots. Behind them, an elderly, stooped woman with snow-white hair was hanging on to the arm of a younger, dark-haired person for support: Liz.

Tabitha's pulse quickened. They'd be here any minute and Luke would expect her to greet them.

'I have to go,' she said, checking herself quickly in the dressing-table mirror and pinning on her best smile. 'I'll call you back as soon as I can.'

Liz was dismayed to discover that they were the first to arrive. She blamed Pat, who'd turned up at Bag End while she, Esme and by then Loveday, too, had been enjoying a glass of wine. Pat had asked the time so often and complained about being late that in the end Liz could stand it no longer and suggested they all set off.

Luke, however, quickly put her at her ease. 'Lovely to see you again.' He passed her coat to a young man in a black shirt and trousers and kissed her on both cheeks. She caught a faint whiff of expensive aftershave. 'I'm so grateful for your help. Without you, of course, none of this would have been possible.'

He turned to the other women, standing awkwardly in the middle of the hall, and introduced himself. 'I'm so glad you could come, and at such short notice, too. We tend to do things quite spontaneously, Tabitha and I. Welcome to The Stables. Let me find you a glass of bubbly!'

'I'm not that keen on champagne, to be honest with you, I'll have sherry,' Pat blurted, rather ungraciously, Liz thought, and she felt herself redden on her friend's behalf.

'She's a bit deaf,' she whispered to her host, hoping that he wouldn't be offended.

Luke looked amused and took the old woman gallantly by the arm. 'One sherry coming up,' he announced, ushering them into a large reception room on the left. 'You must meet my wife.'

She was standing alone in front of the marble fireplace, lit by the rosy glow of flickering flames, and looked quite stunning, Liz thought, in a long, tight-fitting silver dress that showed off her statuesque figure. Her thick, curly black hair just skimmed her bare shoulders and fanned out around her face like candyfloss.

Liz could feel Loveday start, and Pat's eyes opened wide. Glamorous women were few and far between in Tremarnock, especially when the tourists went home, and you certainly wouldn't find a dress like that in the local boutiques, not even Audrey's.

Luke disappeared to fetch the drinks and for a moment nobody spoke, until Tabitha exclaimed: 'Cool boots!'

She was staring down at Loveday's black, platform, knee-length boots, with white laces criss-crossing all the way up the front. These were teamed with fishnet tights, a black PVC mini-skirt and a red satin shirt, open to the cleavage. The overall effect was certainly eye-catching.

For a moment Loveday looked startled, then she smiled with pleasure. 'Aw, thanks. Robert says I can't wear them for waitressing but I wear them loads when I'm not working.'

'They're unique.' Tabitha was still marvelling and, grabbing Esme's arm for support, Loveday raised a foot and tipped it from side to side so that her hostess could take in the full glory.

'I'm not sure I could get away with them,' Tabitha went on, 'but the girls in Manchester would go mad for them. Where did you buy them?'

'Cardiff,' Loveday replied, lapping up the praise. 'I went with my boyfriend for the weekend. You'd never find anything like that round here. The clothes shops are dead old-fashioned.'

Realising what she'd said, her eyes slid left and right guiltily, but luckily Audrey wasn't within earshot.

A helper arrived with a tray of drinks, which they took gratefully, and Loveday, clearly sensing that she'd found a kindred spirit in Tabitha, filled her in on some of the local fashion shops that were worth a look in. 'Royal William Yard in Plymouth's not bad. There's a couple of designer dress places – not that I can afford them.'

While the two chatted, Liz took the opportunity to glance around. The room had been freshly painted and had a low panelled ceiling, pretty leaded windows overlooking the street and interesting wood panelling that went halfway up the walls. The owners had already hung up a collection of framed prints, as well as a variety of modern paintings, and there was a giant rectangular gilt mirror above the fireplace.

The furniture had been pushed back and in each of the four corners was a mahogany table with a heavy lamp on top, their ceramic bases shaped like ivory and silver pineapples with sable shades. The wooden floor was original, and had been polished to a shine.

As more people arrived, the temperature and volume increased and Liz recognised Tony Cutt's loud voice behind her. She turned to find him, with his handsome Brazilian partner, Felipe, chatting to Rick Kane, who was accompanied by the white-blonde lady friend he'd dined with at A Winkle In Time.

Tony worked in PR, and he and Felipe, who was quite a bit younger, divided their time between a flat in London and Tony's cottage in Tremarnock. Felipe didn't work, but he was very artistic and had designed the leaflets and posters for Liz when the whole village community had got together to raise funds for Rosie's proton therapy in Oklahoma. His English was pretty broken, but when he was around he threw himself with gusto into local life and was a keen member of Tremarnock Art Club, which met every Friday afternoon in the leaky church hall.

Tony, who was wearing a rather tight floral shirt, roared

with laughter, and Liz caught Felipe's eye, signalling that she'd join them in a moment, before turning back to her group to excuse herself. Tabitha had taken off a gold bracelet that was covered in charms, and was showing it to Loveday, while Pat and Esme looked on.

'I got this one in Amsterdam,' Tabitha explained. 'Look, it's a tulip. And this here's the hand of Fatima. A friend bought it for me in Egypt. It's supposed to ward off the evil eye.'

Loveday whistled. 'Wow! All those different countries!' She peered at a tiny treble clef on the bracelet, holding it between finger and thumb. 'What's this one for?'

'I used to be in a folk rock band,' Tabitha replied. 'I had a partner who played the harmonica, and there was a guitarist and a sax player. I did the vocals – and wrote some of the music.'

Loveday's eyes widened with interest. 'A real band! What were you called?'

Tabitha shook her head, as if regretting that she'd mentioned it. 'It was a long time ago.' She quickly fastened the bracelet back on her wrist and reached for her glass, which was on the mantelpiece behind her. 'I don't do it any more.'

Now that the ice had been broken, Pat, who'd been very quiet up to now, plucked up courage and took a step a forward.

'I wondered if you'd care to help me with the church flowers? We're a bit low on numbers, you see. We generally meet once a week but if there's a wedding or christening, obviously there's more to do.'

Tabitha inhaled sharply and her face froze. 'Absolutely not.' And without more ado she pushed past the old woman, practically elbowing her aside in her eagerness to get away.

Pat's mouth dropped open and for a moment she was lost for words. They all were. It had been so abrupt. No explanation, apology or excuse. Nothing.

'Whatever did I...?' Pat said at last, but she didn't finish the sentence. The courage that she'd mustered previously had dissolved and now she just looked old, upset and confused.

Liz, seeing her sway, quickly grabbed her by the arm and guided her to a seat by the window, afraid that she might fall. She felt wounded and angry on Pat's behalf, because she knew that the flowers were a big thing for her. The three or four hours that she spent choosing blooms and making beautiful arrangements was practically the only time that she left the house during the week, and it was quite an effort for her even to get to church. It was all too easy to laugh at things like that, but Liz knew better.

'I never meant to offend her,' Pat muttered, plonking down in the chair and shaking her head. She'd gone quite pale and Liz passed her the glass of sherry, which was only half-drunk; she sipped it gratefully, as if it were medicine.

There was scarcely room to move now for people, but Liz managed to crouch at her feet and pat her on the knee.

'Are you all right? What a strange thing!'

She was trying to process what had happened. One minute Tabitha had seemed friendly and quite relaxed, and the next she'd been storming off as if she'd been insulted; it made no sense. Pat's colour, thankfully, was now starting to return, but she'd clearly had a shock. She wasn't used to being snubbed; she was usually surrounded by friends and family, people who knew and loved her.

'I'll tell you one thing,' she said, her voice now sounding a little stronger, 'that's the last time I ask that woman to do anything. As far as I'm concerned, she's a stuck up so-and-so who left her manners in Manchester, or wherever it is she comes from.'

Liz couldn't help agreeing.

The couple from Ashley House came over to say hello and

while they looked after Pat, Liz excused herself and went in search of the loo. She wanted a few moments on her own to collect her thoughts. It had crossed her mind that to cheer Pat up she should offer to help with the flowers herself, but that was the last thing she needed.

She was already a member of the Parish Paths Group, which aimed to keep rights of way open to the public by clearing vegetation, rebuilding stiles and kissing gates and repairing footpath surfaces. What with that, running her own business and helping at the restaurant, too, she had quite enough on her plate.

The trouble was, in a place like Tremarnock there were numerous worthy causes to throw yourself into, from providing hot lunches for elderly residents to driving teenage mums-to-be to and from antenatal appointments. Living as they did so far from the hallowed portals of Westminster, sometimes it seemed as if the rest of the country forgot they existed and they just had to get on and do it all themselves.

There were several closed doors to the right and left of the corridor, and she opened them in turn, hoping to find the bathroom. The final door was locked, probably occupied, so she waited a few moments, resting her back against the wall. She felt tired, suddenly, and uncomfortable. She'd been looking forward to the party and to seeing all her friends, but now all she wanted was to slip away to Bag End.

It was quite clear to her that, however hospitable Luke might be, Tabitha was a tricky customer who didn't really want them there, but Robert had promised Luke that he'd look in after the restaurant closed so, come what may, she would have to hang around.

The door to the kitchen at the far end of the hallway was ajar, delicious smells were wafting out and there was a great deal of activity going on inside. A girl in black, like the other helpers, was standing by the island in the middle, taking things off baking trays and putting them on platters, until a stout, older woman in a white apron pushed her aside impatiently and rearranged what she'd done.

The door burst open and the young waiter that Liz had seen earlier emerged with another tray of drinks. He had sweat on his brow and an air of confusion, and she shot him a sympathetic smile. She knew what it felt like. Sometimes, on a busy evening at A Winkle In Time, it seemed that her feet hardly touched the floor.

Now she could see inside the kitchen more clearly and noticed Tabitha, standing with her back to the stainless-steel fridge-freezer, keeping out of the way. She was fiddling with the bracelet on her arm and appeared not to know what to do with herself. Feeling like an intruder, Liz would have averted her gaze, but the stout older woman barked at one of the girls, making Tabitha start, and she glanced up, catching sight of Liz for the first time.

Their eyes locked momentarily until they both looked away quickly, but not before Liz had noticed something peculiar in the other woman's expression, a flicker that made goosebumps run up and down her spine. She wasn't imagining it, she was certain: Tabitha was frightened of something. No, more than frightened, she was petrified.

Liz hesitated, not quite sure what to do, then the loo door opened and Audrey stepped out, wearing a quirky long, loose, emerald-green dress that had been on one of the mannequins in the window of her shop last summer.

'Liz!' she cried, her cheeks flushed, her lips painted crimson. She had dark hair tipped with platinum streaks, cut pixie-short and artfully mussed. 'I didn't realise you were here!'

She was bubbling with party spirit, having clearly managed to set aside any pique that she might have felt on learning that her catering services had been spurned in favour of someone from Tavistock.

'Fabulous do!' she went on, then whispered in Liz's ear. 'I say, Luke's charming, isn't he? Terribly handsome!'

'He is.' But Liz couldn't help remembering that look on Tabitha's face. Did he know that his wife was terrified of something and, if so, what?

After going to the loo, she strolled back towards the party and joined the guests who'd moved across the corridor to the other reception room, which was less crowded and cooler. Rick Kane had a protective arm round his white-blonde lady friend and they were deep in conversation with some locals, including the leader of the Parish Council, who was an awful bore. Liz couldn't face getting stuck with him, so she turned her attention to another, rowdier group on her right.

This was made up of teens and twenty-somethings, including Jenny and John Lambert's boys, Ryan the fishmonger, Nathan the postman and his girlfriend, Annie, the fitness trainer. Nathan had been a skinny lad until he'd started downing protein shakes, bought himself a home gym and developed an impressive set of biceps and a barrel chest. The only problem was he seemed to have forgotten about his lower half, which was oddly out of proportion with the rest.

Annie, who ran the Mature Movers class at the church hall, as well as Zumba sessions and yoga for pregnant women, didn't seem to mind, though. She had a pretty, lively face, was short and muscly and spent her life in Lycra. They were an ideal match.

Liz was surprised that Loveday wasn't with them. She and Nathan had been an item for a while, until she'd dumped him unceremoniously for someone who'd been dumped in turn for Ryan, but it was all water under the bridge now.

'What are you laughing about?' She smiled, moving over to join them. She caught a faint whiff of fish wafting from Ryan's direction. 'Not me, I hope?'

One of the waiters approached with a tray of canapés and she popped a triangle of toast, spread with pâté, into her mouth.

'Ryan had a date with the au pair,' Nathan said gleefully, 'but when he asked her out again, she said she was going to go back to Spain so there was no point. Seems he frightened her so much she's decided to leave the country!'

Liz glanced at poor Ryan, whose thick black eyebrows were zigzagging across his forehead in a deep frown.

'She's been planning to leave anyway,' he spluttered. 'She said she doesn't like the countryside. She's told the Mallons she'll only stay to settle their little boy in. It's nothing to do with me.'

But Nathan was having none of it.

'What did you do to her?' He smirked. 'Did you wave your cockles and winkles at her?'

The others guffawed. Ryan grew redder in the face and Liz came to his rescue by asking Annie about her mother and grandmother, to whom she was very close.

'My gran, Hazel, she's not been too well.' Annie frowned, then something distracted her on the far side of the room and she didn't finish. Liz spun round and saw Loveday enter with Luke and stop just inside the door. She was gazing up at her host, who was much taller than her and standing very close. He laughed loudly and she twiddled one of her hooped earrings and laughed back.

'They're getting on well.' Nathan sniggered.

Annie poked him in the ribs. 'Shh, they might hear.'

'Where's Jesse?' he asked suddenly, having forgotten all

about Ryan and the au pair now that something more interesting had cropped up.

Liz reminded him that Jesse and the others were working
but that they'd be along later if the party was still going.

'I reckon it will be,' Ryan commented, grabbing another
bottle of lager from a passing waiter and taking a swig, while
Liz helped herself to a second canapé. 'Doesn't look like
they're in any hurry to get rid of us.'

Thinking that she'd been away from Pat for a while and
ought to check on her, Liz wandered back to the other room
and cast an eye around. The old woman was still on the chair
where Liz had left her and seemed to have attracted quite
a gathering, including Audrey, who was kneeling beside her.
Tony and Felipe were standing by the fireplace, still talking
to Rick and his new girlfriend, and Tony beckoned to Liz to
come over. Tabitha, meanwhile, was nowhere to be seen.

'Darling, you look gorgeous!' Tony said, admiring the strap-
less black cocktail dress that Liz had bought for her honey-
moon. She and Robert had had a glorious long weekend in
Paris after the wedding.

Felipe, it seemed, had been telling them about his art club
and the strange chap who'd dropped by to talk to them. An
artist himself, he lived in a cottage on the Polgarry Castle estate
with his young son. Liz knew that his paintings sold rather
well in London and elsewhere, but he rarely ventured into
Tremarnock and had little to do with local affairs. The castle,
high up above the village, had been empty since its eccentric
owner had died. It must have been pretty lonely up there.

'I do not know how he survives,' Felipe said, shuddering.
'So cold, so gloomy. I think he must be, how do you say,
loco?' He put a finger to his temple and twisted it round, as
you would a screw.

'Mad,' Tony said pleasantly, 'bonkers. But we don't know that, darling. Maybe he and his son like the solitude.'

Felipe shook his head. 'Poor little boy. I definitely would be bonking if I lived there.'

Liz stifled a giggle.

'Bon*kers*.' Tony sounded very patient.

'That eez what I said.'

Rick's white-blonde girlfriend, who was called Sylvia, piped up that she, too, had an interest in art and Liz noticed that Rick now had his hand on her bottom.

'My ex used to paint in his spare time. I used to model for him.'

'With or without clothes?' Tony roared with laughter at his own joke.

'Without,' she replied, unembarrassed.

Tony clapped his hands. 'Excellent! You should do some life modelling for Tremarnock Art Club, shouldn't she, Felipe?'

The younger man looked perplexed.

'Life drawing,' Tony explained. 'Painting naked ladies. You'd enjoy that, wouldn't you, darling?'

Felipe looked aghast. 'Oh, no, we do only landscapes and flowers. And fruit in bowls. No one naked.' He shook his head vigorously. 'No, no.'

Their drinks were topped up once more; the waiters really were most assiduous. Tony, who was enjoying himself immensely and was even more of a gossip than Pat, whispered theatrically, 'Luke's a very good-looking man.' He winked at Liz. 'I've noticed all the ladies flirting with him. Tabitha had better watch out.'

'She's a very rude woman.'

Liz turned to find Esme right behind her, raising her sharp

chin haughtily and staring down her pointed nose. Tony stopped in his tracks.

'She was unkind to Pat and she hasn't been out of the kitchen for hours. Haven't you noticed? She's hardly spoken to anyone. She's left it all to her poor husband.'

Liz shuffled miserably. However peculiar Tabitha was, she didn't want to openly criticise someone whose house she was in and whose wine and food she'd been enjoying, and besides, she'd seen that look on her hostess's face. She was about to suggest that she walk Pat home, resolving to call Robert and tell him that she'd had enough and wouldn't be returning, when she heard a volley of knocks and Luke's loud voice in the hall.

Glancing at her watch, she realised that it was almost midnight already. Where had the time gone? Pat must be shattered, she thought, feeling guilty. She'd meant to drop her home after a couple of hours. There again, she must have been having a good time or she'd surely have asked to leave.

All at once, numbers in the room seemed to double as Jesse and the other staff from A Winkle in Time walked in, followed by Luke, with an arm round Robert's shoulder. They were soon joined by Loveday and the group from next door, laughing loudly and pushing each other, as if they hadn't met for years. Robert smiled at Liz but didn't join her because he and Luke were talking.

From a distance they looked quite similar. Tall, slim, handsome and the same sort of age, they were both casually dressed, but while Robert's white shirt was rolled up at the sleeves and crumpled down the front, Luke's sleeves were fastened with gold cufflinks and his pale pink shirt was immaculately ironed.

Tony, who liked a large audience, strolled over with Felipe to greet the young people and Liz joined them. Loveday had an arm round Jesse's hips and was resting her head on his shoulder, but she straightened up when Liz approached and crooked a finger.

'He's amazing!' she whisper-shouted, so that Liz could hear her above the chatter. 'Mr Mallon, I mean, Luke. He's a *huge* businessman. He was telling me about it. He's got loads of people working for him.'

Liz smiled at her enthusiasm. 'He does seem very successful. What does he do, exactly? Aside from setting up the guest house, I mean?'

Loveday shrugged. 'He's got his own company. Financial services or something. I didn't really understand.' She grinned. 'Main thing is...' she leaned towards Liz, her voice lowered, '...he's obviously completely loaded and I reckon there might be an opportunity for me!'

Liz raised her eyebrows. 'Really? What do you mean?'

'Well.' Loveday's eyes were shining. 'He told me he's going to need to take on extra staff over the coming months and asked me a lot about what I do. He seemed very interested.'

Liz frowned. She didn't want to burst the girl's bubble, but it was hardly a job offer.

'Could be worth exploring,' she replied, noncommittal.

Jesse had been chatting to Alex, or rather to his Elvis quiff, which was looking particularly glossy tonight, but he turned to Liz and Loveday, who repeated her story.

'Sounds great,' he said, ruffling his girlfriend's hair. 'But don't jump the gun. Luke's had a few drinks, remember. He might have forgotten everything he said in the morning.'

Loveday huffed. 'Honestly! You're both so negative! I'd be stuck waitressing for ever if I listened to you.'

'Sorry,' said Liz said, feeling mean for having poured cold water on the idea. 'It does sound promising.' Loveday had been at the restaurant a long time and made no secret of the fact that she was bored. Perhaps the Mallons would have something for her, you never knew.

Pleased to detect a glimmer of enthusiasm at last, Loveday started bubbling over. 'He's so cool and suave, like an actor or something. And isn't the house gorgeous? I've never been anywhere so posh in all my life.'

Liz smiled, but a strange niggle had lodged in her stomach and later that night, after she and Robert had dropped Pat off and were climbing into bed, she mentioned what had happened.

'Luke's a go-getter,' he said, smoothing away the wrinkles on his wife's brow with a thumb. 'I reckon the guest house will be really successful. It's just what Tremarnock needs, and I wouldn't be surprised if there's an opening for Loveday somewhere. Let's wait and see. I agree Tabitha's a bit frosty, but if she's married to him she must be all right.'

'She looked terrified in the kitchen,' Liz protested. 'I know I wasn't imagining it.'

He turned out the light and coiled an arm round her waist. 'You're tired and your imagination's running away with you. Now, stop worrying and close your eyes.'

His voice was low and gentle and she felt her shoulders relax, her weary limbs sinking into the mattress. Soon, very soon, she'd slip into unconsciousness.

'Don't you think he's a bit too good to be true?' she mumbled. 'Too handsome and charming? No one can be that perfect.'

'Hush,' said Robert. 'I'm sure he's got his faults just like everyone else. Now, for goodness' sake, go to sleep!'

Chapter Five

'I feel such a fool.' Hazel dabbed her eyes with a cotton handkerchief and stared at her lap.

She was sitting in her favourite armchair in the small front room of her flat, a mug of tea by her side. It was almost midday and she was still in her nightclothes. In fact, she hadn't been out of them since that dreadful event eight days ago, hadn't left the flat.

She'd gone down with a cold and sore throat and had spent most of the time in bed. Jackie had been to the chemist to get her some lozenges and a bottle of cough mixture, but they didn't seem to do much good. Annie had phoned a few times and said she'd visit at the weekend, and Hazel was certain she'd be more herself by then, but, oh! It had been such a shock.

'You mustn't blame yourself,' said PCSO Smith, who'd pulled up a chair from the little dining table in front of the window. 'They're so convincing. It could have happened to anyone.'

Hazel shook her head. 'I was so stupid, like a child. I should have known better. I've caused so much bother for my son and daughter. And the police. And all that money…' She let out a sob and put the handkerchief over her mouth to stifle it.

'It was all the savings I had,' she went on, once she'd composed herself. 'It was supposed to pay for my funeral, so Jackie and

68

Roy wouldn't have to. I never imagined something like this would happen. Never. Barry must be turning in his grave.'

PCSO Smith patted the old woman's knee. It was Sgt Kent who'd told her to come. 'A follow-up call,' he'd said. 'It's what community police work's all about.'

At times like this she felt more like a social worker than a member of Her Majesty's Constabulary, but she was glad that she'd called. 'Come on, now,' she coaxed. 'It could've been worse. At least no one's hurt.'

Hazel hiccupped and the young police officer glanced at her pale, lined face and unkempt hair. There mightn't be physical scars, but the emotional ones were clear for all to see.

'We tried to trace the mobile phone number but it was a pay-as-you-go and they've probably thrown it away,' the policewoman said gently. 'There has been one development, though. It happened to another lady in the Torquay area on Friday. Same story exactly. She drew out twenty-five thousand pounds, if it makes you feel any better. Seems they're targeting around here now. At some point they'll make a slip-up.'

Hazel paused, twisting the hankie round and round her forefinger. She was thinking of something, plucking up the courage to speak.

'You know what really scares me?' she said at last. 'They know where I live, what I look like, everything. I don't feel I can trust anyone. I don't feel safe in my own home any more.'

Her eyes darted to the window, as if someone might be rattling at the lock, trying to get in.

PCSO Smith frowned, wishing that she had some good news to cheer the old woman up, that she could say they'd nailed the bastards and recovered the cash, but unfortunately it wasn't like that.

'I promise you won't hear from them again,' she said

instead. It was something, anyway. 'They're professionals, these people. They make a great deal of money, hundreds of thousands, probably, maybe even more. They're very keen not to be identified. They got what they wanted from you and they won't be coming back.'

Tabitha had been so busy since the party on Saturday that she'd scarcely set foot outside The Stables. For the past five days she'd spent her time in meetings or on the phone and filling in the mountains of paperwork that had to be completed before she and Luke could officially throw open their doors.

When he'd informed her all those months ago that he'd put in an offer to buy a huge, rambling place miles from anywhere, she'd been aghast, and at first she'd tried hard to talk him out of it. She didn't want to leave Manchester or run a guest house, she'd insisted, and what's more, she had absolutely no idea where to begin.

But experience had taught her that arguing with him was pointless. When he got an idea in his head, there was no stopping him.

'I need you to do it, Tabitha,' he'd said seriously, his face up close to hers, so that she could see the pores on his nose and chin. 'There's lots of information online and we'll get people in to help when necessary. It doesn't have to be lucrative, just enough to cover costs. You can furnish it however you want,' he'd added magnanimously, as if that would somehow make her feel better. Then he'd kissed her – quite hard – on the lips. 'I want it to be stunning – just like you.'

If they weren't trying to make money from the venture, she really didn't see the point, but Luke had insisted that it would benefit his other business and give them a reason to be in Cornwall, not that she understood why they needed one.

Once the deal had been signed, she'd felt like a rabbit in the headlights, but as there was no going back, she'd reluctantly set about finding out as much as she could. Though she'd left school early, she'd always been good with figures and fortunately, as Luke had said, there was a great deal of assistance out there in the form of books and online courses.

He'd already obtained permission from the local council to change the use of The Stables from a dilapidated former home into a boutique B & B, but that was really only the beginning. They needed to get fire, gas and food hygiene certificates, as well as special insurance, and Tabitha hadn't even begun to think about marketing and publicity.

The plan was to open in February which, though four months away, seemed frighteningly close. In the past few days, she'd ensured that most of the necessary safety checks had been completed. Now it was time to turn her attention to the interior décor because the visitors' rooms, though freshly painted, lacked furniture and furnishings and those important little touches that would transform a run-of-the-mill lodging house into the really special establishment that her husband required.

This morning, armed with a tape measure, pencil and pad, she went around the house measuring up walls and alcoves for beds and chests of drawers, chairs, sofas, bookcases, side tables and wardrobes. Fortunately Oscar was occupied with Pilar in the playroom, as she'd never have been able to do it with him around.

A little later she sat in the large, square room beside the kitchen, which they'd designated the study, trawled the internet and ordered almost all the furniture that she needed from a well-known London department store. She found the bedding there, too, soft, white Egyptian cotton, and a mass of thick white towels and dressing gowns, plus small, flat screen TVs. Then, her head spinning and already exhausted by choices and costs, she sourced the cutlery and crockery, pots and pans for the breakfasts. By the time she'd finished, she'd spent a small fortune.

She scarcely stopped for lunch and while Pilar took Oscar to the library in the afternoon, Tabitha went through the pile of interiors magazines that she'd brought with her from Manchester and picked out various curtain fabrics, cushions and lamps that she liked the look of. She'd had simple blinds put up in their private quarters before they'd arrived, but they were only temporary, to tide them over until they found something better.

There were to be four guest rooms – three doubles and one twin – that she'd grouped in her mind under the headings 'cosy', 'spacious' and 'luxe', depending on their size, and they were to have an indulgent, contemporary feel with some period features, such as vintage-style lamps, a gilt mirror or a sumptuous chaise longue. She'd have well-thumbed books in bookcases, vases of wild flowers on side tables and ivy twisted around bedposts and across mantelpieces. Luke had said he wanted their visitors to be enchanted as well as comfortable; he wanted the sort of place that reflected owners of style, taste and discernment.

She bit her lip. Who was he trying to fool? She closed the magazine that she'd been looking at and put it down, reflecting sadly that she ought to be enjoying the process. After all, not every woman had the same luxury of time and money at her disposal. Instead, however, it just seemed like a terrible chore that she must finish as quickly as possible or Luke would wonder what on earth she'd been up to.

Pilar and Oscar had returned from the library and it was

already dark outside when the au pair poked her head round the door to inform Tabitha that she had a visitor. 'She is called Shelley Screech, very strange name,' she said mournfully, as if it were only to be expected in a backward place like this.

Tabitha jumped up. So preoccupied had she been that she'd forgotten all about the woman who'd responded to the discreet ad that she'd placed in *The Lady* magazine some weeks ago, asking for help with the cooking, cleaning and general running of the guest house, and at first glance the person who greeted her in the reception room downstairs appeared distinctly unpromising.

Tallish, thin and pale, she had a slot for a mouth, a prominent chin and mousy hair scraped back in an unflattering bun. She'd clearly made some effort to look smart because she was wearing a grey suit, but it fitted badly and she stared disconcertingly at the floor as she shook Tabitha's hand, anxious to avoid eye contact. She couldn't have been more than forty, but her drooping shoulders and lined face suggested a hard life.

Even as Tabitha invited her to sit down, she was thinking that this wouldn't do at all. She'd imagined a neat, efficient type, pleasant and hard-working. Shelley looked as if she might blow away in a puff of wind. In any case, she was only the first person that Tabitha had arranged to see and there were others who'd expressed interest. She'd get the interview over with as quickly as she could and fire off a rejection letter.

While Shelley talked falteringly, in her strong Cornish accent, about her previous jobs as a chambermaid and working in the kitchen of a busy seafront café, Tabitha found her attention wandering. However, her ears pricked up when the woman pointed out that she lived in Callington, some twenty miles and a good forty-minute drive away from Tremarnock.

'It won't be a problem,' she said quickly. 'I've got my own car.'

As far as Tabitha was concerned, this was a distinct advantage, as she'd already made up her mind not to mix with the locals any more than necessary, far less employ them.

'I really want this job,' Shelley said suddenly, staring straight at her potential boss for the first time. 'I've got two kids, you see, and my husband was made redundant a while back and he can't work 'cause of his depression...'

Her voice trailed off and she cracked her bony knuckles nervously. She was perched so precariously on the edge of the chair that it looked as if she might fall off.

'Please...'

Their eyes met and Tabitha gave a start of recognition. She knew that look – it was desperation. In an instant her mind was made up.

'When can you begin?' she asked, straightening. If she were making a mistake, so be it; she'd far rather the job went to someone who needed it.

Shelley's face broke into a smile for the first time and she looked almost pretty. 'You mean you're going to take me on? I'll work really hard, I won't stop, and you won't have no complaints. I won't let you down, I promise.'

It was after six by the time she left and Tabitha, who felt that she'd go cross-eyed if she looked at one more interiors magazine, decided to take Oscar in his stroller for a quick walk around the village. The dark streets were almost empty and she pulled up her hood and kept her head down, glancing left and right to check her surroundings, keen not to have to speak.

She was relieved, as she headed along the seafront past The Lobster Pot, that no one went in or came out. The tide was high, submerging the beach, and the restless water slapped irritably up the sea wall while the moon, partly obscured by cloud, cast a long thin light like a silvery streak across the surface.

Oscar pointed. "Ook, Mamma.'

'Moon,' said Tabitha, without stopping, and he repeated the word wonderingly.

As they left the front and strolled up South Street, they spotted Rosie, Liz Hart's slightly frail-looking girl with the limp and pale blue glasses, who'd come to the house with the pot plant. She waited for them at the corner of Humble Hill and bent down to speak to Oscar, but soon went on her way when Tabitha explained that he was cold and hungry. She didn't ask why the girl was out at this time or where she'd been.

Anxious not to follow her, Tabitha continued on her path a little way before turning right into Towan Road, where The Victory Inn pub was, not that she'd been inside. About halfway down a man was getting out of a silver car and she hoped to slip by unnoticed but a voice boomed, 'Tabitha!', and there was nothing for it but to stop.

'We've just arrived,' said Tony, stretching his arms above his head and yawning. 'Took absolutely hours.' He lowered his arms and breathed in deeply. 'Ahh! Sea air!' His partner, Felipe, went round to the back of the car, opened the boot and heaved out the luggage.

'Wait a moment, darling,' Tony called over his shoulder, 'I'll give you a hand!' But he made no move while Felipe staggered up the front path of their cottage, Ebb Tide, humping two heavy suitcases.

Tony turned back to Tabitha and rubbed his hands together. He was wearing jeans and a dark, V-necked jumper that hugged his tum just a little too tightly.

'So what's been happening? Any scandal? Been any murders?' He chuckled at his own joke, checking to see if Felipe had heard, but the younger man had opened the door of the cottage and disappeared inside.

Tabitha smiled back thinly. 'Not that I know of. I've been so busy getting the guest house ready.'

'Poor darling. Glass of wine?' said Tony pleasantly. 'There's a nice bottle of Sauvignon chilling in the fridge. I won't take no for an answer.'

'No—' Tabitha said, regardless, but Tony waved a hand in the air.

'Nonsense, it's Thursday night. The weekend's practically started!' Then he grabbed the handle of the stroller from her and half pushed her and her son up the garden path.

'Felipe will park the car,' he said casually, leaving it stranded in the middle of the road, the driver's door still open. 'He's much better at it than me. Rio has the third worst traffic in the world, you know. You have to learn to park on a five-pence piece.'

As soon as they'd walked through the bright blue stable door into the living room, Oscar struggled to be let down, and while Tony fetched the wine and glasses, Tabitha took the opportunity to glance around.

The ceiling was very low, giving the cottage a warm, cosy feel, and everything seemed, to her, to be in miniature: the small rectangular sash window with freshly painted shutters that looked out on to the street; the rough, whitewashed fireplace, which was little more than a square hole hewn into the thick wall; the narrow, softly lit alcoves on either side housing books and CDs.

There was a shiny oak floor, a small cream sofa with jolly blue and white striped cushions, an armchair, a TV, a few prints and watercolours on the walls and not much more, but you didn't need it. The place was simple, tasteful, welcoming and spotlessly clean. If Tabitha hadn't been a city girl at heart, she thought that she could have moved in straight away.

'Like it?' said Tony, reappearing with their drinks and a

bowl of crisps balanced on a wooden tray. 'I bought it as a bolthole about fifteen years ago. Best thing I ever did.'

He fetched a little oval table and set it in front of the sofa before passing Tabitha her glass. Oscar, who hadn't yet eaten, spotted the crisps and she seized him by the wrist before he could make a dash for them, making him yelp in fury.

'Sorry, young man,' Tony said, as if noticing the boy properly for the first time. 'Would you care for one of these?'

Hunkering right down, he proffered the bowl and Oscar stopped protesting, his eyes lighting up greedily. Tabitha gulped, fearing that he'd grab the lot, but, on the contrary, Tony's manners seemed to have rubbed off and he took just one crisp rather elegantly between finger and thumb before shoving it whole in his mouth. She was immensely relieved.

'Scrummy!' Tony said, smiling indulgently before passing Oscar another, then he rose and sat beside Tabitha, patting the space between them for her son to climb up.

So, she thought, warming, Tony has a gentle side, and despite herself she opened up a little and started to tell him about her day, the themes she had for her guest rooms and the furniture that she'd bought. He listened very attentively and made enthusiastic noises. 'Divine...! Sumptuous...!'

When Felipe returned from parking the car, he poured himself a glass of wine and settled down with Oscar on the rug in front of the fire to show him his collection of pebbles and shells. The boy watched, enchanted, as he took them out of a cardboard box, one by one, and rolled them in his hands or held them up to the light before passing them over.

'Felipe adores babies.' Tony smiled, noticing Tabitha's eyes on him. 'He's got dozens of little brothers and sisters back home. I can't keep count. He's awfully fond of them.'

'Look, spiral like staircase,' Felipe said, handing Oscar a

round, cream shell with diagonal stripes. 'And this one eez a snail. Pretty.'

'Pretty,' Oscar repeated, gazing at the object with wide brown eyes. 'Snail.'

'What are you doing about advertising, darling?' Tony asked Tabitha suddenly, changing the subject. 'You do realise it's crucial? You could run the most charming guest house in the country but if nobody knows it's there, I'm afraid it's doomed to failure.'

Tabitha frowned. 'I guess I'll hire someone. To be honest, I haven't looked into it yet.'

Tony took a slurp of wine and held up his glass to admire the pale yellow-gold hue. 'I could do it for you. You know I've got my own PR business in London?'

Tabitha's mouth went dry and she shook her head. 'I had no idea.'

'Eez very successful,' Felipe piped up from the floor. 'He has many clients, all sorts. Tony's the best.'

He beamed. 'I don't know about that, but I helped some friends who opened a little hotel in St Mawes and I'm glad to say they're doing very well, always booked up. It wouldn't be much work and I'll give you mates' rates. It would be a pleasure, honestly. Any excuse to spend a bit more time down here!'

Had Tabitha received prior warning, she'd have marshalled her excuses. As it was, her only thought was that under no circumstances must her new neighbour become involved.

'No,' she blurted, rising suddenly and nearly knocking over the little table with the tray on it. 'I don't want... I've already found... a friend's firm in Manchester...'

It was a lie and it came out quite wrong, but she didn't stop to correct herself. Instead, sweeping Oscar up, she pulled their coats off the peg by the stable door and hurried out into the night, shoving her son into his pushchair and strapping him in before he'd had a chance to work out what was happening.

The stable door was still wide open as she wheeled him down the path and her hosts must have followed, because she heard Tony exclaim, 'What on earth got into her? Did I do something wrong?'

He sounded hurt, wounded; not surprising, the way she'd behaved.

'Eez not you, it's *her*,' Felipe hissed loudly. She quickened her pace, hanging her head in shame. 'Mad. Loco! I think she must have – how do you say? – nail missing.'

After Oscar had gone to sleep, Tabitha padded into the reception room where the party guests had gathered the previous weekend and put on some music. The incident with Tony and Felipe had upset her and she wanted to put it to the back of her mind.

There were no curtains on the windows and the light from the streetlamp opposite flooded in, cutting a path through the central space while leaving the corners dark and mysterious. She settled into one of the armchairs in the shadows, rested her head against the back and closed her eyes, allowing the hypnotic, melancholic chords of Diamonds and Rust by Joan Baez to flood through her.

It was a song that Tabitha knew off by heart, having listened to it so often. Joan was one of her heroes, along with Janis Joplin and Bob Dylan. In the early days, she'd begun working the clubs and pubs of Liverpool, Hull, Leeds and Manchester with the band, adapting the old classics to make them relevant again so that soon they'd had quite a following.

It had only been later that she'd plucked up the confidence to perform some of her own compositions and by then their fans had been ready for something new and different. They hadn't minded that some of the music was a bit raw and in need of polishing, they'd just wanted to get a sense of the direction in which the group was heading.

She remembered how on one particular night the club in Liverpool had been packed out, so full that people had been standing in the street, listening at the windows and doors, determined to be part of it even if they'd been unable to buy tickets. That had been the evening that Jez, a scout for MLS Records, had approached them in the bar afterwards, saying he wanted to introduce them to his boss.

'I've told him all about you,' Jez explained. 'He's very keen to meet up.'

She was spaced out, on such a high, but in his enthusiasm he didn't seem to notice. The haunting line about eyes bluer than robin's eggs pierced Tabitha's consciousness and made her shiver. Baez had such a way with words and always sounded vulnerable to her, like a beautiful bird that's terrified and doesn't know why.

Suddenly the music stopped and her own eyes fluttered open. 'Luke!'

Her husband had snapped off the sound and was standing just a few feet away, in the middle of the light, shoulders back, fair hair gleaming. From this angle he looked ten feet tall.

'What are you doing?'

Tabitha sprang up and he held out both hands, enclosing hers in his.

'I've got something for you. Come.'

Silently, she followed him upstairs to the bedroom, where he walked swiftly to the side lamp and put it on. 'Look.'

Tabitha inhaled sharply. There, laid carefully on the bed as if someone had just stepped out of it, was an evening dress covered in red, gold and blue sequins. It had wide, padded shoulders, a low-cut V-neck and the long sleeves bent upwards at the elbow as if the spectral wearer was waving at someone, or dancing, perhaps.

'Where did you—?' Tabitha started to say, but Luke shushed her.

'Aren't you going to put it on?'

Swiftly, Tabitha pulled off her grey sweater, the white shirt underneath and her jeans and shoes and climbed into the dress, which had a zip running all the way down the back.

'Here, let me.' Luke did it up. The gown fitted perfectly and he stepped back to admire his purchase.

'Beautiful.' He smiled, looking her up and down. She hadn't had a chance to see herself yet. His hands circled her waist and he drew her to him, pushing his cheek against hers, so that she could feel his moist breath in her ear. 'I knew it would suit you. It was very, very expensive. It looks as if it's been made for you.'

As soon as she could, Tabitha pulled away, stumbling slightly on the hem of the dress, which was a little too long as she wasn't in heels.

'Where did you get it? Can we afford it, on top of everything else?'

Luke pressed a finger to her lips. 'Stop worrying. Business is booming.'

She frowned, thinking of the vast sums that she'd shelled out today on furniture and suchlike, not to mention the architect's fees that, as far she knew, hadn't yet been settled in full. Despite what she'd told Tony, she still had to find a publicist, Shelley would soon be on the payroll and they hadn't even begun to take bookings…

'So? Do you like it?'

There was an edge to his voice that put her on alert.

'I love it!' She hurried to the mirror, moving from side to side so that she could view herself from different perspectives. 'You're so clever!'

She coiled up her hair with one hand and held a sparkling diamond earring to her lobe with the other. He'd bought her the earrings a while ago, and a matching necklace. She'd queried the cost then, too. Then she tilted her head a little so that she could watch him watching her in the shadows.

'You wouldn't have had that, back where you come from.' His voice was very low.

The memory of a small, dark terraced house invaded her mind; that constant sense of shame, dull hopelessness and fear. Her father's angry face: 'Tabitha, stand up straight... Tabitha put on your headscarf. You won't enter His house without covering yourself properly.'

The regular beatings. Her two brothers had suffered as well; thank God she'd had them, because at night they'd huddled together for comfort, like orphaned puppies or cubs. But the boys weren't as bad as her, it seemed, because she alone had been adopted, taken in as a baby, and look how she'd repaid her parents' selfless generosity! With ingratitude, surliness and disobedience.

She could still hear her mother's thin, hard, hectoring voice: 'God gave you hands to work with, and work you shall. Make your bed... Do the washing up... Sweep the front step...' She could still recall the endless bible meetings and prayers. No music or TV. No parties, Christmas or birthdays. Destined, it seemed, to gaze at the neighbours' children playing in the street from her locked bedroom window.

Later, in her teens, she'd had to wear bras so tight that she could scarcely breathe in order to disguise the swell of her growing breasts, as if her very femininity had been a disgrace that she must pay for. Plain hair, plain clothes, ugliness and misery. This had been her lot in life, this had been what she'd deserved.

But she must have had some spark of courage, of defiance, because she'd started to slip out and jump over the garden fence to meet the one normal friend that she'd managed to make of her own – Molly. Secretly, they'd practised their songs in Molly's parents' garage and formed the band together. Tabitha had even tasted cider and snatched kisses from the sweet, gentle guitarist, Dave.

Finally, though, they'd been caught out and her mother's blank expression, words that she'd learned by heart, had hissed from her lips.

'"But now I have written to you, if any one called brother be fornicator, or avaricious, or idolater, or abusive, or a drunkard, or rapacious, not to mix with him; with such a one not even to eat."' Eyes blazing, she'd pointed at the door. '"Remove the wicked person from amongst yourselves…"'

It hadn't been some random person she'd been throwing out either, it had been her, Tabitha, because she'd dared to blossom into a beautiful young woman, play music and kiss a schoolboy. She'd been barely sixteen and she'd never seen her family again.

She shook her head, trying to brush the bad thoughts away. Thank God Oscar had two parents who loved him. She must hold fast to that.

'Our boy won't want for anything,' Luke said carefully, as if reading her mind. He seemed to have a knack; sometimes she thought there was nowhere to hide. 'You're quite safe so long as you're here with us.'

She looked at her husband, whose blue eyes glittered shiny and hard, like knives.

'I know.'

Chapter Six

IT WAS MOVING-IN day for Loveday and Jesse, and no one at Bag End was to be excused duties. The girl turned up at seven in the morning with bird's-nest hair and dark circles under her eyes; she wasn't accustomed to glimpsing light before at least nine and it didn't agree with her.

Liz, who'd been in a deep sleep beside her husband, took a moment or two to register that it was Saturday. 'Goodness!' she said, pulling her robe around her, tying the cord and running downstairs. Her feet were bare and although it was warm inside she shivered as she opened the door and the cold air whistled round her ankles. She rubbed her eyes. 'I thought you couldn't pick up the keys till ten?'

'Well, Uncle Robert's got to drive me there, and we should bring the bags down and put them in the hall.' Loveday pushed past her aunt and marched into the kitchen, where she opened the fridge door, took out a carton of orange juice and proceeded to pour herself a large glass. 'We've got masses to do.'

Rosie, woken by the noise, came and joined them at the kitchen table. She was wearing a blue and white spotty nightdress and her fair hair was tangled on one side where she'd been sleeping on it. It used to reach almost to her waist but it had been shaved for the operation, then the follow-up therapy had made it all drop out again. Now, it was chin-length and would take a while to grow back fully but, to her relief, it was just as thick and shiny as before. Liz thought she looked sweet and young, but she didn't say so.

'We'll need to clean the place properly,' Loveday went on, pulling off her hoodie and hanging it on the back of a chair. She was in uncharacteristically practical jeans and trainers. 'And put up the pictures and blinds. Jesse and me don't know much about DIY.'

Liz plonked some cereal on the table and fetched brown bread, jam and butter. 'Eggs and bacon for starters, anyone?' She was thinking that this would be a long day. 'We're going to need plenty of energy.'

The smell of sizzling bacon brought Robert down and soon Jesse arrived, too, so that Liz had to fetch more eggs from the fridge. She'd bought them, as usual, from Pendean Farm, and smiled at the names on the carton of the hens who'd laid them – Penny, Polly, Poppy, Samantha, Gertie and Maud. Pendean's eggs seemed to be creamier and fluffier than any others, with bright yellow-orange yolks; she couldn't imagine going back to supermarket ones now.

Jesse's blond curls tumbled round his face and he gave a lazy grin. 'Ahh, breakfast,' he sighed, pulling out a chair next to Loveday and shuffling in close, so that their shoulders were almost touching. Robert, who was leafing through the paper, failed to notice, but Liz did. She often spotted them gazing at each other when they thought no one was looking.

Rosie seemed to have lost her tongue and Liz suspected that she had a bit of a crush on Jesse, not that he'd noticed, but, then, so did most of the girls in the village. Fortunately he seemed to have put his playboy days behind him because Loveday wouldn't have stood for any nonsense.

'Will you teach me how to cook?' she asked Liz, as she wolfed down scrambled eggs on toast. 'I want to make us nice dinners and I can only do cakes.'

She lived mainly off takeaways, but she'd learned to make delicious cakes for the sales she'd put on to raise funds for Rosie's therapy. Liz had been incredibly touched.

''Course I will.' The image of Loveday and Jesse sitting at their own dinner table made her smile, though she did worry that they were very young. She'd tried to coax Loveday into waiting a year or two, but she'd been adamant, so Liz had resolved instead to support them as much as she could.

Jessie glanced up from his plate. 'You're good at making toast as well as cakes,' he joked. 'We can live on that.'

Loveday's face fell. 'We'll get bored of toast.'

He cuffed her on the arm. 'Don't be silly, I'll teach you how to cook. I don't mind doing it all, if you want, or we can get fish and chips from Bob's On the Beach, or pizza.' He winked at Robert. 'Or raid A Winkle In Time for leftovers.'

Loveday perked up. 'I got some gorgeous plates at the discount store, and matching mugs. We can get pizza when we've unloaded the stuff!'

After carting down the bags from upstairs, Robert drove her to her friend's place to collect her luggage, then on to the estate agent to pick up the keys while Liz and Rosie dressed. Then they all walked together, carrying as much as they could, to the flat in Towan Road, which ran parallel to Humble Hill as you headed from the village in the direction of Polgarry Castle.

Loveday quivered with excitement as she put her key in the lock and insisted that she and Jesse enter first, so that they could invite the others in. It was a little place, not unlike the cottage that Liz and Rosie had lived in before Bag End, only smaller, and its new incumbents had the top flat, while a single man was renting the ground floor.

The narrow entrance smelled of stale cooking, and you had to slap a switch on the left to turn on the dull overhead light, so that you could see where you were going. Once they'd climbed the cramped flight of steps, however, a second door opened straight into a reasonably sized, square room with a window overlooking the street. A brown plastic sofa with a hole in the seat and a matching armchair huddled round the electric fire, and there was a small white table pushed against the left-hand wall and two wooden chairs.

'Quick, get the throw on!' Loveday exclaimed, rootling through one of the carriers she'd brought and pulling out a plastic bag containing a pink and blue striped blanket. Once she'd unwrapped and arranged it artfully over the torn sofa, the place already looked cheerier, and the addition of two fuchsia cushions in either corner and another on the armchair improved matters further.

'How do you like it?' Loveday stood back to admire her work.

'It's very pink,' said Jessie.

Liz thought, He's got no idea. He hadn't yet seen the pink towels, sheets, pillowcases, duvet covers, lampshades and crockery. 'Let's have some fresh air,' she said quickly, walking to the window and opening it an inch or two. She was hoping that she wouldn't be around when Loveday produced her candy-coloured stuffed animal collection.

While the men returned to Bag End to fetch Robert's car, loaded with carriers and suitcases, the others rolled up their sleeves, donned Marigolds and got down to cleaning the kitchen. It was only a tiny space, just off the sitting room, but it took a while as the cupboards were sticky and the work surfaces, cooker and microwave were coated in grease.

Liz, who was a bit of a pro, had to show the girls which products to use.

'You need to give it more welly,' she scolded, when she caught Rosie dabbing with her good hand at the stained sink, using one shrivelled corner of damp cloth. 'And plenty of stuff down the drain, please.' She was a great believer in bleach.

Loveday and Rosie were too squeamish to tackle the loo, so Robert manfully stepped in. Meanwhile, Jesse insisted that he could put up the new roller blinds and Liz stood at the bottom of the ladder, looking on anxiously as he ripped down the faded curtains and bored messy holes in the wall using Robert's power drill.

'Are you sure you don't want a spirit level – or a ruler?' she enquired.

'Nah,' said Jesse confidently, 'I can do it by eye.'

Once he'd fitted the blind into its mounting brackets, he came down from the ladder and stood back, hands on hips, to examine his work. There was a pause while he put his head first on one side, then the other, to view the blind from different angles.

'Does it look straight to you?' he asked at last.

'Um…' Liz didn't want to hurt his feelings. 'Perhaps it's just a teeny bit higher on the right?'

Jesse screwed up his eyes, as if that would make a difference. 'I think we've just been looking at it too long.'

Neither of them noticed Loveday arrive with a feather duster in one hand, a can of furniture spray in the other.

'It's wonky!' she cried, making them both start.

'No, it's not,' Jesse said hotly. 'It's only because you're standing so far back. Come closer and you'll see it's fine.'

Loveday took a few doubtful steps forward before waggling her feather duster bossily. 'Look, it's definitely up on one side, down on the other. D'you need glasses?'

Liz thought of the large holes in the wall that would need to be filled in if he started all over again, not to mention his wounded male pride.

'Well, I think it gives the room character.' She glanced sideways at Loveday, whose lip curled cynically. 'And it's a gorgeous colour!'

That seemed to do the trick.

'It is, isn't it?' She grinned. 'And it matches the pink and blue blanket.' She tickled Jesse's cheek with the duster before linking arms. 'I couldn't ever of put that up, I wouldn't know where to begin.'

'It was nothing,' he said modestly, but he seemed to have grown a couple of inches in height. Liz, meanwhile, decided that she might just ask Robert to do the next blind on the quiet.

When the flat had been cleaned from top to bottom and smelled of bleach and lavender polish, they hung some pictures on the walls, put flowers in the small vase they'd bought and set it on top of the TV. Then Robert and Rosie went for groceries, while Loveday and Jesse made up the bed with new sheets, pillows and duvet.

Liz, who was in the kitchen, putting cutlery in the drawer, could hear giggling and when she poked her head round the door they were throwing cuddly toys at each other across the room.

'That's Puff!' Loveday screamed, as a pink and yellow dragon hit her on the head and a large stripy zebra flew in the other direction, making Jesse dodge. 'Don't hurt him!'

'Puff?' Jesse said delightedly. '*Puff?* What kind of name's that?'

It was late afternoon by the time they'd finished and they plonked down on the sofas and armchair, exhausted, while Jesse called for pizza. They hadn't had anything since breakfast and the food, which they ate on their laps, tasted more delicious than a gourmet meal.

'I'm so happy, I could explode!' Loveday sighed, when she'd had as much as she could manage. She cuddled into Jesse, beside her. 'I never ever thought I'd have my own place, with my own kitchen and bathroom, all my own things – and my own boyfriend,' she added shyly. 'My room at my parents' was so tiny and there was no privacy. You could hear everything anyone said – especially the arguing.'

Jesse put down his plate and wrapped an arm round her shoulder. 'We won't argue, babe. Well, not much, anyway.'

Liz looked at Robert, who smiled. 'I think you're going to be very happy here, I can feel it in my bones. And I'm looking forward to dropping by frequently, unannounced, to make sure you're behaving.'

Loveday shifted uncomfortably while Jesse stared hard at the floor.

'Only joking,' Robert added. 'Sort of.'

They washed and dried up, using the new tea towels that had made Rosie so cross, and when at last it was time to go, Loveday was quite tearful.

'Thank you so-o-o-o much.' She gave Liz and Robert a hug and planted a sloppy kiss on Rosie's cheek. The younger girl looked embarrassed and pleased at the same time. 'You've been really brilliant. I'll never forget you.'

Liz laughed. 'We're not emigrating to Australia! We're only round the corner. In fact, you're nearer here than you were before!'

'I s'pose so, but it feels different, like everything's going to change because I'm an adult now.' Loveday said 'adult' as if it were a dirty word.

'I don't think so,' Robert teased. 'Not until you stop wearing those skirts like bandages, anyway.'

Rosie's foot was dragging a bit more than usual as they

strolled back to Bag End, so they had to take it very slowly. It was after seven and the streetlights were on, and they agreed it was a good job that they hadn't anything planned because all they wanted was a hot shower and maybe a good film on TV.

'What do you think they'll do tonight?' Rosie asked her mother. 'Stay in?'

'I expect they'll go for a drink,' Liz replied. She'd noticed that there was a karaoke night at The Victory Inn and was pretty certain they'd be at the front of the queue.

As they entered Fore Street, they saw Tony and Felipe just a few yards down, walking arm in arm, and they turned when Rosie cried, 'Hello!' and Tony's face broke into a smile.

'Hey, how's my favourite girl?' he said, approaching to give her a hug and ruffle her hair. He had a soft spot for Rosie.

Liz, who hadn't seen the couple since the previous weekend, explained about the new flat and Tony clapped his hands in excitement.

'We must get them a housewarming present. What do they need? Some glasses, perhaps? Or bed linen?' He glanced at Felipe, who nodded enthusiastically. They both loved presents. 'They're having a party, I hope?' They loved celebrations, too.

Liz laughed. 'I should think so. I just hope Tremarnock can stand the noise. I don't suppose it'll be quite like the do at The Stables, not as tasteful.'

'Much nicer, though,' Tony replied, and Liz would have asked what he meant but Felipe got in first.

'Tabitha has very bad manners,' he said darkly, pulling a face. 'She snub Tony when he offered to help with advertising. She made a stupid excuse, like he is not good enough for her. I think she can stick her guest house up her—'

'All right, darling,' Tony interrupted. He lowered his voice.

'The husband's charming but, if you ask me, there's something the matter with her. She's not *normal*.'

There was a pregnant pause while everyone reflected on the truth of this statement, then Felipe gave his partner a nudge.

'We must go, we will be late.' He checked the time on his phone and Tony explained that they were on their way to The Lobster Pot, where they were meeting up with Rick and his girlfriend, Sylvia.

'She's a bit of a goer, that one.' He winked at Liz, who raised her eyebrows. 'I hear she's *very* demanding, if you know what I mean.'

'Lord!' Liz was conscious of Rosie, ears pricked, listening to every word. 'I hope Rick can keep up!'

She took Robert's hand as they said goodbye and rounded the corner with Rosie into Humble Hill, each lost in their own thoughts.

'What a strange woman Tabitha is,' Liz observed at last, while Robert rootled in his pocket for the key. 'I can't fathom her at all.'

'Not everyone's as friendly as you, Lizzie,' he replied, opening the door and waiting while she and Rosie stepped inside. 'But Luke's great, so I guess they balance each other out.'

Liz almost said something more but changed her mind.

Thanks to the unusually mild weather, Rick was able to keep up his early morning swim all through October. Come rain or shine, for as long as anyone could remember, he'd been heading down to Tremarnock Beach two or three times a week before opening his shop. He only stopped when the water became too rough or the outside temperature dropped below freezing.

He was a peculiar sight, in a pair of flappy blue trunks, his hair pulled up in a white plastic swimming cap that covered his ears, his sideburns forcing their way out like an unruly thicket. His body was bulky and pale, and he had funny little bandy legs and a mass of grey chest hair that trailed down his tummy like seaweed when he left the water.

He didn't believe in wetsuits, though he stocked a few in his shop, along with masks, snorkels, flip-flops, postcards and the Cornish fudge and fairing biscuits that were among the few items Liz had ever seen anyone actually buy. He claimed that the shock of plunging into the freezing ocean worked wonders for the heart and lungs and although so far Sylvia hadn't joined him, she'd been spotted by Jenny Lambert watching adoringly from the sea wall. Jenny, who sometimes walked Sally on the beach first thing, said whatever was in Rick's theory, it certainly seemed to be doing the trick as his girlfriend was clearly smitten.

On this particular Sunday Rick was joined by Audrey, who claimed that she needed to get in training for the annual Christmas Day swim, which, though some way hence, was a big event in the village. She and Tony had known each other since childhood, as their mothers were old friends, and Liz used to wonder why they'd never got together as in some ways it would have been ideal. The mystery had been solved one evening when Audrey had become a little tipsy in the pub and revealed that, as fond as she was of Rick, she couldn't possibly cope with his lack of sartorial style.

'He's always had the most appalling dress sense,' she'd explained. 'You can change certain things about a man, but not that.'

Fortunately, the problem didn't seem to bother Sylvia.

Audrey and Rick met on the shingle at 9 a.m, a little later

than usual, Audrey in a white towelling robe that she soon discarded to reveal a daring pink and white spotted halter-neck swimsuit that showed off her statuesque figure. Sylvia stood watching from a safe distance in a black, fake-fur coat and dark trousers tucked into knee-length boots. Due to the brisk wind, she frequently had to push her white-blonde hair off her face to stop it sticking to her mauve lipstick.

'They're crazy,' Tony said to Liz, who'd bumped into him in the General Stores, buying a newspaper, and had agreed to take the scenic route home. They slowed to a halt beside Sylvia. 'I'll force myself to go in at Christmas but only because I'd feel like a ninny if I didn't.'

Rick, who had on rubber aqua shoes, like pixie boots, trotted down to the water's edge and plunged in first, while Audrey picked her way more gingerly across the gritty shingle before entering the surf. Although the air wasn't cold, the wind was whipping up choppy grey and white waves, and she squealed when a mini-breaker caught her unawares, splashing up her thighs and torso almost to waist level and covering her in foam and salty spray.

Realising that any further delay was pointless, she dived in herself and disappeared completely for a moment, but soon re-emerged and swam towards Rick in her ladylike breast-stroke. He was some distance out now and trod water until she caught up, then led the way purposefully towards one of the orange buoys, bobbing gently on the slate-coloured sea.

As they moved further and further off, it became difficult to tell where the grey sky ended and the water began and Liz began to wonder if they'd ever come back. Then their pace slowed, Audrey caught hold of the buoy, looked back at the shore and waved. Liz, waving back, could just make out her high-pitched voice, punctuated by the odd laugh from Rick, mingling with the cries of seagulls and the swish, swish of the incoming tide.

'They've gone a long way,' Liz commented. 'It can't be that cold, or at least they must have got used to the temperature by now.'

'Rick absolutely loves it,' Sylvia purred. 'He says it keeps him young and I think he must be on to something. He's got the energy of twenty-year-old.'

Liz caught Tony's eye and the corners of her mouth twitched. Remembering his comment last night about Sylvia's 'demands', she feared that at any moment he'd make a rude innuendo and she wasn't sure that she'd be able to cope.

'Lucky him!' she said, clearing her throat quickly. 'You're never tempted to go in yourself?'

'Oh, no,' Sylvia replied, patting her hair. 'As I told Felipe in the pub last night, I far prefer indoor pursuits.'

Tony coughed and Liz felt her shoulders start to shake. Luckily, they were interrupted by a loud bang and turned to see John Lambert slamming shut the door of his fishing-tackle shop, clutching a heavy-looking shovel in one hand, a smaller spade in the other. The price tags were still on them.

'Everything all right?' Liz called, because he looked harassed.

'Sally's gone to ground. Stuck in a rabbit hole. Can't get her out!'

'Oh, dear.' Sally was always getting lost; she wasn't exactly well trained. After a frantic search involving most of the village, Liz had once discovered the little dog in the back garden of her old cottage, having slipped in unnoticed when she'd opened the door.

'Are you planning to dig her out?' Tony asked doubtfully, staring at the shovel. 'With that?'

John nodded. 'Nothing else for it. She's been gone two hours and we can hear her yelping. Jenny's frantic.'

Tony offered to help and Liz, who decided that Robert would have to wait for his newspaper, said that'd she'd come, too. Meanwhile, Sylvia announced that she and the swimmers would catch up as soon as they could.

'I'll tell Rick to bring his spade as well. He'll be good at digging. He's very strong.'

Tony elbowed Liz in the ribs and she pinched his side as they hurried up Fore Street. 'Stop it!'

John was enormously grateful for their company, explaining as they went that Jenny had been out with the dog since 6 a.m. and they'd already tried coaxing her from the rabbit warren with her favourite squeaky toys and doggy snacks, to no avail.

'She's disappeared down a hole before, but never for this long. Normally food does the trick. Jenny thinks she's stuck. I said she was getting too fat. Sally, I mean,' he added quickly, 'not Jenny.'

They took a right turn in the direction of Cardew Heights and the Catholic church, and as they passed the car park Luke sauntered towards them, swinging a key from his forefinger. He drove an enormous black four by four, very shiny and new, unlike most of the muddy old vehicles round here.

They stopped for a moment to say hello and when he found out what had happened, he, too, insisted on accompanying them. It was turning into quite a party.

'It's my pleasure,' he said when John tried to dissuade him. 'I love dogs and Sally was one of the first villagers I met!'

Halfway up the steep, winding lane Tony had to stop to catch his breath, and John produced a hip flask from his back pocket and passed it round.

'Jenny will be so grateful. She'll be amazed when she sees I've brought the whole cavalry.'

Luke took a large swig of brandy and Liz couldn't help thinking that he wasn't exactly dressed for a country walk, let alone digging, in pale chinos, tan leather loafers and a smart navy pea coat, but of course he hadn't been in Cornwall long. It had taken her a while to work out that her old, city wardrobe simply wasn't suitable for Tremarnock and little by little she'd replaced it with more suitable garments.

Now she barely ever wore heels and her waterproof mac and walking boots were among her most prized possessions. Luke would learn, she thought, especially when he returned home with sticky reddish mud caked up his trouser legs and all over those nice clean shoes.

The Catholic church, founded on the site of a sixth-century monastery, stood on its own, perched on the top of the hill and surrounded on all sides by fields. Liz had been inside many times with Rosie, who loved to light a candle before gawping at the old wooden village stocks in the south-west corner, and examining the names on the crumbling tombstones in the overgrown graveyard.

'Jenny's over there!' John said, pointing towards a wooded area to the right of the chapel. 'I expect she's on her hands and knees, that's why we can't see her.'

They tramped over damp grass, keeping their eyes peeled, until they heard a shout: 'John!' And his wife stood up in front of a stubby old oak, waving frantically.

She had on a green quilted gilet and Wellington boots, and her blonde hair had largely escaped from the black Alice band that was meant to be holding it in place. As they approached, Liz could see dirty streaks across her cheeks and noticed that her eyes were red. She'd been crying.

'I'm so glad you're here!' Jenny said, grabbing the spade off her husband as soon as he was close enough. 'She's stopped barking. I hope she's all right.'

She started to stab her spade in the earth, sending clumps of sticky mud flying, until Luke stepped forward and suggested that they'd have to be careful that the hole didn't collapse, suffocating poor Sally.

'Wouldn't it be better to widen the entrance?' He scratched his chin. 'Whereabouts do you think she is? There's no point making a hole if she's in a completely different section of the warren.'

He bent down and shone the torch on his mobile phone into the cave, before shaking his head. 'Can't see anything.'

Jenny's face crumpled. 'It's hopeless. She might be three feet underground.' She turned to John. 'What are we going to do?'

He put an arm round her shoulder and frowned. 'Let's think about this for a moment. We must be logical.'

Jenny squeaked Sally's toy mouse at the entrance again and called her name, but there was no response, so she plonked onto her backside disconsolately. 'It's all my fault. If only I'd kept her on the lead.'

'We could call the fire brigade or the RSPCA,' Tony piped up. 'They might have better tools. Heat-seeking equipment or a JCB or something.'

'Not easy to get one up here,' replied Luke, 'and it might take ages. I reckon our best bet is to dig round the mouth of the hole and try to open it up.'

He threw off his coat, took the shovel from John and pushed it into the soil around the narrow entrance of the warren, groaning as he did so and using his right foot for maximum leverage. Every now and then he'd stop and shine his torch again, but as his spade got further into the tunnel it became clear that Sally must, indeed, be a long way beneath, because there was absolutely no sight or sound of her.

'Here, let me take over,' said John, when Luke paused for a moment to roll up the sleeves of his pale blue shirt, but he was having none of it. 'I'll do it. You stay with Jenny; she needs you.'

'He's marvellous, isn't he?' Tony commented to Liz, who nodded, though she wasn't entirely convinced that Luke's was the right strategy. She couldn't help thinking that he was putting in a lot of effort for dubious gain and his attempts seemed as much about show as anything, but perhaps she was being uncharitable.

Just then they heard a cry and saw Sylvia, Rick, with another spade, and Audrey hurrying towards them, followed by Felipe, carrying what looked very much like a pair of bellows and a heavy saucepan.

'What the—?' said Tony, but there was no time for speculation because Rick had jogged ahead of the others and come to a halt in front of the group, panting and red in the face.

'Not found her yet?' He was still wearing his swimming trunks, now clinging wetly to his hairy thighs, plus a grey sweatshirt and old trainers. Luke continued digging.

'Felipe's got an idea,' Rick puffed. 'His mother breeds terriers in Rio. Very popular there apparently.'

Tony raised his eyebrows and Audrey, who'd now caught up, elucidated. 'Brazilian terriers. They're quite famous.' She was still in her soggy towelling robe and, though bedraggled, managed to bat her eyelashes when Luke glanced up and give a fetching smile.

Felipe, behind, pushed forward so that he was standing next to Luke at the mouth of the warren. 'My mother's terrier are always getting stuck. Most annoying. But they are very good for catching rats and mice – and skunks. Also for crowding chickens.'

'Herding,' Tony said helpfully, but his partner, brandishing the bellows, didn't hear.

'This is what we use in Rio.' He gestured for Luke to move out of the way, set the saucepan down in front of the hole and lifted off the lid, releasing a waft of meaty steam.

'That's my soup!' exclaimed Tony, only just realising. 'What are you doing with my soup?'

Liz peered into the saucepan, filled with grey-brown liquid, barley and bones. It didn't look much but smelled delicious.

'I was going to have it for lunch,' Tony added ruefully, but everyone was watching, fascinated, while Felipe crouched down and proceeded to pump soupy steam down the shaft with the bellows.

Liz wanted to giggle but managed to control herself. Meanwhile Sylvia sidled over to Luke and asked in a low voice if he was cold in just his shirtsleeves.

'Would you like to borrow my coat?' she offered, and he laughed. 'I don't get cold. I'm a man.'

'I can see that,' she simpered, and Audrey shot her a dirty look.

There was silence for a few moments until they heard a short, sharp yip, followed by a furious scrabbling.

'It's her!' Jenny cried joyfully, jigging up and down on the spot. 'It's working!'

Felipe nodded sagely. 'It works every time, I tell you. Much better than digging.'

Liz glanced at Luke, who seemed almost annoyed, or was she imagining it? But he quickly rallied, standing over Felipe and shining the torch down the cavity.

'I can see her! She's right there. Come on, girl, that's it, there's a good dog.'

He took a step back and while Felipe pumped a bit more,

Jenny's nose suddenly popped out of the opening, followed by her front paws and upper body. She was covered in earth.

'Quick, grab her!' said John, and as Luke leaned forward and tried to seize the collar he accidentally knocked into Felipe, who tumbled backwards, sending the saucepan and its contents flying.

Sally, who couldn't believe her luck, quickly heaved herself out of the hole and fell on the food, licking and gobbling up as much as she could before anyone could intervene.

'Oh!' Jenny cried, alarmed. 'She'll choke on the bones. Quick! Somebody stop her!'

Now it was Sylvia's turn to lunge forward, but her foot hooked round Luke's ankle, and he keeled over and landed flat on his face in the mound of sticky mud that he'd dug from the hole.

There was a collective gasp, then she bent down and tried to yank him up by the arm as she grasped Sally's collar.

'Leave me alone!' he roared, shaking Sylvia off, and she backed away, still hanging on to the dog for dear life.

'Are you all right?' she squeaked, ignoring Rick, now hovering by her side, but Luke didn't say anything as he got on to his hands and knees and rose slowly, turning only when he'd reached his full height and everyone could see the damage.

He was literally covered in thick wet muck, all down his clean blue shirt, over his chinos and nice tan shoes and across the palms of his hands. But the worst part was his face, which was caked, too. Even his eyelids were encrusted in goo so that he could scarcely open them.

Laughter bubbled inside Liz again, it was all too much, and this time she simply couldn't stop.

'Are you hurt?' she spluttered, hoping that he'd see the funny side and join in, but instead he stood stock-still, trembling with anger. If a body could glower, then his was incandescent with rage, which somehow only made it funnier.

'Oh, dearie me,' Tony tutted, 'oh, lordy lumpkins,' which made Liz snort again. 'Here, take this.' He produced a clean white hankie from his trouser pocket which he offered Luke, but he couldn't see so it had to be placed in his hand.

The others now sprang into action and began casting around for more tissues and Liz managed to find a small pile in her coat pocket. Meanwhile, Sylvia fussed and flapped around, trying to get at Luke's face with a corner of her sleeve.

'I'm so sorry,' she was saying, 'I didn't mean... I was trying to grab the dog...'

Luke raised his arm like a shield to fend off her advances – 'I can do it. Leave me alone!' – while Audrey stood back and watched the show, looking suspiciously as if she was enjoying her rival's discomfort.

Jenny now had Sally in her arms and was stroking her affectionately. 'Bad dog!' She wasn't fooling anyone. Sally, though filthy, didn't seem any the worse for wear and yelped and wriggled furiously, but her mistress held fast while John attached the lead.

'Thank God for that,' he said, slapping Felipe on the back. 'We couldn't have done it without you!'

Felipe gave a modest shrug while Tony grinned from ear to ear.

At last, when Luke had cleaned his face enough to be able to see properly, Sylvia plucked up the courage to ask again if he was all right. 'Let me wash your clothes,' she said abjectly. 'It's the least I can do.'

'We'll come back to your place and you can give them to us,' Rick chipped in. 'The mud will come off those shoes no problem. I've got a special brush.'

Luke stamped his feet and shook the dirt off his hands. He seemed to have regained at least some of his composure. 'I'm fine. No damage done.'

Then he smiled; his handsome face lit up and he was the old Luke again, charming, relaxed, friendly Luke, everyone's friend. 'What an adventure, eh? Thank goodness we found the dog!'

He turned to Sylvia, hovering by his side, and congratulated her on catching Sally. 'If you hadn't made a dash for it, she might have disappeared down that hole again!'

Sylvia's shoulders relaxed and there were no objections when he put his arm round her waist and gave her a squeeze, despite the fact that it made her fake-fur coat dirty. All, it seemed, was forgiven, though Liz thought that if he'd snarled like that at her, she wouldn't forget in a hurry.

As they headed back to the village, Sylvia and Audrey stuck close to his side, chatting and laughing. If Rick minded, he didn't show it, but Liz did wonder if he'd have liked his girlfriend to walk with him.

The others trailed behind, talking about what had happened, and Jenny commented that Sally must have been terribly frightened down that hole. 'I've heard of terriers getting stuck for days. She might have starved to death!'

John harrumphed. 'If you ask me, that dog was having a grand old time and had no intention of coming up till she was good and ready. We should have saved ourselves a lot of trouble and left her to it.'

'Rubbish!' said Jenny. 'How can you be so heartless?'

Liz rather suspected that John might be right, but she hung back and waited for Tony and Felipe to catch up, sensing that it would be imprudent to get involved.

Chapter Seven

ROSIE BROKE UP from school a few days before Christmas, and she and Liz had a happy time wrapping presents, writing cards and putting up decorations. Liz's father, Paul, wouldn't be joining them, having promised to spend the festive season with his wife in London. Liz and Rosie didn't mind too much, however, because they'd enjoyed his company so much last year and were content just to be with Robert. They'd fix up something with Granddad in the spring.

The lights went up in the village in early December, amidst much fanfare as usual, including the annual carol-singing in the market square led by the Methodist church choir and a big brass band. Everyone joined in, and it gave Rick an opportunity to show off his booming baritone. Barbara, from The Lobster Pot, kindly provided free mulled wine and mince pies, and quite a few people got tipsy, including a number of teenagers whose parents either failed to notice or turned a blind eye.

When the singing finished, it was the turn of the local Morris dancers, including Barbara's son, Aiden, who created a stir in his splendid Cornish kilt, tattered jacket and black top hat adorned with leaves and feathers, bell pads jangling merrily from his shins. Some while back, he'd managed to persuade

Alex to join the ranks, on the basis that he'd only have to stand in a corner, playing his accordion, but little by little Alex had become more involved and now he jigged, stepped, bashed his stick and waved his multicoloured handkerchief like the best of them. No one had ever seen an Elvis-style Morris Man before.

A Winkle in Time was open on Christmas Eve, so Liz and Rosie stayed at home while Robert worked, and Pat joined them for a glass of her favourite green ginger wine. Liz kept a bottle in especially. They were joined by Jean and Tom, who were alone this year as their married children were staying with the families of the other halves. They weren't exactly bereft, however, having booked ten days in Florida, leaving on the twenty-seventh. Jean was quite beside herself with excitement.

They were sitting round the fire in Liz's cosy front room, in one corner of which stood a lusty green tree covered in lights and glittering baubles. Rosie had also strung white fairy lights round the mantelpiece and tucked sprigs of holly with deep red berries behind the picture frames on the walls, and there was a spray of mistletoe tied to the ceiling lamp in the centre of the room. The place looked very jolly.

'I really shouldn't. I've managed to lose half a stone,' said Jean, eyeing the plate of smoked salmon triangles on brown bread that Liz passed across. 'I don't want to look like a whale in my swimming costume.'

'You couldn't possibly. You always look lovely,' said her husband gallantly. He was sitting beside her on the sofa, nursing a pint of lager. 'Have one if you fancy it.'

'Oh, go on, then,' said a relieved Jean, helping herself to a canapé. 'It's only small.'

They chatted for a while about village life and Jean wondered if anyone had seen Tabitha recently.

'Not for ages,' replied Liz. 'It's extraordinary. I don't think she ever leaves the house.'

Jean sniffed. 'Perhaps that's the custom in her culture. I wouldn't know.'

Liz shot her a look. 'I don't believe the customs are any different in Manchester, are they? She was born and brought up in the North.'

Jean was a dear friend, but Liz couldn't abide the casual racism that sometimes slipped out of her mouth, and unfortunately she wasn't the only one around here. It was important to challenge ignorance because only then would people start to change.

Pat, who thought well of everyone unless disappointed and was generally pretty broad-minded, would normally have backed Liz up. Instead, however, she shook her head.

'Tabitha doesn't belong in Tremarnock, that's for sure. She doesn't understand our way of life.'

'Maybe she's just shy,' Rosie chipped in, sensing the frostiness that had crept into the atmosphere. 'Anyway, Luke fits in well. I really like him.'

'Excellent fellow,' Tom agreed. 'Always stops by to admire the garden and say hello.'

Liz rose swiftly and took the empty glass out of Pat's hand. 'Time for a top-up? It is Christmas after all.'

When the guests left, she and Rosie made their way up Humble Hill to the Methodist church, pausing for a moment to gaze at the myriad stars glittering in the night sky.

'Can you see Santa and his reindeer?' Liz asked, knowing that Rosie was really way beyond such childishness.

'I think so!' she replied, amused. 'I hope he doesn't forget me!'

As they approached the little steps that led up to the main

entrance, a gang of rowdy youths passed by, laughing and swaying on their way back from the pub.

'Don't get too drunk!' they shouted, and Liz gave a wry smile in return.

The church was quite plain inside, with simple wooden pews and an unadorned altar, and she half expected they'd be the only ones there, as many people preferred the candlelit service at the Catholic church. But in fact there was a decent crowd, the place smelled of polish and was cheered up by one of Pat's displays of red and white flowers near the pulpit, as well as a sweet nativity scene and a big Christmas tree with an angel on the top. She and her helpers had been busy.

Rosie spotted Audrey and her aged mother right up front, wearing magnificent fur hats, as well as Barbara and a female relative. A few minutes later, a visiting family arrived with their two handsome teenage boys, and Rosie sat up straight and peeped at them out of the corner of an eye. Liz felt a pang, because she was certain that the boys hadn't registered her. Never mind, her time would surely come.

The minister was a strange-looking fellow with a bald head, little round glasses and a stubby nose that was almost swallowed up by his big red cheeks. Rumour had it that he enjoyed a glass of port or three, but no one held it against him as he worked hard and kept a close eye on his admittedly dwindling flock. He spread his arms wide to welcome the congregation before they sang the opening carol, 'O Come, All Ye Faithful!', and a warm feeling spread through Liz, like hot tea on a cold day. Christmas was finally here!

Rosie yawned a few times during the sermon and rested her head against her mother's arm, but she perked up for 'Away in a Manger', then had to stifle a giggle during Communion when Audrey's old mum's fur hat fell off into the aisle and she made a huge song and dance about retrieving it. To crown it all, she put it back on skew-whiff, giving her the appearance of a tipsy Hussar.

Everyone tried not to notice, but it wasn't easy, and one of the visiting boys snorted, much to his mother's disgust. Fortunately, they were rescued by a rousing rendition of 'Ding Dong Merrily on High!', before everyone trooped out into the night, wishing each other a 'Happy Christmas!'. All in all, it had been an excellent service.

Thankfully, the restaurant was closed on the twenty-fifth and at 9.15 a.m. Liz, Robert and Rosie went together to collect Pat before making their way to the seafront. It was a grey day – no hint of sunshine – but the temperature was well above average for the time of year, which was a blessing.

Most people dressed in silly costumes for the annual swim and Liz and Rosie were wearing pink swimsuits with white tutus under their winter coats, and cheap toy tiaras on their heads. By the time they arrived, there was already quite a crowd gathered in front of The Lobster Pot, including Jean and Tom dressed as Father and Mother Christmas, Audrey in a wimple and veil, Barbara in a green spotty dress, the Lamberts and their teenagers in Disney outfits, Tony in a Harlequin outfit and Rick, who always made the most effort, in a silver bikini, complete with fake boobs, a long blonde wig and lashings of make-up.

Sylvia, meanwhile, was standing a little way back from the swimmers, well wrapped up in her fake-fur coat, beside Esme and Felipe, who thought they were all quite mad. There were others, too, friends and relatives, some of whom Liz didn't recognise, who'd come along to watch the fun.

'Are you sure you want to?' Pat asked Rosie, who was shivering in her coat. She turned to Liz. 'I really don't think she should do it, do you? She might catch a cold.'

Liz couldn't help agreeing, but wouldn't say no. For the previous two years Rosie had been too ill to join in and she was determined to today. She'd never been one to shirk a challenge; it was part of what made her who she was.

They were distracted by a shout – 'Merry Christmas, friends!' – and turned to see Luke strolling towards them in some bright red swimming trunks decorated with sleigh bells, a pair of goggles perched on his head. Behind him, Tabitha was wheeling Oscar in his pushchair, nodding hello only when she caught someone's eye. She was fully dressed in jeans, boots and a puffer jacket and clearly had no intention of swimming herself.

Luke had a most impressive physique – slim and toned, with broad shoulders, narrow hips and a washboard stomach. You could tell that he worked out. Audrey's mouth dropped open and Sylvia quickly muscled through the crowd towards him; she couldn't help herself.

'Where's your towel?' she asked breathlessly, glancing at Tabitha almost as an afterthought to see if she was carrying one. 'Would you like me to get you one? It's no trouble at all.'

Luke grinned and shook his head. He seemed to have forgotten his muddy tumble and the unfortunate tussle. 'I'll dry off on the way home.'

'Goodness!' gasped Sylvia, who couldn't take her eyes off him. 'You're so hard!'

She didn't seem to notice anything amiss, but Tony sniggered while Liz stared determinedly at her feet.

'No wig?' Rick shouted at Luke, keen to divert attention. 'Keeps the head warm!' He patted his blonde mane girlishly and Audrey giggled.

'He can borrow my wimple,' she joked, but Sylvia, oblivious, continued to gawp at Luke's manly chest, drinking it in.

'I think Rick's had it,' Pat whispered mournfully. 'Look at the woman. She's gone absolutely gaga!'

Someone indicated that it was time and the swimmers in coats or towels dropped them on the ground or handed them to their families and stepped on to the beach. Then the whistle blew once, twice, three times, and all of a sudden there was a mad dash towards the waves.

Luke, who was a fast runner, speeded ahead and plunged in first, creating a tremendous splash and swell, but Rosie couldn't hurry and Liz held her hand tightly as they made their way more cautiously to the water's edge.

'Are you sure you want to do this?' she asked hopefully, but Rosie wasn't to be deterred.

'Of course!'

The pair braced themselves, closed their eyes and hopped into the waves, still holding hands and gasping as the cold water hit them. Rosie lost her footing and tumbled in first before bobbing up almost immediately, her eyes goggling like a fish's. 'I can't breathe!'

But she was laughing, so Liz clenched her teeth and ducked under. 'It's like ice!' she screamed, feeling her skin shrink and her lungs contract. 'I can't stand it!'

Some of the others thrashed around for a while, creating a tremendous spray, and Luke swam out quite far, stopping to wave at the onlookers, but Liz and Rosie had had enough after just a few strokes and skipped as fast as they could back to the shore, where Robert was waiting with their towels.

'Well done!' he said, rubbing Rosie vigorously before starting on his wife. 'Quick! Into the shower with you!'

Barbara had already said that they could use her bathroom above the pub, because she knew that Rosie needed to get warm quickly, and as they entered The Lobster Pot, Robert handed over the bags that they'd brought along with a change of clothes.

'See you in a minute. What'll you girls have?' he asked as they disappeared up the windy stairs that led to Barbara's flat.

'A stiff gin, please!' Rosie quipped.

She took ages to get changed, and by the time they went back down, the pub was humming and there was scarcely room to move. There was a big blaze going, so that everyone's cheeks were rosy, and Liz stopped for a moment on the second to last step to check who was there. She could see Robert in the far corner, talking to Pat and a now wig-less Rick. A younger crowd was hovering by the door, including Loveday, in lashings of black eye make-up, Jesse, Ryan, Alex, Nathan and Annie. Over by the fire, Tony was holding court with Felipe, Tom, John Lambert and Audrey's aged mum, while Barbara and her son Aiden were busy serving at the bar.

In the middle of the room, standing in a rapt circle, were Sylvia, Audrey, Esme, Jean and Jenny, and right in the centre of them all, holding back his head and laughing loudly, was Luke. He looked more striking than ever, Liz thought, in a clean white shirt, his fair hair still damp and slicked back off his smooth, shaven face. He was clearly enjoying himself immensely. Tabitha, meanwhile, was nowhere to be seen. Perhaps she'd already gone home.

Rosie pushed past her mother and started to weave her way through the crowd towards Robert, but Liz remained glued to the spot, reluctant to budge. From a distance, the women surrounding Luke appeared to her so silly, fake and simpering that Liz was tempted to shout at them to pull themselves together, yet they were her friends and it troubled her to be thinking this way. Perhaps she was the one at fault, but of one thing she was absolutely certain: she would not be joining their fan club.

She might have stayed like that for some time, wondering how to reach Robert without being noticed, but then she glimpsed Loveday breaking away from her group and making for the bar. Liz stood on tiptoe to try to attract her attention, thinking it would be the perfect way to dodge Luke's posse, but something made him turn and he spotted the girl himself.

Her eyes lit up and she made a beeline for him, the older women fanning out so that she could enter their inner sanctum. As soon as she was close enough, Luke bent down, rested a hand on her shoulder and kissed her on both cheeks and she smiled back coyly. Then he took her arm and led her back a few paces so that they could talk, just the two of them, while the rest looked on enviously. Unable to watch any more, Liz seized her moment and hurried towards Robert, keeping her head down. What on earth was the matter with them all? They seemed to have lost their senses.

On reaching her husband at last, he handed her a glass of red wine that she took gratefully. 'You've been ages. What have you been doing?' But she didn't know how to explain and shook her head. By now Pat was flagging, and they agreed to finish their drinks quickly and head for home. In any case, the turkey had to go in and Rosie was keen to open the presents; she'd been extremely patient.

'It's so hot in here,' she complained, as they made their way towards the fresh air, 'I can't wait to get out.'

But of course they had to stop and chat to the younger ones, still huddling by the door. Jesse said he and Loveday had gone to a party after the restaurant had closed last night and hadn't got to bed till 5 a.m. He looked a little pale but was in remarkably good spirits.

'What did they put in your drink?' Liz laughed. 'A magic potion? I think I could do with some myself!'

Annie, who was wearing a little black dress instead of Lycra for a change and looked extremely pretty, mentioned that she and Nathan were driving to South Devon shortly to spend the day with her mum and gran, who was eighty and needed a bit of TLC.

'Only eighty?' said Pat. 'She's a spring chicken!' Annie laughed.

Next Loveday arrived, brimming with excitement, and she grabbed Liz's arm and insisted that she stay a moment longer.

'Amazing news!' she whisper-shouted, so that Liz could hear her above the chatter. 'The Mallon's au pair's left 'cause she can't stand Tremarnock and Luke's asked if I want to be their nanny!'

Liz's heart fluttered and her mouth dropped open; she couldn't help it. It was so sudden. He'd hardly met the girl – and did Tabitha even know?

'But you've no experience,' she blurted. 'You've never worked with children. I wouldn't have thought it would be your thing at all.'

Loveday frowned, having clearly expected a quite different response.

'He said his wife can train me,' she huffed. 'Apparently their little boy's really easy and he said whatever I earn now, he'll top it.' Her eyes were shining. 'And when Oscar's asleep or at nursery, I can help run the guest house, take bookings and that. I'd be like a personal assistant.'

Jesse and Robert, who'd been chatting to the others, turned now and listened to the news.

'Sounds great,' Jesse said, ruffling his girlfriend's hair. 'Well done, babe. I'll miss you at the restaurant, though.'

The corners of Loveday's mouth drooped. 'I'll miss you, too.' Then a new thought perked her up. 'But I like little kids and Luke's got a big financial advice business so he won't have time to do the guest house.' She puffed out her chest. 'It's not like being a waitress is a proper career, is it?'

She glanced sideways at Robert to see if he was offended, but he put an arm round her shoulder.

'It's fantastic,' he said, bending down to kiss her on the cheek. 'It could be just what you need.'

Liz bit her lip. Loveday wasn't exactly a natural at wait-ressing and it was probably time to move on, yet still she felt a deep misgiving that she couldn't put into words. But it was mean to pour cold water on the girl's enthusiasm. Jesse and Robert were enthusiastic, so she should try to be, too, especially as she couldn't think of a rational objection.

'You're right,' she sighed, reaching for Rosie's hand. 'Just make sure you know what you're getting into and you have a proper contract before you start.'

Chapter Eight

PILAR'S ABRUPT DECISION to leave had been a terrible blow and the prospect of having to get to know someone new filled Tabitha with dread. She'd begged the au pair to stay, offering extra money and promising more time off, but to no avail. Pilar liked Manchester and hadn't wanted to come to Cornwall in the first place.

'I am sorry,' she'd said, when she'd handed in her notice and announced that she'd be leaving just before Christmas, 'but I prefer the city. I do not like being in such a small place. I feel choked.' She'd made a gagging sound to hammer the point home.

Tabitha couldn't help agreeing, but hadn't let on. 'It'll get better. There are lots of people your age, you just need to get to know them.'

'I do not think,' Pilar said gravely, 'that they are my type of people. I have bought my plane ticket and I will not change my mind.'

When Luke had told Tabitha that Loveday was to take over, Tabitha had felt slightly sick. It went completely against all her resolutions, but she hadn't bothered to argue – there was no point.

'Does she have any experience of looking after children?' she'd asked quietly, careful not to criticise.

Luke had waved a dismissive hand. 'She says she likes them and you can teach her. It won't take long. In any case, we're in a hurry. We haven't got time to interview lots of people and she's only on two weeks' notice.'

Now, three days after Christmas, the girl was due to arrive for a 'getting to know each other' session. You couldn't even call it an interview, really, because she'd already been offered the job.

'Make her welcome, Tabby,' Luke had said when he'd left home early that morning to go to his new office. He'd squeezed her shoulder before running a palm slowly down her face and cupping his fingers round her jaw. 'She's going to be very useful.'

Oscar was having his afternoon nap when Loveday turned up five minutes early, and Tabitha ushered her into the kitchen and closed the door. The girl had made an attempt to look smart in a tight navy V-necked jumper that might once have been part of her school uniform, a green skirt that reached almost to her knees and remarkably sensible black pumps. She had no coat, though, and her bare legs were blue with cold.

'Liz and Robert tell me off about it,' she shrugged, when Tabitha asked if she were chilly. 'I don't much like coats, never have. The one I've got makes me feel like I can't breathe.' She grinned. 'Sounds weird, doesn't it? I guess I'm just a weird person.'

Tabitha found herself smiling, remembering their brief conversation at the party about the crazy boots, and it occurred to her now, as it had then, that there was something very appealing about her. She was argumentative, sure, a bit silly and ignorant and no doubt extremely annoying at times, but beneath the surface, Tabitha guessed, lay a fierce pride, vulnerability and a desire to be loved that she did her best to conceal. She seemed like someone unused to praise and encouragement but who might just blossom in its warmth. She reminded Tabitha of herself.

'I think we're going to get on just fine,' she announced suddenly, and Loveday's face lit up.

'I'm so glad. I was worried you weren't into the idea. To be honest, I thought maybe Luke, er, your husband, had talked you into it and really you hated my guts. I'll do my very best for you, Mrs Mallon, honest I will. I'll look after your little boy like he's my own and work every hour God sends if you want me to.'

Her enthusiasm was infectious and Tabitha smiled again. 'That won't be necessary. We're not slave-drivers, I hope. We'll draw up a proper contract explaining your pay and working hours. Now, let me show you where everything is before I take you to meet Oscar.'

They strolled around the kitchen, opening cupboards and drawers so that Loveday would know where to find the little boy's plastic cutlery, plates, beakers for his milk and juice and so on. Tabitha explained what he could and couldn't eat. 'No sweets. Vegetables with lunch and tea. I want him to get used to a variety of tastes.'

She said that she'd like the girl to take Oscar for a walk every day. 'Just around the village, though, I don't want you going far.'

'I could find out about local toddler groups,' Loveday suggested, 'and baby gym, that sort of thing. I can ask Jean. She looks after little children, she knows everything.'

Tabitha frowned, 'I don't think—'

But Loveday wasn't listening. 'I can't believe you're going

to pay me to do fun things with him,' she said, practically twitching with excitement and sounding for all the world as if she'd been offered a free trip to Disneyland.

Next, Tabitha showed her the utility room behind the kitchen, because it would be her job to wash and iron Oscar's clothes and keep his room tidy. Shelley would be taking care of the guest rooms. The reception rooms were out of bounds, but there was a playroom in the family quarters full of books and toys.

'He loves picture books,' Tabitha explained. 'Please read to him often and don't let him watch too much TV. Half an hour or so before tea's fine.'

By the time they went upstairs, Loveday, who'd been so animated earlier, was looking a little dazed, as if she'd never before received so much information all in one go.

'What time did you say he has his lunch again?' she asked, frowning. 'Maybe I should've written it down.'

They were at the door to the apartment and Tabitha touched her lightly on the arm. 'Don't look so worried, you can't absorb it all at once. I'll be here most of the time, remember, and you can ask me anything.'

'Won't you want to go out? After you've finished the breakfasts, I mean? To meet people for lunch or...' Loveday scratched her temple, as if racking her brains to try to imagine how rich ladies filled their time '...or to have facials or massages or whatever?'

Tabitha shook her head. 'I'll have far too much to do here.'

The little boy was already standing in his cot, peering over the wooden bars, when they entered his room, and Tabitha scooped him up and balanced him on a hip. Loveday opened her arms wide but he shook his head and buried his face in his mother's shoulder.

'It's beautiful!' Loveday sighed, taking the opportunity to gaze around and admire the walls, painted with dark green trees, exotic flowers, brightly coloured parrots and butterflies, like a tropical rainforest. Beneath one tree sat a smiling tiger, and there was a green canopy over the wooden bed, like the roof of a tent. A large, stuffed grey elephant stood in the corner and a monkey was swinging from a rope attached to the sky blue ceiling.

Tabitha looked pleased. 'It's the first room we did up here. We wanted it ready for when Oscar arrived, to help him settle in.'

The small boy clung to her while she opened his wardrobe, but he was watching Loveday closely.

'Trousers, dungarees, shorts, shirts.' Tabitha riffled through the row of child-sized hangers, groaning with clothes. 'And there are T-shirts and jumpers in the chest over there.'

Loveday opened a drawer and pulled out a stripy woollen sweater, glanced quickly at the label and put it back carefully. Then she turned to Oscar and smiled.

'Who's a handsome, smart boy?' She tickled him in the ribs and now, at last, the dimples in his cheeks appeared. 'You and me are going to have a great time, aren't we? Loveday's going to find lots of nice things for us to do!'

He jumped down and fetched a toy train to show her, and Tabitha left them for a while when it was clear that he wouldn't object. When she popped back, Loveday was on her hands and knees, chasing him round the carpet, to squeals of laughter. The bonding experiment seemed to have worked.

'Come with me,' Tabitha said when she finally caught the girl's attention. 'I need to show you something.'

Loveday took Oscar's hand as they followed his mother down the corridor and into the rest of the flat, including the playroom, sitting room, Oscar's bathroom and Tabitha's own bedroom, which was more like a hotel suite really, with a cream-coloured sofa and armchair at one end and a bathroom to the right.

'It's enormous!' Loveday marvelled, gazing at the queen-size bed and fitted wardrobes, the white walls that perhaps needed another coat or two. 'What colour is it going to be?'

'I haven't decided yet. I need to complete the guest rooms before I can put the final touches to it.'

When at last they'd finished, Tabitha said she wanted Loveday to start as soon as possible and it was arranged that they'd speak again the next day. The whole interview had taken so long that she was late for work and had to run to A Winkle In Time, flinging the door open and practically tripping over Robert in her eagerness to reach the cloakroom.

'I'm sorry,' she said, noticing his look of disapproval. 'I didn't have time to get changed.' Waiting staff were supposed to wear black and white.

'Well, at least you've got sensible shoes on, and for once you're not showing half your backside.'

Loveday scowled and might have said something rude back, except that Liz arrived, carrying a big bunch of flowers to go in the stone vase at the end of the bar.

'You won't believe what a brilliant time I've had!' Loveday announced, forgetting her annoyance and grabbing Liz by the arm. She scarcely had time to lay down the flowers before she was being pulled into the kitchen to hear the news.

It was hot, steamy and noisy in there, despite the fact that the back door was open, and Jesse was at the hob, stirring a hollandaise sauce to go with one of the starters. His handsome face lit up when he saw his girlfriend burst in, dragging a startled-looking Liz.

'Hey, babe! How did it go?'

The other boys stopped what they were doing and Alex put his hands on his hips. Meanwhile, Liz, who didn't think that she'd ever seen Loveday so animated, hung back a little to allow her to bask in her moment of glory.

'The little boy's gorgeous and his mum seems really nice. And the house is amazing. You should see his bedroom, and Mrs Mallon's. And Oscar's got loads of clothes, all designer ones.'

She was talking so fast that it was hard to keep up.

'And Mrs Mallon – she says to call her Tabitha – she wants me to take Oscar out. And when he's having a nap I can do stuff for the guest house. She says the job can be what I make it, they're going to need lots of help.'

She paused for a moment to catch her breath before launching off again. 'I'll be like her right-hand girl. I can't wait to start. It's going to be the best opportunity ever. I can't believe they've picked me!'

'Oh, my!' Liz said when Loveday drew to a halt at last, and Jesse left off stirring and gave his girlfriend a hug.

'What's she like, then, Tabitha?' asked Alex, running a hand through his quiff. The sleeves of his black and white checked overall were rolled up and he had sweat on his forehead and upper lip. 'I heard she was a bit la-di-dah.'

Loveday broke away from her boyfriend and shook her head vehemently. 'Oh, no, she's really friendly and nice.'

Friendly wasn't the adjective that Liz would have chosen, but she was relieved that the pair seemed to get on. Perhaps Tabitha preferred young people; she certainly hadn't taken to Pat – or herself, come to that. She just hoped that Loveday wasn't being hasty in accepting the job. It could be awkward if it didn't work out.

When she returned to Bag End, she took off her coat and headed straight upstairs to see Rosie, guessing that she'd be reading. English was one of her favourite subjects and she devoured good books. Liz tiptoed into her daughter's room, not wishing to interrupt, and was surprised to find the girl sitting on her bed, leaning against the pink pillows, the phone clamped to her ear.

'Rosie?'

She looked startled when her mother spoke, pressed the hang up button and threw the phone down.

Liz was confused. 'Who was that?'

But instead of replying, Rosie jumped up, hurried to her desk where an exercise book was open, plonked down and started writing. She didn't look round once or catch her mother's eye.

Liz's heart started to pitter-patter, remembering the bullying her daughter had once suffered at school. 'Is everything all right?'

Rosie waved her away crossly. 'I'm busy. Can you go now?' It was more of a command than a question.

She wasn't usually rude and Liz might have picked her up on her manners, but instead withdrew, wanting time to think. As she wandered downstairs, she found herself pondering, uneasily, on the fact that she and Rosie had always been so close; they'd told each other everything, which was hardly surprising, given that it had been just the two of them for so long. This strange, secretive behaviour was an entirely new state of affairs.

Although tired, she waited for Robert to return from the restaurant and cornered him in the bathroom while he cleaned his teeth, watching his reflection all the time in the mirror.

'She looked shocked when I walked in and threw down the phone.'

Robert leaned over and spat into the washbasin before

straightening up. 'Did she?' He seemed amused. 'She's done it to me a couple of times, too.'

Liz was annoyed. Why hadn't he mentioned it? If Rosie had a problem, she, Liz, needed to know.

'Do you think I should talk to her? Do you reckon something's up?'

'I think it's called being a teenager,' Robert replied, turning off the tap and screwing the lid back on the toothpaste. 'She's nearly thirteen, remember. She's not a baby any more. There'll be all sorts of things she doesn't want us to know.'

New Year came and went, Rosie got through her next scan with flying colours and before long it was the first day of the spring term. Liz had already said goodbye to Robert, who'd gone to the restaurant to take an early delivery, and as Rosie was later than usual she went to find her.

'You're wearing make-up!' she said, as her daughter clomped down the stairs, dragging her bag stuffed with everything that she needed for the day.

'I'm not!'

Rosie tried to push past her mother but it was too late; Liz had already spotted the smudge of blue eye shadow, the black mascara. It was reasonably well applied, she'd give her that.

'I thought you weren't allowed to wear make-up to school.'

'It's only a tiny bit,' Rosie whined. 'They won't even notice. All the other girls wear it.'

Liz shrugged. 'If you get a detention, don't say I didn't warn you.'

'There's no time to take it off now anyway.'

It was true. Spending extra long getting dressed had worked to her advantage; Liz knew her game.

'I'll give you a lift,' she said. 'You won't make it otherwise.'

In truth, Liz would have liked to drive her daughter to school every morning and collect her, too, but she wasn't allowed. It was quite a hike up the hill to the nearest bus stop and she hated to think of Rosie limping all that distance with her heavy bag, then doing the same trip in reverse at the end of a long day. Since September, however, she'd begged to be allowed to make her own way like the other children and Liz had reluctantly concurred. She recognised that the journey had little to do with getting from A to B, but was rather an opportunity to show independence and socialise. She'd been that age once herself after all.

The Lexus was parked in front of Bag End and they both clambered in. They'd finally said goodbye to their ancient old banger, Eeyore, when Robert had insisted it was dangerous, and they now used his car. It was fairly new and very smart, with all the mod cons including built-in satnav, although that hadn't worked for a while and they'd been meaning to get it fixed. Even so, Liz still missed Eeyore; she'd had him when she and Rosie had moved from London all those years ago, and they'd been through so much together that they were almost like old friends.

Rosie sat silently beside her mother as they left the village and headed along country roads so narrow in places that there was no room for other cars to pass. Brambly hedges swished against the sides and Liz kept an eye open for dogs, rabbits and wild deer in her path. At one point they had to wait while a farmer drove his herd of lowing cows from one field to another. There was no point getting stressed, it wouldn't make the cows any faster, so she turned off the ignition and watched as, plump and glossy, their udders swayed rhythmically as they walked, the animals jostling each other in their eagerness to reach pastures new.

'Poo, they stink,' Rosie said grumpily as the pungent smell of manure and sweat filled her nostrils, and Liz felt wistful for the times when they used to sing at the tops of their voices when they made the same trip, but she mustn't complain. Rosie had been born with a sunny nature and it would shine through again, for sure. It wasn't her fault that her hormones were beginning to ramp up, making her cranky.

As they approached the school gates, Rosie flipped down the sun visor and checked herself in the mirror. It was then that Liz noticed Tim Butler, one of her daughter's classmates, hanging back by the iron railings while dozens of other pupils in identical blue and grey uniforms streamed past. He hadn't been at the primary school and Liz didn't know much about him, except that he had a bad stammer; Rosie had told her. He looked quite cute from a distance, smallish and neat, with short brown hair and symmetrical features.

'You can leave me here,' Rosie commanded, beginning to open the car door.

'Hold on, we're still moving.'

Once Liz had parked, Rosie hopped out with a quick 'Bye' and hurried, lopsided, towards the boy, who was strolling in her direction. He smiled shyly until he caught sight of Liz then looked away, embarrassed. She quickly checked her mirror before pulling off; she'd be in trouble with her daughter otherwise.

The way home was in the same direction from which she'd come, but she decided against doing a three-point turn as it would have prolonged her daughter's mortification. Instead, she set off up the road, intending to take the next turning and double back, grinning to herself as she gained speed and left the school far behind.

Ever alert to the possibility that Rosie was being bullied or that her illness had returned, it had never in a million years occurred to Liz that she might have a boyfriend, or someone she was keen on anyway. Perhaps it was Tim that she'd been on the phone to; it would certainly explain the secrecy. Liz couldn't wait to tell Robert.

In her excitement she somehow managed to lose her way. It had happened many times when she'd first moved to the area, when all the country roads had looked the same and she'd frequently had to stop and ask. Now, however, she felt like a native and couldn't remember the last time she'd been confused.

This morning, though, she was distracted and managed to take a wrong fork and ended up on an A road heading in the wrong direction. She drove several miles without coming to a roundabout, then decided that instead of pushing on, she'd take a left and double back along the lanes. It couldn't be too difficult.

Before she knew it, however, she was in an unfamiliar territory, on tiny country roads with no signposts. The more she went down, the more bewildered she became so that she started to wonder if she was going round in circles. On either side, she couldn't see over the tops of the hedges, which were broken up only occasionally by identical wooden gates leading to identical fields, where the January weather seemed to have leeched all the colours into indistinct browns, tans and greys. There wasn't a soul in sight.

After a while she began to feel tired, nauseous and a little desperate, and cursed herself for failing to fix the satnav; she'd talked about it often enough. It was cold out and the heating was on full blast, but that only made her woozy so she decided to stop for a moment in a lay-by and gather her thoughts. She wound down the window and gulped a few deep breaths of fresh, chill air, telling herself to keep calm.

Feeling a little better, she pulled her phone out of her bag and noticed, as she'd suspected, that the battery was dead. There was nothing to do but soldier on until she reached a sign or familiar landmark, or came across a real live person at last. Had she passed this sharp bend before? She had no idea because there were so many others like it. She thought that if she weren't so cross and weary she'd find it funny, and wondered if she was going mad. Either that or she was unwell; she certainly wasn't thinking straight.

The road swerved to the left and she accelerated up a short, steep hill. Just before reaching the top, a battered blue car careered over the brow and screeched to a halt in front of her, narrowly avoiding a collision. They'd both been going too fast and Liz unlocked the door, preparing to jump out, apologise and ask where they were at the same time. Before she could do so, however, the driver, a bald, red-faced man, slammed a fist on the horn and flashed his lights furiously. Thinking better of it, Liz turned and reversed halfway back down the slope until she could pull in and let him pass. The last thing she needed right now was a fight with a foul-tempered motorist.

As he went by he lowered his window and swore at her and she surprised herself by bursting into tears. This wasn't like her; normally she'd have shrugged it off, or shouted something rude in return. Come to think of it, she hadn't been quite herself for several days. It was hard to describe what the matter was, but she'd felt out of sorts – weak, vague, tearful and, yes, a little queasy. She'd imagined that it was the time of year, that post-Christmas blip when everyone seemed to pick up coughs and colds and complain about nasty bugs going round, as well as the weather. It usually passed when the first daffodils poked their heads through the hard earth and pale green leaves started to appear on the trees.

A thought flashed through her mind and her stomach

lurched, as if she were on a boat. It couldn't be, could it? The idea was at once so terrifying and thrilling that she could scarcely entertain it, and she felt like screaming at the top of her voice at the distant cattle and sheep in the fields beyond. But she might be wrong, of course, she shouldn't leap to conclusions. There was one sure-fire way to find out...

Newly refreshed, she set off once more until at last she came to a sign saying 'Netted logs and ducks for sale'. She pulled hard on the wheel, swooped into the turning and there in front of her was a white farmhouse with a barn alongside, housing a muddy red tractor. The place looked deserted but she could hear a dog bark so she rang the bell and soon, to her relief, a small woman in jeans and a green sweatshirt appeared. Liz blushed slightly, embarrassed to have to admit that she was lost, but the woman was unruffled.

'I know what it's like,' she said with a smile, resting some paper against the wall and drawing a sketchy map. 'I've got no sense of direction whatsoever.'

She slipped on a pair of clogs and walked to the gate, pointing to her left. 'Follow the road a few hundred yards until you reach a wooden stile and a notice saying public footpath.' She indicated where it was on her map. 'Turn sharp right after that, then second left, then first right and you'll see a sign marked, "Caution! Otters crossing".'

Liz thought she knew the sign; she and Rosie had passed it once and commented. They'd opened the windows and craned their necks, looking for evidence, but much to their disappointment hadn't spotted a single animal. From the sign, it wasn't far to the A road that she'd taken earlier and once there she could find her way back to Tremarnock.

'Thank you so much,' she gushed. 'I was beginning to think I'd be driving in circles for ever!'

She felt like cheering when she reached the crucial fork and spotted the sign, and vowed to phone the garage that very day about the satnav. She was itching to go home but instead took a well-known detour into the local town and parked the car in the high street. As she put money in the meter she saw Esme, pulling a lurid pink and black zebra print shopping trolley on the opposite side of the road, but pretended not to notice. Then she hurried into the supermarket to buy a few items for Pat, followed by the pharmacy, hoping that she wouldn't spot anyone else she knew.

Anxious to reach home, she was planning to just drop Pat's groceries off without going in, but when the old woman came to the door it was obvious that something was wrong. Pat pulled a strange face, then gestured with a thumb in the direction of her front room and mouthed words that Liz couldn't decipher.

'Are you all right?' she asked, thinking that Pat must have lost her voice. 'Have you got that nasty laryngitis again?'

Pat shook her head vigorously and pointed once more to her front room. Realising that her plans would have to wait, Liz plonked the groceries on the floor and ventured in, bracing herself as she had no idea what to expect.

Her eyes fell immediately on Felipe, who was sitting in one of Pat's armchairs, beneath her porcelain lady collection on the window shelf behind, weeping quietly into a tissue.

'What is it?' Liz cried and he looked up, red-eyed, and blew his nose.

Pat, who was right behind, found her voice and answered for him.

'He's had a tiff with Tony,' she explained breathlessly. 'Tony accused him of having an affair with that Bungle from the art club. Tony's gone to London and taken all his clothes with him and he's not answering his phone. Felipe hasn't slept a wink and he can't eat a thing and he's going mad with worry. Oh!' She wrung her hands and sighed.

Liz's head had started spinning. Bungle, so called because of his fondness for rescuing items found in skips and junkyards and restoring them to some sort of dubious usefulness, was a local artist who had run the club on Friday afternoons for years. He was very popular, owing not just to his skills as a painter but also his whacky sense of humour, but Liz had never thought him a Casanova. For starters, he'd always seemed more interested in animals than relationships to her. He owned four mongrels, to whom he was devoted, and, as far as she knew, had never had a partner. Besides, Felipe and Tony adored one another, for goodness' sake. It made no sense.

She racked her brains, trying to think of something helpful, but could only come up with platitudes. 'All couples have rows and they usually blow over. Sometimes it's good to clear the air.'

Felipe looked at her reproachfully. 'Eez not just a little row, is a huge bust-up.' He clenched his fists like a boxer to demonstrate. 'Tony has removed his wedding ring. He says we are finished.' He sobbed again and Pat, still hovering behind Liz, passed him a box of tissues from the little lamp table displaying some of the items from her precious owl collection.

'He's very upset,' she said, as if Liz hadn't noticed. 'I think he's going to have a nervous breakdown. He'll end up in one of them mental hospitals if he's not careful. Like Tina Pocock. She wasn't the same again, poor soul, after they took her away.'

Felipe flinched and Liz considered it wise to halt Pat's flow right there. 'Why don't you put the kettle on and make us all a nice cup of tea?'

The old woman shuffled off and Liz returned to Felipe.

'*Are* you having an affair? I mean, you don't need to tell me but—'

It seemed so unlikely, but she was about to say that if she knew the truth she'd be in a better position to advise. She didn't get the chance, however, because he sprang up, red-faced, and dropped the box of tissues on the floor.

'I would never do such a thing. Tony is my, how do you say, spirit mate?'

'Er, soul-mate?'

'Yes, soul-mate,' he repeated hotly. 'I would never love another man. My heart is his alone.' He look at Liz reproachfully. 'I thought you knew me better than that.'

'I'm sorry,' said Liz, gesturing for him to sit down. 'I never imagined you would. So why has Tony jumped to the wrong conclusion?'

Felipe sighed mournfully and stared at Pat's swirly carpet. 'Because I said Bungle has pretty eyes. I said I wish I had nice blue eyes like him because mine are brown and brown is a boring colour. Everyone in Brazil has brown.'

'Oh, dear. What colour are Tony's eyes?' Liz couldn't remember but had a nasty feeling that she knew the answer.

'Brown,' Felipe snapped. 'I wish I had kept my teeth shut.'

'Mouth.'

'Mouth, teeth, it makes no difference. English is a stupid language anyway.' He whacked the side of his head with the base of his palm.

Liz frowned. She knew how sensitive Tony was and that he had a tendency to fly off the handle, especially in matters of love. He'd had a string of failed romances before meeting Felipe, but had been so happy of late and she'd become very fond of Felipe, too. She couldn't bear to think that this little misunderstanding might drive them apart.

'What did you say to him when he accused you?' she wanted to know.

'I tried to explain. I said blue is like the sky and brown is like mud. It's true, no? I am not telling lies. But Tony started packing his bags and would not listen when I begged him to stay. He says it is obvious I prefer Bungle and I must go to him, but I do not want to.'

'You must get the next train to London,' Liz insisted. 'And on the way buy him something brown – a present, chocolates or something.'

Felipe looked doubtful. 'He does not like chocolates because they make him fat, he prefers savoury things.'

'Well, his favourite blend of coffee, a brown jumper, anything. And wrap it up beautifully. You know how he loves gifts. Take his wedding ring, too, and ask him to put it back on. He'll relent, I'm sure of it. He adores you, Felipe, he'll be missing you dreadfully.'

By the time Pat returned with the tea, Felipe had calmed down and was already talking about the brown leather jacket that Tony had spotted in Plymouth and that he'd nearly bought, before concluding that it was too expensive. Apparently it matched Tony's colouring perfectly.

'I will buy it for him before I board the train. It's a very nice brown, very soft leather.'

'Well, I never,' Pat said to Liz when he finally left, with a new-found spring in his step. 'I had him down as a basket case, I really did. Thought they'd be carting him off in one of them straitjacket things. Thank the Lord it hasn't come to that.'

Of course Liz had to stay and calm Pat's nerves, too, then hear about her friend Elaine, from Saltash, who had another friend, Beryl, who knew Rick Kane's girlfriend Sylvia, or knew of her, more like. It seemed that she had a bit of a reputation.

'Apparently she's been married and divorced three times. *Three times*,' Pat repeated, 'fancy that! She's had more husbands than I've had hot dinners!'

'Gracious! She sounds like Elizabeth Taylor!'

Pat pulled her chair closer to Liz's.

'Elaine says she only married the last one for his money. He was a wealthy solicitor but he packed in his job because he didn't like it so she ditched him. Made sure she got a good pay-out first, though. You saw the way she was gawping at Luke Mallon on Christmas Day. That Rick had better watch his step or she'll have his shop off him.'

Liz snorted. 'It can't be worth much and, anyway, Rick's not keen on getting married again, he told me. He's having too much fun playing the field.'

'You mark my words,' Pat said darkly, 'she's a gold-digger. You should never trust a woman with that brassy-coloured hair, they're always after something.'

By the time Liz managed to escape it was almost midday and she was desperate to complete her mission. With trembling fingers she unwrapped the pregnancy kit that she'd bought and read the instructions, forcing herself to slow down and do it properly. This wasn't something you wanted to mess up.

She tried again to remember when she'd had her last period but couldn't. It must have been a while ago, though, well over a month. The dates would probably fit with that evening when Robert had got a bit carried away...

Of course they'd discussed having a baby, but had both agreed that now wasn't the right time. Rosie had been through so much with her illness, then there had been the wedding and getting used to having Robert around permanently. No, they'd decided, there was no hurry and, what's more, they were blissfully happy as they were. A baby wasn't on the agenda.

The result of the test only took five minutes but it seemed like for ever. Liz couldn't bear to sit and watch, so she paced around her bedroom, glancing out of the window every now and again to distract herself. She saw Barbara scurry past in a plum overcoat, carrying two heavy shopping bags. Then Jean trundled by, wheeling a double buggy. Liz jumped back, not wishing to prompt a visit.

She plumped the cushions on her bed and checked her watch for the umpteenth time, feeling quite light-headed. What if it was negative? She'd get rid of the evidence immediately. She wouldn't tell Robert, or anyone. She'd feel a fool. Maybe she couldn't have another child. Perhaps Rosie was destined to be the only one.

What if it was positive? Robert might be appalled. Rosie had begged for a brother or sister but might not be so keen if it actually happened, and what about cerebral palsy? In her head, Liz knew that it wasn't genetic, it was just incredibly bad luck, most likely caused by lack of oxygen during the pregnancy or birth. In her heart, however, she feared that if she were to conceive another child, she'd be anxious for the entire nine months.

She looked at the time again and nearly ten minutes had gone by. Was she going to chuck it away without even checking? She was made of sterner stuff. Steeling herself, she ventured into the bathroom, where the white stick was balanced innocently on the edge of the washbasin where she'd left it. Who would have thought that such a simple piece of technology could hold the key to your future?

She picked up the applicator, grasping it between finger and thumb, and walked gingerly next door, settling on the end of the bed where the light was good. She took a deep breath – this was it – and squinted at the oval window, half closing her eyes as if hoping the information might seep in more slowly.

PREGNANT. One little word, eight letters. She looked once more, eyes wide open this time, aware of the pulse vibrating in her temples, her wrists, the sweat prickling on the back of her neck. PREGNANT again. There was no mistaking it.

She remembered how she'd felt when it had happened all those years ago, when she'd thrown up for the third morning running and popped out in her lunch hour to the chemist. Then, she'd more than dreaded Greg's reaction. With reason, as it had turned out. He'd been horrified, urging her to have an abortion, but she wouldn't. Having lost her mother at just sixteen, she couldn't destroy the new life inside her that might look a little like her beloved mum, sound a little like her even. That might just ease the loneliness inside that time couldn't seem to heal.

And how right she'd been to continue with the pregnancy! Rosie was the light of her life and now she had Robert, too, gorgeous, loving, kind, generous Robert, who'd made her life complete.

She shivered, thinking that perhaps a baby would destroy what they had; it would certainly change their family. And yet... She grinned, hugging her arms around herself, feeling as if her heart might burst with fear and delight wrapped into one.

Frantic suddenly, she jumped up and ran downstairs to her bag, which she'd abandoned in the hallway when she'd come in. It was terrible timing; he'd be in the middle of serving lunch. There again, he'd never forgive her if she waited. She fumbled for her mobile, only to remember that it was dead, so she grabbed the landline with trembling fingers instead.

There were two, three, four rings then at last she heard his voice. 'Hey, darling.' His pleasure warmed her through.

'Oh, Robert,' she said breathlessly. 'I've got something to tell you.'

There was a sharp inhalation. 'Is everything all right?'

'Yes! At least, I think so. Don't worry, I'm fine!'

She could hardly bear it any longer. She wanted him there, with her, or she might explode like a shaken soda bottle.

'I can't speak on the phone. You'll understand why. You've got to come home *now*!'

Chapter Nine

As soon as she hung up, Liz regretted her haste. She should have waited till he returned at four-ish. It wasn't fair to disturb him at work and she'd no doubt worried him. She picked up one of Rosie's books, which was lying on the sofa in the front room, and tried to read, thinking that a cool, calm, collected woman would have bided her time until the right moment, preferably when her husband was sitting down at the end of the day with a glass of wine or a stiff whisky.

Instead, she'd lost her way, then summoned poor Robert with no explanation. She stared at the words on the page, all the while listening, ears pricked, for the sound of his feet coming down the hill, the turn of the key in the lock. Wondering what his response would be, unable, hard as she tried, to picture his expression when she broke the news.

It didn't take him long to arrive and as soon as he entered the house she abandoned any last shred of composure and ran to find him.

'Liz!' he said, holding out his arms to catch her as she hurled herself in. 'What's happened?'

'I'm sorry, I couldn't wait...'

Then she practically dragged him into the sitting room, took his hands in hers and stood, facing him, before the unlit fire.

A cold winter light flooded in, illuminating a vase of creamy white lilies with pale green leaves on a table in the corner, and the air smelled sweet, heady and alive with expectation. Mitzi, the cat, who was snoozing on a warm patch of carpet underneath, flicked her tail and sneezed.

'We're going to have a baby,' Liz whispered, gazing steadily at her husband.

'What?'

'I just did a test.'

His expression froze, his body tensed and his hands tightened in hers. What was he thinking? The silence seemed to last for ages, though in reality it was only a few seconds, then she noticed that his eyes were damp, though whether with gladness or dismay she couldn't tell.

'Is it true?' he said at last. 'Are you sure?'

But there was no time to reply, because all at once his handsome face broke into a smile that made her think the sun had toppled from the sky and made a home in his heart; it was so dazzling that it practically gave her sunburn.

'Oh, my!' he cried, crushing her against his chest. 'I never thought…!' Then he leaned down and kissed her on the mouth with such tenderness that it seemed as if his very soul had slipped inside to mingle with hers. This, she thought, feeling her own eyes fill with emotion, was how it was meant to be.

'Are you positive you don't mind?' she asked, when she'd pulled away at last. She was checking for the tiniest chink of doubt, the merest hint of misgiving. 'I thought you might say it's too soon. I mean, we'd decided to wait.'

'Mind, Lizzie?' She loved it when he called her that because it's what her mother used to say. Never Eliza, her real name, always Liz or Lizzie. 'I only suggested waiting because I didn't want to pressure you. You've made me the happiest man alive!'

Then he took her in his arms again and did a sort of waltz round the room, and by the time they came to a halt she was exhausted and her sides ached from laughing.

'You must get back to work,' she said breathlessly. 'They'll be wondering where you are.'

But whether he heard or not was unclear because the next thing she knew he was half pushing, half pulling her to the sofa, where he grabbed a cushion and jammed it behind her back, before dragging up the little footrest by the fire and placing her legs, one by one, on top.

'You must relax... What was I thinking? Would you like some tea – or juice? You must eat. Protein. That's it, steak... I'll buy some...' He was talking so fast, more to himself than her, that she could scarcely keep up. 'Fish, too, and plenty of milk, cheese... no, not cheese.' He scratched his head. 'Is it only soft cheese you can't have? Pickles!' he cried suddenly. 'Gherkins!' He frowned. 'Or are you craving something else? Bananas? Curry?'

Liz giggled. 'Stop it! I'm not ill! And, no, I don't have any cravings yet.' She looked at him seriously. 'You mustn't tell anyone. Not a soul. Not even Rosie until we've had the three-month scan. Promise me you won't.'

Robert paced the room, swinging his arms to and fro like one of those Nordic walkers, minus the poles. He looked as if he needed to let off steam, otherwise he might burst like an overfilled balloon.

'Not tell anyone? It won't be easy... the boys are sure to guess... and Loveday...' His voice trailed off as he completed another circuit.

Liz smiled. Communication had never been his strong point, at least not until he'd met her. In the old days, he'd have had no trouble keeping his thoughts to himself; in fact, half the time it was impossible to work out what was on his mind. Now he sounded like a leaky tap.

'Well, you'll just have to try,' she said firmly.

Loveday started her new job the following Monday. She was very nervous, but fortunately her first day proved an unmitigated success. She rushed round to Liz's that evening to tell her all about it, and said that she and Tabitha had got on like a house on fire. Luke hadn't been there, but Oscar was gorgeous and she adored him. All in all, she claimed, the new post was a dream come true.

Liz couldn't help wondering how she'd cope with the domestic side of things – making Oscar's meals, doing his washing and ironing and keeping his room tidy – but could only hope that she'd manage somehow, or that Tabitha would be a patient teacher.

She'd also been told how to take bookings, so that when Oscar was having a nap she'd be able to answer the phone and field emails. The Stables was due to open for business on the first of February and apparently there had already been a fair amount of interest and a few firm reservations. It was unlikely that the place would start filling up immediately but, with luck, word would soon spread.

Robert was convinced that this could only be good news for A Winkle In Time and Liz hoped that he was right. The village pubs served simple food like ploughman's lunches and steak and chips, but if you wanted something more adventurous, A Winkle In Time was the place to go. Otherwise you'd have to drive to one of the surrounding villages or venture into Plymouth.

On Red Letter Day, Liz was on her way back from the supermarket at about 11 a.m. when a big silver Mercedes pulled in outside Bag End and nabbed her space, so that she had to do a loop, stop up the hill and walk down. Just as she passed Pat's cottage, a tall, elegant woman with a chestnut-brown bob emerged from the passenger seat and buttoned her long camel coat to the collar. She was wearing black sunglasses, which seemed rather unnecessary on a grey winter's day, and high tan boots. As she closed the door a man got out as well, walked to the rear of the car and proceeded to pull out two big black suitcases.

'This way,' he said to his partner, as he headed towards Fore Street. The woman followed, walking gingerly in her heels on the uneven road surface before turning right by Jean's place, Dynnargh.

Liz guessed that they were the first guests, and tried to imagine how nervous Tabitha, Shelley and Loveday must be. Luke too, maybe, though he was more laidback. Loveday had mentioned that she'd been instructed to keep Oscar well away from the reception areas downstairs as Tabitha wanted an air of calm, sophisticated relaxation.

'They're coming here for a holiday,' she'd explained to the girl. 'They won't want a small boy running around making a noise. He needs to get used to behaving a bit differently with guests.'

Loveday had been asked to arrive extra early in the morning so that she could entertain Oscar while Tabitha and Shelley finished the preparations. She'd been intending to take him to the park, but then it had started raining and before she knew it there was a loud rap on the door so she decided it would be best to wait while the guests settled in.

In the end, she didn't leave until after lunch, resolving not to disturb Tabitha, who was busy in the kitchen and had quite enough to think about. She couldn't, however, resist peeking into the main reception room to see what the newcomers looked like. She'd heard that they were from London, which was pretty exotic as far as she was concerned as she'd never been there.

The door was ajar and she could see the guests, sideways on, settled in front of the glowing fire, having already visited their room and unpacked their bags. Either Tabitha or Shelley had taken them a tray of coffee and cakes, which was placed on a little table between the pair, and they were now studying some leaflets about local places of interest. The woman had removed her high heels and was rubbing her feet together. You could almost hear her purring. The man, in a thick navy cable-knit sweater, pushed up at the sleeves, was talking to her in a low voice, occasionally interrupted by the crackle and thud of a log splitting and falling as it surrendered to the flames.

'This walk looks beautiful,' he said. 'Along the coast.' He passed her a leaflet. 'I could do with some sea air.'

'I fancy a trip to the Lost Gardens of Heligan,' the woman replied. 'Looks as if we'll need a whole day, though.'

Oscar squawked in Loveday's arms and the couple turned their heads.

'Sorry,' she said, 'we're just going to the swings. We didn't mean to disturb you.'

The woman smiled. 'What a cutie!' The little boy did look very appealing in his red hooded jacket and matching pompom hat, his round face flushed from wearing so many clothes indoors. 'Is he yours?'

'Oh, no! I'm the nanny.' Saying this made Loveday glow with pleasure. 'This is Oscar. He's Tabitha and Luke's son, I mean Mr and Mrs Mallon's.' She kissed him on his squidgy cheek for the umpteenth time.

'Sweet,' said the woman, turning back to her leaflets. Loveday fetched the pushchair from the cupboard to the left of the front door and strapped her charge in, before heading up the cobbled street. It was a revelation to be given so much responsibility and although the job was hard work sometimes, she was blissfully happy.

She'd already begun to establish a routine at home, with finger painting one day, baking another, but couldn't help feeling that Oscar would benefit from the company of children his age. Jean had mentioned a good toddler group in the nearby village, to which she took her own charges, and it was easy to get to by bus, but Tabitha had seemed reluctant so Loveday had dropped the idea. In any case, come the summer she could take him to the beach, where there'd be plenty of little ones.

'Some mums are very protective,' Liz had said when Loveday had raised the matter. 'Particularly with first children. You know how I am with Rosie; I can't help it.'

As Loveday wheeled the pushchair up the road, she found herself blinking in the light as she breathed in the sights, sounds and smells of the village. Now that the rain had stopped, the birds were tweeting and the world seemed to have come alive once more. People's voices could be heard above the noise of an occasional car starting up, and lazy trails of smoke billowed from chimney pots before wafting away on the wind.

When they reached the corner of Torren Street, Sally, the Jack Russell, came scampering down the hill with John in hot pursuit. His hair and clothes were damp and he gave a wave but didn't stop.

'Heel!' he shouted, but as usual the dog took not a blind bit of notice.

'Woof,' said Oscar excitedly, kicking his legs. 'Woof woof.' He craned his neck so that he could watch the animal until it ran out of sight.

They were about to resume their journey when a voice

behind them cried, 'Wait!' and Loveday swung round to see Tabitha hurtling towards them in the smart beige sweater and dark trousers that she'd put on that morning, her black hair streaming behind her like a waterfall.

'Where are you going?'

Loveday hesitated. Had she done something wrong? 'Only to the park. Do you want me to—?'

Tabitha shook her head. 'You didn't tell me. I thought...' She was panting. 'Everything's fine.'

It didn't seem fine, though. Her eyes slid left and right, as if searching for something in the little side roads and alleyways, behind a garden wall or under a wheelie bin. Anyone would think the Beast of Bodmin had escaped from the moor and was roaming the area in search of prey.

'Are you sure?' Loveday pressed, and Tabitha looked shifty. Anxious to do the right thing, Loveday offered to come back but her boss refused.

'Just be careful, that's all. There are bad people in the world.'

Loveday was taken aback. Crime was rife in London, she knew, but down here graffiti in the public loo made front-page news.

Not in this village, she almost said, then decided that it might seem impertinent and shut her mouth.

Tabitha cursed herself inwardly. She shouldn't have given the girl a fright like that. She was being stupid and panicky and Luke would be furious if he knew. And yet...

The guests were still by the fire as she tiptoed past and Shelley was in the kitchen with the door shut, so she padded silently to her bedroom, picking up the phone on the side table and dialling the familiar number.

Molly didn't reply at first, but rang back almost immediately when she spotted the missed call. She was good like that.

'What's up? Everything OK?'

Tabitha's mouth felt dry and she took a sip of water from the glass beside the bed. She was so relieved to hear her friend's voice that she almost wept.

'I thought I saw him, Moll,' she whispered, checking the door to make sure that no one was about. 'Just now. Outside the house. He was wearing a padded black jacket, like the one he used to have. And a baseball cap. When he saw me at the window he walked away quickly. It all happened so fast, I couldn't be sure, but oh! What if he's found me? What if he tries to hurt Oscar?'

She let out a sob that muffled Molly's reply.

'What makes you think it was him,' she was asking, 'other than the jacket? Could you be mistaken? Could it have been someone else?'

Tabitha bit the back of her hand, leaving tooth marks on the skin. It was the only way to stop herself crying.

'I might be wrong. I couldn't see his face properly because of the hat. It's just that he was the right sort of height and size, and there was something about his manner... And if it wasn't him, what was he doing hanging round the house anyway?'

Molly cleared her throat. 'Maybe he was thinking of renting a room?' She'd swung into practical mode. 'He could have read about the guest house and wanted to check it out. Honestly, it's very unlikely he'd have followed you to Cornwall. Besides, he knows you're with Luke.'

Tabitha took a deep breath. Molly always managed to sort her out, she was a pro.

'You're right,' she said, feeling the damp cloak lifting from her shoulders. 'Anyway, he hates the countryside and he's hardly ever been south. I'm just being silly.'

'That's the spirit.' Molly paused, and Tabitha thought that she could hear another voice, someone at the video company where she worked. She came back on the line. 'I've got to go, sorry, but try not to worry. Call back soon. Love you, Tabs.' And she was gone.

Even so, Tabitha couldn't help sneaking back to the window and flicking to one side the temporary blind that she always kept closed. Satisfied that the man hadn't returned, she lay on her bed and shut her eyes for a moment, repeating Molly's words over and over: 'Renting a room... Checking out the guest house... Knows you're with Luke.'

As she lay there, feeling the soft, cool sheets against her cheek and the palms of her hands, her mind flipped back to another time, thirteen years ago. She wriggled, turning her head backwards and forwards on the pillow restlessly, but to no avail. She seemed destined to repeat the story over and over, until the day she died. Beyond, even...

It had all started, really, after she had been kicked out of home and had gone to stay with Molly. Not in her house, Molly's mum and dad wouldn't have allowed that. They'd taken against Tabitha's adoptive parents, saying the fundamentalist religion that they'd joined was weird and Molly should keep well away.

'They indoctrinate children and force them to marry within the sect,' Molly's mum had told her. 'They can't even go to university – imagine that! Maybe Tabitha's got a chance, because she's from different stock and she's more feisty, with a mind of her own. But the younger two look like zombies or robots in their funny clothes and with that weird way of speaking. They're not allowed to think without checking with their parents first.'

Back then, there had been a great deal that Molly and

Tabitha hadn't understood. Molly had said if the council found out that Tabitha was on her own, they'd send her to a horrible children's home or put her with a foster family, who might be even worse than the other lot. So for nearly a year Tabitha had hidden in the garage, sneaking in and out via the alleyway at the back, peeing in bushes and waiting for Molly to return from school and bring her food that she'd managed to scavenge from her parents' cupboards and fridge.

She'd found an old mattress for her friend, a sleeping bag, candles, books, paper, writing things and a little heater for when it got cold. And whenever her mum and dad went out, she'd signal to Tabitha that the coast was clear for her to come inside and have a wash, go to the loo and change her clothes.

The garage, which had been made into a sort of studio for Molly to practise with the band, was quite clean, but no one could pretend it was luxurious. Tabitha remembered lonely hours spent huddling in the sleeping bag, hugging her knees to her chest and wondering when it would be safe to venture out and wander the streets.

She had been permanently afraid that Molly's parents would discover her, or that her own would come looking and drag her back. It had been years before she'd realised that, in reality, if she'd bumped into them in the street they'd have averted their gazes and walk on by. The only respite she'd been able to find had been in writing music, and at weekends, when the boys had come round, they'd have jamming sessions, just like the old days, only Tabitha had had to sing quietly in case someone heard and recognised her.

As it happened, she and Molly had been clever and Molly's parents had truly believed that their daughter's friend had run away.

'Doesn't she keep in touch?' Molly's mum would ask

occasionally, and Molly would shake her head. 'That's a shame, because you were such good pals. I wonder what she's doing now. I hope she's made a better life for herself away from that peculiar family.'

They could have continued like that for quite a while longer had not Molly's dad decided to set up his own company and announced that he needed to convert the garage into a study for himself.

'You hardly use it now, Moll,' he'd argued when she protested. 'Only at weekends, and next year you'll be working hard for A-levels and then you'll be off to college or university. It'll make the perfect office space for me. Sorry, love, you'll have to practise at someone else's house from now on.'

As soon as Molly broke the news, Tabitha realised that she'd have to get a job and a room somewhere fast. Time was of the essence. In truth, she'd been planning to do it for a while, only the thought of being on her own had frightened her so that it had been easier to put it off. Plus, Molly kept saying that if she waited, they'd land a record deal and everything would be hunky-dory. Of course it was unlikely, but somehow Tabitha had made herself believe what she wanted to believe, that there was a rainbow with a pot of gold at the bottom and it wouldn't be long before they found it.

Finding a job with no experience, no fixed address and an anxious look in your eye, as if you had something to hide, was never going to be easy. Molly cobbled together the money for a deposit on a poky room in a run-down house, but Tabitha soon realised that delivering leaflets wasn't going to pay the bills; she'd have to get something more lucrative.

There were jobs going at the student pub up the road but they wouldn't have her front-of-house, she was too young and green.

'You can work in the kitchen, washing the dishes,' the manager, Alf, told her, eyeing her up and down. 'I don't want no trouble, mind. Whatever happens in my pub stays in my pub, understand? Good girl. Then I think we're going to get on famously.'

He squeezed her waist as she walked by as a token of their new-found camaraderie.

The hours were long and the job was mind-numbingly dull, apart from when she had to spring into life to dodge Alf's wandering hands. The only chink of light was when she and the band managed to get together at Matt's or Dave's house once or twice a week to rehearse. Then she could lose herself in her singing and imagine that she was someone else entirely, a famous musician like Joan Baez, travelling the world and performing to audiences who appreciated the passion in her voice, the depth of feeling in every word she uttered. They even started to get regular gigs in pubs and clubs around the area, though it was difficult to fit them in, what with her job and the others' schoolwork. But they managed somehow.

For a while, things improved further when Carl got a job as a barman at the pub. He was in his late twenties, small, strong and wiry, with close-cropped dark hair, a permanent six o'clock shadow and clever little black eyes that seemed to miss nothing.

He took a shine to Tabitha and would look out for her, glaring at Alf, who was lazy and drank too much, and cracking his knuckles at him. At first Alf would find fault with him, so that at any moment Tabitha suspected he might give him the sack. But before long he began to fear and rely on the younger man to run the place, and the other staff began to forget who was the boss and who the employee. It was Carl who ruled the roost, Carl whom they deferred to. More and more, Alf would retire with a bottle of whisky to his flat upstairs, while Carl kept the tills ringing and the customers happy with more than just drinks. He always had a supply of something to hand – heroin, coke, whatever they fancied.

So lost was Tabitha in her thoughts that at first she didn't hear the noises in the corridor outside.

'Come on, little man, let's get your coat off.'

Her eyes snapped open and she felt a surge of relief. Loveday and Oscar back from the park! Home safe and sound and, what's more, they'd drag her from the dark place that she'd been in.

'Can I come in?' Loveday tapped at the door before entering the room with the little boy in her arms. 'He loves that roundabout so much! He doesn't seem to get dizzy and he found a little friend to play with.'

'What friend?' Tabitha checked herself. 'I mean, did you know him?'

Loveday looked at her strangely. 'Only one of Barbara's granddaughters. You know? Barbara from The Lobster Pot? Her son Aiden's got two kids who live in Launceston. He's divorced but he brings them here quite often.'

Tabitha felt her shoulders relax. 'How nice!' She took her son from Loveday's arms and pressed her cheek against his. He smelled of milk and baby soap and soft young skin.

'She's called Matilda,' Loveday went on. 'She's two, like Oscar. They were chasing each other round and round and going on the slide together. I only came back because he's tired.'

He yawned on cue, gave a grouchy moan, and Tabitha settled him down to sleep before suggesting a cup of tea. Shelley would have left by now, she wasn't the chatty type anyway, and Tabitha enjoyed these one-to-one moments with Loveday and could tell that she did, too. At times like this, the age gap seemed to melt away and they were more like friends than boss and employee. Tabitha didn't have a lot of friends.

They sat on stools round the kitchen island and spoke about clothes and music – and Jesse.

'He's got a great six-pack.' Loveday grinned. 'And he can cook! Perfect combo.'

Tabitha laughed. 'The ideal man! Does he have a brother?'

Loveday didn't have time to reply because Luke strode in, halting the conversation in its tracks.

'What's so funny?' He took off his coat and threw it on a stool.

'We were just discussing Oscar's new word,' Tabitha replied, quick as a flash. 'He says "bests" for "guests". I rather like that.'

She glanced at Loveday, who nodded almost imperceptibly. She was good like that, loyal, even if she didn't understand.

Luke fetched a bottle of distilled water from the fridge and poured himself a glass.

'I've had some bad news. I came home early because I need to discuss something with you.'

He pulled up a chair and the women listened intently while he explained that his main financial advice business, still based in Manchester, was principally run by his partner. Now, however, the new venture that he, Luke, had started in Plymouth had begun to take off, but unfortunately the wife of one of his key employees had fallen ill and he needed to go back up North, where she and the family still lived.

'Hopefully he won't have to stay long but in the meantime I'm short-staffed at a crucial time.'

Tabitha looked worried. 'What are you going to do?'

Luke crossed his arms. 'That's why I wanted to talk to Loveday.'

She looked surprised. 'Me? What do you mean?'

He went on to explain that he and Tabitha were very pleased with the work that she'd been doing so far, with her attitude and maturity, and her potential for greater things, and he was certain that Tabitha could spare her from Oscar duties for a couple of afternoons a week to lend him a hand, just until the other man returned.

'It's interesting work,' he went on, 'and you'll learn a lot. I can pay you a bit extra, too, plus your fares, of course.'

Loveday was amazed; she hardly knew what to say.

'What is your business? What is it you do?'

'Come in tomorrow and I'll explain,' he replied, 'it's highly confidential.'

'Highly confidential? Wow!' Her eyes shone. 'It sounds like spying or something.'

Tabitha's heart fluttered. 'Luke?' But he gave her a look that made her throat constrict, the words freeze in her mouth, so she got up to put the empty tea mugs in the dishwasher.

'What do you say?' he went on. 'I know I can trust you. Are you up for it?'

There was a pause and Tabitha, standing by the sink with her back turned, felt Luke's eyes on her. She could hardly breathe.

'Would you mind?' she heard Loveday ask her in a small voice. 'I mean, can you manage without me? You've only just opened the guest house.'

She sounded young – and so trusting. Tabitha's head swam and she gripped the edge of the work surface, turning her knuckles white.

One, two, three, she thought, before spinning herself round and giving a dazzling smile.

'I think it's a wonderful idea! We're not exactly busy yet. Shelley's a great help and it's only for a couple of days a week. It sounds like a fantastic opportunity. Go for it!'

Chapter Ten

Two weeks later, Liz stood in front of the bathroom mirror, put the toothbrush in her mouth and heaved. How could such a little thing cause her to retch? She took the brush out quickly, thinking it would almost be funny if she didn't feel so bad. She wasn't throwing up every morning like last time; instead, she felt tired and nauseous all day long. Even certain smells – like peanuts, oddly – made her gag.

According to the old wives' tales, it was the sign of a strong pregnancy, but knowing this didn't seem to make it any easier. She peered at herself in the glass and decided that the dark circles under her eyes were getting bigger and her skin, pale at the best of times, was positively sallow. Ugh.

Disgusted, she abandoned the toothbrush and swilled mouthwash around instead. It might have tasted foul but at least it didn't make her want to vomit. Honestly, the things women had to put up with. Robert did his best to sympathise but, really, he couldn't hide his excitement about the baby; she reckoned he secretly regarded morning sickness as no more than a tiresome but necessary irritation. He had no idea…

Of course she'd stopped using the e-cig and she'd tried ginger and nibbling on dry biscuits, to no avail. She was losing weight, despite her husband's best efforts, and it was a miracle that Rosie hadn't noticed but, there again, she was so wrapped up in school, and Tim Butler, that a Vietnamese pot-bellied pig might have taken up residence at Bag End and she wouldn't have noticed.

'We're not going out together,' she huffed, whenever Liz tried to probe. 'We're just friends, that's all.'

But the secretive phone calls continued, plus trips into Plymouth at weekends when she wouldn't let her mother drop her anywhere near the meeting-up point, or wait for her in the same street when it was going-home time. As far as Liz knew, Tim was a nice boy; she reckoned his interest in her daughter would give her confidence and the fact that he, too, had a disability, his stammer, had no doubt brought them together. She wished, however, that Rosie would invite him home, or at least allow her to meet him somewhere neutral. Liz wanted him to know that Rosie was more vulnerable than other girls and needed to be taken care of. Most of all, she didn't want her to get hurt.

After saying goodbye to her at the garden gate, she set her sewing machine on the kitchen table and sat down to a few hours of making hair accessories. She'd come up with a new range of yoga sweatbands in bright colours that could double up as scrunchies, and she'd managed to sell quite a few through her friend in Birmingham, who owned a women's dress and accessories shop, and whom she'd met in Oklahoma when Rosie had been undergoing treatment.

The woman, Sam, had a daughter, Lottie, who'd hit it off with Rosie and the families had also become close, travelling to see each other every few months since their return. Recently, however, doctors had revealed the dreadful news that Lottie's tumour was growing again and she was undergoing another round of aggressive chemotherapy. Naturally, Sam was devastated, although she tried to put a brave face on it, and Liz had been doing her best to cheer her up.

At around two o'clock she strolled slowly up the hill to the church hall, where Tremarnock Art Club was holding a show of their work. She'd promised Felipe that she'd be there and was delighted to find him sipping tepid coffee with Esme and Tony, who had left London early that morning in order to enjoy a long weekend in the village.

Thankfully, Tony and Felipe had recovered from their contretemps and, indeed, Tony was sporting the brown leather jacket that his spouse had bought him as a peace offering, zipped up to his chest and straining a little over the tum.

'Darling!' Tony cried when he spotted Liz. 'You look absolutely ghastly. What on earth have you been doing to yourself?'

Liz, who immediately felt ten times worse, was about to mutter something about 'a bad night' when Bungle shuffled over and offered to explain something about the work on display.

She sensed Tony bristle in his presence, but he said nothing. To be fair, despite Bungle's nice enough blue eyes, there wasn't much competition; he smelled slightly stale, had a scratchy beard and wispy grey hair with a bald patch in the centre, and was wearing a navy smock and brown sandals, out of which peeped knobbly toes with thick yellow nails.

Liz walked slowly round the exhibition. The paintings, which were mounted on wooden display boards, were mostly fairly samey, featuring fruit, flowers, crockery and other day-to-day objects, competently drawn but with nothing that would really make you sit up and take notice.

'We used acrylics for these,' Bungle explained in his Cornish burr, stopping by a picture of an orange and a beer bottle artfully arranged beside a shiny stainless-steel kettle. 'It's the layering of colour that produces the depth and richness.

Otherwise the picture can look flat and contrived. I say to my pupils that every picture should tell a story, like a novel.'

She nodded, trying to think of something intelligent to say, but her eye kept wandering across the room to another painting, quite different from the rest. It looked a bit like the layered petals of a crimson flower against a pale pink background, with black whiskery stamens protruding from the top.

'Who did that?' she asked, quickly regretting her question because the more she stared, the more she feared that the image might, in fact, bear a rather strong resemblance to a certain part of a woman's anatomy.

'Rick Kane,' Bungle said proudly. 'He only recently joined the group and he's doing very well. As a matter of fact, he painted this one at home. It's different from what we normally do but I accepted him at the club straight away on the strength of it. It's wonderfully rich and symbolic, don't you think?'

At that moment she heard Rick, behind her, introducing Sylvia to some other visitors. They were still together, it seemed, despite her ill-disguised passion for Luke. Keen not to get drawn into conversation with him about the subject of his oeuvre, Liz told Bungle that she was gasping for a drink and headed swiftly towards the teas and coffees that were being served by Jenny Lambert, standing behind a white, linen-clad trestle table.

'It's a bit risqué, isn't it?' Jenny laughed, having clocked Liz's hasty exit. 'Rick's telling everyone Sylvia modelled for him and she seems quite proud of it. She's not embarrassed at all!'

'Don't.' Liz shuddered. 'I'm not sure we're ready for it in Tremarnock. I wouldn't fancy it on my wall, would you? Give me a nice bowl of apples or a bunch of cornflowers any day!'

The room was filling up and she noticed Audrey make a beeline for the enigmatic artist from Polgarry Castle. He was quite striking, tall and well built with jet-black hair, and he looked somewhat taken aback by Audrey, who had a tendency to talk loudly and stand very close to people. She fancied herself as a bit of an artist, too, and perhaps hoped that some of his talent might rub off.

Liz felt a little sorry for him and might have gone to his rescue, had she and the others not been joined by an unknown, middle-aged couple, who revealed that they were staying at The Stables.

'Lovely place,' the woman cooed. 'So comfortable and tastefully done, and Luke's delightful. Full of amusing stories.'

'Yes,' the man agreed. 'Perfect for a weekend break, or a week, come to that. The wife's very quiet, though, isn't she?' he added, more to his own wife than Liz. 'Hardly says a thing.'

'She's probably got her hands full with their little boy,' said Liz, wondering why she was defending the woman yet again. Loveday did give her glowing reports, though.

'We have the best chats,' she'd said recently, before going on to describe some of her boss's tastes and mannerisms. 'She never has milk in her tea, she says it kills the flavour. And she doesn't eat carbs, or only sometimes, anyway. That's why she's got such an ama-a-a-zing figure.'

Liz, who wasn't feeling all that positive about her body right now, had felt a stab of jealousy. 'I don't like tea without milk,' she'd snapped back, pulling a face. 'And everybody needs carbs for energy.'

Then she'd checked herself and backtracked, remembering Tabitha's frightened expression at the party. 'She *is* in fantastic shape,' she'd added. 'I wish I had a minuscule waist like that.'

Jenny poured more boiling water from the kettle into one

of the giant urns and asked the unknown couple where they'd come from.

'West Sussex,' the woman replied. 'Near Chichester. I don't know if you've heard of it?'

Liz smiled to herself, thinking it was funny how often outsiders assumed they didn't have a clue about anywhere else in the country, as if Cornwall were some backward colonial outpost.

'Oh, yes,' said Jenny, 'I know it well. I grew up in Sussex, actually. Near Eastbourne.'

The woman seemed almost put out. 'We like it very much. We're not as cut off as you are here – but of course we don't have as much space, or your magnificent coastline,' she added quickly.

'Have you walked to Hermitage Point yet?' Jenny asked politely, deftly steering the subject in a less competitive direction. 'It's not far, only a mile or so, and there are magnificent views. There's a footpath leading out of the village that'll take you right there.'

The woman turned to her husband. 'That must be the place we read about in the *Western Morning News*. I said we should go.'

Liz would have stayed longer, except that she noticed Nathan admiring the exotic crimson flower and as Rick was elsewhere, decided to excuse herself.

'I'm surprised to see you, I didn't think painting was your thing,' she said, adding mischievously, 'How do you like this one? It's by Rick. Apparently it's of Sylvia.' It was naughty, she knew, but she couldn't resist it.

Nathan frowned, trying to work out what she meant, then, as the truth hit him, 'What? You don't mean…?'

She nodded.

'That's disgusting.'

Liz giggled; young people seemed to think sex had been invented just for them and adults weren't allowed to talk about it, far less paint it.

'It's art, Nathan,' she replied, fake-innocently, glancing around to check no one was listening and lowering her voice. 'I wonder if it's a good likeness.'

'Stop!' the young man spluttered. 'I don't want to hear any more.' And with that he hotfooted it on his big body and skinny legs over to the nice, safe, still lives on the far side of the room. The story would, of course, be all around the younger members of the community in no time, which was probably a good thing as it might swell visitor numbers.

Once she'd complimented Felipe, Audrey and the other artists on their work and made appropriate noises about their choices of colour, subject matter and so on, she decided to take a quick detour to The Stables, hoping to find Loveday there with Oscar.

She hadn't been to the guest house since the party before Christmas, not wishing to intrude on Tabitha or make things awkward for her niece. However, having tried Loveday on the mobile a couple of times without success, Liz thought that a quick visit wouldn't do any harm. After all, the girl had pretty much settled in now and they seemed happy with her. Surely they wouldn't begrudge a five-minute conversation on the doorstep with her aunt?

It was cold, wet and windy and just before the turning to Market Square Liz was overtaken by a bedraggled group of strangers, striding purposefully in cagoules and muddy boots, with backpacks strapped to their shoulders. They were talking to each other in accents that definitely weren't from around here, and one of them was holding a map in a protective plastic cover.

Liz wondered if they, too, were staying at The Stables, like the couple that she'd met at the exhibition. It was still early days but so far Luke's and Tabitha's guests seemed slightly different from the tourists who packed Tremarnock in summer. They were older, for a start, with no children, wealthier, less noisy and more refined, perhaps. It wasn't sun, sea, sand and kid-friendly pubs they were after, but scenic walks, historic churches and stately homes. And fine dining, it seemed, because A Winkle In Time, once quiet in winter months, was certainly benefiting.

After another successful midweek evening when the restaurant had been almost full, Robert had suggested that the Mallons must be doing a good job and were just what Tremarnock needed to make the place an all-year-round draw.

'They're good news, Lizzie,' he'd proclaimed. 'We're lucky to have them.'

Liz tucked her hair into the hood of her waterproof jacket and walked slowly after the group, keen to allow them plenty of time to get home before she turned up. She was thinking that it would be nice if Loveday wanted to spend the evening with her and Rosie, having fish and chips and watching a film perhaps. Not that she, Liz, much fancied fish. A plate of chips might go down OK, though.

Robert wouldn't be back until well after eleven and it was fun to have company, especially on a Friday night. If she'd thought about it earlier she would have invited a few others: Hannah, her glamorous accountant friend from Dolphin House, where she used to work as a cleaner, though she'd be sure to be busy; or Kasia, boss of Krystal Klear Office Cleaning Services, if they could cope with her manic chat.

Liz felt sad suddenly, remembering Iris, who used to run the newsagent in Plymouth where she'd bought her weekly lottery ticket on her way to Dolphin House. Once Iris would have been first on the guest list for tonight. They'd been such good friends, sharing jokes and cheering each other up, until the older woman had cruelly betrayed her.

She reached the guest house and rapped a couple of times with the brass knocker on the heavy oak door. It opened almost immediately and Tabitha peered round the edge.

'Oh!' she said, widening the gap just a fraction. 'Loveday's not in.'

Now it was Liz's turn to look surprised, because the girl couldn't be with Oscar. He was balanced on his mother's hip, sucking his thumb and staring curiously at the visitor.

'When will she be back? I wanted to give her a message.' She realised that she sounded nervous and foolish. Why did Tabitha have this effect on her? She wouldn't bite.

'She's with my husband,' Tabitha replied. 'In Plymouth. They'll be back around six.'

'In Plymouth?' For some reason Liz felt a prickle of alarm.

'Yes,' said Tabitha. 'Didn't you know? She's working for him for a couple of afternoons a week at the moment. I don't need her to mind Oscar full time.' The door was still only half-open and it was quite clear that, despite the filthy weather, she wouldn't be inviting Liz in.

'Would you mind asking her to ring me when she returns?' Liz said, 'or, better still, call in on her way home?'

'All right.' The door swung to almost immediately, practically trapping the toggles of Liz's jacket as it slammed shut.

Rude woman, she thought, walking away quickly. She really didn't know why she bothered to stick up for her, and to think she'd once imagined that they might be friends. Give her manic Kasia, wild Hannah or any of the villagers, come

to that; she didn't need Tabitha in her life. She just hoped that
Loveday had her head screwed on tight.

Loveday was on a high when she turned up at Bag End in
nothing but a denim mini-skirt and thin black cardigan, and
Rosie seemed to catch her mood.

'Let's not stay in,' Loveday pleaded. 'Let's go to The Victory
Inn. I feel like celebrating.'

'Can we?' Rosie begged. 'It'd be more fun and there aren't
any good films on. Please, Mum? Don't say no. It *is* the weekend.'

Liz had been looking forward to collapsing, but crumbled
before the expectant faces of her niece and daughter.

'All right.' She'd been eyeing up her sofa and the empty fire,
longing to get a good blaze going. 'You'd better borrow one
of my coats, Loveday, or you'll freeze to death.'

The pub, which had once been a seventeenth-century
cottage, was little more than a single room with low ceilings
and wonky floors. Inside, it was filled with nautical bric-a-
brac recovered from the treacherous Cornish coast, such as
ships' figureheads, cutlasses and bits of canon. There was
even an old pair of sailor's trousers and a battered tricorn hat.

There were only five or six rough benches and tables and
the place really came to life in summer, when chairs spilled on
to the pavement. Luckily, though, the threesome were early
enough to nab a couple of wooden stools at the bar, where
Liz and Rosie sat checking out the menu, while Loveday
scrutinised some seated men on the left who'd finished their
pints and were on the point of leaving.

By the time Liz ordered they'd gone, and she settled down
gratefully next to her daughter while Loveday, over a Bacardi

and Coke, recounted the day's events – or as much as she was allowed to, anyway. It seemed that she could only indicate in very broad brushstrokes what this temporary new job entailed, as the detail was hush-hush.

'I've been mostly just listening so far,' she explained. 'Luke's been telling me what to do. He's dead patient, answering my questions and that, and he's showed me how to use the computer and listened while I practised on the phone. His first job was working in a call centre. Imagine that! Selling phone contracts. He's got such a good way of talking to people. He's given me a list of things to say and he's a great teacher, he doesn't get irritated, he's not like that.'

'But why is it so...?' Rosie paused, searching for the right word '...*confidential*?' She had a wide vocabulary and liked words, although she sometimes used them in the wrong way. 'I don't understand what you're doing. Can't you give us a clue? We won't tell anyone, promise. You can trust us, you know you can.'

Loveday gave an enigmatic little smile; she was enjoying being mysterious, the Mona Lisa of Tremarnock.

'It's a secret operation and it's very important work. It's helping people.' She looked exceedingly pleased with herself. 'I can't say anything more 'cause I'm not allowed. It might blow our cover, then the whole operation would be ruined.'

Liz frowned. From the way Loveday was talking, you'd think that she'd been hired as a Bletchley Park code breaker, but she, Liz, shouldn't leap to conclusions. The girl was an adult now and hadn't asked for advice. The last thing she needed was her aunt dumping on her enthusiasm.

'It sounds fascinating, but who are you and Luke working for?' she asked carefully. 'Is it a private company? Can you at least tell us that?'

Loveday glanced left and right and shook her head. 'I've probably said too much already.'

'That's so annoying!' Rosie's thick blue glasses had steamed up and she took them off and wiped them with a corner of her sleeve. 'I wish you hadn't said anything about it now. It's not fair.'

Loveday took a sip of her drink. 'Sorry, I know I'm being a pain, but I've promised not to breathe a word. I've even signed a legal document.'

She rested her elbows on the table, looking very solemn. 'I've never been asked to do anything like this before and no one's ever taken me seriously. My mum wouldn't even let me go to the shops for her without writing everything on a piece of paper and checking the receipt. Even Uncle Robert wouldn't allow me to take bookings or go anywhere near the till.' She was focusing her kohl-rimmed eyes on Liz, willing her to understand. 'Luke believes in me and I don't want to blow this. I can't let him down. You do see, don't you?'

Liz took a deep breath, trying hard to keep an open mind. 'Where are you based?' It seemed a safe enough question.

'The outskirts of Plymouth,' replied Loveday, tapping her nose. 'Can't give you the exact location, that's confidential too.' She perked up. 'Guess what? I've got my own office, with my own laptop and mobile, everything! I get a new phone each time I go in, and there's even a swingy chair!'

She looked so delighted that Liz couldn't help smiling. Who was she to look for trouble? Loveday was a bit naïve and had a lot to learn. Perhaps this would be the making of her.

'And today Luke took me to lunch at the Theatre Royal restaurant. Imagine that! We shared a charcuterie board for starters, then I had teriyaki salmon.' She wrinkled her nose. 'Didn't like it much, but I pretended to. It was much posher than Uncle Robert's place and the waiter called me "Madam". I wondered who he meant!'

Their food arrived – great big plates of battered fish and fat, steaming chips, with a pot of ketchup each in a little white bowl. Rosie tucked in immediately but Loveday was unusually restrained, having eaten more than usual earlier on.

'You know,' she mused, picking up her fork, skewering a chip and watching the column of damp steam rise towards the ceiling, 'I feel so lucky to have met Luke and Tabitha. I didn't mind being a waitress, not so much anyway, but I was stuck in a rut, I didn't feel like I was going anywhere.'

Liz nibbled on a corner of her own chip, which tasted surprisingly good, then dipped the remaining end in ketchup and popped it in her mouth. She was thinking that she knew what Loveday meant. It was fun chatting to the staff and customers at A Winkle In Time – the nice ones, anyway – but working for herself was far more satisfying.

'Have you told your mum and dad?' With luck, her niece would listen to them if they had any doubts; it wasn't really *her* place to voice them.

Loveday pulled a face. 'Nah, they don't care.'

'Yes, they do.' Liz liked Sarah and Andy and was sorry about their divorce. She wished that they weren't so focused on their own problems, though, and would make more effort with their daughter. She still needed them.

'You should call them. When are you going to Penzance?'

'No time soon. They're so busy rowing over who gets the telly, the dog and the frigging washing machine, they've forgotten I exist. Anyway, there's nothing to stop them coming here, is there? 'Specially now I've got my own flat. But they can't be arsed.'

Thank goodness for Jesse, Liz mused, popping in another

chip. He seemed to adore Loveday and had even talked about trying to get a mortgage with her once he was a fully trained chef. It might be possible when his wages went up, and her pay rise would help, too.

'So who's this lad you're seeing?' Loveday said suddenly, licking ketchup off her fingers and fixing on Rosie.

Liz flinched. She'd giggled about Tim with Robert's niece, but had warned her not to let on; Rosie wouldn't like to think they'd been gossiping behind her back.

'What lad?' She glared at her mother, who pretended not to notice and nibbled guiltily on another chip. 'I don't know what you're talking about.'

Loveday poked her across the table with a finger. 'I think you do. I've noticed that twinkle in your eye. Go on, what's he like? Is he your *boyfriend*?'

Rosie stuck out her tongue but, to Liz's relief, followed up with a shy grin.

'He's called Tim Butler. He's in my class and he makes me laugh.'

'Great start,' Loveday replied. 'Is he handsome?'

Rosie pretended to examine the three coloured bangles on her good arm, twisting them round and round. 'I think so. He's not very tall, though.'

'Well, that doesn't matter,' said Liz, 'so long as you like him. Boys grow later than girls anyway. He's bound to catch up.'

Loveday drained her Bacardi and Coke but didn't suggest going up to the bar for another; she was enjoying herself too much.

'So where does he live, this Tim?' She put down her knife and fork. There was a good deal of food on her plate still; they really were big portions.

'Near the ferry,' said Rosie. 'His mum's divorced and he's got a brother called Mark, who's much older, like nineteen.'

'Mark Butler?' A flash of recognition crossed Loveday's face. 'Does he work on the ferry?'

Rosie nodded. 'He shows the cars where to go and collects the money.'

'I've probably seen him many times,' Liz mused. 'They all look similar to me – blond and tanned with lots of tattoos.'

She was hoping that Loveday would manage to prise more out of Rosie, but she rose purposefully to go to the loo, bringing the line of enquiry to an abrupt close. Once she was well out of hearing, Loveday leaned in towards Liz, who proffered her ear.

'Bad news,' the younger girl whispered.

'What do you mean?'

'That family, the Butlers. The mum's a lush and Mark's been done for assault. He got six months suspended. Everyone thought he'd go to prison.'

'Assault? Blimey! What did he do?'

'Broke someone's nose in a fight,' said Loveday. 'Outside the pub. They were having an argument and Mark lost it. He's a total nutter.'

Liz shuddered. She couldn't bring herself to stamp on an insect, let alone break a man's nose.

'But he's all right, Tim, isn't he? Rosie really likes him.'

Loveday shook her head. 'Bad influence, I'd say. You should keep her well away.'

Liz swallowed. She'd only eaten half her chips and hadn't touched the fish, but she wasn't remotely hungry now. Rosie and Tim were in the same class, they saw each other every day and they'd become such good friends. How on earth was she supposed to separate them?

She took a sip of orange juice and quickly changed the subject when Rosie returned, but she wasn't stupid; she knew something was up.

'What's the matter?' She glanced from her mum to Loveday and back again. 'What were you talking about?'

Liz sighed. She'd always tried to be honest with Rosie, who'd spot a lie a mile off anyway. Best to broach the subject now, she decided, while she had support. She started very gently, allowing Loveday to interrupt with the odd incriminating anecdote: 'My friend saw his mum staggering back from the pub on her own. She could hardly walk, she was completely rat-arsed'; and, 'Mark used to be called "panda face" at school because he was always scrapping and getting black eyes.'

'It's not true!' Rosie said hotly when the pair had finished. 'I've met Mark and he's really nice. And I've never seen the mum drunk. Tim would have told me, they're really close.'

Loveday made a cross sign across her chest. 'God's honest truth. The court case about Mark was in the papers – you can look it up.'

'Well, you can't blame Tim for something his brother did,' Rosie went on, teary now. She fixed on her mother, eyes blazing. 'You don't blame me for what my dad did to us, do you? And maybe it's all just rumours anyway. I don't believe any of it. You shouldn't judge people till you've met them.'

They were a dejected pair as they said goodbye to Loveday and headed back to Bag End in silence, the evening ruined. As soon as they got in, Rosie marched upstairs as fast as she could on her wonky leg and banged her bedroom door shut. She'd never done that before and Liz was left alone.

Rosie was right about not judging people, she thought as she sat, miserably, waiting for Robert's return. They hadn't been judged by the villagers when they'd arrived all those years ago in their ancient car with scarcely a pot plant to their name, they'd been welcomed with open arms. But, still, alcoholism and crime? She couldn't ignore the warning. She mightn't be able to stop Rosie from talking to Tim at school, but it was in her power to forbid their weekend activities and, harsh as it might seem, that was what she'd have to do.

'Wasson, me cock?'

Jesse grinned at Loveday, who glanced at him through half-closed eyes before turning back to the TV screen. It was gone midnight and she'd had several more Bacardi and Cokes with Nathan and the gang, who'd joined her after Liz and Rosie had left. She'd given them a blow-by-blow account of her meal at the Theatre Royal and the deferential waiter; they'd been very impressed.

'Yeeuch! You're all sweaty,' she declared, pushing Jesse away when he tried to pounce on her. 'Go and have a shower.'

He backed off and went to fetch a glass of water, calling from next door, 'You'd be sweaty if you'd been in the kitchen all night.' But she didn't reply.

He peeled off his shirt and flung it on the kitchen floor by the washing machine before re-joining her. It usually worked; the minute Loveday caught sight of his surfer's six-pack she was putty in his hands. He waited for something, some small sign of appreciation, but none came. Unusual. He tried another tack.

'Had a good evening?' He yawned loudly, stretching his arms above his head so that she could take advantage of his biceps. 'We were really busy. Full house. My salmon soufflé went down a treat.'

She continued to stare at the TV, though you could tell she wasn't really watching.

He was puzzled now and scratched his head. 'Have I done something wrong?'

'Nope.' She looked as if she had a bad smell under her nose.

Muttering under his breath, he sloped off to wash and when he'd finished, Loveday was in bed, eyes firmly shut, the pink duvet pulled tight under her chin. Something was definitely up.

'What is it, babe?' he asked, climbing in beside her. His limbs were aching and he'd been thinking about her all the way home, hoping that she might give him one of her sensational massages. It seemed that he wouldn't get an answer but then she sat up, propping herself on her elbows.

'I hate it when you say that.'

'What?' He couldn't think what she was talking about.

'Wasson,' she replied. 'It's so...' She frowned, searching for the right word. 'So *common*. It makes you sound like a Cornish yokel with a piece of straw sticking out of your mouth.'

Jesse roared with laughter. 'I am a Cornish yokel – and proud of it, me 'ansum!'

She huffed and turned to face the wall.

'Anyway,' he said, rolling her over again and pulling tight so that she couldn't wriggle away, 'what's brought this on, my lover? I never heard you make no complaints about my Cornish voice before.' He was deliberately exaggerating now.

'*Any* complaints,' Loveday corrected. He was squeezing hard and she was gasping for air. 'Not *no* complaints, that's ungrammatical.'

'Ooh, gone all hoity-toity, have we?' Jesse tickled her in the ribs, making her squeal. 'Madam at The Stables been giving you lessons in talking posh, has she?'

'Don't!' Loveday gasped, struggling to push him off, but

he only clamped tighter, like a boa constrictor, and tickled harder. 'I can't bear it!'

'Do you still hate my Cornish accent, then?' he teased. 'I won't stop till you take it back.'

'I love it! I do! Mercy!'

At last he let her go and Loveday sighed with relief. She was all hot and sweaty herself now. Of course, after that it was hard to resist the smell of his smooth man-skin, his firmness beneath her fingertips, his blond curls, still damp from the shower. The light from the streetlamp outside filtered through the curtains, illuminating his face and body, and at moments like this she always thought that he resembled one of the Greek heroes in a storybook that her teacher had read to the class when she'd been a child, about Perseus and Jason, Theseus and Hercules. She'd loved those stories with a passion, and could remember the colourful pictures as if it were yesterday.

'Sexy beast,' he said, kissing her forehead, her nose, her mouth. 'I could gobble you up.' He made a growling sound like a wild animal.

'Stop it!' She giggled then, putting on her best upper-class drawl to wind him up, 'I had lunch at the Theatre Royal today.'

She wanted to tell him about the teriyaki salmon, the coffee and chocolates, the polite waiter; to be honest, she wanted to impress him like the others in the pub earlier. Instead, though, Jesse pulled away and looked at her seriously.

'Babe?'

She wondered what was coming next.

'You didn't mean it, did you? About the way I sound?'

''Course not.' But images of Luke had seeped into her mind – his smile, the perfectly ironed cuffs of his expensive shirt, the gold watch on his wrist. 'I just think...'

'What?'

'It would be nice if you didn't act the clown all the time. I mean, the way you lark around and make crude jokes, and that chain around your neck. It's not very sophisticated. You should try wearing a smart shirt sometimes. A suit, even.'

'I don't need a suit. I don't have that sort of work. You never complained about my clothes before.'

'It just occurred to me, that's all. Men look good in nice shirts and cufflinks, that sort of thing.'

'Men like Luke.' The name danced in the air between them like a leaf on the wind.

She hesitated. 'He never swears or farts and he opens doors for you; he's a real gentleman.'

'God, Loveday.' Jesse pushed her off and moved to the opposite side of the bed, creating a cold, hard space between them. 'Since when have you cared about all that stuff? If you want a bloody gentleman you'll have to go and find one.'

She knew that he was waiting for her to apologise, to make up to him, but she wouldn't. Instead, she lay there for some time, pretending to sleep, tuned in to the ticking of his over-active brain.

She wasn't being unreasonable, was she, wanting him to dress a bit smarter, act more classy? After today she'd decided that she, too, needed to upgrade her wardrobe, and had resolved to go into Plymouth at the weekend to buy new gear.

The truth was, she'd felt a bit self-conscious in her tight blouse and skirt at the restaurant and had wished that she'd had a jacket with her and wasn't wearing so many earrings. None of the other women had big hoops like hers, or hair shaved up both sides, come to that. Perhaps it was time to grow it out.

Luke had looked so suave and handsome, all the women fancied him, you could tell. And he kept saying she had a very good telephone manner. 'You're going be brilliant at the job, I can see.'

Jesse moaned quietly, having dropped off at last. He must have been exhausted after his long day. She was knackered, too, as a matter of fact, but felt restless, maddeningly wide awake.

No, she thought, turning over to find a more comfortable position, she couldn't pretend that things hadn't changed now she'd started the new job, and Jesse needed to understand. She was moving on, making something of herself, whereas half the time he still acted like a big kid.

Luke, on the other hand, well, he was a different matter. Luke was refined and successful, practically perfect, as far as she could see. What's more, he'd chosen *her* above all the other girls in the village when he could have had the pick of the lot. She hugged her arms around her, feeling very special, and couldn't seem to get him out of her head all night long.

Chapter Eleven

'I'M SORRY TO have to tell you that your bank card has been cloned and an attempt has been made to use it fraudulently.'

Doris gasped. 'Oh!'

It was a fine, sunny March morning and she'd been enjoying watching 'Homes Under The Hammer'. Instinctively, she rose from her chair in front of the TV and peered out of the net curtains of her tiny bungalow, as if expecting to find a stranger lurking in the front garden.

'Fortunately, the card wasn't accepted,' the policeman explained.

Doris plonked back in the chair. Her hands were trembling so much that she nearly dropped the phone.

'Are they watching me?' she whispered, scanning the four corners of the room, listening for noises upstairs. She wanted to scream, only she knew that would make it worse. She wanted to summon her neighbour, Sheila, immediately, preferably Sheila's husband, too. Doris felt alone and really frightened.

'Don't be anxious,' the policeman said. 'You're quite safe. They won't come anywhere near your home.' He had a gentle voice, warm and kind, very polite, and she felt herself relax a little.

'Nothing's been stolen from you and we think we might know who the culprits are. We're hoping to make some arrests soon.'

His words reassured her but, still, she was worried about her pension. Sheila usually drove her to the bank on Tuesdays to withdraw her money for the week; Doris couldn't get there by bus, not with her dodgy hips. She needed every penny to pay for the gas and electric, not to mention food, the phone bill. She couldn't do without her pension. It was a struggle to get by as it was.

And what about that twelve thousand pounds? Her chest tightened. Sheila had always said she should transfer it to a special savings account, where she'd get more interest, but she didn't want that; she liked to be able to see it all there, in one place. It had taken a lifetime to build up. What if she needed a new boiler or roof? What if there was a leak in the pipes and she had to get the plumbers in?

'What c-can I d-do,' she stammered, 'to stop them?' She was imagining them right now, trying to use her cloned card somewhere else. They might pinch the lot.

'I'm going to give you a helpline number,' the policeman said. 'They'll be able to cancel the card for you, and transfer your money to a safe account while we complete the investigation. Do you have a pen and paper?'

Doris wrote the number down very carefully before hanging up and redialling. It was a nice young woman with a Cornish accent who answered, ever so sympathetic.

'It's rubbish, isn't it?' she tutted down the line. 'You're the third lady who's contacted us this afternoon.'

The pleasant young woman took Doris's bank details, card details, pin number and so on, and said that she'd transfer the cash for her straight away.

'It's going to be all right,' she promised. 'Now, you've had an awful shock. I should go and make yourself a cup of tea.'

Sheila popped by shortly after, with a couple of leeks and some Brussels sprouts from her husband's allotment, and rang 999 as soon as she heard the news. Sheila had lots to do; her son was supposed to be coming for supper and she wanted to tidy up and make a macaroni cheese, but she couldn't leave Doris. The poor woman was in a terrible state.

The police told Sheila that someone would be there soon to take a statement, a local officer. 'Can you stay with her tonight? She shouldn't be left, not with the fright she's had.'

Sheila glanced at Doris, who was blowing her nose. She was all alone since her husband had passed away. No children, no relatives close by. Pale pink scalp poked through her sparse white hair, and her neck was so thin it looked as if it might snap in the wind.

Sheila sighed, half wishing that she'd never called in with those damned Brussels, she'd been looking forward to catching up with her son. But what else could she do? She'd known Doris for as long as she could remember, some thirty years, probably, since they'd moved in next door.

'Yes,' she replied, giving Doris a reassuring smile, 'I'll stay.'

Loveday sat back in her swingy office chair and gave herself a mental pat on the back. She'd done it again! That poor old lady had sounded so worried. Who wouldn't be, thinking their life savings were about to be stolen? But she'd managed to put Doris at her ease and her money was safe. Job well done.

Ahmed strolled in with a can of Fanta for her; he knew the way to her heart. 'How did it go?' he asked casually. He was a small man in his late thirties, clean-shaven and slim, with a penchant for sharp jackets and carefully ironed shirts, very well spoken. He had a family somewhere, like the bloke who'd gone away because his wife was ill, but Loveday hadn't met them.

'Great,' she said. 'Couldn't be better. I transferred twelve thousand. She was so relieved.'

Ahmed grinned and ruffled her hair. 'Good girl. You're doing the public a real service, you know. You should be very proud of yourself.' His praise warmed her through.

There were four of them in the office – her, Ahmed, Sam and Luke, though he came and went as he had numerous meetings to attend. She didn't mind that it was all men, because everyone was so friendly and easy to talk to. They each had their own room on the top floor of a small office block in a business park just outside Plymouth city centre, and they were known as Henry Mount Financial Services, or HM for short, though in reality they were nothing of the sort. There was a firm of architects below, but she hardly saw them.

The others kept their doors shut most of the time, only emerging to brief her on a caller, go to the loo or just poke their heads in for a chat and to see how she was. Sometimes her work was quite stressful, because the elderly victims tended to need a lot of hand-holding, like little kids, really. Often they were in tears, but she was good at comforting them and liked to leave them in a better state than when they'd first spoken.

In between calls she was doing a good deal of online research, compiling lists of names and addresses, getting credit reference checks and marketing data. It was amazing how much you could find out about a person – their date of birth, where they banked, how much money they owed and what sort of things they liked to purchase. She'd had no idea. She typed up big lists and passed them to Luke, who'd distribute them round the team. There were others working for him, she knew, in different parts of the country, though she didn't have anything to do with them, and Luke was always very encouraging about what she did.

'You're a star!' he said sometimes, or, 'What would I do without you?' She liked pleasing him; his compliments made her work extra hard.

She had to pinch herself sometimes to convince herself that it was true, that she really was involved in his important, top-secret operation, even if only for a few weeks. Her! Loveday! On her first day, Luke had explained that HM was just a cover, that because of his financial expertise, the Metropolitan Police had asked him to assist their fraud unit on a special investigation into nationwide telephone scams, mainly targeting elderly, vulnerable people. Her head had swum, until he'd brought her down to earth.

'It's big, Loveday,' he'd said solemnly, forcing her to focus, 'really big and complex, spanning many continents. It's going to take a long time to track them down because there are so many of them, and they mustn't know we're on their trail.'

Often, he said, bank staff themselves were involved in the fraud. Loveday could hardly believe that. It was crucial to secure the pensioners' money fast, before it disappeared, and it was up to her to persuade them not to talk to anyone at their bank, because it might scupper the investigation.

'The poor victims are frightened out of their wits,' he'd continued. 'They feel like they've been burgled in their own homes. And make no mistake, the scammers are very dangerous. They've got a great deal at stake. They know if they get caught, the police have the power to confiscate their homes, their property, everything they've built up over the years, and they'll go to almost any lengths to stop that happening.'

Loveday had squealed, she couldn't help it. Almost any

lengths? They sounded terrifying, and the next thing Luke said had only made her more afraid.

'I don't want to scare you,' he'd insisted, lowering his voice and doing just that, 'but you must understand that idle talk could put not just you but your friends and family at risk, too.'

Loveday had found herself wondering if she should have got herself into this in the first place. She had visions of threatening-looking men with stiletto knives in their pockets, lurking in the shadows, waiting for a signal from the big boss to silence her for ever.

She'd been about to suggest that maybe she wasn't the right person to help after all, but Luke had put a reassuring hand on hers. 'We need you, Loveday, and I have every faith in you. You'll be perfectly safe so long as you keep your mouth shut.'

'I will,' she'd promised, thinking that from now on she'd be far too nervous to spill any beans. She wasn't generally known for her discretion, but Luke had put the fear of God into her and nothing on earth would make her blab.

It had taken her a while to process everything he'd told her, but later in the afternoon, when he'd been looking at one of the list of names she was compiling, she'd plucked up the courage to ask a question.

'Why did you say yes – to helping the police, I mean?' It had struck her that it would have been a good deal easier, and safer, to concentrate on his very successful business and leave the undercover work to someone else.

Luke had sat on the edge of her desk, swinging a trousered leg to and fro. He was wearing a crisp, white, open-necked shirt and slip-on shoes in soft, tan leather. He seemed to have this aura around him, she thought, and you could tell at a glance that he wasn't just any old Tom, Dick or Harry.

'I guess I wanted to put something back,' he'd replied,

gazing at her with eyes so blue that she thought she could drown in them. 'I've done very well for myself, I've got everything I need – nice home, nice car, beautiful wife and son. But not everyone's so fortunate.' He'd sighed and shaken his head. 'There's a lot of suffering out there and I just thought, I've got the skills and the time. I could retire now if I wanted, but I wouldn't fancy sitting around on my backside, getting on Tabitha's nerves or playing golf all day, it's not my scene. I'm good at what I do – I might as well put it to some use.'

Loveday had nodded, feeling humble and inspired at the same time. 'You're an amazing man.' She'd hoped that didn't sound childish, but it was true. Then, to her surprise, he'd leaned over and cupped her chin in his warm hand, gazing at her again with breath-taking intensity. 'And you're a very brave young woman.'

She'd never forget it. The feel of his soft skin, the whiff of expensive aftershave, those periwinkle-blue eyes fixed on hers. She'd felt giddy with pleasure and thought at that moment she'd do anything for him, anything at all.

'I must be off,' he'd said, rising suddenly and breaking the spell. 'I've got a catch-up meeting with the fraud squad chief. You wouldn't believe some of the stories he tells...'

And with that, he'd gone, leaving her alone once more.

Ahmed reappeared, jolting her back to the present, and told her to expect a call from an elderly gentleman.

'He sounded pretty cut up. Do your best to calm him down.'

This time he patted her shoulder, before making his way back down the corridor to his own office. He was gorgeous, Loveday thought, really kind and supportive, like a big brother, almost, or an uncle. He didn't dazzle like Luke, though. No one else did that. She pushed herself off the edge of the desk so that the chair swung round and round, making her giddy.

Ahmed and Luke had worked at the same call centre in Manchester years ago, selling mobile phone packages; she'd once heard them joking about it in the corridor outside.

'You always won salesman of the month,' Ahmed had laughed, 'and I always came second, no matter how hard I tried. I only ever won when you were off sick or on holiday, you bastard.'

'D'you remember how the prize was vouchers for crap shops?' Luke had replied, laughing back. 'Dunno why any of us bothered. I guess in those days we thought a watch from Argos was the height of sophistication.'

Loveday had felt herself blush because she'd been looking online at watches from Argos only recently. She'd thought there were some really nice fancy ones, if only she could afford them, and made a mental note not to buy anything from there again.

She was drifting once more. She'd never been such a day-dreamer, not until she'd started here. Her phone rang once, twice, three times and she gave herself a mental shake, cleared her throat and picked up.

'Metropolitan Police Helpline,' she said in her most efficient voice. 'How can I be of assistance?'

At first she couldn't understand the caller fully because he was talking very fast, in short, panicky sentences like little gasps: 'Over fifteen thousand pounds... savings account... cash card... robbed...'

'Please don't worry, sir,' she soothed, imagining him at the other end, rocking backwards and forwards, scarcely able to think. Poor old bloke, it really wasn't fair. 'We'll put it in a special police account for you. It'll be quite safe.'

She could hear the relief in his voice and almost picture the fog in his brain starting to clear. She listened patiently while he went over the whole story with her, beginning way before the call, when he'd been taking his dog for a walk round the block, popping into the newsagent's for his newspaper and a packet of soft mints. She didn't mind; as far as she was concerned, it was all part of the service.

'What a terrible shock,' she said, when at last he'd slowed down. 'Who'd have thought this was going to happen, eh? Well, thank goodness it's been discovered before it's too late and we can put that money away for you. Now, why don't you read me those numbers?'

Some time later, over at Devon and Cornwall Police Headquarters in Exeter, Inspector Royce called a meeting to explain what had happened.

'We've got a lady in Bideford who's lost twelve thousand, a gentleman in Dawlish fifteen thousand, and two more women in Barnstaple – one ten grand, one forty.'

His colleagues raised their eyebrows. You could almost see their noses twitching, like hounds scenting a fox; they needed something to get their teeth into. They were part of a new, dedicated anti-fraud unit, and they had everything to prove.

'We're going to be seeing a lot more of this type of crime,' Insp. Royce warned. 'They've worked out there are more than your average number of retired people down here in the South West and pockets of cash.'

He told the team to 'follow the money', and they nodded in agreement. It was the only way. Problem was, a lot of accounts were set up using stolen identities, or bought off foreign students for a small sum before they left the country. Banks were supposed to look out for suspicious activity, but they didn't do it.

'First things first, we need production orders from the court and notices served on the banks. I want proof of identity used for the fake accounts, handwriting samples, telephone numbers, anything you can lay your hands on.'

Insp. Royce knew full well that the crooks would most likely have used unregistered, pre-paid mobile phones that they'd already chucked away, but it was still worth a try. He scratched his head. Experience told him the money would have been moved by the time they got there, too. It was probably at this very moment spidering out into numerous other accounts all over the country and abroad. Soon it would be invested in property, luxury goods, fake foreign businesses, you name it, and they wouldn't have the resources to track it all the way.

But if they could just catch a few suspects, some of the small guys who'd allowed their accounts to be used for laundering purposes, get them in for questioning, that would be something. No point pretending Mr Big was the end goal. He'd be sitting pretty somewhere, enjoying his mansion and his fast cars. Bastard.

Insp. Royce sighed, wondering if his bosses wished they had left things to Action Fraud, the national, London-based clearing-house that normally dealt with these crimes. This special unit was already costing a fortune and so far they'd got precisely nowhere. Still, you had to be positive. Good, old-fashioned police work, that's what was required, and who knew? One day someone, somewhere might make a mistake or cough.

'What are you waiting for?' he said, watching the young officers push back their chairs and spring to their feet. The older ones, all too aware of the obstacles, took their time.

'C'mon, people,' Insp. Royce went on, clapping his hands. Rallying the troops was an important part of the job. 'Let's get to work – and there's a pint in it for the first one who brings me a proper lead.'

*

Liz held Robert's hand as they waited to be called for the scan. Her bladder was full to bursting and she was feeling light-headed, because she hadn't eaten for hours. She was half sick with nerves, too.

'I hope they hurry up,' Robert said, nodding to the young woman sitting opposite, her head resting on her partner's shoulder.

Liz didn't reply because she was frightened she'd say the wrong thing. He was so excited but the truth was all she could think was that something might be the matter. Everyone, from her GP to Pat to her father in London, had tried to convince her that there was no earthly reason why she shouldn't have a healthy baby this time but, still, she couldn't quite believe them. After all, lightning had struck twice with Rosie.

'Eliza Hart?' the nurse called, and she found herself springing to her feet, ready to bolt for the door.

'Darling,' Robert said, rising, too, and putting a comforting arm round her back. The closeness calmed her a little. 'It's going to be all right,' he whispered, as the nurse ushered them into the darkened ultrasound room. 'We're going to meet our baby!'

As she lay back, allowing the female sonographer to rub chilly gel on her small, naked bump, she watched Robert stare eagerly into the screen, as if searching for some hidden truth. She couldn't bring herself to do the same yet; she'd rather study his face for tell-tale signs.

The sonographer passed the probe over her abdomen and soon Liz heard a rapid drumming, like fairy feet tap-dancing on a wooden floor. Robert's eyes were so wide that she almost forgot her anxiety and laughed.

'There we are,' the sonographer said comfortably, refocusing Liz's thoughts. 'That's baby's heart.' She took a few measurements and scribbled them down on a form. There was another pause while she moved the probe, then, 'That's the head.' Robert seemed to be drinking in the image, his gaze never once leaving the screen. 'There's the shoulder, arm, the vertebrae, the bottom,' the woman continued, before jotting down something else. 'You've got an active one here, look! Did you see the toes wiggling?'

At that, Liz could resist no longer and turned to stare at the fuzzy picture. Her pale, ghostly baby squirmed a little before flicking its leg, as if to prove that he or she was very much alive, and she felt a surge of love so powerful that it threatened to blow her away.

'Oh,' she heard Robert say, 'it's so beautiful. There's its fingers, and its nose. I wonder who it's going to look like? Me or you?'

The sonographer, still busy making notes, chuckled. 'Not the postman I trust!' And Liz giggled, thinking of Nathan and the rumpus *that* would cause.

A shadow crossed her mind and the heaviness that had been weighing on her descended once more. 'Is it all right? Is everything OK?'

The sonographer patted her arm. 'Completely normal, love. Good, strong heartbeat, good size, all its bits and pieces.'

Liz exhaled; she hadn't realised that she'd been holding her breath.

'Now, stop worrying,' the woman went on. 'Go away and enjoy your pregnancy.' She turned to Robert, a playful glint in her eye. 'And I hope hubby's going to do his bit and tell her to put her feet up now and again?'

He gave a mock salute. 'Yessir, rightaway, sah!'

Clutching the black and white photograph, they strolled back to the car, each lost in their own thoughts.

'Shall we go for a coffee?' Robert asked at last, climbing into the driver's seat and buckling his belt.

Liz nodded. 'I could murder a homemade scone, too. I think my appetite's returned.'

He switched on the ignition and checked the mirrors. 'We can let people know now, can't we? I'm sure Alex has twigged already, he keeps asking me how you are. And Jesse's been making comments about buns in the oven, I'm sure he's guessed, too.'

'Really? I didn't think the bump was that obvious.'

Liz stroked her tummy and smiled, feeling the on-off anxiety of the past couple of months melt away, and she could swear that deep within her baby stirred.

'Tell anyone you like,' she said happily, as Robert pulled off. 'The whole village if you want, starting with Rosie, of course. Let's give her the news together when she comes home from school.'

They waited and waited, and by the time Rosie showed up, an hour and a half later than usual, Liz was such a bundle of nerves that she almost forgot about the baby and started berating her daughter instead.

'Where on earth have you been? I was worried sick. Why didn't you call? We were about to come looking for you in the car.'

Rosie plonked her enormous black bag on the hall floor and rolled her eyes.

'Mu-um! I had an audition for the school play. I had to wait ages before it was my turn. You shouldn't fret so much.'

She pushed past her mother and headed for the kitchen. 'I'm starving.'

Liz trailed after her. 'Why was your phone turned off? You could have texted me at least.'

'Sorry,' said Rosie, opening the fridge and reaching for a carton of juice and one of those cheese strings that she made Liz buy. She didn't sound sorry. 'You know I always turn it off in school and I forgot to switch it on again. There wasn't time to text before the audition, I had to get in the queue.'

Liz sighed. Rosie wasn't usually forgetful and, anyway, she was home safe and sound, which was what really mattered. Liz opened her arms wide 'Come here, I haven't had a hug' And in Rosie walked, wrapping her own arms round her mother's waist, resting her head against her breast and making everything seem all right.

'I didn't mean to worry you,' she said in a small voice.

''S OK. That's better.' Liz breathed in her daughter's familiar scent and smoothed down her thick fair hair, which had largely escaped from its stubby ponytail. 'But please don't do it again.'

She glanced at Robert, hovering by the door, and held up a finger to indicate that she needed a minute. He nodded, but she sensed that he was ready to explode, shifting from one foot to another as if continual movement was the only way to maintain control. He'd just have to wait. 'Now, what's this about the school play? Sounds exciting!'

They all sat at the table while Rosie stuck a straw in her drink, unwrapped the cheese string and started pulling off rubbery strands and popping them in her mouth. They were going to do a musical version of *Alice in Wonderland*, it seemed, and she was hoping to land a part.

Liz was both surprised and thrilled; Rosie had been so shy at her previous school, but she'd come out of herself recently. Even so, Liz would never have imagined in a million years that her daughter would want to act and sing. She'd have thought she'd prefer being behind the scenes, helping with the props or lighting perhaps. Rosie's grandmother, her own mum Katharine, would have been so proud, having been a bit of a performer herself.

'When are we going to be able to see it?' Robert wanted to know, but Rosie was vague, explaining that they hadn't fixed a date yet. Sometime next term, probably.

'If I get a part, there'll be loads of rehearsals after school. One of the sixth formers is directing – it's got nothing to do with the teachers. It's all her idea. She wants to be a director after university.'

Liz thought the project could only be a good thing, so long as Rosie didn't get too tired, as it would surely help to take her mind off Tim. The pair had stopped meeting up at weekends and Liz was surprised, actually, by how easily her daughter seemed to have accepted the new state of affairs; since that night when Liz had warned her to keep away from the family and Rosie had stormed off to her room, she'd hardly mentioned the boy at all.

When at last they'd finished chatting about the play, homework and what was for supper, Liz gave Robert a meaningful look and he cleared his throat.

'We've got some news.' He sounded nervous; they both were. After all, they had a pretty momentous announcement to make and they thought Rosie would be pleased, but you never quite knew.

She stopped slurping her drink and put the carton down, her eyes narrowing suspiciously. 'What?'

Robert nodded and Liz took a deep breath, pulling back her shoulders. 'You're going to have a brother or sister.' She peeped at her daughter through her dark brown fringe to gauge the reaction, and Rosie's mouth fell open.

'It's true.' Robert produced the photo of the ultrasound

scan from his wallet and placed it on the table in front of his stepdaughter. 'Look. It's only tiny at the moment, but it's already got all its little fingers and toes. You're going to be a big sister!'

Rosie stared at the picture, tracing a line around the dome of the head, over the forehead, nose and mouth, along the curved back, and one small tear trickled down her cheek before she wiped it away with a sleeve.

'I can't believe it,' she whispered, 'it's a dream come true.' Then she scraped back her chair and hurried to her mother, planting a hot kiss on her face before engulfing Robert in a damp bear hug.

Liz patted her lap and Rosie perched on the edge; she hadn't done that in ages, she considered herself far too old.

'We'll have to think of names,' she murmured, more to herself than the others. 'And buy a cot and a pram and things. I can take him or her for walks, can't I? I'll be old enough.'

Liz gave her a squeeze. 'Of course.'

'What shall we call it?' Rosie went on. 'How about Mia for a girl? I like Mia.'

'I prefer Robertina,' Robert teased. 'I think we should name her after me.'

Rosie's face was a picture, so he pushed it further. 'And how about Ninian for a boy? That has a good ring about it.'

Rosie was horrified. 'Are you serious?' She wasn't a hundred per cent sure.

'Absolutely. Ninian was a saint, you know. He could be Ninny for short.'

Now she twigged. 'Or Marvin. Or Hubert,' she said delightedly.

'I've always liked Gaylord,' Liz chipped in.

Rosie frowned. 'That's just silly.'

'Dudley!' Robert suggested.

'Ermentrude!' Rosie squealed.

'Eglentine!' Liz offered. 'Eggy among friends.'

And so it went on and on until they ran out of suggestions and Robert had to leave – late – for work and Liz said that it was time to prepare supper. Rosie, meanwhile, disappeared to do her work and the house fell quiet. The silence seemed to settle in every room, under the floorboards, between the thick stone walls and up into the old slate roof, filling the place with warmth.

This, Liz thought, while she made a salad and rolled three chicken pieces in breadcrumbs – one for Robert for later – was surely the closest that you could get to bliss. It's what she'd known back in Balham, before her mother had died and everything had changed. For many years after she'd feared that, try as she may, she'd never find such contentment again, that it would always elude her. But she'd been wrong.

Rosie seemed to read her mind because later, as Liz tucked the pink duvet around her daughter's slim shoulders and under her chin and turned out the bedroom light, she asked her mother if she'd ever been so happy.

'Yes,' Liz replied carefully, 'when I found out I was pregnant with you.'

The room was dark but Liz could imagine Rosie's pale face, her furrowed brow.

'But you and my dad weren't getting on, so it can't have been the same. I mean, this time everything's just how it should be. Perfect.'

Liz paused, searching for the right words. Rosie wasn't a jealous child but, still, you had to tread softly.

'No,' she said slowly, 'it wasn't the same because your dad and I weren't right for each other. But you were the first, and everything was totally new. I'll never forget when I saw you on the scan. I cried, because you were so beautiful. You'll always be exceptional, my special Rosie. Nothing will ever change that.'

She stooped to kiss her daughter's forehead. ''Night, darling.'

Rosie yawned. It had been a long day. 'I can't wait for it to be born,' she mumbled, rolling onto her side.

'It'll come soon enough. Now go to sleep.'

''Night, Mum.'

''Night.'

Liz was tiptoeing towards the door when a voice called, 'Soon there'll be two of us to tuck in, isn't that weird?'

'Very.'

'Maybe sometimes I'll put him or her to bed.'

'I'm sure you will.'

I love you, Mum.'

Liz's heart swelled with both pain and pleasure; pain because she knew that before long it wouldn't be just Liz and Rosie, Rosie and Liz. They'd been such a tight-knit pair, but that era was drawing to a close. Pleasure because, well, they'd been lonely, too, and now Rosie would have someone who'd be there for her always, even when she and Robert were long gone.

A dog barked outside and the floorboard creaked, as if in response to Liz's over-active brain. She could hear Rosie's mind slipping into blissful unconsciousness.

She wanted this baby to know that it, too, was part of the special moment and that it was so very welcome, though they hadn't yet met.

'I love you too,' she whispered to them both.

Chapter Twelve

THE FOLLOWING MORNING, Oscar was in a grumpy mood, having slept badly and woken especially early. He wouldn't eat the scrambled eggs that Loveday, who was on nanny duty that day, made him for breakfast, and threw his plate across the room, where it landed with a squelch on one leg of Tabitha's designer jeans, which had to go straight in the washing machine.

'Can you take him for a walk?' she asked Loveday, who'd noticed the bags under her boss's eyes, the creased jumper. 'Maybe he'll drop off in the pushchair. I'd rather he had a big sleep now than this afternoon. I couldn't stand another night like last night.'

'Sure,' said Loveday, but before she could leave, Shelley, who had been taking tea and toast to the guests next door, came bursting in, ashen-faced.

'She had the dream!' she squeaked. 'That red-haired lady with the vet husband, she saw them go through the wall!'

'It's all right,' Tabitha sighed, pulling out a chair for her and inwardly cursing Luke's bad judgement.

Before he'd left for work the previous morning, he'd told the red-haired lady about the old inn and the smugglers' tunnel that used to lead from one of the bedrooms upstairs all the way down to the cellar beneath the breakfast room and under the road to the house opposite. For years, it had been a successful escape route from customs men, and rumour had it that several people who'd stayed in The Stables before the Mallons arrived had smelled strange tobacco smoke and dreamed they'd seen shadowy figures in old-fashioned clothes walking through the wall and into the tunnel.

Unfortunately, Shelley, who was nervous at the best of times, had overheard the conversation and had talked of little since. This latest revelation was the last thing that anybody needed, least of all Tabitha, who wasn't a bit afraid of ghosts, only real people.

'Calm down,' she said, signalling to Loveday to put on the kettle. 'I should think the woman's imagination was running riot after talking to Luke.'

Shelley wasn't to be assuaged. 'What if I see them? I'd drop dead with fright, I know I would!'

'Maybe they're friendly ghosts?' said Loveday, trying to be helpful.

'Ghosts aren't ever friendly,' Shelley snapped. 'They jump out and wrap their white, clammy hands round your neck and squeeze.'

She made a ghastly choking sound by way of proof.

'Why don't you go for that walk now?' suggested Tabitha, thinking it would be better if she handled this alone. 'Oscar needs some fresh air.'

As Loveday left the room, she could hear Tabitha talking in a low voice, trying to persuade Shelley that, whatever the red-haired woman might or might not have dreamed, there was no chance of bumping into any phantom smugglers now, because they only came out at night when the lights were off.

'Are you quite sure?' Shelley sounded doubtful.

'Absolutely positive,' replied Tabitha firmly.

Loveday enjoyed her perambulations round the village. She always bumped into someone and often ended up going for coffee and a chat. Oscar was everybody's darling; all the villagers loved his big brown eyes, chubby cheeks, ready smile and funny words and expressions. He was a real cutie, especially favoured by the elderly ladies, though they mightn't be as impressed with him today.

Of course he refused to put on his coat and woolly hat, chucking it on the floor angrily, then he wouldn't climb in the pushchair. He was making such a noise outside the breakfast room, where the four guests were still sitting at the new, round oak table, that Loveday had to do a fireman's lift and bundle him outside, pushchair and all, before shoving him in the seat, where he went rigid with fury until she strapped him in so tightly that he realised further resistance was futile.

Finally she pushed him, squawking, up the street towards the play park, but she didn't get far because Luke rounded the corner and sauntered towards her. She was surprised, because she'd thought he'd gone to the office.

As he came nearer, she noticed something slightly different about him; he didn't seem in any hurry and was swinging his arms casually, his head held high and a jaunty smile playing on his lips. He was clearly having a very good day.

He stopped short when he saw Oscar, bending down to ruffle his curly hair, which only made the boy screech louder and harder. 'What's got into him?'

Loveday explained that he'd been out of sorts all morning and that Tabitha had needed a break.

Luke chuckled. 'He *was* up with the larks and it was poor Tabby who had to deal with him; he wouldn't let me anywhere near him. Thank God you're here to pick up the pieces.'

Still stooping over his son, he looked up, fixing Loveday with his startling blue eyes, so that hot red spots blossomed on her cheeks and she glanced away, hoping that he wouldn't notice.

'I don't know what we'd do without you.' He grinned, which made her suspect that he *had* noticed. She wished he wouldn't tease her like that, but she sort of liked it, too.

She was about to continue her journey when he rose and patted her on the arm. 'Wait there a moment. I'm going to fetch Tabitha. I've got something to cheer her up.'

Intrigued, Loveday hung back until she saw the pair re-emerge from the house. Luke was grinning while Tabitha, a step or two behind, just looked harassed.

'Come,' he said, when they were alongside, and before Loveday knew it he was leading both women up the street and into the gravelly car park near the swings, where villagers who couldn't park outside their houses paid a small annual charge to reserve a space.

Loveday had no idea what was coming, but didn't have long to wait because Luke pointed – 'There!' – and her eyes fell on a gleaming sports car, a low-lying beast of a vehicle that made the others round it look like old-fashioned charabancs, apart from his own silky black one, of course, which was in the corner.

She didn't know anything about cars, but could tell that this one was special; brand-new and shining in the morning light, and so white that it almost hurt her eyes. She'd never seen anything quite like it, only in photos anyway, with glamorous male celebrities clambering in or out in dinner jackets and shades, or women in glitzy dresses and sky-high heels.

'Wow!' she said, glancing at Tabitha, whose eyes had opened very wide. 'It's amazing!'

Luke nodded. 'It's a Porsche Boxster.' He stroked the bonnet lovingly, as you would a sleek Siamese or a glossy thoroughbred, all the while looking at his wife intently. 'I've just picked it up. Happy anniversary, darling. You'll look great in it.'

Loveday glanced down at the number plate, which said T4BBY, before turning to her boss. She was trying to imagine how she would feel if someone had just bought the car for her, and couldn't.

She half expected Tabitha to scream in delight and rush into Luke's arms, or burst into tears of joy perhaps, but instead she stood there for what felt like an age, staring hard at the car, not moving an inch, and Loveday shuffled from one foot to another, waiting for a response.

Luke was the one who finally broke the silence.

'What do you think, then? Cool, eh? Seven years on Saturday. Quite an achievement!'

'I don't want it,' Tabitha blurted. 'You'll have to take it back.'

Loveday's mouth dropped open; she couldn't believe it, and Luke's face turned to stone.

'What do you mean?'

Tabitha shook her head several times, working her mouth in a strange way. She seemed upset and, weirdly, very, very angry.

'It's ridiculous,' she said at last. 'I can't possibly drive it.'

The air between husband and wife was so tense that you could cut it with a knife and Loveday, confused, was half-inclined to run away.

'C-could you swap it, for one you p-prefer, I mean?' she stammered, hoping to lighten things, but they ignored her, standing bolt upright, a few feet apart, like opponents in a duel.

'Shall I—?' she started to add, thinking, Please, let me make myself scarce. But there was no time to finish because Luke lunged forward and grabbed his wife by the tops of her arms, squeezing hard.

'Who the hell do you think you are?' he hissed, pushing his face up close, and Tabitha gasped, 'Oh!'

Loveday was so shocked that she remained rooted to the spot, unable to speak or move. Luke seemed cold, hard and terrifying, and her heart started hammering erratically in her chest.

'How dare you!' he went on through gritted teeth, still grasping his wife's arms. She struggled to pull away, but he held fast and shook her several times so that her head swung back and forth. Loveday felt her own knees buckle, her body start to sway.

All of a sudden Oscar yelped, 'Mamma!' distracting Luke, who swung around. His eyes fell on Loveday and he seemed surprised, as if he'd forgotten she was there. Instantly his arms dropped to his sides, his stance relaxed and his face softened. Seizing the moment, Tabitha backed off quickly and bent down to comfort her son while Loveday exhaled.

There was only a moment to catch her breath again, though, because Tabitha stood up, her brow furrowed: 'I'm sorry, I didn't mean it. I was just being stupid.'

Her eyes, still flashing, told a different story, but Luke seemed almost himself again.

'That's better. You'll love it once you get the hang of it.'

He turned to Loveday, grinning, as if it had all been a big joke.

'She's a beauty to drive.'

Loveday was so shaken that all she could do was nod pathetically, but he didn't notice because he was focused once more on his wife.

'Come and see the interior. It's all leather.'

Tabitha took a few reluctant steps forward and he opened the driver's door so that she could look inside.

'Nice,' she said mechanically, when she re-emerged.

'Nice?' Luke repeated. 'I buy you a forty thousand pound car and that's all you can say? *Nice?*'

His voice was sharp but he was grinning at Loveday.

'We'll take you for a ride in it sometime,' he told her. 'There's room in the back for Oscar, too.'

The boy had gone very quiet and when she checked, he'd stuck his thumb in his mouth and his eyelids were drooping. Luke, meanwhile, noticing a smear on the car windscreen, took a pale blue silk handkerchief out of his top pocket and wiped it off. 'That's better.' He gave both women a flash of his dazzling white teeth.

After that, Loveday decided to postpone her trip to the park and call on Liz instead. The truth was, she felt jumpy and wanted desperately to talk to someone about what had happened. Before she could leave, however, Luke took her to one side.

'Don't mention this to anyone, will you?' he said, putting an arm round her shoulder, and she shivered, hoping that he wouldn't notice.

'Tabitha's a bit funny about presents and she thinks I'm extravagant. It annoys me because I like buying things for her, but she's happy now. Everything's fine,'

He turned back to his wife, who was still standing by the car, and beckoned her over, putting his other arm round her so that the two women flanked him.

'See,' he said, pulling them close, 'that's more like it. We're all friends.'

But, still, the hair on the back of Loveday's neck prickled, and somehow she just knew in her bones that she wouldn't be recounting what she'd witnessed to anyone at all, though she wasn't quite sure why.

Even so, Loveday was keen to see a friendly face and as Liz was out she knocked on Pat's door instead. It didn't take the old woman long to reach the door and she ushered Loveday and Oscar in quickly. 'Hurry up and bring in that pram. It's blowing a gale out there. You must be perishing.'

Loveday parked the stroller in the narrow hallway, unzipped Oscar's coat and eased off his hat, taking care not to wake him.

'It's not that cold.' She kissed Pat's cheek. 'And it's a push-chair, not a pram, by the way.'

'Pushchair, pram, whatever. Mums didn't have all these new-fangled things in my day, you know. Now, there are so many thingamijigs for babies it's a wonder anyone knows how to work them.'

Loveday smiled, grateful for a dose of normality. 'So what did they put babies in back then? Kangaroo pouches?'

Pat huffed. 'All I know is, raising a child wasn't anything like as complicated as it is now. Plenty of fresh air, sleep, homemade cooking and a firm hand when needed. Simple as that, and they didn't give half so many problems neither. There was none of those juvenile distinctives, or whatever you call 'em.'

'Delinquents,' Loveday corrected, but Pat wasn't listening. She was bending over Oscar now, gazing at his adorable, slack mouth, his long, curling black lashes that swept down his cheeks like a fringe. You'd never guess that he'd been such a tyrant earlier in the day.

'What a lambkin,' she said softly. 'A little peach.' She straightened up. 'Unlike his mum.'

Loveday frowned, but Pat didn't notice. 'Time for a cuppa?' and, without waiting for a yes or no, she shuffled off down the corridor to put on the kettle.

Once settled in the little front room with mugs of tea in their hands, Loveday was able to tell Pat about Luke's present, though she was careful not to mention Tabitha's reaction, or his response.

'It's about so big.' She opened her arms wide to demonstrate the length and width. 'And bright white, brand new.'

She was expecting Pat to be impressed but instead the old woman was silent until the girl had finished, then shook her snowy head.

'Sounds like he's up to something,' she said darkly, wagging a finger. 'If you ask me, men don't go buying their wives expensive gifts like that unless they've something to hide.'

Loveday swallowed. She wanted so badly to hear Pat's opinion about the argument, and to be told what to do.

'I don't think you're right about him,' she said instead, anxious to convince herself as much as anyone. He was still her boss after all, and up until a few moments ago she'd thought he was God. 'He's very generous and he does a lot for other people, you know.'

Pat made a rude snorting sound.

'Anyway, why shouldn't he give his wife a present on their wedding anniversary? I wish Jesse would buy *me* things like that.'

Pat's sparse grey eyebrows knitted together and her mouth set in a thin, hard line.

'Now, don't you go finding fault with your Jesse. I'd sooner have him than ten of your Lukes, or whatever his name is. You hang on to that fella, my girl. If you don't, there's a dozen others who'd happily take your place just like that.'

She leaned forward and snapped her fingers under Loveday's nose, making her flinch.

She pursed her lips. Pat was full of homespun wisdom and it was surprising how often she got things right, but a ticking off wasn't what was needed right now; it was comfort she'd been after.

'I'm taking Oscar to the swings,' she said, rising quickly. If she didn't go this second she might burst into tears and spill all the beans.

'Is anything the matter?' Pat asked, making to stand, too, but Loveday gestured for her to stay put. 'Nothing at all. Thanks for the tea and biscuits. I'll let myself out.'

She didn't want to go back to The Stables but of course she must, and she sensed a peculiar atmosphere the moment she walked through the door. She'd been hoping that the row would have blown over, and half expected Tabitha and Luke to be out, taking a spin in the new motor, but her coat was still hanging on a peg in the hallway. There was no sign of either of them, though, and only the quiet chatter of guests in the reception room and Shelley vacuuming upstairs, so that Loveday almost jumped when the kitchen door swung open and Tabitha emerged. It seemed that she'd been crying.

'Are you all right?' Loveday asked.

'Bit tired, that's all.' But Tabitha's eyes were bloodshot and Loveday couldn't help noticing that her hands trembled as she tried to unbuckle her son from his pushchair.

'Let me do it,' the girl offered, taking over. 'He had a really long sleep. He ate half a banana at the park but that's all. He'll be ready for his lunch now.'

Tabitha picked Oscar up and perched him on her hip as

she watched Loveday put a jacket potato in the microwave, grate some cheese and raw carrot and chop a few slices of cucumber. While she worked, she was acutely aware of the older woman's eyes on her and could tell, in that instinctive way, that she wanted to say something.

Loveday was tempted to raise the subject of the car herself, but she was too nervous and bit her tongue. She strapped Oscar into his wooden highchair and was relieved when the microwave pinged because it broke the awkward silence.

'There,' she said, putting a plate of colourful food in front of her charge and he beamed obligingly, showing off his dimples. He'd completely recovered from his bad mood of earlier in the day.

Tabitha drew up a stool and watched Loveday pop a spoonful of potato into his mouth, before blurting, 'I hate that car.'

Loveday stopped in her tracks, the plastic spoon suspended in the air.

'Why?' she asked tentatively, and Tabitha dabbed her eyes with a tissue that she'd pulled from the sleeve of her sweater.

'We don't need it,' she said, blowing her nose, 'and God knows what it cost.'

She looked pale, almost fragile, and hiccupped – or was it a sob? Loveday put an arm round her, because it's what she herself would have wanted under the circumstances.

'Don't be upset.' She sounded more grown-up than she felt. 'It's a present, isn't it? If he wanted to buy it for you, what's the problem?'

It was a stupid question, given the way he'd treated her in the car park, but Loveday didn't even begin to know how to broach that.

'He bought it for himself, not me,' Tabitha replied. 'He's

always buying me expensive things I don't want. He likes the idea of me in it, he doesn't care what I think.'

'It's a gorgeous colour,' Loveday commented, hoping to cheer her up.

'It's flashy and it makes me look like a show-off.'

Loveday swallowed, unsure how to respond. *She* wouldn't mind attracting a few envious looks now and again, but she wouldn't want Jesse to shake her or shout in her face. She didn't understand and felt she must surely be missing something, some vital link in the chain.

'Could you ask him to change it, when he's calmed down, I mean? Swap it for something you prefer?'

Oscar whacked his plastic spoon on the tray, sending bits of cheese and potato flying, and she stooped to pick them up.

'You don't see, why would you?' said Tabitha, fiddling with the hem of her sweater, picking at an imaginary piece of fluff. 'I've no idea where he gets the money.'

Loveday threw the food in the silver swing bin by the sink and almost laughed. This was easy to solve! 'But his company's doing brilliantly, he told me. He could probably buy six of those cars if he wanted.'

'Forget it. I shouldn't have mentioned it again, sorry.'

They switched subjects and Loveday made her boss smile at last, but when she asked as she was leaving what time Luke would be home, the corners of Tabitha's mouth drooped, her eyes filled with tears and she shook her head.

As Loveday walked swiftly back to the flat at around 6 p.m., she found herself thinking for the first time that perhaps it had been a mistake to leave A Winkle In Time. The job might have been boring, but at least she had been safe there and surrounded by friends. She could hand in her notice, but was one nasty scene between the boss and his wife enough of a reason to throw it all in? Tabitha and Oscar would miss her and, besides, she had an uneasy feeling that Luke wouldn't let her go without a fight.

At around half past midnight, Liz yawned and snapped off the TV, too tired to watch any longer. It wasn't unheard of for Robert to be late back from the restaurant and he didn't know that she was waiting up for him but, still, she'd hoped to catch him, because something was preying on her mind.

Pat had rung at around three thirty, just after Liz had put down the phone on Rosie, who'd been brimming with excitement, having just heard the news that she'd got the part of one of the Playing Cards in *Alice*, and there was a rehearsal after school that very day. Pat, meanwhile, had sounded so het up that at first Liz couldn't understand what she'd been on about, until she'd heard the names 'Loveday' and 'Luke' so often that she'd managed to pick up the thread.

'I reckon Loveday's had her head turned,' Pat had said breathlessly. 'It's Luke this, Luke that, and she wasn't very nice about Jesse neither. What's she doing at that office? That's what I want to know. Why can't she talk about it? And where does his money come from for that posh car? It seems fishy to me.'

Liz didn't give two hoots about the car, but she did care about Robert's niece. She'd played devil's advocate on the phone for a while, trying to persuade Pat that all was well, but knew that she hadn't done a very convincing job.

'I don't like the sound of it,' Pat had muttered ominously when Liz had tried to hang up. 'You talk to that husband of yours and see what he thinks.'

The last of the embers on the log fire had died and Liz

shivered, feeling suddenly chilly. She rose, picking up the remains of a packet of dry biscuits that she'd been nibbling on, and was about to turn out the lights when she heard Robert banging on the door and shouting through their letterbox, 'I can't find my key!'

When she opened up she was met with a boozy blast and her husband staring down at her with a sheepish grin on his face. 'Shorry, Lizzie, musht've left them at work.'

She stood back while he entered the house, almost tripping on the step, and watched him sway down the hallway and into the front room.

'Luke came by and we had a few drinks to toasht the baby,' he hiccupped, plonking on the sofa and gazing at her blearily. 'I think I'm going to regret it in the morning.'

It wasn't the right time for a discussion, but hearing Luke's name once more was too much for Liz and, against her better judgement, she sat beside her husband and recounted the conversation with Pat.

'What do you think?' she asked at last, prodding Robert in the ribs to make sure that he was still awake. 'Pat's pretty sharp, she wouldn't have spoken without good reason.'

Robert clumsily took her hand, and traced the thin blue veins that threaded along the back of her wrist with a forefinger.

'You worry too much. He's a good bloke.'

'But do you really believe all this top-secret stuff? It sounds so implausible.'

Robert shook his head several times, rather harder than necessary.

'You don't understand. Loveday's young, she exaggerates everything. You know what she's like. Luke's in finance, that's his real job. It just happens he's helping the government because they asked him to.' He had difficulty with 'government' especially, over-emphasising each syllable like a child testing out a brand-new word. 'Apparently it's normal for them to get in outside help when they need it. He can't discuss it but it's all above board.'

Then he closed his eyes, worn out with the effort.

Liz sighed. It had been a mistake to raise the matter now, and she tried, without success, to heave him up from sitting. She'd never seen him quite like this before; it must have been some celebration. He looked ready to nod off on the sofa, but he'd only wake up cold and stiff. 'I can't carry you, you're too heavy.'

At last he got the message, groaned, and she heard him stagger upstairs, while she fetched him a large glass of water from the kitchen. He was going to need it. Later, when he'd crashed into bed fully clothed and she'd had to help him off with his shirt and trousers, she lay awake listening to his heavy breathing. She thought he'd passed out, but he must have sensed her brain whirring.

'I'm shorry about tonight,' he mumbled. 'Shouldn't have stayed so long. Luke really rates Loveday, y'know. He knows she's had a difficult time. He wants to help.'

Liz swallowed, wondering whether to speak. She couldn't stop herself.

'If he's such a saint then how come Tabitha's so miserable?'

Robert paused, before letting out a strange sound, some-where between a yelp and a grumble. 'Look, Liz, maybe she's just not a very happy person.' He seemed to have sobered up a little and sounded sharp, like a sting. 'Loveday's finally found a job she's good at and enjoys. For heaven's sake, don't go and poke your nose in and spoil it for her.'

Chapter Thirteen

'He's still furious with me about the car, Moll. He stormed off and I don't know where he's gone.'

Tabitha was lying on her bed, propped up against a pile of cushions. It was the early hours of the morning but she was wide awake, every sense on alert.

She heard Molly take a sip of something. Wine? Water? How would she know, when her friend was so far away? She'd been trying to contact Molly all evening, but she'd been out having fun. Tabitha didn't know the meaning of the word.

'He'll be back,' Molly said calmly, 'He's probably driving round the countryside, letting off steam.'

Tabitha scarcely heard. Her mind was jumping all over the place. 'I should've pretended I liked it, I'm a fool. I can't bear to think where the money's come from.' She bit her lip. 'I don't want to drive round in a big, fuck-off car, I want to blend into the background.'

'Not easy with your looks,' Molly remarked drily, 'but don't worry about the cash, that's the least of your concerns. As long as you don't know anything about it, you're not involved, right? Anyway, it might be legit.'

Tabitha glanced instinctively at the window, even though it was dark outside and the blinds were drawn. 'It's not, I'm sure.' She shivered. 'God knows what he's up to. I just wish he wasn't using Loveday, I don't want her getting into trouble.'

'If only I could help,' Molly sighed, and at that moment Tabitha missed her so much it was like a physical pain.

'Don't ever leave me, Moll.'

'You know I won't.'

Afterwards, Tabitha sat in the gloom, too tired to read, too anxious to rest. There were four guests staying, two couples who complimented her on everything, from the cooked breakfasts that Shelley helped her prepare to the carefully designed bedrooms, but it was unlikely they'd hear if Carl broke in, and would they know what to do anyway? Luke would, she'd give him that.

She padded over to the cream-coloured armchair, pulled up her legs and wrapped her arms round her shins, staring into the shadows, feeling her aloneness like the slow movement of the hands of a clock, the empty space between stars.

Looking back, she thought she'd been such an obvious target for Carl – young, isolated and vulnerable. Pretty, too; she supposed that was a factor, and she'd been putty in his hands.

He'd used a set routine on her, she recognised that now, winning her trust, then worming his way into her heart so that she'd come to believe she was in love and couldn't exist without him. Later, he'd offered her drugs, crack cocaine mainly, and taken away her pub earnings so that she'd had to ask him for cash. Finally, after months of grooming when all she'd really cared about had been her next fix, he'd brought in the punters. It had been so well planned.

She could remember the first time as if it were yesterday. She'd tried to protest, struggling from Carl's grip and shouting that this was her red line, but he'd hit her with enough force to ensure that she'd never forget. Before long, there had been men every other night and she'd stopped complaining, believing it when Carl had said that she was worthless and deserved it.

Molly had tried to save her, but it had been no use. It must have been heartbreaking, watching her friend's downward spiral, deaf to all advice, bullying and pleading. But she'd stuck by Tabitha and had somehow managed to get her to their gigs, once a fortnight or so, in a fit enough state to sing. By then, the band had been performing in pubs around Liverpool, Manchester, Hull and Leeds. It would have looked odd if their main vocalist hadn't been there. Besides, Carl had liked the money, though he'd had nothing but contempt for the music.

Tabitha rested her cheek on her drawn-up knees, recalling how every so often she'd have glimpses of what she'd become. It had been then that her mother's final words to her would ring in her ears: '"Remove the wicked person from amongst yourselves."' At the time it had seemed deeply unjust, though she'd never have dared argue back. Now, filled with self-loathing, she'd have killed herself if only she'd had the guts.

When she'd first set eyes on Luke, he'd been standing by himself in the middle of the tightly packed room at the back of the pub in Manchester's Oldham Street. Even then, he'd stood out from the grungy students in their jeans, faded T-shirts and shabby trainers. He had been so tall and elegantly dressed, in a crisp blue and white striped shirt, his fair hair swept back, his face smooth. And those blue eyes, fixed on her the entire night, so that when she'd sung, she'd felt as if it was for him alone.

She'd covered up her bruises with make-up but couldn't imagine that he liked her, not really. Somehow, though, she'd suspected when she left the pub that he'd be waiting for her. She'd already made up her mind to say she couldn't talk, that she had a boyfriend, only Carl had noticed the stranger, too, and hadn't liked what he'd seen.

'Fucking slag,' he'd said, jumping out of the shadows at her, grabbing her hair and pulling her into the dark alleyway beside the pub. There had been no time to cry out, because he'd punched her so hard that her head had flown back and smashed into the wall behind. 'Think you're something, do you? Well, you know what? You're a piece of shit.'

It had been some weeks before she'd seen Luke again, but she hadn't forgotten him. He'd stood right up front, his eyes boring into her so that she'd felt almost as if she were naked. Her heart had sunk and her hands had trembled, because she'd known that Carl would be watching and she'd hurried from the building at the end so there was no way he could say she'd led him on. Even so, her teeth jangled and her nerves were shot to pieces as she'd waited at the corner of the dark street, well away from the crowds.

Carl hadn't taken long. She'd felt a sharp pain on the left side of her face and staggered a few paces. 'Bitch,' he said, and she'd closed her eyes, anticipating another blow. It had never come, though, because Luke had appeared, smashing Carl hard in the head with his fists so that he'd fallen to the ground, groaning. Gone was the slim, suave man who'd been making eyes at her in the pub. Now he was all muscle and brute strength. A wild animal.

He'd kicked Carl again and again, until she'd screamed at him to stop because she'd thought he'd finish him off. Then he'd knelt beside his victim, whispering, 'If you go anywhere near her again, I'll rip you to pieces.'

While Carl had whimpered, Luke had calmly taken a business card out of the wallet in his trouser pocket and tucked it in his fist, crunching the broken fingers round it tightly.

'Remember my name,' he'd said quietly, before adjusting his pale grey jacket and taking Tabitha's hand.

'Come,' he'd said, leading her towards the shiny silver car parked a few metres up the road, and she'd been too shocked and dazed to resist.

After her poky place in Liverpool, his Manchester flat was breath-taking: a posh, bachelor pad at the top of a brand-new, high-rise block with giant windows and an amazing view. She'd had a bath, put on the white towelling dressing gown that he'd given her and allowed him to examine the painful swelling on her temple, rubbing in some arnica that he'd found in his bathroom cabinet.

She'd been amazed when he'd given her the double bed and taken the sofa next door for himself, and when she'd woken the next morning, he'd brought her tea and gone to work, telling her to rest, make herself at home and help herself to anything she fancied from the fridge.

'We'll go for dinner later,' he'd said, 'if you're feeling up to it. There's a great little restaurant nearby.'

All morning she'd wandered around the flat, opening drawers and cupboards, eager to find out as much about him as she could, but there was precious little to go on: no letters or photographs, nothing to indicate if he was married, or had been, who his parents were or where he was from.

His clothes were neatly pressed and tidied away, his bath-room contained just one brand of shower gel, shampoo and soap, a single toothbrush, some plasters and painkillers, arnica and two bottles of upmarket aftershave. The place felt more like a hotel suite than a home, but his fridge was well stocked with foods, some of which she'd never tasted before – French cheeses, wholemeal bread, cured meats, olives, smoked salmon and freshly squeezed fruit juice. She'd been hungry, not having eaten for hours, and had tried a little of everything.

Every now and again she glanced out of the window, frightened that Carl would come, but she was so high up that the people below were faceless blobs and she told herself that he'd be in no fit state to track her down just yet. Later, she slept, took a shower and climbed back into the things that she'd worn the night before. She had nothing with her save those clothes and her handbag with a comb and some loose change.

She was fine until about four, when the jitters started. She would have called Molly, but she was at college. She turned on the TV and tried to focus, nibbling on biscuits, bread, anything she could find to take her mind off the cravings. Carl would have sorted her out, but not until she'd taken her punishment and this time, she'd thought, he might kill her.

When Luke finally walked in at about 7 p.m. she almost wept with relief.

'Are you OK?' he asked, noticing her jerky movements and anxious, darting eyes.

Instead of taking her out, he made pasta, poured them both a glass of red wine and insisted that she tell him everything, every last detail. She paced the room, unable to sit still, but he was quiet and patient, nodding every now and again and prompting her gently to go on.

When at last her story was over, she fully expected him to throw her out. After all, she'd left no stone unturned. She'd felt that somehow he'd have known if she'd tried to gloss things over and in any case it had been a relief to speak the truth. Even Molly didn't know the full story. Carl – and now Luke – were the only ones.

For a moment Luke paused, knitting his eyebrows, and Tabitha thought this was it. She was mentally hurrying from the flat, wondering where to go and how to hide. Then he got up from where he was sitting and took her in his arms, and she was so surprised that she shook and sobbed until his shirt was wet and she thought that she had no more tears left.

After that, he drove her to the out-of-hours doctor who handed her a prescription for diazepam and something to help her sleep.

'We'll get you off that stuff,' Luke promised as they climbed back in his car, and he seemed so sincere that she almost dared to believe him.

The first few weeks of withdrawal were hellish; she felt so depressed that she could scarcely get out of bed. Fury and fiery restlessness came in waves, followed by lapses of lethargy and hopelessness. Luke insisted that she stay indoors with him the entire time. 'You're safe here,' he told her. 'I'm going to make you well.'

He took her to support group meetings and picked her up at the end and when she mentioned Carl he told her not to worry. 'I've got my eyes on him. He won't come anywhere near.'

As she became fitter and stronger, she began to think about re-joining the band because composing and singing was what she liked to do more than anything in the world. They'd found a new lead vocalist, they'd had to, but Molly promised to take Tabitha back in a heartbeat. Luke, however, said no. 'You don't need to work now, Tabby, you've got me.'

Molly visited when she could and to begin with Luke seemed to like her, but when she, too, raised the issue of the band, his face clouded over. The life didn't suit Tabitha, he said, the late nights, parties, drugs, the whole seedy scene. Molly tried to argue that Carl was the problem, not the music, but Luke wouldn't have any of it.

'She's bad news,' he warned, when Molly left. 'I don't want you seeing her.'

After that, Molly and Tabitha only met when he was away;

it was easier when Molly got a job in Manchester. She'd either visit the flat or later, when Tabitha had begun to relax a little about Carl, they'd go for a meal in the city centre, taking care to keep to busy streets and venues, constantly checking that they weren't being followed. Although they never saw Carl, they always had the feeling that someone was watching. Molly said they were Luke's men, too, but they let them be.

Tabitha was happier than she'd ever been, wasn't she, with a stunning home and a boyfriend who showered her with expensive presents: a ring here, a gorgeous pair of shoes there? He loved it when she dressed in beautiful clothes and she'd never been the object of such praise and admiration. It was almost too much. And yet... little by little she began to wonder about her rescuer, whom she could never quite pin down. He left for work each day but she never saw his office, neither did he give her his business address or phone number.

Then there were the strange friends, who rang at odd times of the night or at weekends, when he'd shut himself away to take the calls, emerging later with a frown or a grin, but he wouldn't say why.

After a while, she started to push a little, wanting to be part of that side of his life and curious, too. 'Tell me,' she'd beg. 'I'd like to know about your work, I want to be supportive.'

But he smiled coolly and snapped the TV on. 'I don't like mixing business with pleasure. When I'm with you I just want to relax.'

Frustrated, she began again to wish that she had something more in her life. She wanted for nothing materially because Luke paid for everything, but singing and composing had been her passion. As she became more confident in herself, she wanted to know why Luke wouldn't let her go back to what she did best. Surely, with Carl under control, he couldn't deny her that?

She waited till the end of the evening after they'd been for a meal and made love. They were lying in bed, her head on his chest, breathing in and out deeply, listening to the sounds of the still busy city below. But as soon as she spoke, she could feel Luke's body tense.

'I've told you, Tabby. I don't want you doing it.'

Something made her bold; perhaps it was the wine she'd drunk earlier.

'You want me to be happy, don't you? What's the harm?'

Without warning, he pushed her off, sprang out of bed and stood in the doorway, facing her. His fair hair gleamed white in the half-light and he looked taller than usual, and menacing.

'Watch your step, or you'll be on your own again.' His voice was hard, his mouth small and tight, and for a moment she'd been reminded of the way he'd spoken to Carl that night when he'd been lying in a bloody mess at his feet.

'I–I'm sorry,' she stammered, 'I was being silly.'

And just as if someone had flicked a switch, the light came on and he turned into the old Luke, kind, protective, loving Luke.

'That's my girl,' he said, sitting beside her once more, running his palm down the side of her face and squeezing her jaw just a shade harder than she'd have liked.

She wondered whether it was pure coincidence that two days later she saw Carl for the first time in months. He was on the other side of the road, right across from the flat, leaning casually against the wall, smoking a cigarette, and when his eyes bored into her, her knees went weak.

She stood, paralysed, watching him flash in and out of sight as cars and lorries rumbled past in both directions.

Then, when there was a lull in the traffic, he pointed at her slowly and deliberately, before aiming two fingers at his own temple and staggering slightly. She was in no doubt what he meant.

Two burly men in jeans and dark bomber jackets walked past, staring at him the whole time, and he slunk away. But after that she didn't feel like going to the shops, as she'd intended, and hurried home, waiting for Luke's return.

'Good day?' he asked cheerfully as he plonked his briefcase on the floor and took off his coat, then he gave her a look and she knew that he knew and that he'd been teaching her a lesson.

They married a year later. It was only a quick, register office affair. His parents were dead and he said he'd invited his sister, who lived in Glasgow, but she couldn't come. Two of his friends were witnesses, but they couldn't stay for a drink, so Luke and Tabitha went on their own to his favourite restaurant in Salford. Soon after, they moved to their new townhouse in Manchester and six years after that Oscar came along. Luke said that she'd made him proudest man in the world.

She'd always suspected that there were other women, but she never mentioned it. She'd rather he had twenty mistresses than abandon her to her fate, for she was certain that Carl would neither forgive nor forget. She'd been devastated when Luke had told her they were moving to Cornwall, not only because she'd have to leave Molly and the city she now called home, but also because she'd felt safe there, surrounded by his minders.

'He won't follow,' Luke insisted, 'not when he knows I'm around.'

But she couldn't help thinking that he didn't know the man as intimately as she once had, or how deep his resentment ran.

In any case, she had no choice. Luke had bought The Stables without her seeing it and she was to run a guest house.

The door creaked, making her jump, and she cried out, 'Oh!' She was so relieved when her husband walked in that she almost forgot about their argument and rushed towards him. 'I thought... Where have you been? I didn't know if you were coming back.'

She wanted him to hug her, to tell her it was all right, but his eyes were mean and bloodshot.

'Ungrateful bitch,' he said, grabbing her by the jaw and squeezing so tight that she squealed in pain. He pushed his face close to hers in that way he had and she could smell alcohol on his breath. 'I'll throw you back on the streets where you belong. You'll never see Oscar again.'

When he finally let go, she sank to the floor. 'Don't, Luke, I beg you. I swear to God it'll never happen again.'

She grasped his ankles but he shook her off, took a step back, and she wondered if he might kick her. She didn't care, as long as she could stay. Instead, however, he turned on his heel and made for the bathroom, where she heard him switch on the tap and climb in the shower. Familiar sounds. The reassuring noise of everyday life. He'd come round, surely? If she behaved...

She rose slowly, ignoring the twinge in her legs from kneeling in that cramped position, the smarting arm from where he'd grabbed it, and she slunk into the bedroom, crawling under the duvet and curling up, foetus-like, so as to occupy the least space possible, to give him all the room he required. By the time he returned and clambered in wordlessly beside her, she sensed that he'd calmed a little. He switched out the light and she heard his breath become slow and heavy until finally a short, rhythmic sequence of juddering snores, followed by a gasp, told her that he was asleep.

He rolled on his back, stretching his arms and legs wide so that she had to scrunch up even smaller, but she didn't try to move him. This she could endure, she thought, running her hand down the knobbly seam of the mattress, reminding herself of just how close she was to the very edge. Oscar needed her and for him, the light of her life, she'd put up with anything.

Chapter Fourteen

IT WAS ROSIE'S thirteenth birthday at the end of March, and although she didn't want a party, she'd asked for money to take some friends to a film in Plymouth and for pizza after.

Liz was still unused to having cash in her pocket, having had to scrimp and save for so long, and had found herself budgeting out loud in front of Robert one Monday morning when the restaurant was closed and Rosie had left for school. 'Roughly five pounds on petrol, nine pounds-ish per ticket, seven pounds or so for a pizza.' She'd frowned at him over his breakfast cereal. 'How many friends do you think she can invite? Can we afford it?'

He'd reached out and touched her hand. 'Darling, she can have as many as she likes. You don't need to worry about money any more.'

But, still, Liz found it hard to splash out, even where her daughter was concerned. Thriftiness was in her blood and Rosie's, too. They weren't used to treats.

'Can I have three people?' Rosie had enquired later, ticking their names off on her fingers. She hadn't mentioned Tim, though. These days, his name never crossed her lips.

Liz had said that she could have a few more if she wanted,

but Rosie had shaken her head. 'Three's the perfect number. If I have any more I won't get to talk to them all.'

Saturday arrived, the day of the party, and when Liz returned home midmorning from dropping the girls at the cinema, Robert was at the restaurant and the house was quiet. She was intending to do some work herself and had just plonked her sewing kit on the kitchen table when the phone rang: Pat.

'How the babby?' the old woman wanted to know. She was as excited about the forthcoming arrival as anyone, and was already busy with her balls of wool and needles, knitting bootees, cardigans and shawls.

'All good,' Liz replied, stroking her bump. 'It's definitely starting to show now.'

Pat told her to look after herself, before turning to the *real* reason she'd called. 'Guess what?'

Liz recognised that breathless tone and, suspecting that this would be a long one, filled the kettle and settled down.

Pat cleared her throat and announced solemnly that she'd had a call from a Detective Constable James Burgess. 'From the Met, you know.' She tended to put the police on a pedestal, alongside the Queen and the Archbishop of Canterbury. 'Such a charming man. Perfect manners.'

The bad news was that someone had been hacking into accounts at her bank and stealing people's money, the good was that her own was quite safe. A very helpful gentleman – not James Burgess, someone else – had transferred the lot into a special police account for her until the investigation was over.

'Just imagine if they'd gone off with all my savings,' Pat muttered. 'It doesn't bear thinking about.'

Apparently, the police were close to making some arrests,

she went on, while Liz listened quietly. 'They think there's quite a few involved, the dirty dogs.' They'd asked her not to contact the bank herself for fear of jeopardising the operation. 'I said of course I'd do anything I could to help. Can you believe it? Me? Caught up in a fraud investigation? Fancy that!'

The next few minutes seemed to pass in slow motion as Liz carefully went through the details again. She was trying to sound calm but it wasn't easy. Even as the old woman repeated the sequence of events, doubt crept into her voice as the story sounded more implausible with each retelling.

'I've been duped, haven't I?' she said at last, sounding hollow with regret. 'All my savings.' There was a strange noise, a bang and the line went dead.

'Pat?' No reply.

Liz froze. 'Are you there?' Then, forgetting coat or shoes, she tore up the quiet street and hammered on her neighbour's door, letting herself in with the key that she kept for emergencies. Her heart was pumping furiously as she hurtled into the front room, to find Pat sprawled and unconscious on the carpet in front of the window, her right arm twisted at a strange angle and blood trickling from the corner of her mouth.

For a moment Liz thought she was dead, but bending down she felt for a pulse in her wrist that confirmed she was still breathing. Grabbing the phone that was lying at Pat's side, Liz dialled 999 and cradled her friend's head on her lap, smoothing her white hair, the deep lines on her forehead, while she waited for the ambulance to arrive. She didn't dare move her, scared of causing further damage, but whispered gently again and again, as much to reassure herself as anything, 'They're coming now, they're on their way. You're going to be all right.'

Pat stirred and moaned as the paramedics examined and

moved her carefully into the ambulance. It seemed that she'd broken her poor arm badly. She was clearly in a lot of pain and Liz went with her on the journey to hospital, talking to her in a low voice and stroking her hand, though the old woman was bewildered and scarcely knew what was happening.

It was only when Pat was being wheeled into Casualty that Liz was able to ring Robert and ask him to collect Rosie from the cinema, as well as alert the police to the fraudulent call.

'I've no idea how long I'll be,' she told him. 'I'll keep in touch. You know,' she went on, thinking of Pat's broken bones, her kind heart, the way she'd do anything for anyone, 'I hate those people. I don't know how they can live with themselves. If I bumped into them in the street, I swear I'd strangle them with my bare hands.'

That evening, Loveday sat in the corner of The Lobster Pot, sipping a Bacardi and Coke and waiting for the others to show up. She loved having her weekends free, particularly Saturday nights. They'd always been very busy at A Winkle In Time and although there was usually some house party or other going on afterwards, it wasn't the same. She'd arrive tired and sweaty in her waitressing clothes, smelling of fish, garlic, herbs, wine and all the other fancy ingredients that went into the dishes. Whereas today she'd risen at noon and mooched about listening to music, calling friends, munching on crisps and toast, having a long bath and spending hours getting ready.

She fiddled with her phone for a while, playing Candy Crush Saga and avoiding Barbara's son Aiden's eye. He was quite a bit older than her, and they'd had a brief romance until she'd grown tired of his frequent trips to Launceston to see his kids. Truth to tell, she wasn't that keen on his Morris dancing either. Looking back, she'd been a bit of a cow, dumping him by text. Awkward. But she had been less mature back then. Now she was sure she'd handle it better.

Barbara sashayed over to take her empty glass. 'Top-up?' she asked, smiling. A widow in her fifties, Barbara wasn't the type to bear grudges. In any case, Aiden had a new girlfriend, an estate agent from Lostwithiel, who was closer to him in age and far more suitable. He was still annoyed with Loveday, she could tell, but he wasn't exactly dying of a broken heart.

Tony and Felipe strolled in, wearing V-neck sweaters in different colours and matching white Converse trainers. They waved at Loveday and ordered drinks from Aiden at the bar before settling down at a table on the other side. It was 6.30 p.m., still early, and the place wouldn't start filling up for half an hour or so. Loveday hoped her friends would hurry so that she wouldn't have fight off customers wanting the seats that she'd bagged. She knew what it was like.

When Barbara returned, she handed Loveday her drink before pulling up a chair. She was dressed to the nines in a scarlet frock, cut low at the front, high black heels and big, gold earrings. Her blonde hair didn't move, thanks to quantities of lacquer; if you lit a match she'd go up in flames.

'Isn't it awful about Pat?' she said, wiping water from the bottom of the glass off the table with a cloth and shaking her head.

Loveday, who had no idea what she was talking about, listened quietly while the older woman filled her in. Pat, she said, was at that very moment undergoing a nasty operation to pin the broken bones in her arm back together. Surgeons could work wonders nowadays but, given Pat's age, even the general anaesthetic was a risk.

'Liz said she was in awful pain, poor thing, very distressed. Seems she was the victim of a telephone scam.'

Loveday's ears pricked, she wanted to know all the details, and Barbara described how the 'so-called police' had offered to transfer Pat's savings into a special, safe account. 'Looks like she's lost the lot. It was the fright that made her collapse.'

The temperature in the room seemed to drop and Loveday felt a bit woozy. Transferring victims' money into a special, safe account was her job, and the words that had been used to Pat sounded like the ones that she'd been told to say. She gave herself a mental shake and almost laughed. It had probably been Ahmed on the phone – or even Luke – busy with their investigation!

'Her money's fine!' she cried. 'She can have it back whenever she wants, she just needs to ring the number they gave her.'

Barbara looked at her strangely. 'Robert spoke to the *real* police. They said it's been happening all over, same story exactly. There's no "safe account". The cash disappears as fast as you can click your fingers and when you try to ring the number it's dead, the phone's been chucked away. I'm afraid the money's gone. To be honest, though, that's the least of our worries. Money can be replaced – but Pat can't.'

Loveday thought of the new mobile phone that she was given every time she went to the office, which she'd never thought to question, of Tabitha's strange reaction to the Porsche and of Luke's frightening treatment of her. To be honest, Loveday hadn't felt quite the same since; she'd been more guarded around him, though he didn't seem to have noticed. Her chest tightened as Pat's words flashed through her mind: 'Sounds like he's up to something,' she'd warned. 'If you ask me, men don't go buying their wives expensive gifts like that unless they've something to hide.'

Her hands started trembling and she tucked them under the table so that Barbara wouldn't see. She felt confused and didn't like the path down which her thoughts were leading her. Pat was like another grannie. She was part of Tremarnock; you couldn't imagine a time when she wouldn't be there. Now the old woman was frightened and in pain.

'Liz said he called himself Detective Constable James Burgess,' Barbara informed her. 'Scum.'

Loveday felt sick. That was one of the names Ahmed used. She knew because the old people quoted it back when they got through to her. Her thoughts turned to all the elderly men and women that she'd spoken to at HM Financial Services. Luke had taught her to be gentle and reassuring but firm, too, because it was in their interests to do as she said.

'Don't worry, your savings will be quite secure,' she'd insisted, taking care to call them 'Mr' or 'Mrs', unless they gave her permission to use their first names. Ahmed and Sam always shut their doors so that she couldn't hear what they were saying. And those lists of names and numbers that she'd compiled so willingly and handed over, complete with ages, addresses, credit ratings. Luke had told her to concentrate on Devon and keep well away from Tremarnock. She hadn't asked why. 'It's an ill bird that fouls its own nest', that was one of Pat's sayings. Maybe Ahmed had slipped up.

She'd thought she'd been helping to protect the old people. She could taste acid in her mouth and tried to tell herself that she was being silly, adding two and two together to make five.

'She will be all right, won't she?' she asked Barbara desperately, attempting to disguise the crack in her voice.

'We just don't know, to be honest. Fingers crossed.'

She must have noticed Loveday's eyes pooling with tears because she touched her hand, which made her want to cry even more. 'I'm sorry to be the bearer of such bad news. She's old, you see, and the arm's very badly broken.'

Loveday found herself gripping the edge of the table. Might Pat *die*? What's more, if the police were on the case maybe she, Loveday, would go to prison. The voices around her faded in and out.

'Are you all right?' Barbara asked suddenly, signalling to Aiden at the bar for assistance. 'You've gone as white as a sheet.'

Loveday could feel the sweat on the palms of her hands and upper lip; she had to get out. She pushed back her chair and stood up shakily, pausing just long enough to ask Barbara to pass a message to her friends that she was feeling ill and had gone home.

'Let Aiden walk with you at least,' Barbara called after her, but she was too late. Loveday had already stumbled from the pub, not caring about the stares. She hurried up South Street, past the familiar houses and shops, past Rick and his girlfriend, coming from Market Square, past Jenny Lambert and her dog, and across Humble Hill. All the while her brain was in overdrive, trying to work out what to do.

Talk to Robert and Liz – and Jesse, too. Of course! They'd go together to the police and sort everything out. And once Pat was better, Loveday would pay her and all the others back. She'd save her money, every last penny, for however long it took – the next fifty years if necessary. For a moment she almost laughed with relief.

Then something that Luke had said came back to her and she staggered, as if she'd been hit: the scammers were very dangerous, they'd go to great lengths not be caught. 'I don't want to scare you, but you must understand that idle talk could put not just you but your friends and family at risk, too.'

She started to run as fast as she could up the alley that

separated the gardens in her street from the ones that backed on to them, cutting her arms and face on the twigs and spiky brambles and knocking down wheelie bins. Her hands trembled as she rammed her key in the lock and lurched into the house, slamming the door shut behind her. Then she turned off her mobile, and climbed, in all her clothes, under the duvet, covering her head completely so that all she could hear was the thumping of her own anxious heart.

It was a complex operation to put Pat's arm back together, involving wires, screws, rods and metal plates. Afterwards, the surgeon declared it a success, but pointed out that they weren't out of the woods yet. There was always a danger that the arm would become infected or refuse to heal properly, and Pat was going to need lots of care.

'It'll take a good few months to get better and she'll need plenty of rest,' he warned Liz, who was there with Pat's favourite niece, Emily, when Pat came out of Theatre. 'She can't use the arm for while, so she'll be in hospital for at least a week and she'll need someone to look after her when she goes home.'

Word spread fast and soon everyone wanted to know what they could do to help, and Liz became the main point of contact. Before long, Barbara, Jean, Tony, Felipe, Esme, Rick and all the rest were taking it in turns to visit Pat in hospital and keep up her spirits. She was in bandages, uncomfortable and looking very frail, but she appreciated the company, though she did miss home.

'I've never been away so long,' she said sadly, and Liz promised that she'd water her pots and keep everything clean and tidy.

Emily said she could stay with her aunt for the first week

after she left hospital, but after that she'd have to return to her husband, who was in poor health himself. In between her own hospital trips Liz drew up a rota to ensure that her friend wouldn't be on her own for more than an hour or two once she was discharged, and all her meals would be provided. Even the young ones offered to help: Nathan and his girlfriend Annie, Ryan, Jesse and the boys at A Winkle In Time. After all, everyone adored Pat. Only Loveday failed to volunteer, which was peculiar, given that the pair were very fond of each other.

However, Liz was so busy that for several days she scarcely had time to think, then on Thursday morning, before he left for the restaurant, Robert told her he'd heard from Jesse that Loveday was ill and hadn't been to work.

'Flu, I think,' he said. 'She's been in bed for days and still isn't right. I said she should see a doctor, don't you think?'

Liz was puzzled. Normally Robert's niece would phone or drop by almost every day. Either that or they'd bump into each other in the shops or street. Loveday tended to wear her heart on her sleeve and would share even the slightest problem, yet now she'd gone completely quiet. It was most unusual.

Liz decided to postpone seeing Pat and check on Loveday at the flat instead. She rang the bell and rapped on the door several times but there was no answer, and, thinking that the girl might be sleeping, she went away and came back in the early evening.

When there was still no reply, Liz became increasingly concerned and shouted through the letterbox, 'It's me. I'm going to fetch Jesse. Are you all right?'

She put her ear to the door, thinking she could detect movement, and sure enough soon Loveday herself appeared on the step in a pink dressing gown and grubby white slippers.

'Why didn't you answer?' Liz asked, confused, and the girl scowled.

'I'm sick, didn't Jesse tell you? I've been in bed all week. I can't talk to anyone.'

She was so rude that for a moment Liz was tempted to turn round and go home, until she reminded herself that she was unwell.

'Can I get you anything? Food? Medicine? Something to read?'

Loveday shook her head and replied, Greta Garbo-ish, 'I want to be alone.'

She looked pale, it was true, but flu wasn't the end of the world. Liz thought of poor Pat, stuck in hospital after a shock that could have killed her, and felt her sympathy ebb away.

'Have you heard about Pat?' she asked, expecting some acknowledgment, a question at least, to find out how she was doing.

'I don't want to talk about it,' snapped Loveday.

Chapter Fifteen

As SOON AS Liz left, Loveday padded upstairs and sat on the
end of her unmade bed, her head in her hands. She'd wanted
nothing more than to tell Liz everything, but she mustn't, and
it had been the same with Jesse. All week long he'd been so
thoughtful, bringing her cups of tea, offering her massages,
but she'd given him the cold shoulder and turned away.

'Leave me alone. I'm ill.' If she'd once told him how she
actually felt, the floodgates would have opened and she
wouldn't have been able to stop.

He'd come back to check on her after every lunchtime when
she was in bed, the curtains closed. 'Can I make you some
soup or something?' But she'd grunted no. 'Pat seems to have
turned a corner,' he'd added today, making conversation, and,
'See you later, babe,' as he'd headed out again for the evening
shift. 'Hope you feel better soon.' She hadn't replied.

She wished he wouldn't be so understanding; his kindness
was killing her.

The sun dipped below the horizon, the shadows lengthened
and she was still lying there in the dark, almost in the same
place where he'd left her, when he returned again at eleven
that night.

'Boss let me off early,' he said cheerfully, strolling into the room and switching on the light because he could tell that she was awake, 'so I could come home and look after you.'

Loveday bit her lip. 'You shouldn't have bothered.'

'What?' He stood still, waiting for her reply, clearly unsure if he'd heard her correctly.

She sat up, eyes blazing. 'I said you shouldn't have bothered to come back. There's nothing you can do.'

His expression changed from one of surprise to anger as something in him finally snapped, and she watched his body tense, his eyebrows lower. It was inevitable, really. You could push him so far then – bam! He'd explode like a volcano. She was just as bad.

He stalked over to the window and flung it open to let fresh air into the stale room.

'What the fuck's the matter with you? You're acting like you're dying, so why don't you call a doctor?'

She could tell that he was hurt more than anything. Who wouldn't be with the way she was behaving? But instead of saying sorry she shouted back.

'Thanks for the sympathy. I've got a stinking headache and all you can do is yell.'

Tears dribbled down her cheeks but, of course, she didn't say why. He claimed she was shutting him out, then accused her of being obsessed with Luke, and that really set her off because he was right, but not in the way he thought.

'Stop trying to control my life,' she screamed. 'I don't want to live with you any more.'

His face fell and she thought that he might burst into tears. She hated what she was doing to him, but she hated herself even more.

'Babe,' he said, suddenly quiet. 'This is stupid. Why don't we—?'

'Get out, for God's sake! Just leave me alone!'

She lay on her stomach, her face buried in the pillow, and heard him hurl something across the room that hit the wall. When she peered round, he was smashing a chair leg against the paintwork. 'See what you made me do?'

'Stop it!' she cried, and he whacked the wall once more before storming out and slamming the door behind him so hard that the walls shook.

Of course she hardly slept that night, hoping he'd come back but knowing that he wouldn't. He'd have gone to his mum's to cry on her shoulder. Thank God she was there because he was going to need her. As she lay there, feeling the darkness pressing down, tears welled up yet again; she'd wept so often that you wouldn't think she'd have any left. She couldn't bear to think how much Jesse would detest her if he found out the truth.

She shivered, picturing Luke's bright blue eyes that she'd once found so mesmerising, his smooth skin, the gold cuff-links on his crisp designer shirts. She'd once measured him up against Jesse and had found her boyfriend lacking, and she couldn't believe that she'd been such a fool. It was too late now. Everything about Luke had become ugly and tainted, including The Stables and all those tasteful things in it that she'd marvelled over, wishing that she had the style to pick them out herself. Only little Oscar still gleamed bright like a star, but Tabitha was a different matter.

Loveday balled her fists, not sure whether to get up and punch the wall like Jesse, or wail. She assumed that Tabitha must be involved, too, which meant that every kind smile and word had been fake. Perhaps even that scene in the car park had been staged, to win her sympathy or something. Loveday had adored their chats and confidences; she'd even flattered herself that they were friends, yet all along Tabitha had been buttering her up to make her do exactly as she wanted.

As daylight filtered through the thin curtains, she got up with a sigh. Time was running out. No doubt Liz would be round again soon with Robert, probably, anxious to find out what was going on. And what if Tabitha called by, or even Luke himself? If she wasn't back at work on Monday, he'd want to know why.

She rose slowly and went to the wardrobe, fishing out a big black suitcase, the one that she'd used to bring her clothes here when they'd moved in. She and Jesse had been so happy then, almost unable to believe that they had their own place at last. Life had seemed pretty near perfect. How rapidly it had gone sour! Whatever happened to her, at least she was going to keep him out of danger.

She threw in what she could – bras and knickers, socks, jeans, sweaters, make-up; her waitressing clothes, she might need those. She thought of one more thing and guiltily slid open the drawer containing Jesse's T-shirts. He had three white V-necks, almost identical, and she took one, hoping that he wouldn't miss it. She held it to her face and it smelled of washing powder – and him. Quickly, she plonked it on the other things and tried to zip up the bulging suitcase, but it was too full so she dragged it to the floor and sat on it, working the zip around.

It wasn't easy and she caught her left forefinger in the metal teeth, drawing blood. The sharp pain made her wince and she stuck the finger in her mouth. No time to search for a plaster now. She was about to carry the bag out when she noticed her stripy zebra, propped up against the pillow beside Puff, the pink and yellow dragon. She paused for a moment then grabbed Puff with her injured hand, stuffing him in her fabric shoulder bag because there was no way she was going to open up the case again.

In the kitchen, she found a pen and an old leaflet advertising story time for toddlers at the local library; she'd picked it up for Oscar, thinking he might enjoy it. She was going to miss that little boy. On the back of the leaflet she scribbled a quick note. It was for everyone, really. Jesse, of course, and Robert, Liz, Rosie and all her other friends in the village. It had to be final, leaving no room for doubt. There was so much to say, so it was easier to say practically nothing at all:

'I've gone away to start a new life. Don't try to contact me. Please send my love to Pat and tell her to get better soon. Loveday x'

She left it on the worktop by the microwave, where she knew it would be found, along with her mobile phone, from which she'd hurriedly erased the content. She'd dispose of her bank card later, so she couldn't be located that way, and borrow what she needed. Then she dragged the case down the stairs and waited.

Ten minutes later, the unlicensed cab arrived and parked a few metres up at the end of the street. The driver was an Indian guy who ran a corner shop near one of the Plymouth nightclubs that she used to go to, and he did a bit of ferrying on the side; he'd given her his number when she popped in once for chewing gum and she'd figured that he was a good choice because he wouldn't want to be traced.

It was very early and the street was silent, save for an old man putting out an empty milk bottle. He didn't see Loveday or the driver, carrying her suitcase in the opposite direction towards the car. As they moved off, Loveday gazed out of the back window, keen to soak up every last detail of the little village that she'd made her home and in which she'd been so happy.

Her very last view was of Tremarnock's higgledy-piggledy rooftops, some with smoke curling comfortably from skew-whiff chimneypots. They reminded her of warm kitchens and loving company, laughter and cups of tea. Would she ever be back? She had no idea. She forced herself to turn towards the windscreen, the road ahead and whatever future lay beyond.

The upstairs flat at Jack's Cottage stood silent and empty for two nights, but no one noticed. As it happened, the tenant downstairs was away, too, visiting his girlfriend in Gunnislake. He was a self-employed plumber, on the road a good deal, and it often suited him to stay at her place because it was more accessible. Truth to tell, he was hoping she'd ask him to move in and he wasn't much interested in Tremarnock any more, or the two young people; he wasn't even sure he'd recognise their faces.

While he and his girlfriend lay in bed, listening to the church bells summoning the faithful to the Sunday morning service, and luxuriating in the fact that they didn't have to go anywhere, Jesse was clutching the TV remote, flicking aimlessly through channels at his mum Karen's house, and contemplating his own unhappiness. Karen had been doing her best to put a smile on his face, but he missed Loveday and didn't know how to patch things up. If only someone would wave a magic wand to make it all OK again. If only he were better with words, like Luke...

Jesse had turned up, white-faced and weepy, at his old home in the early hours of Friday morning and Karen had welcomed him in with open arms. She could tell that he didn't want to talk – she was brilliant like that – so she'd made hot chocolate and they'd sat and half watched an old film until his eyelids had been drooping, then she'd made up the bed in his old room and he'd fallen into a deep sleep.

It had been hard, going to work on Friday and Saturday, and Robert must have realised something was up because he'd kept looking at him to check that he was all right, but Jesse had pretended not to notice. After all, Robert was Loveday's uncle and he was bound to take her side. Families were like that.

On Saturday morning, over breakfast, when his little brother, Finn, had already gone to football practice, Jesse and Karen had had their first proper chat and she'd been super-sympathetic. Now, though, she was getting fed up; you couldn't blame her.

'For goodness' sake, stop moping,' she said, standing at the living-room door, her arms crossed. 'Go and see her and sort it out.'

Jesse flicked the channel again and turned up the volume. It was something he'd done as a boy and it had always driven her mad. The house was filled with the smell of bacon that she'd cooked for breakfast, along with sausage, fried egg and beans, a Sunday morning ritual.

'I want to play X-box!' Finn grumbled, trying to grab the control himself, but Jesse held it above his head so that he couldn't reach it.

'She doesn't want to see me,' he said, not looking at Karen because he didn't want her to see his bloodshot eyes.

Karen snapped at Finn, 'Get dressed – now,' before sitting down beside her big son and patting his knee.

'Look, love,' she said gently, 'I've told you, there's not a couple in the world who haven't fallen out. I know it feels like the end of the world, but sulking won't make it better. You two need to talk and it's your day off, so you've got the perfect opportunity. Why don't you swallow your pride and go to the flat? She's probably desperate for you to make the first move.'

Jesse pulled a face, remembering Loveday's cruel words.

'She's the one who should apologise, she's been a complete cow. Anyone would think she's the first person to have flu and I don't even think she's been that bad. She's making it up—'

'Hush,' Karen interrupted. 'There must be something else bugging her, but you won't find out unless you ask. You can be the bigger person.'

Jesse considered this for a moment. He was very close to his mum, who'd mostly been on her own since his dad had left when he was four. She'd had one boyfriend since, and Finn had been born when Jesse was fourteen, but his father had been a waste of space, too, and soon it had just been the three of them. Karen had always been there for Jesse and now was no exception.

'Have a shower then head on over,' she coaxed, sensing that she might be getting through at last. 'It's still early, she should be in now.'

Jesse flicked off the TV and rose, stretching. 'You're right.' He was trying to sound nonchalant but felt as if he had a bag of frogs in his stomach. 'Will you be round later – in case I need to come back?'

Karen smiled. 'Of course, love. I've got a pile of ironing upstairs like you wouldn't believe. I'm not going anywhere today.'

'Hello?' He walked gingerly into the front room, half expecting Loveday to leap out from the kitchen or behind the sofa, screaming abuse. She could be a wildcat when roused. When he couldn't see her he went into the bedroom, noticing the broken chair and dents in the wall and glancing away guilt-ily; he shouldn't have done that.

The bed had been made up tidily and there were no clothes strewn across the floor or socks, pants and bras drying on the radiator. Swiftly, he bent down and picked up the pieces of chair and shoved them at the top of the wardrobe underneath some towels, not wishing to be reminded of his bad temper.

He checked the loo – empty – listened at the bathroom door and, realising there was no one there, opened it and walked in. Everything was the same, yet different. There was that familiar, musty smell because the extractor fan didn't work, and his blue towel was hanging beside her pink one on the rail, which was dry. He bent down and checked the bathmat; dry too, and there was no water in the basin either. You didn't need a detective to tell you that she hadn't been in here this morning.

When he noticed that her toothbrush was gone, his heart started to pitter-patter. He opened the wonky cabinet where she kept her make-up to find that the pink plastic bag covered in fluffy kittens was missing, too. She never went anywhere without that. Perhaps she'd moved out, gone back to live at her friend's mum's place, or with Liz and Robert. Or maybe there was another man.

Jesse swallowed, feeling sick, as the image of Luke swam into his head. He remembered how one of his mates had been cheated on and he'd pitied him, wondering how he'd been stupid enough not to notice what was under his nose. He'd never thought Loveday would do it to him, though, not in a million years. There again, Luke was some competition.

Emptiness washed over him, followed by blind fury that made him want to punch Luke in his stupid, smarmy, grin-ning face, but what good would that do except break his mum's heart? It wouldn't bring Loveday back. He groaned, as the reality of losing her sank in. He loved that girl; he'd thought they'd grow old together.

He walked into the kitchen, dreading finding some clue there: an empty bottle of wine and two glasses? A strange pair of boxers in the washing machine? His eyes fell on a piece of paper on the worktop and beside it Loveday's white phone in the pink case covered in gold hearts. He used to tease her, saying it was silly, but now it made him miss her more.

Picking up the paper, he focused on her big, messy, un-joined-up handwriting and tried to make sense of what was there. She'd gone to start a new life, but where, and with whom? He checked her phone, thinking it might tell him something, only to discover that she'd returned it to the manufacturer's settings.

Anger welled up again, and hopelessness, and he banged his forehead on the worktop until his eyes stung. Then he replaced the note and, with her mobile still in his hand, wandered into the front room and slumped on the sofa.

He felt paralysed with indecision, too frightened to call anyone, not even his mum, imagining that the whole world knew she'd left him and was laughing behind his back. He wrapped his hand round the phone tightly and stroked the keys, imagining Loveday's fingers. She was so quick, she could tap out one of her soppy messages to him in no time at all, using those silly emoticons that made him smile.

Would Luke really have left his wife and son to go away with her? And what about his business and that secret work he'd been doing that no one, not even Jesse, was allowed to ask about? A new emotion engulfed him – fear. What if she wasn't with Luke at all and something had happened to her?

He sprang up, tucking her phone in his back pocket, left the flat and walked swiftly down Fore Street towards the harbour, looking left and right, hoping not to see anyone he knew. Further down, a chubby man in a grey suit was standing outside the empty Hole in the Wall pub, brandishing a set of keys, accompanied by a younger, taller man with a ponytail, in jeans and a khaki jacket: a potential buyer? They weren't interested in Jesse.

His stomach lurched when he reached The Stables and he almost turned round and retraced his steps, but that would be cowardly. Taking a deep breath, he took hold of the old iron knocker and banged loudly once, twice, three times before taking a step back. He'd done it now. It wasn't long before the heavy oak door swung open. Tabitha appeared and Jesse quickly scanned her face for evidence.

She didn't smile, though that wasn't unusual, but neither did she appear upset. Her dark hair was tied back, businesslike, and she was in jeans and a white shirt, rolled up at the sleeves. Jesse glanced down and saw Oscar peeping out from behind her leg, fixing him with inquisitive brown eyes. In his hand was a red plastic car that he brandished proudly. To be honest, it all seemed quite normal.

Jesse opened his mouth to speak but nothing came out, and Tabitha raised her eyebrows. How could he ask if her husband had left her for the nanny? What form of words could he use to make it sound all right? He was saved by none other than Luke himself, who came striding down the hallway towards them, grinning widely, arms outstretched.

'Jesse, my good man! Come on in! What brings you here? How's our Loveday? Feeling better, I hope?'

Bewildered, Jesse followed Luke to the kitchen, passing the guests eating breakfast in one of the reception rooms, past the helper, Shelley, looking like a frightened rabbit, with a large jug of orange juice in her hands.

'Tea, coffee – or something stronger?' Luke asked, checking the expensive gold watch on his wrist. 'Or is it too early for that? We've been up so long I've lost track of the time.'

Like his wife, he was wearing jeans, and a blue and white striped shirt, open at the collar, and his hair was damp and slicked back, as if he'd just come out of the shower.

'Nothing, thanks.' Jesse frowned and Luke stopped smiling.

'How can I help?'

'Do you know where Loveday is?' Jesse cursed the wobble in his voice as he explained in rapid sentences about the note. 'She didn't say where she was going and she hasn't taken her phone.' He pulled it from his pocket to show them. 'Did she tell you her plans?'

There was a pause when no one spoke and Luke's face clouded over, then he stroked his chin thoughtfully.

'How odd.' He fixed on his wife. 'She didn't say anything to you, did she?'

Tabitha shook her head slowly.

'Wait a minute.' He tapped her hand several times as if restarting a clock. 'Didn't she tell you she was bored of Tremarnock? I'm sure that rings a bell.'

Tabitha hugged her arms around her and stared at the floor. 'I think she might have said something like that.'

Shelley had reappeared and was frying eggs on the giant silver cooker. Jesse was sure that she must be listening, but her back was turned and it didn't show.

'I'm so sorry,' Luke sighed, above the sound of hissing fat, the steam rising from the hot pan. 'I thought she liked working for us and Oscar will miss her badly – we all will.'

He shifted from one foot to another, before gazing at the younger man with bright blue eyes.

'Was everything all right? Between you and Loveday, I mean?'

The question seemed to come from nowhere and Jesse flinched, as if the other man was shining a torch in his face.

'Fine.' He wasn't going to say that she'd frozen him out all week, or that they'd argued; it was no one else's business.

Oscar whimpered and Tabitha picked him up and hugged him close. She looked anxious and the corner of her mouth twitched in a strange way. 'Should we call the police?'

Luke drew himself up tall and his face and neck reddened. 'Absolutely not.' Then, softening, 'I mean, it's not up to us, is it? That's a decision for Jesse and Loveday's family.'

Jesse shuddered, remembering. 'I have to tell them, they don't even know yet.' And with that he turned on his heel and let himself out into the cobbled street, which now seemed strange and hostile. Even the air felt different – sharp, grey and unfamiliar. He longed to be older and wiser and wished that someone would tell him what to do. Most of all, he just wanted his girlfriend home.

Chapter Sixteen

It was Rosie who answered the door, still in her nightclothes and clutching Mitzi, who peered at Jesse through the folds of her mistress's pink dressing gown.

On seeing him, the girl's greeny-grey eyes, behind her pale blue glasses, opened very wide, and a hand flew up to cover her face. For a moment he was confused, until the cat jumped out of her arms, the hand dropped down and he realised that she was trying to disguise an angry red spot on the side of her nose. Some other time he might have found it endearing, but not today.

'Are Liz and Robert here?' he asked, and Rosie followed him into the toasty front room where the fire was lit and the pair were sitting at either end of the sofa, leafing through the Sunday papers, mugs of coffee on the floor beside them. Liz was in a skimpy white nightie, Robert a navy robe, and their bare legs met in the middle, wrapping round each other like vines.

'Look at us, such slobs!' Liz exclaimed, swinging her legs down and narrowly missing her drink. You could see the outline of a neat baby bump through the cotton gown. 'We don't normally slouch around like this.'

'Yeah, yeah,' said Rosie, standing at the door, crossing her arms. 'Sometimes Mum doesn't get dressed at all on Sundays.'

'And why not, if you don't have to work?' Robert scratched his head. 'Speaking of which, I'd better get my show on the road. We've got a party of eight arriving at twelve forty-five.' He looked at Jesse. 'You're off today, right? How's Loveday? Any better? Got any nice plans?'

Jesse shuffled miserably.

'What's up?' said Robert, and Liz signalled to Rosie to make herself scarce.

She pulled a face, Liz mouthed, 'Go,' and a moment later the door clicked shut.

Now that the three of them were alone, Jesse, unable to hold it together any longer, buried his face in his hands. A tissue was produced from somewhere and when he was seated and had composed himself he started to explain what had happened.

'I thought Luke and Loveday might have gone off together, but they couldn't have, could they, if Luke's still home?'

Robert shook his head.

'And she told Tabitha she was bored of Tremarnock, but she never said that to me. I don't understand.'

His mouth trembled; he pretended to cough and Liz put a comforting hand on his knee.

'She seemed the opposite of bored,' she said, puzzled. 'She was thrilled with the job and the flat – and living with you. Why would she lie to us?'

'It's bizarre,' said Robert, rising to fetch the phone. When he opened the door, Jesse caught sight of Rosie out of the corner of his eye scuttling down the hallway.

They could hear Robert next door, pacing on long legs round the kitchen, first telling the boys at the restaurant that he'd be late then talking to his sister, Sarah.

'Calm down… Are you sure she hasn't left a message? Have another check…'

They looked up expectantly when he returned but he shook his head. 'Sarah says they haven't spoken for two weeks. Like the rest of us, she thinks it's very out of character.'

He stopped pacing suddenly and Jesse wondered what was coming next. 'Did you and Loveday have an argument?'

That question again. Jesse inhaled sharply.

'No, nothing like that.' His mum had talked to him about respecting women and he shouldn't have thrown that chair.

Robert seemed satisfied. 'Right,' he said, straightening up, 'I'm going to have a word with Luke myself. You two call around her friends, everyone she knows. That friend she was living with before, the postman—'

'Nathan,' Liz interrupted. Robert was hopeless with names.

He went to fetch his coat from the hall then came in again, zipping it tight and turning up the collar.

'Do you think we should call the police?' Liz's voice cracked for the first time.

'Not yet.' Robert patted Jesse's shoulder. 'Don't worry, you know how impulsive she is. My guess is she's got some mad idea into her head and she'll soon realise she's missing you and come home, tail between her legs.'

He laughed, trying to lighten the atmosphere, but it didn't work. Rosie, who'd crept in quietly, sneaked into her mother's arms and snuggled up close.

'D'you think she's all right?' she asked, looking first at Jesse, then Robert, then Liz.

'Of course,' Liz replied, giving her a squeeze. 'She'll be back in a day or two, wondering what all the fuss was about.'

'But what if she's not?' said Rosie.

*

245

By the time Robert returned from The Stables, Liz and Jesse had either spoken to Loveday's friends or left messages. In reality there weren't that many to contact; she hadn't travelled much beyond Cornwall and had only kept in touch with a few people from her childhood. No one had the faintest idea where she could have gone. Jesse wanted to see his mum to fill her in, and promised to return soon. Meanwhile, Rosie and Liz got dressed at last.

'What did the Mallons say?' Liz asked Robert, cornering him in the hall the moment he walked through the door.

'Nothing much.' He kissed her lightly on the lips and she and Rosie followed him back to the front room, where he slumped on the sofa. 'They were both under the impression that she enjoyed her work.' He rubbed his stubbly chin; he hadn't yet shaved. 'Luke did mention one thing, though.'

Liz's ears pricked. 'Yes?'

'He said he thought Loveday and Jesse were having problems.'

'Really?' Liz, sitting opposite her husband, leaned forward and rested her elbows on her knees. Rosie was perched on the arm of the chair beside her. Liz knew that the couple were hot-headed, Loveday especially, and that they'd had a big bust-up a couple of years ago, when they'd been dating first time round. But they had been younger then and less sure of their own minds, and since they'd got back together and moved into the flat they'd been like a pair of lovebirds.

'She didn't tell me anything about it – and neither did Jesse.'

'No,' said Robert, knitting his brows.

'Where did Luke get that from, then?'

Robert seemed distracted and she wasn't sure that he'd heard so she poked his leg with a finger.

'Luke said Loveday had a heart-to-heart with Tabitha,' he

explained at last. 'You know they get on very well. Loveday was quite upset and said Jesse frightened her.'

Liz sat back and crossed her arms. 'Nonsense. I don't believe a word of it.'

'Nor do I,' chipped in Rosie, who'd been as quiet as a mouse up to now. 'There's no way she's afraid of Jesse, she'd have told me. We talk about everything.'

The phone rang and Robert rose to answer it, returning to inform them that Sarah and her estranged husband Andy were on their way from Penzance by car. Liz took a deep breath; Sarah wasn't the easiest person, but she, Liz, would have done the same under the circumstances.

'Where will they sleep?' she asked, and Robert said he'd prepare the spare room while one of them would have to take the sofa. Then Rosie announced that she had a rehearsal.

'On Sunday?' Liz was surprised, but her daughter explained that they needed to fit them in whenever they could.

'You don't mind, do you? I'll stay if you want me to.'

Liz shook her head. It was probably better if she escaped the anxious atmosphere for a few hours; it wasn't as if there was anything she could do. After she left, Liz went to find her husband, who was standing by their bedroom window, gazing at the street below.

'I rang the police,' he told her, as if continuing a conversation he'd been having with himself. 'They said we should wait forty-eight hours and if she doesn't contact us, they'll make enquiries. The problem is, she's nineteen and won't be classed as high priority. And she left a note stating her intentions. They seem to think she'll turn up anyway. Most do.'

He turned to face her and she stared, noticing the strained expression, the deep lines around his mouth and eyes that hadn't been there earlier. 'Oh, Robert, you don't think—?'

'Something doesn't feel right, Lizzie. This conflicting information, Luke saying one thing, Jesse another.'

The blood rose to her cheeks and started pumping in her ears, her temples, so that she felt as if her skull might burst. 'I've known Jesse half his life. He'd never touch Loveday and I'd trust his word over Luke's any day.'

Robert stood very still, his tall frame and broad shoulders silhouetted against the light. 'You're completely wrong about Luke.'

Liz's eyes narrowed. She'd never argued with Robert, not in all the time that they'd been together, but she could let rip now.

'No, *you're* completely wrong,' she shot back.

The arrival of Sarah and Andy a couple of hours later only seemed to increase the tension, because Sarah was in a terrible state and practically collapsed into Robert's arms.

'My baby,' she was saying, 'where's my baby?'

Andy, a short, stocky man of about thirty-five, stood back awkwardly while she soaked Robert's shirt in tears.

'She's been like this all the way,' he told Liz. 'I said crying won't do no good but she won't listen.'

Liz put the kettle on while Robert did his best to calm his sister down. Liz had only met her a handful of times but had quickly gleaned that she wasn't very good at coping. In the early years, after their parents had died, Robert had had to manage for them both, then Andy had taken over as best he could. Now that he and Sarah were getting divorced, however, he seemed to have lost whatever skills he might once have possessed and was useless in the eye of the storm.

They sat at the kitchen table and went through everything

again, though Liz wasn't convinced that Sarah was listening. She had a box of tissues in front of her that she was pulling out one by one and shredding, before squishing them together and plonking them in a messy, wet heap on the wooden surface.

She was quite different from Robert in looks as well as personality; about five feet five inches tall and well covered, her blonde hair pulled back and fastened with a plastic clip. She was wearing a baggy white T-shirt over black leggings, and Robert was looking at her with such love and concern that Liz's anger cooled a little; he was extremely fond of his sister, warts and all.

Jesse returned from seeing his mum and it was quickly decided that he, Robert, Liz and Andy would go to the flat and have a hunt around. Maybe Loveday had left a receipt somewhere, a postcard, anything that might indicate where she'd fled to. It was better than doing nothing, for sure.

'I'll come too,' said Sarah, and Liz thought it was ironic that the very first time she'd see the place was when her daughter was missing from it. Still, she'd been going through a difficult time.

News travelled fast and by now, it seemed, the whole of Tremarnock had heard, so it took a while just to reach the bottom of Humble Hill. Jean, who was in her front garden, hung over the gate, trug in hand, soon to be joined by Tom.

'What a shock!' she said, shaking her head. 'I told Tom I hadn't seen her since the week before last when she popped in with Oscar for a cuppa. She was fine then, full of the joys of spring.'

Tom offered to accompany them to the flat, but Robert said no. 'There's enough of us, and it's only small.' Meanwhile, Jean said she planned to visit Pat in hospital and Liz asked her to pass on a message. 'Tell her I'll come again as soon as I can.'

There was a cry and, turning, they saw the imposing figures of Audrey and Esme hurrying towards them. They were both tall and Audrey was wearing a long, bright green coat with black frogging up the front, while Esme, in her trademark navy fisherman's smock and flapping purple skirt, was waving frantically, her wispy grey hair flying round her face.

'I heard about it from Rick,' Audrey said breathlessly, drawing to a halt beside them. Is there anything we can do, anything at all?'

Liz thanked her but said not for the time being, and would have walked on had not Tony and Felipe appeared, shrouded in gloom.

'Young people go missing all the time,' Tony said mournfully. 'Most reappear but some are never found.'

'In Rio, is fifteen people missing every day,' added Felipe. For once, Tony didn't correct him. 'Many of them are murdered. They burn them so no one knows what's happened. Just gone. Pfft.'

'Well, nothing like that's happened to Loveday,' Liz said firmly, taking Sarah by the arm and starting to lead her purposefully up the hill. When they were out of earshot she whispered in Sarah's ear. 'Felipe's very sweet but he's talking rubbish. Tremarnock's not Rio de Janeiro, no one's been murdered and we'll soon have Loveday home.'

The empty flat seemed cold, dark and unwelcoming and at first everyone wanted to read the note that was crumpled and still sitting on the worktop where Jesse had left it. Sarah then wandered around, sighing like a lost soul, while the others set to, opening every drawer and cupboard, checking on shelves, behind photographs and under rugs, sofa and chairs.

Robert called to Liz from the bedroom. 'Can you come here?'

She found him standing in the middle of the floor, staring

at the right-hand wall, where there was a gash in the pale yellow paintwork and chunks of plaster had come away.

'It wasn't like this before, was it?'

'We were trying to move the wardrobe.'

They turned to find Jesse right behind them, chewing on the corner of a nail.

Robert frowned and knelt down to look under the bed, the chest of drawers, beneath the pillows, leafing through the pile of books on the side table and holding them upside down to see if anything was hidden inside the pages. Meanwhile, Andy flung opened the wardrobe and took out a pile of Loveday's clothes on metal hangers, placing them carefully one of top of the other on the bed.

'Can you see what she's taken with her?' he asked, and Jesse went through the clothes carefully, pointing out the missing things. When he'd finished he bent down to pick something up and called out: 'Look!' He was holding a stuffed zebra that had fallen on the floor beside the bed. 'I think she's got Puff, that fluffy dragon thing. His face crumpled. 'She loves Puff. She wouldn't go anywhere without him.'

'It's a good sign,' Liz said gently, 'it must mean she's safe.'

Robert inspected the room one more time and noticed the pile of towels on top of the wardrobe. Stepping over, he reached up and pulled out several pieces of wood, which he placed on the floor in front.

'They look like chair legs,' he said, glancing at Jesse. 'What are they doing up there?'

'The chair broke,' Jesse replied quickly, 'I haven't got round to fixing it yet.'

Robert removed another leg, which had split in two, turning it round and round in his hands, like a master carpenter. 'I don't think you could mend this, it's too badly smashed.'

Something about his expression made Liz angry again. 'Why are we discussing an old chair? Surely we've got better things to do?'

After replacing everything carefully, they left the flat in silence, and Liz's heart sank when she spotted the tall figure of Luke, in a smart navy raincoat, talking to the landlord of The Victory Inn at the other end of the street. There was no getting away because Luke saw them, too, and started walking quickly towards them. He wanted to know if they'd found anything at the flat, before going on to explain that he'd been making enquiries of his own.

He glanced back at the landlord, who nodded, then leant towards Robert and asked for a word in private. Liz reluctantly walked away. Just before rounding the corner, she looked over her shoulder to see the three men huddled close together, their heads almost touching, and pricked her ears, hoping to pick up a few words. Unfortunately, though, their voices were so low that she couldn't catch anything at all.

Jesse looked exhausted and Liz suggested that he go back to his mum's for the night. It was getting on for 6 p.m. and it had been a long day.

'There's nothing more you can do now. I'll call if we hear anything.'

'I still can't believe it,' he said miserably. 'I keep hoping it's a bad dream.'

He looked so lost, and far too young to be carrying this weight on his shoulders. Liz gave him a hug.

'Try and get some rest. Who knows? She might call us in the night.'

'Do you think so? Really?'

She nodded, but now that she'd seen the half-empty flat and read the note for herself, she was full of doubts. It was important, though, to try to keep spirits up, including her own.

Andy and Sarah took their bags upstairs; having opted temporarily to put aside their differences and share the comfy double bed; neither fancied the sofa. Meanwhile, Liz stood at the hob, frying some mince and onion for a spaghetti Bolognese. She didn't suppose that anyone was hungry but they'd need to eat, particularly Rosie, who had school tomorrow.

Rosie. She started, realising that she'd virtually forgotten about her daughter, who hadn't yet returned from the rehearsal. Liz wondered whether to drive to school to find her, until she realised that it would be shut today and Rosie hadn't said whose house she was going to.

She was about to grab her phone when Robert arrived with Rosie herself, having met her on the doorstep.

'How was it?' Liz asked, thinking that her daughter looked tired and awfully pale, though her eyes were sparkling.

'Great. The director was really happy.'

'I can't wait to see it.'

Rosie lifted the lid off the spaghetti Bolognese, bubbling on the hob, and sniffed. 'That won't be for *ages*. We still needs loads of practice.'

She vanished upstairs, leaving Robert and Liz alone, and he perched on the edge of the kitchen table and cleared his throat. The landlord, it seemed, had heard Loveday and Jesse rowing late on Thursday night. Their bedroom window had been open and they'd been shouting and screaming.

Andy and Sarah appeared at the door and stood, listening quietly, as he went on.

'Then there was a noise, like a big bang, followed by some

thuds. Apparently Jesse yelled, "See what you made me do," then everything went quiet.'

Liz's brain started racing, trying to process what she'd heard. 'So did the landlord call on them to check they were OK? That's what I'd do.'

'He thought about it, then decided it was none of his business,' Robert replied. 'It was all quite quick and he only remembered when he found out Loveday had gone.'

He looked at Liz, then Andy and Sarah, whose mouth was open, her eyes staring. 'You know what this means, don't you?'

Andy nodded, grim-faced. 'We call the police again – right now.'

Liz felt the hairs on the back of her neck rise as the reality of Robert's words started to sink in.

'They used to squabble like mad at the restaurant,' she found herself gabbling, 'but it didn't mean anything. Jesse just forgot to tell us about the argument, that's all. He's got a lot on his mind.'

But Andy wasn't listening. He balled his fists and growled, a strange, menacing sound that came from the back of his throat. He was a builder by trade and you could see the muscles through the sleeves of his shirt, the veins of his neck bulging.

'If he's done something to our—'

Robert raised a hand. 'Don't jump to conclusions. We must try and stay calm.'

Sarah burst into tears again.

'Leave it to us, girl,' muttered Andy, patting her back awkwardly. 'Once the coppers are involved, I'm sure that lad'll start talking, and if he doesn't, I'll pay him a visit myself.'

Chapter Seventeen

AFTER THAT, EVERYTHING seemed to go into fast-forward. Two police officers arrived to take statements, before visiting Jack's Cottage with Robert and Andy. Liz, Sarah and Rosie huddled together at home, trying to distract themselves with inane chatter, but always returning to the same subject: where was Loveday and why had she gone?

Having done a thorough examination of the flat, the officers concluded that there were signs of a struggle and set about making enquiries around the village, retracing the steps that Liz, Jesse and Robert had taken, calling on Luke and Tabitha, Jean and Tom, Esme, Rick, Audrey, Tony and Felipe and, of course, Jesse himself. In the meantime, their colleagues started to ring round local taxi firms to see if anyone had picked Loveday up.

'If she's gone somewhere, she had to have got out of the village somehow,' the woman police officer reasoned, explaining that they'd also check the bus companies, CCTV footage at the railway station, hospitals and her bank account to see if it had been used.

The minutes seemed to blur into hours and when Liz next looked at the clock it was nearly midnight, way past Rosie's bedtime.

'Go to sleep,' she said, shooing her daughter upstairs. 'You'll be exhausted in the morning.' She was exhausted herself; she could hardly put one foot in front of another. She half expected Rosie to beg not to have to go to school, but she didn't. How things had changed! Only a short time ago she'd have done anything to wangle a day off.

Liz and Robert didn't get to bed themselves till about 3 a.m. and they were far too troubled to sleep. The police would return first thing and had said if they'd no more information and Loveday hadn't rung, they'd start to search the area. Robert lay on his back, staring at the ceiling, and Liz rested in the crook of his arm. There was a light on in Sarah's and Andy's room that she could see through the chink in her door, and she heard one of them go to the loo. They were wide awake, too.

'You don't honestly believe Jesse has anything to do with it, do you?' Liz asked. It made no sense to her; she'd worked with him at A Winkle In Time for years, as had Robert, and neither of them had ever seen a hint of violence in the young man's character.

Robert stroked her shoulder with a finger, drawing imaginary rings in ever widening circles. 'I don't know, Lizzie. Luke says—'

That name on his lips again. 'Stop talking about Luke,' she snapped, shuffling away. 'He's only been in the village five minutes.'

Robert tensed, she could feel him stiffen just a few inches from her side. 'I don't understand why you're so hostile towards him. It's not helpful. In fact, it's embarrassing how cold you are with him. He must have noticed.'

'I don't care what he thinks,' Liz replied hotly. 'He means absolutely nothing to me. He doesn't know Loveday and Jesse like we do, and I don't know how he dares cast aspersions. In fact, I think it's peculiar, the way he's so involved. Really odd.'

'He's being supportive, Liz. It's called community spirit.'

He sounded so patronising; it made her blood boil.

'Oh, for God's sake, Robert, Loveday's *your* niece and Jesse's practically family, too. You seem to be more worried about hurting Luke's precious feelings than you are about them. I can't figure it out. I don't know what's come over you.'

She wanted so much to get through to her husband, to make him see straight, but the air between them crackled and spat with enmity.

'Robert?' she said after a moment, wishing that she hadn't been quite as aggressive; it wasn't the right way to win an argument after all. But he rolled over and turned his back on her, leaving a gap between them that felt wider than the Sargasso Sea.

'Time to get up, Tabitha.'

Luke's voice drifted through her mind and for a moment she thought that she was still dreaming.

'Wake up, Oscar's calling you.'

Her ears pricked. 'Mamma!'

She opened her eyes, noticing the cold, grey light seeping through the blinds, and remembered that it was Monday. It should be like any other day of the week except...

'Mamma!'

The sound of her small son's cheery voice again cut through the bleak stillness. He was generally happy when he woke and that made her smile, too. But not today.

'What time is it?'

'Six thirty.'

Luke's tone was cold and formal; he'd been like that since their argument about the car, despite her best efforts to backtrack. He was keeping her on her toes, she could tell, cracking the whip and forcing her into line. It would be some time before things between them returned to normal. Well, she'd wait.

She swung her legs out of the duvet and padded across the room to open the door.

'I hope Loveday's home,' she said, without looking at him. She'd gone to sleep worrying about her and it would be the same day in, day out until there was good news.

'I'm going over to Robert's,' Luke responded, adding that he'd hang on till after Oscar's breakfast and take him, too.

Tabitha was surprised, because he rarely offered to help. Since last week, when Loveday had gone off sick, she'd had to look after their son as well as the guest house and it hadn't been easy. Now, it seemed, there was no end in sight.

'I suppose I'll have to find someone new,' Luke commented, more to himself than her, and she nodded, thinking him heartless. He seemed very concerned about Loveday in front of others but, in truth, the only person that he really cared for was himself.

She hurried along the landing to her son, almost bumping into him as he raced to meet her. Then she sat him on the bed while she dressed quickly in jeans and a clean white T-shirt before carrying him downstairs.

Shelley was already in the kitchen, fetching eggs, bacon, sausages, tomatoes, mushrooms and fruit juice from the section of the giant fridge that they reserved for guests. She'd gone even quieter since the red-haired lady's dream, as if the less noise she made, the less likely it was that the ghosts would bother with her. Now she went about her work so silently that Tabitha sometimes forgot she was even there.

'Morning!' she said, putting Oscar in his special seat and pouring him some cereal, and Shelley merely nodded.

Luke sat beside his son while he ate, leaving his wife to lay the round table in the breakfast room. It was hard trying to perform normal tasks with a knot in her stomach, and her hands trembled slightly as she took the guests' crockery and cutlery from the heavy mahogany sideboard opposite the window, placed spoons, knives and forks in the right places and folded linen napkins.

As she arranged fresh flowers in a little vase to put in the centre of the table she found herself thinking yet again that she was pretty certain Luke had something to do with Loveday's disappearance, and that it was somehow connected to his Plymouth office and whatever went on there. After all, he'd lied first to Jesse, Liz and Robert and then to the police when they'd spoken to him last night. What's more, he'd made her lie, too.

'Just do it,' he'd told her on the quiet. 'It's what Loveday said to me in the office but it sounds better coming from you.'

She'd opened her mouth to protest but he'd squeezed her jaw so tight that it had made her eyes water, twisting her neck at an angle that had sent sharp pains shooting down the side.

'Repeat exactly what I've said, word for word.'

'Yes, Luke.' It was what she knew best.

She felt an overwhelming sense of dread, yet despite her suspicions couldn't quite believe that he'd harmed Loveday. For a start, he'd been with *her* on Thursday and Friday nights and most of Saturday, around the time when it seemed she'd gone missing. What's more, she was useful to him and surely the last thing he'd want would be to draw attention to himself, having come here to blend into the community and be seen to lead a normal family life?

Perhaps she'd discovered something about him and his business, got scared and run. That thought gave Tabitha momentary comfort, but then the clouds descended again. Suppose he went looking for her – or got someone else to do it for him? He had plenty of 'friends' after all, and was certainly capable of vile acts if he felt that his interests were compromised. Tabitha shuddered, feeling fearful, weak and hopeless and wondering where it would all end.

The smell of bacon and sausages soon brought the first guests down, a middle-aged Australian couple visiting the UK on the initial leg of a European tour. Tabitha hated small talk but they filled the gaps, helping themselves to cereal and fruit juice while they recounted their previous day's visit to Boddinick. From there, they'd walked across hilltops and through woodland and creek to Polruan, before catching the ferry to Fowey.

'There were the most glorious views,' the woman said, tipping milk on to her cereal and adding spoonfuls of nuts, raisins and chopped banana. 'And at Fowey we had our first ever cream tea.'

'Lived up to all expectations,' her husband added, slugging back a second glass of orange juice. 'I'd like to send some of that clotted cream to our folks before we leave Cornwall. They'll go mad for it.'

Tabitha suggested a mail-order shop before taking their requests for cooked breakfasts, and when she returned they asked about the missing girl. They hadn't met Loveday, having only arrived two nights ago, but they'd seen the police in the village.

'What a worry,' the woman said. 'Her parents must be frantic.'

Tabitha made to leave, but the woman wasn't content to

stop there. 'This seems such a safe, welcoming place. Do you think she's run away? But the police must suspect something bad or they wouldn't be here, would they?'

'I've no idea,' Tabitha snapped, then, checking herself, 'I mean, I'm sure she'll turn up soon. She probably just wanted a break, she's a bit like that.'

The other guests appeared in dribs and drabs: a German woman with very short hair and a no-nonsense air; an Irish couple; and a businessman from Nairobi and his daughter, who was at university in Plymouth. The businessman asked if, instead of a cooked English breakfast, he could have rice, potatoes and salad, and Tabitha hurried next door to see what Shelley could rustle up.

Before long, the room was humming with noise and laughter as everyone shared tips and stories. At the same time the phone rang frequently, with people enquiring about accommodation, and Tabitha longed for Loveday, who'd become so adept at answering calls and checking dates on the computer in the study by the kitchen.

When at last the guests had finished, Shelley helped clear away and started on the rooms while Tabitha took payment from the Australian couple, who were leaving, before checking the emails and online bookings. It was almost midday before she could finally scoot upstairs, knowing that Luke would no doubt be home soon, so she'd have to be quick.

She opened the blinds just a chink and checked outside before calling Molly's number.

'Can you speak?'

There was a crash, as if Molly had broken something, then, 'Bugger. I've just spilled coffee all over my desk.' She was silent for a moment before coming back on the line. 'I'm so glad you rang.'

Molly said she'd seen Carl in town and Tabitha's heart missed a beat, as it always did at the mention of his name.

'He was on his own, he didn't see me, but it was definitely him. So he's not in Cornwall, for sure. You're safe.'

Normally, the news would have filled Tabitha with joy, but today it scarcely registered. In short, breathless sentences she explained about Loveday's disappearance, her own lies and fears that Luke was involved. She knew that she didn't have long.

At the end, Molly let out a pained sigh. 'You'll have to tell the truth.'

Tabitha started, almost dropping the phone. 'I can't. You know what Luke would do. He'd throw me to Carl or finish me off himself.'

She expected Molly to agree, but instead she hesitated before clearing her throat. 'Between a rock and a hard place, eh, Tabby?'

Tabitha's shoulders slumped. 'As always.'

'Except that this time someone else is involved – a young girl.'

Tears sprang to Tabitha's eyes and she dug her nails into the palms of her hands, wishing that the pain would wash her misery away.

'Do you think I don't know that, Molly? Do you imagine I'm not ashamed? I have to live with the guilt twenty-four seven. If it weren't for Oscar, I promise you I'd call the police right now – and to hell with the consequences.'

Jesse's mum stood at the door of his old bedroom and wrinkled her nose.

'Shouldn't you be getting ready for work?'

He didn't answer.

The room was pretty much as it had always been – single bed, small desk and chair, a few shelves on the wall proudly displaying his childhood sports trophies, various books on surfing and an assortment of annuals, including the football ones that he'd devoured as a lad.

The only real change since he was small was that Karen had replaced his old spaceman duvet with a plain blue one, and the walls, once covered in posters and stickers, were now painted a neutral shade of cream. It was a right mess today and smelled stale. She was itching to get in there with the vacuum cleaner and furniture spray.

She repeated herself, louder this time, and Jesse took out his earphones. It was after 4 p.m. on Tuesday and he was sitting on his bed, still in the boxers and crumpled T-shirt that he used as nightclothes. He hadn't felt like changing, hadn't felt like getting up at all, to be honest.

'I'll be down in a minute,' he said, plugging the earphones back in and bobbing his head in time to the music that he was pretending to listen to.

He could tell his mum was annoyed, she hated what she called 'slovenly behaviour', but she wouldn't scold him like she used to when he was a kid, not today. She knew he was unhappy and she was being really kind, keeping off his back, bringing him drinks and snacks, but it didn't help, not really. He was glad she was there, though; he didn't know if he could cope on his own.

The police had been round yesterday and again today, a man and a woman, with the same questions they'd first asked on Sunday night, only put in a slightly different way: what was Loveday like as a person? What was her state of mind before she left? How was his relationship with her? They'd kept homing in on the fact that he hadn't been entirely honest about the argument. They were very interested in that.

'Why did you tell Robert Hart you hadn't argued when you had?' they'd repeated this morning. 'Why did you imply the chair had broken by accident and the hole in the wall was caused by moving a wardrobe?'

Jesse had explained that he was ashamed for having lost his temper and hadn't wanted anyone to know, not Luke or Robert, least of all his mum.

'My dad used to shout at her a lot and throw things and I hated it,' he'd said. 'I don't normally yell at Loveday, well, only when she yells first, and then it's usually over really quick and we make up. I've never chucked anything at her in my life.'

'Are you sure you didn't chuck the chair at her on Thursday night?' the policeman had enquired. He'd been very polite, as if it was the sort of thing you'd ask anyone any day of the week, but Jesse knew what he was getting at and it had been all he could do not to holler at him then, out of sheer upset and frustration. Couldn't they see that he wanted her back more than anyone? Didn't they realise he was missing her like crazy, like a hole in the heart?

'Never!' he'd replied wearily, because he'd said it all before. 'I hurled it at the wall and it smashed. That's why there's a dent there.'

'Can you explain why Loveday told Tabitha Mallon that she was frightened of you? Why would she say that if it's not true?'

The first time he'd heard it Jesse had been so surprised he'd honestly thought they might be winding him up, but they'd looked deadly serious. Jesse's mind had started racing but he'd told himself to keep calm. Don't let them rattle you.

'I've no idea,' he'd replied slowly. 'It must have been a joke. I mean, we love each other. I thought I'd spend the rest of my life with that girl.'

The policewoman had scribbled something down in her notebook before smiling at him, as cool as a cucumber.

'Are you jealous of Mr Mallon?'

'Jealous? Why would I be jealous of him?'

'You told Mr Hart you thought he and Loveday were having an affair.'

Jesse felt as if he'd been punched in the stomach because it hadn't been easy for him to admit that to Robert and it was supposed to be private; he'd thought Robert was his mate, well, sort of, as much as a boss could ever be your friend.

He removed his earphones again and switched off the music because nothing, not even loud noise, could distract him from his thoughts. Surely Robert didn't believe...? And what about Liz? He got up and stared at himself in the little mirror above his desk, thinking that he scarcely recognised the person staring back.

He flattened his uncombed hair and tried to pull himself together, reasoning that of course Robert and Liz had felt obliged to tell the police everything they knew. But the knowledge that they'd spoken about him behind his back, and revealed something that could be taken in the wrong way, made him feel alone and scared.

'What made you think they were having an affair?' the police had asked. By then, Jesse had been scarcely listening. He walked back to the bed and punched his pillow hard.

'See what sort of person I am?' he muttered under his breath, 'I punch stupid, fucking pillows.'

He waited a few moments before padding down the corridor to the bathroom because he didn't want his little brother to see that he'd been crying. He'd be upset; he hero-worshipped Jesse.

'Have a good evening,' his mum said as he left the house. 'It'll be nice to see the lads again.'

She was trying so hard to cheer him up but it didn't work. He grunted goodbye before flinging his bag over his back, blinking in the light as it was the first time he'd been out all day.

He hadn't been to work since Saturday, when the restaurant had been chock-a-block and they'd been rushing round like headless chickens. They'd somehow coped without him or Robert on Sunday and yesterday they had been closed. Jesse hadn't been able to do lunchtime today because the police had been with him, but Robert needed him now. The show had to go on.

As he strode down the hill past the Methodist church, he passed a parked police car and two officers knocking on someone's door. It seemed as if the whole place was buzzing with coppers, though in reality there weren't so very many; they were still acting relatively low-key, which must be a good thing because it meant they thought she was OK. They did seem awfully interested in him, though.

He'd offered to help, of course. He wanted to do anything he could. He'd given them photos of Loveday, the name of her doctor and dentist, plus a few of the clothes she'd left behind. It had felt weird, that. They'd sealed off her bedroom so no one could go in, but it didn't bother him because there was no way he'd be returning. The place only held bad memories now. They'd also wanted the names of his previous girlfriends and it had been quite hard to remember them all.

'What were those relationships like?' the policewoman had asked again this morning. 'Did you ever hit any of them?'

Jesse had felt like getting up and walking out, but he'd gritted his teeth. 'I told you, I don't hurt women.'

Jenny Lambert was outside Gull Cottage, searching for something in her handbag, and he thought she spotted him before hurrying inside, but he might have imagined it. In every house, he fancied he saw curtains twitching, eyes watching, people whispering, 'There he is, that's him, Jesse Lacy. The one they're questioning.' He fixed on the cobbled street, looking neither left nor right, and glanced up again only when he heard a shout – 'Oi!' – and turned to find Alex running down South Street towards him in black drainpipes and brothel-creepers, his Elvis quiff bobbing.

'All right, mate?' Alex said, slapping Jesse on the back, who stumbled slightly and almost lost his footing. It was as if his strength had washed away in the past few days, leaving him like a half-uprooted tree that might crash to the ground in the slightest wind. He was pleased to see Alex, though, with his honest, open face.

The two walked the final few steps side by side, Alex's arm round Jesse's shoulders, pressing down. Inside, Jesse was relieved to be told that Robert wouldn't be here till later because he was dreading the encounter; he wouldn't know what to say.

'Sorry about Loveday,' said one of the lads, passing Jesse a black and white checked overall. Was he deliberately avoiding his gaze? It might just be awkwardness. Callum the pot washer was at the sink, peeling spuds, his sleeves rolled up as usual to reveal the naked lady tattoos. He looked up briefly, giving Jesse a nod before continuing with his work. The atmosphere felt cool, despite the smallness of the room and the number of bodies in it, and Jesse felt more grateful than ever for Alex's greeting, because it seemed that others weren't so well disposed. Jesse felt wounded, but what could he do? If their girlfriends had gone missing, he might look at them differently, too.

They worked in silence, Jesse preparing a vat of their popular fish curry, made with sea bass, coconut, tamarind, tomatoes, chilli and other spices, while the sous-chef made mayonnaise to go with the crab. The local fisherman had caught three live lobsters earlier in the day, which were sitting in open cardboard boxes in the fridge, packed with damp seaweed to keep them moist, and they were on the menu, too, waiting for the first lucky customers.

As all the fish was locally sourced, once it ran out, that was that. Most people understood and quite liked the fact that you never knew what would be available from one day to the next or whether, by the time you arrived, you'd have missed some particular delicacy that had been served up earlier; only a few made a fuss and they tended not to return. Robert always said that was a good thing. You had to understand and appreciate the way the restaurant operated or you shouldn't come at all.

Soon the two waitresses turned up and Jesse could hear the clanking of cutlery and chinking of glasses next door. One of them popped her dark curly head round the door to say hello and ask Jesse if there was any news.

'Nothing,' he replied, conscious that all ears were on him. 'Zilch.'

The girl frowned and said, 'I wish I could do something,' before retreating, and Jesse wished that she'd had a few kind words for him, but there had been none.

'She'll turn up, mate,' said Alex, taking pity, but it only seemed to make things worse because no one else joined in.

Several customers wanted the hot shellfish starter with garlic, olive oil and lemon juice, and Jesse enjoyed stirring the mussels, winkles, scallop and oysters, testing the sauce to make sure that it was just so. He liked his job and being busy helped to take his mind off things. However, when Robert walked in at around seven thirty he jumped, as if he'd seen a ghost, and reality crashed back in.

His boss looked harassed, wavy hair tousled, as if it hadn't seen a comb for a while, white shirt crumpled and skin pale. Once upon a time that hadn't been unusual, but since he'd got together with Liz he'd seemed calmer, a different person, really. This was more like the old Robert, unhappy and on edge. He had every reason to be.

'How's it going?' he asked. He was addressing Jesse, but his eyes slid away, resting on a spot near his feet.

Jesse would have answered but Alex got in first with a fake-cheery, 'OK, boss, what's the latest?' He was jumpy, too, and had guessed that Jesse would have trouble responding.

'They've contacted all the local taxi firms now and drawn a blank. No one remembers picking her up. And it turns out the CCTV at Plymouth railway station wasn't working all weekend, so there's nothing there either.'

'Bummer,' commented Callum.

Jesse swallowed. No one had told him this, yet he couldn't help feeling that he should have been the first to hear. After all, Loveday was his girlfriend; he was closer to her than anyone.

'What's next?' he asked, hanging his head and feeling like a fool for having to enquire.

Robert shifted from one foot to another and rubbed his cheek several times as if something was there.

'Media coverage, I think. An appeal for information, though it's still only a few days, bearing in mind we don't know exactly when she went. You were the last one who saw her, of course...'

He looked at Jesse with wide, unreadable eyes and Jesse stopped stirring, the spoon suspended in mid-air. He couldn't help it; he felt cold suddenly, despite standing over a bubbling saucepan.

'No one else has seen hide nor hair of her since Liz went round on Thursday afternoon...'

Jesse looked down at the saucepan and stirred vigorously, willing himself to act normal, not to appear suspicious. He was beginning to feel like he'd done something bad even when he hadn't.

'Personally,' Robert went on, 'I think they should go for all-out media coverage right away, but they have their own method of doing things and they're the experts. We have to trust them.'

Alex attempted to lighten the atmosphere by offering Robert a spoonful of Jesse's fish curry – 'It's perfect' – but Robert shook his head and disappeared into the backyard, so he popped the spoon in his own mouth instead.

'Bad business,' he said mournfully.

Jesse had heard that meaningless phrase a million times in the past few days and something in him snapped. His face and neck heated up and he backed away from the hob and wheeled round, wooden spoon in hand.

'Look,' he said, as everyone turned to stare, 'I know you all think this has got something to do with me. Well, it fucking well hasn't.'

There was a sharp intake of breath and an embarrassed cough, which upset him even more.

'Why don't you just ask outright what I've done with her? Go on, I dare you.' He glared at them in turn, but they wouldn't meet his eye.

'C'mon, Jess, mate, you're upset.' Alex patted his back and

tried to take the wooden spoon from his hand, as if Jesse might launch an attack, but he pushed him off.

'I've got no idea where she is, all right?' he blazed. 'We had an argument, then she fucked off. I never thought she'd do something like that. I miss her so much…'

There was a catch at the back of his throat and he spluttered, as if he'd swallowed something down the wrong way.

Alex spoke again. 'No one said…'

But Jesse had seen the tight faces and he flung the spoon down, splattering sauce across the tiles. Then he ripped off his checked overall and stormed out of the restaurant, ignoring the gawping customers already seated and pushing past a group of others coming through the door.

Tears trickled down his cheeks and he clenched his fists as he stalked back up the hill towards home, realising that he'd left his bag and jacket in the cloakroom, but there was no way he was going back now. His key was in the bag so he had to ring the bell, and when his mum saw his expression she took him in her arms, closing the door quickly behind them.

'What happened, son?' he heard her say, and then, when he didn't reply, 'There, there, you're home, safe and sound. No one's going to disturb us tonight. I won't let them.'

Finn appeared in his pyjamas and, without a word, wrapped his arms round his brother's waist and rested a cheek against his side. The three of them stood like that in the hallway for quite some time, huddled together, an isolated unit, finding consolation in the silence of understanding, comfort in the closeness of their warm bodies. Knowing that it wouldn't last.

Chapter Eighteen

THE NEXT MORNING Jenny Lambert rose at six, leaving her husband, John, still asleep. It was the first of April and sunlight was creeping through a chink in the curtains; she wanted to be out, enjoying her first proper taste of spring.

She dressed quickly in an old pair of jeans and a sweatshirt and pulled her blonde hair back in a scrappy bun. No one would see her at this hour. Then she crept downstairs, past the kids' bedrooms. They were both at college now, doing A-levels, and mightn't be up for a while. Their hours were unpredictable and she could no longer keep up.

When she entered the kitchen, Sally barked joyfully and leaped out of her basket, running round her mistress's feet in circles, wagging her stumpy tail.

'Shh,' said Jenny, bending down to stroke the dog's wiry back. 'You'll wake the others.' But Sally continued yelping as Jenny climbed into her wellington boots, which were by the back door, grabbed her Barbour jacket, and fastened Sally's collar and lead. Then they strolled out together into the chilly morning air.

There were few signs of life, only wisps of smoke rising from the odd chimney, which was just how Jenny liked it. Soon it would be Easter and she always slighted dreaded the annual influx of tourists, filling the streets with their noisy chatter. Of course they weren't all bad and the fishing-tackle shop did its best business from April onwards but, still, peaceful mornings like these were to be savoured.

Her normal route was down South Street to the beach, then along the cliff top to Hermitage Point, from where the view of the ocean was so clear and unspoilt that you felt as if you were standing on the very edge of the world. Today, however, she decided to head past the Methodist church and up the road that led towards the ferry, before cutting down into the dense woodland that was home to thousands of interesting species of trees, wildflowers and fungi. It had been a relatively mild February and March and if she was lucky she might even spot some bluebells.

She loved this time of year, when everything was growing and bursting into life. The air smelled of wild garlic, birds were singing at the tops of their voices, leaves unfolding, and mammals beginning to wake from their winter sleep. The trees seemed to be alive with busy squirrels, and she kept her eyes open for queen bumblebees, seeking nectar and pollen from the spring flowers, as well as frogs, toads and lurking grass snakes.

Sally was in heaven, snuffling around tree trunks and damp, fallen logs and poking her head down burrows, yapping excitedly, as if some rabbit would be foolish enough to pop up just for her amusement.

At one point Jenny feared she'd lost the dog again, so she blew her whistle. The shrill sound echoed around the valley and sent thousands of birds flapping wildly into the sky. She felt guilty for having alarmed them. Sally ignored the summons but reappeared some minutes later with muck on her back, having found something disgusting to roll in. At least she hadn't got stuck down another wretched hole.

They were having such an enjoyable walk that Jenny completely lost track of time. It was only when she heard the church bells strike eight in the distance that she remembered John had asked her to open up the shop as he wanted to get to the bank first thing. He'd be annoyed if she forgot.

Realising that she'd come much further than she'd thought, she decided that she'd better take the short cut up the steep bank to her right and walk back along the main road that led in and out of Tremarnock.

'C'mon, Sally,' she said, feeling for the lead in her coat pocket, and the dog sprang up the overgrown hillside in front of her while Jenny trudged behind.

'Wait!' she called, when Sally's tail disappeared into a clump of brambles, then, more loudly, 'Stop! Heel!'

Of course it was useless. Jenny could hear crunching noises as the dog jumped into patches of vegetation, snapping off twigs and stems, then paused to sniff around before leaping on.

In the distance came the rumble of a van or lorry, making its way to or from the village, and Jenny was frightened that Sally would forget herself and race on to the road.

'Sally!' she shouted, scrabbling around in her pocket once more for the whistle. She was out of breath now, not nearly as fit and nimble as her pet. She blew as hard as she could and waited, ears pricked. Sally seemed to have stopped moving. Good. Perhaps she did have a bit of sense after all.

Jenny was nearly at the top of the bank when Sally yapped again, three short, sharp yips, more excited than before. Jenny knew that sound; the dog had found something. Jenny hoped that she hadn't put up a rabbit or stumbled across one of the unsuspecting wild deer that roamed the countryside and sometimes strayed into people's gardens.

Jenny quickened her pace, pumping her arms and legs and panting heavily. She was boiling hot now and would have liked to throw off her coat and sweater. At last the trees thinned and she spotted Sally just a few yards ahead in a little clearing. She had something brightly coloured in her mouth and was shaking her head to and fro with the object between her teeth, and growling,

'Drop it!' Jenny commanded, but Sally had no intention of giving up her prey, so Jenny bent down and wrestled it from the dog's jaws, smacking her sharply on the nose to show that she meant business.

Damp and soggy as Sally's find was, once safely in her hands, Jenny could see that it was a child's cuddly toy dragon, with a pink head, yellow tummy and purple and pink horns and wings. Dirty and torn, one eye was missing while the other stared at her, black and mournful, and Jenny was tempted to throw it away or hand it back to the dog to finish off completely, but something stopped her.

It could have belonged to any one of the children from around here, who'd perhaps been out on a walk with their parents and mislaid it. Jenny had seen things like it in toyshop windows and knew that it wouldn't have cost much; just a few pounds. No mother would want it back in that condition, surely? It would make more sense to buy a new one.

She looked at it again and it seemed to wink at her with its one glass eye and smile enigmatically. A gust of wind whispered through the leaves, making them hiss and tremble, and Jenny shivered. Pink was one of Loveday's favourite colours. Liz had told Jenny about all the pink items she'd chosen for her new flat; they'd laughed about it, wondering how Jesse would feel. Loveday liked to pretend that she was hard, with her thick, black eyeliner, her bolshie attitude and punky hairstyles, but she wasn't really, she was a softie; wouldn't hurt a fly.

Jenny dug into a pocket and pulled out a plastic carrier bag. Her hand quivered slightly as she dropped the wet toy in and tied a knot. She fastened Sally's lead and kept her close as they walked swiftly back along the road to the village. She was being silly, she told herself. It was nothing, just some kid's lost or discarded plaything, valueless. But Loveday was missing, police were swarming round the village asking endless questions and there was a new air of tension and mistrust. Every little piece of information was important, officers insisted, and Jenny, for one, wanted to do all she could to help.

As soon as she reached home she grabbed for the phone and dialled the number that they'd been given. She was standing in the middle of the kitchen, hadn't even taken off her coat or wellington boots.

There was a pause while the woman at the other end spoke to the supervisor. Would they tell her just to chuck the toy, it was nothing, of no significance? Jenny certainly didn't want to waste their time.

'Someone will be with you straight away,' the woman said. 'Don't leave the house or mention this to anyone until we've arrived.'

Jenny could feel her pulse, which had slowed since the vigorous walk, start to rise again and the blood whooshed in her ears.

'Oh, Sally,' she said to the little dog, who was waiting patiently at her feet to be unleashed. Sally cocked her head to one side and whimpered enquiringly. 'I think we might have found something.'

*

There seemed to be a new, stranger mood in the village and Tabitha sensed it immediately. It was early afternoon and she was on her way to the supermarket, but when she went to fetch her car from the car park there were no signs of police and the place was so quiet that she might have mistaken it for calm. However, glancing left as she passed Dynnargh, she saw Liz, Esme and Jean, huddled together and deep in conversation. Jean's face was grave and Esme shook her head a couple of times while Liz spoke. Tabitha was curious but merely nodded when they looked up and continued on her way.

Later, while she was preparing Oscar's tea, Luke came home in a hurry and said the police had 'found something'.

'What?' asked Tabitha, alarmed.

'Something in the woods, I think.' Luke ran a hand through his floppy fringe. 'Robert said it's gone for analysis. Even he doesn't know what it is.'

'Oh, God.' Tabitha's head started to swim and she clutched the edge of the worktop for support.

'Stop being dramatic, it's probably nothing.' He fetched himself a beer from the fridge.

But he was on edge that evening, she could tell, and drank a lot and barked at Oscar when he whinged, making him cry. He seemed to find fault with everything she did, too: the steak for supper was tough and he only ate half, throwing the rest in the bin; there was no loo roll downstairs, which annoyed him, and even her appearance was wrong. Her hair was frizzy and she was wearing too much 'slap' on her face. She'd only put it on to try to disguise the dark circles under her eyes, and she went straight upstairs to wash it off.

In the end, he disappeared into the study to make phone calls and she hovered outside, her ear pressed to the door, listening while he talked very fast, his voice angry and insistent.

'I don't want... Just a girl... Can't be that difficult... Oh, for fuck's sake...'

Then she heard something that made her heart stop and her mouth go dry.

'Good... Hurry up... Let me know when you've done it...'

His chair creaked and she jumped back, stifling a cry, but the door remained shut so she sneaked away and took herself off to bed where she tossed and turned, plagued by black thoughts. Luke came in much later and he, too, was restless; she could hear his brain whirring. She lay quiet as a mouse, so he wouldn't guess that she was awake, and eventually they must both have fallen into a fitful slumber.

The following morning he rose early and left before breakfast, saying that he was heading to the office because 'some of us have to go to work to pay the bills'.

It was about 8.30 a.m. when the first guests appeared and put in their orders, and while Shelley cooked, Tabitha switched on the DAB radio in the kitchen. Tuning into the local news station, she heard the presenter announce that a woman out walking her dog yesterday had discovered a toy dragon, believed to belong to Loveday, in the woods near Tremarnock. The toy had been sent for analysis and results showed that there were traces of the girl's blood on the dragon's head. A local man, Jesse Lacy, had been arrested in connection with her disappearance.

Tabitha's own blood ran cold. She wanted to scream but instead listened with mounting dismay as the presenter said there would be a press conference at 2 p.m. that day, and police were preparing to undertake an extensive search of the village and surrounding areas using helicopters, divers and sniffer dogs. She turned down the volume a little. Could she hear helicopters overhead already? Her mind flitted to Luke and she wondered what he'd be thinking right now. She was sure that he'd have been listening to the report, too. Had he got to Loveday already? She felt sick. There again, the pink toy had been discovered before he'd spoken on the phone last night. Perhaps she was all right – for now.

Tabitha felt a quiver of hope, then fury bubbled when she remembered the lie about Jesse that Luke had made her repeat. Loveday wore her heart on her sleeve, there couldn't be much that Tabitha didn't know about her, and she didn't for one moment suspect Jesse of having harmed her. Was an innocent man to be condemned and, most importantly, where was Loveday?

She went about her morning chores like a robot, smiling mechanically at the guests, clearing away plates, fetching dishes from the kitchen scarcely knowing what she was doing. Then, just before two o'clock, she sat Oscar on the sitting-room floor in front of her with a pile of toys and a plate of chopped-up apple, and turned on the TV.

It was a shock to see Loveday's parents, Sarah and Andy, sitting solemnly in front of the flashing cameras. Robert was on Sarah's left. Andy looked pale and uncomfortable in a brown tie and white shirt, the collar of which was slightly too big. Clean-shaven, the remaining hair around his bald head cut close, he looked as if he'd spent some time getting dressed and ready, preparing himself as carefully as you would for a job interview. There was something poignant about the way his broad shoulders were pulled back, his chin jutting, as if he'd made up his mind to project an appearance of steely manliness, however he felt inside. He took a sip from the glass of water on the pale wood table in front of him, and his big, workman's hands shook.

Loveday's mother, Sarah, a plump woman of about

thirty-five in a dark, long-sleeved top, was close beside him, their upper arms just touching. Her small hands were resting on the table, clutching a scrunched-up white tissue, and her eyes were wide and darting. Robert, meanwhile, in a pale blue shirt, jacket and navy tie, sat very still and upright, staring gravely ahead.

The cameras clicked, lights flashed and Andy, gazing into the lens, began to speak.

'Loveday, darling, we miss you very much and we want you to come home. Please, sweetheart, if you're watching this, call me or your mum, or Robert or one of your friends, it doesn't matter who. Just get in touch and let us know you're safe. If you're in any trouble, we can sort it out. There's no problem big or small that we can't deal with.' His voice cracked and he shook his head to indicate that he couldn't go on.

Sarah took over. 'Baby girl,' she whispered, fixing on a spot at the back of the room, 'we miss you so much, your cheeky grin, your jokes, even your stroppiness.' She smiled before dabbing her eyes with a tissue. 'It's killing us not knowing where you are. No one's angry with you. We just want to know you're safe.' Then she raised a hand to show that she, too, had no more words and Andy put a comforting arm round her shoulder.

Now it was Robert's turn; the camera panned to his face and he cleared his throat.

'Loveday – that's my niece,' he explained formally. 'She's a bright, bubbly person, full of love and laughter. We can't see any reason why anyone would want to hurt her.' He stopped and took a sip of water. 'No one's seen her since last Thursday night, a week now, and we're desperately worried.' You could tell that it was an effort to keep his voice tight and contained. 'If anyone has any information, however small, please get in touch. We need to find her as soon as possible.'

After that, the scene switched to a street outside the building full of parked cars, people and more cameras. A young male reporter announced that there'd just been 'an emotional appeal' for Loveday's return from her parents and uncle. This was followed by shots of circling helicopters, lifeboats waiting to be launched and uniformed police officers with dogs on leashes, eager to begin their search.

Tabitha snapped off the TV and stared into space, scarcely aware of her son, still playing at her feet. Her eyes were unfocused, her thoughts jumbled, and she found her mind darting forward then back, back, to every encounter that she'd had with Loveday, starting with the very first time that she'd met the girl and commented on her way-out boots.

Tabitha remembered how wary she'd been at first, not wishing to employ Loveday, Luke's choice. Little by little, though, she'd softened, won over by the girl's openness and funny ways. She'd seen through the spiky exterior to the kind soul within and, despite the difference in age, background and circumstances, they'd become firm friends.

Oscar got up and started tugging on the leg of Tabitha's jeans, bored now and wanting attention. She decided to take him for a walk and strapped him into his pushchair, thinking all the while, hoping that something, some useful piece of information might be hiding in the dim recesses of her mind if she could only tease it out, like a winkle from its shell.

She marched swiftly along the seafront, ignoring Oscar's shouts of protest, because he wanted to run about. Outside The Lobster Pot, a group of locals had gathered and Barbara was in the centre, padded red jacket zipped up tight to keep out the chill and clipboard in hand. To her right was a uniformed woman police officer and to her left stood Luke, wearing the smart pale blue suit in which he'd left for work this morning.

Tabitha might have asked him why he was back from the office so soon, but she knew the answer. Barbara was speaking and everyone shuffled aside to make room for her as she joined the group. She soon spotted the faces of Ryan, Nathan and Annie, as well as Tom and Jean, standing behind a double buggy, plus Felipe, Jenny, John and the boys from A Winkle in Time.

Tabitha quickly gleaned that Barbara was co-ordinating a search party of local volunteers, working with the aid of the WPC by her side.

'Lots of people have been wondering what they can do,' she was saying. 'We've all been feeling so helpless, but now we can assist in a really positive way. Police say they need as many feet on the ground as possible to help them cover a wide area. We're going to follow a line of search starting here.' She held up a map and pointed to the open area of fields to the right of the dense woodland where Loveday's toy had been found. Everyone was listening intently; you could have heard a pin drop.

'We'll need to move slowly,' Barbara went on, 'at roughly the same pace and with reasonable spaces between. We'll have help from Dartmoor Rescue Group and Cornwall Search and Rescue Team. Obviously they've got plenty of experience and they'll go through everything again before we start.'

There was a murmur of approval and a man said, 'Thank God something's happening at last.'

Barbara held up a hand to quieten him down. 'Felipe's going home to design some flyers and we need volunteers to deliver them this afternoon and tonight. Obviously we want as many as possible to join in the search. We meet at 6 a.m. tomorrow to begin.'

'I say we should start right away, not wait till the morning.

Surely the sooner the better?' another man shouted. Tabitha craned her neck and spotted Rick, beside the tall figure of Esme. More and more people were arriving now, many of whom she didn't recognise, and there were rumbles of assent: 'Here, here!'; 'Arr!'; 'No point hanging about!'

She could just see Luke over the throng, aware that he was listening to everything that was being said. Close beside him was Sylvia, gazing up in rapt silence, while just behind stood Audrey, jostling for space and craning over his shoulder. Tabitha's lip curled involuntarily. If only they knew...

'It'll be dark by six. Best to start at first light,' Barbara hollered. She could do with a megaphone.

'We've got torches,' Rick boomed. 'She might be injured out there, needing hospital treatment. We can't wait the whole night, we've wasted too long already.'

There were more mutterings and someone yelled, 'Criminal, how long it's taken.'

Barbara, becoming flustered, blew her fringe of her face and opened her mouth, but the policewoman stepped in.

'Rest assured, we're already searching.' She pointed to a helicopter in the distance. 'We've got hundreds of experienced guys on the case and they won't stop through the night. It can be pretty hazardous out there when you can't see what you're doing, we don't want members of the public getting hurt. As Barbara says, we need you guys to start first thing tomorrow. In the meantime, the most helpful thing you can do is recruit as many able-bodied volunteers as possible.'

Her words seemed to have a calming effect and a few folk seemed poised to shuffle off, until Luke stepped forward. His presence, tall and commanding, stopped them in their tracks.

'I'll co-ordinate the delivery of leaflets. Who's willing to help?'

At least twenty people raised their hands, including Sylvia and Audrey, of course.

'Great,' he said, before asking Felipe how long it would take to design and print them. 'I guess we want several thousand.'

'Give me a couple of hours,' Felipe said with a nod. 'I will bring them to your house as soon as they're ready.'

'Perfect,' said Luke, then facing his volunteers. 'Meet me at The Stables in…' he glanced at his watch '…half an hour. That'll give me time to work out a plan.'

'Thank you, Luke,' said Barbara, her equanimity restored. She turned once more to the crowd. 'If you've any more questions, talk to me or WPC Fletcher. Otherwise, see you all at the top of the hill opposite the bus stop at 6 a.m. sharp.'

As folk started to disperse, Tabitha heard Jean say, 'Luke's a star, isn't he? We're lucky to have him – and Barbara, of course.'

'You can guarantee they'll do a good job,' Tom agreed. 'You know what they say? If you need something done, ask a busy person.'

Luke didn't stop to speak to Tabitha when the meeting wound up, didn't even look at her, but strode back in the direction of The Stables, a man on a mission, with Sylvia and Audrey in hot pursuit. One or two people glanced at Tabitha, as if expecting her to follow, but her mind was in turmoil and she needed time to ponder.

She waited for a few moments while Oscar ran on the beach and picked up pebbles, before continuing up South Street past A Winkle In Time. It was nearly 4 p.m. now and she guessed that Robert and the other staff would be arriving soon to start preparing for the evening. She'd only ever eaten there once herself, with Luke, but he popped in quite often.

A trendy young woman in a pink coat with black hair came down the hill towards her before disappearing into the turning to Market Square. For a moment Tabitha thought that it was Loveday, and her heart missed a beat. This would have been the route that the girl had taken every day as she'd made her way to the restaurant to work. How much better things would have been if she'd stayed there, close to Jesse, Liz and Robert!

Loveday often spoke about her time there, gossiping about the waitresses. She'd met the new one through Jesse, and she was OK, but the other girl was fussy and annoying and the one before her – what was she called? Tabitha racked her brains but couldn't remember, only that she was a lazy, stuck-up cow.

Oscar squawked, making Tabitha start. She'd been standing stock-still in the middle of the road, staring through the restaurant's darkened windows.

'Sorry,' she said, staring up again, and the boy stopped fussing and settled down.

There was a sense of busyness, people coming in and out of houses, talking in tense voices about their plans for tomorrow and what they'd need. But for some reason all Tabitha could think of, as she headed towards home, was how desperately she wanted to recall that girl's name – and how important it suddenly seemed to be that Luke didn't find it first.

Chapter Nineteen

THE FOLLOWING MORNING there must have been at least five hundred people at the bus stop, which was perched high on the hill beside a lonely red post box on the road that led out of Tremarnock. On one side was a sharp drop down to dense woodland while on the other, empty fields stretched as far as the eye could see.

The sun hadn't yet risen, the air was cold and folk were dressed in coats, gloves and woolly hats, wellies or walking boots, many with shooting sticks or canes in hand, torches to use in wooded areas, crowbars to flip rocks, or walkie-talkies. Some were hugging their arms around themselves and stamping their feet, puffing out wisps of smoky air as they chatted quietly in the half-light.

Liz reckoned that practically the whole village had turned out, plus others who'd no doubt received a leaflet through the door or heard about the search in some other way. She stayed close to Robert, Sarah and Andy, who was holding his wife's arm as if suspecting that without his support she might stumble and fall. The past few days had taken their toll and she was looking frail and exhausted. She said she'd hardly slept and Liz worried that if they didn't receive some positive news soon, she might collapse.

Robert had asked Liz not to come, saying that it was too much for her and she must be sensible, but she'd insisted. She needed to help and said there was no way that she could hang around at home on her own after Rosie left for school; she thought she'd go mad.

'Why don't you visit Pat instead?' he'd suggested. The old woman was still in hospital, making a slow recovery. Liz felt bad that she hadn't been able to pop in as intended, but was reassured by the fact that Pat's niece, Emily, had visited, and other locals were doing their bit, too. In a way, it was a blessing that doctors were keeping Pat in because with all this going on, Liz couldn't have helped to look after her at home.

Barbara and a few others had set up a centre contact point by the roadside, with trestle tables and bottles of water, snacks, blankets and warm sweaters in case volunteers became cold. There were also chairs for people to take a rest when needed.

A man from Cornwall Search and Rescue Team gave a short briefing and asked everyone to sign the time sheet that Barbara had prepared, so they could keep track of search-party members and make sure no one was out for too long. It was important, he explained, to take regular breaks and eat something. An overtired, hungry or physically exhausted volunteer could miss an important clue and endanger themselves and others, too.

When everyone was finally ready, the first searchers, including Luke, Sylvia and Audrey, stood in a straight line, side by side, and set off together across the damp fields, soon followed by the next wave, keen to ensure that nothing was overlooked. As they walked, some people linked arms while others used their sticks to beat down the vegetation and check for buried objects. Few spoke and there was an air of calm resolve, a determination to establish the truth, whatever it might be.

Liz and her group were in the fifth or sixth batch of searchers, behind Alex and the other boys from A Winkle In Time. Liz had spotted Jesse's mum, Karen, by the bus stop; she'd chosen not to join her and Robert but was walking with strangers instead. Liz understood why, but it made her sad and uncomfortable. Robert didn't even acknowledge Karen and that felt wrong, too.

If she stopped to think too much about what they were doing and contemplate the possibility that they might actually find something, she feared she'd be sick, so it was easier just to focus on the task in hand, keeping her eyes fixed on the ground beneath her feet, never losing concentration for a second.

They worked like this for a couple of hours but could only have covered about half a mile as they were being so methodical. Liz would have continued for much longer had not Luke jogged up and insisted that she take a break. 'It would be irresponsible not to,' he claimed, 'in your condition. The others should only do another hour then they'll need a rest, too.'

She suspected that Robert had had a word with Luke, knowing full well how stubborn she was and that she'd search all day, given the chance. It annoyed Liz to think of the two men discussing her behind her back and, besides, she didn't feel like doing anything Luke asked.

'I'll just have a quick cup of tea,' she told her husband, and Luke strode off to re-join his line while she headed back to the centre contact point. It wasn't easy, as she was going against the flow and had to weave her way in and out, trying not to distract volunteers from their task.

She was weary by the time she reached the edge of the road, and was grateful to see a small huddle of people holding out polystyrene cups for Barbara, Jean and Esme to fill with hot liquid from Thermos flasks. Liz nipped quickly behind a tree on the other side of the road to relieve herself, before joining them.

'Tea or coffee?' Jean asked, passing her a cup. 'You must be ready for one. It's not exactly warm out here.'

Esme pulled up a chair for her, while Barbara wrapped a tartan blanket round her shoulders.

'You must be dead beat,' she said kindly, 'in your state, too.'

'I'm not ill!' Liz protested, but the older woman shook her head. 'Here, let's get you another one.' She tucked a second blanket over her knees and this time Liz didn't complain. As the hot tea trickled down the back of her throat and into her empty stomach, she felt suddenly as if she could sleep for a week. She must be worn out, as much from the emotional stress as the physical effort of searching. After all, she hadn't been out that long.

Soon they were joined by Audrey, who'd tripped on a tree root and fallen. She wasn't badly hurt, just a bit shocked, and had been advised to sit down. She drew up a chair beside Liz and for a few moments they discussed the search and how difficult it was to stay focused.

'My mind kept wandering and I had to drag myself back,' Audrey said, rearranging her artfully mussed pixie-crop. 'It'd be so easy not to notice something, wouldn't it? Thank goodness there's so many of us.'

'Everyone's doing their best,' Liz agreed, 'it's marvellous.' Her eyes clouded over. 'I can still hardly believe it, though, can you? You see this on screen but it doesn't happen in real life.'

Audrey nodded then, leaning towards Liz, 'I say, Luke's terrific, isn't he? A real hero. Getting all those leaflets delivered, rallying the troops, right up there this morning at the front of the queue. That's real community spirit for you. Says he won't stop till they've searched every nook and cranny and I believe him.'

Her face fell. 'That's if *a certain someone* would only leave him alone to get on with it, instead of following him round like a love-sick puppy.'

Liz remained silent. She wasn't blind to the rivalry between Sylvia and Audrey who, like most of Tremarnock's female population, wouldn't hear a word against Luke. She just hoped that Rick wouldn't get hurt.

'There's no sign of *her*, though, is there?' Audrey continued.

'Who,' asked Liz, feigning ignorance.

'His wife, Tabitha. She wasn't at the leaflet meeting last night and, as far as I can see, she's not here now. Don't you think that's extraordinary?'

'Well, she does have a two-year-old,' Liz pointed out reasonably.

Audrey wrinkled her nose. 'You'd think she could find someone to mind him for a few hours, though, wouldn't you? Pat's niece Emily, for instance. She can't join the search because her knee's bad and she's got Pat to look after, but she'd have the little boy, for heaven's sake.'

'Maybe he's not good with strangers,' Liz replied. 'I don't think I could have left Rosie with someone she didn't know at that age.'

Privately, she agreed that it was odd, but then so was everything about Tabitha: her jumpiness; the way she seemed always to be looking over her shoulder; the fact that she was so different from Luke, so withdrawn, yet Loveday had only good things to say about her and heaven knows! She could be difficult to please.

'The poor girl was working for Tabitha,' Audrey persisted,

shaking her head. 'That woman ought to be first in line, doing everything she can to find her. Thank goodness for her husband is all I can say. I can't imagine what he sees in—'

'I'm going back,' Liz said, rising quickly. She turned to Barbara, Jean and Esme, still busy pouring drinks and handing out biscuits.

'Are you sure you're up to it?' Jean asked. 'Don't you think you've had enough?'

'I'll just do another hour or two.'

It was around half past three when she returned to Bag End, thinking that she'd make a casserole with lots of veg. Robert, Sarah and Andy would no doubt be starving when they arrived home and Rosie would need a good meal, too. She was always hungry after school.

Liz hadn't checked her mobile all day and when she looked now, there was a message from her daughter: *'I've got a rehearsal. Back around six. Luv u XX.'*

Liz frowned. She seemed to have seen so little of her daughter since Loveday had vanished and, today of all days, she wanted her close. She was glad that Rosie had the play to take her mind off what was happening, but the director would understand if she left early, given what was going on at home. It had been bleak out there in the fields and frightening, not knowing what they might find, and Liz needed a hug. Besides, no one could accuse Rosie of lacking commitment; she'd been to every single run-through; she hadn't missed one.

Liz rang Rosie's number but of course the phone was switched off. Hopefully, though, the school could pass on a message. Liz strolled into the kitchen, picked up the landline and after two or three rings a grumpy woman answered, 'Marymount Academy, can I help you?'

It was the end of the day and she must be keen to go home,

so Liz kept it brief. 'Do you know which room they're in? Would you mind going to find her?'

There was a pause while the woman consulted a colleague, before coming back on the line.

'We don't know anything about that play here. I'll try the drama department.'

Liz waited, tapping her fingers impatiently on the work surface, until at last the voice returned. It seemed that the head of drama hadn't heard about the production and couldn't help either.

'One of the sixth formers is directing,' Liz persisted, thinking there must be some mistake. 'I assumed they'd be rehearsing at school but maybe it's in a pupil's house. If you can tell me the director's name I can probably find a phone number.'

'I'm sorry,' said the receptionist briskly. 'It's got nothing to do with us.'

Liz hesitated, feeling confused. 'But lots of children are involved. Someone must know something.'

'You'll have to keep trying her,' the receptionist went on, increasingly impatient. 'She's probably gone somewhere with her friends.'

Liz was stung. 'She'd never do that without telling me.'

But she was met with a sceptical silence that made her blood boil, and it crossed her mind that she might have strangled the woman if they'd been in the same room. There was no point discussing it with her further, though, so she hung up and took a deep breath, trying to control the anxious drumming in her chest before she called Rosie again. No luck.

Still telling herself that there'd been a slip-up and for some reason the school wasn't in the loop, she scrolled down her list of contacts to find Rosie's friend, Mandy, who was watching TV. You could hear it in the background.

'I thought she went home?' the girl asked, surprised. 'She was at the bus stop. She should be back by now.'

'She's at a rehearsal,' Liz said uncertainly. 'For *Alice in Wonderland*. Do you know whose house she went to?'

'*Alice?*' said Mandy. 'What's that?'

Liz felt dizzy, as if she were standing on the edge of a cliff, looking down. 'One of the sixth formers is putting it on.'

'I wonder who. No one's told me about it.'

At that moment the penny dropped, and Liz knew for certain that there was no *Alice* and there had been no rehearsals. Rosie had made it all up. Liz's mind began playing tricks, planting lurid images in her head and conjuring frightening scenarios. She raced into the kitchen, the phone still in her hand, and grabbed the class list that they'd all been given at the start of term. Mandy was waiting.

'Is she still friends with Tim?' Liz asked and Mandy said, yes, they were very close. Then, in a small voice, 'I think they see each other outside school sometimes. She might be there now.'

Liz jumped back in the car, her palms sweaty as she switched on the ignition and pulled out of the space in which she'd parked only fifteen minutes or so before. One minute she felt angry and bewildered, scarcely able to believe that Rosie would lie to her, the next, frightened. Tears sprang to her eyes so that she could hardly see the road ahead. She'd thought that she and Rosie told each other everything. How wrong you could be! And why would her daughter lie, when she surely knew that there was no subject on earth they couldn't discuss?

There again... Liz remembered how quick she'd been to condemn Tim and cursed herself for dealing with the situation badly, but she'd only been protecting her daughter and doing what she felt was right. In any case, none of this mattered, so long as Rosie was well. Once back in Liz's arms, she thought that they could work through anything.

She hurtled down the country lanes, passing Barbara, Esme and Jean at the centre contact point en route, but they didn't notice her, and within twenty minutes she'd reached the small town that was separated from neighbouring Devon by a stretch of river. She wove her way through the narrow, dingy streets and on reaching her destination parked a little way up before doubling back on foot via a row of down-at-heel terraced houses. Number 24 was smarter than the rest; neat and well cared for, with a newly painted pink front door and white roller blinds in the bay window.

Liz rang the bell, realising that she hadn't worked out what to say, but there was no time to ponder because soon, a slim, attractive woman with a dark brown bob came to the door, wearing a flowery apron. Tim's mother? A welcoming smell wafted from the house and Liz's tummy rumbled, despite herself; she hadn't eaten for hours.

The woman, of about forty, wiped her hands on her apron and smiled. 'Can I help you?'

'Is Rosie here?' Liz blurted then, ashamed of her rudeness, 'I'm her mother, Liz.'

The woman held out a hand. 'Come in! Rosie's told me so much about you!' A shadow crossed her features. 'Your husband's niece? Have they...?'

'No. Nothing like that.'

Relieved, the woman broke into another smile. 'Thank goodness. For a moment I thought—' She stopped herself again, mid-flow. 'I would have joined the search but I couldn't swap my shift. I only got back from work an hour ago. I can do tomorrow morning, though. I don't start till two.'

Liz followed her down the hall, noticing the carefully arranged family photographs in matching white frames on the cream-coloured walls. She hadn't known what to expect, but it wasn't this, and it was hard to equate what she could see with Loveday's description of the family.

'I'm Debbie, by the way,' the woman said, 'It's nice to meet you at last.' Then she paused at the bottom of the stairs and shouted, 'Rosie, love! Your mum's here!'

Liz, who'd been mentally preparing for a confrontation with Tim, his brother, the mother and Rosie herself, perhaps, felt as if she'd been pricked like a balloon, all her fighting spirit gone. Upstairs there was a scuffling, the sound of a chair being scraped back, whispers – and silence.

'They're so busy, bless them.' Debbie laughed. 'Have you time for a quick cuppa while they finish off? I've just baked a Victoria sponge.'

She guided Liz into the small, white kitchen at the back of the house and indicated for her to sit at the pine table in one corner, while she put on the kettle. A window above the sink looked out on to a small, paved garden that was little more than a backyard, really, with ivy climbing up the walls and assorted ferns in pots. It didn't feel like the home of a hopeless alcoholic with a criminal son.

'Me and the boys have been here almost three years now,' Debbie explained, popping two teabags into mugs. A large, golden cake covered in white icing was cooling on a rack by the cooker. 'I'm divorced, you see. I expect Rosie told you.'

Liz felt her face heat up and said nothing.

'My ex got bored and went off with someone else,' Debbie went on, raising her eyebrows. 'The boys took it badly, especially Mark, he's my oldest. He missed his dad and went a bit wild for a time. Teenagers, you know? But he's over it now.' She passed Liz a mug. 'I was pretty shaken up, too, to be honest, but I'm OK now, too. Moving here was the best thing for all of us.'

She cast her eyes around. 'There's still lots of work to do. The kitchen's all right but the bathroom needs replacing. It'll be an expensive job, though. You've moved quite recently, haven't you? Just up the road from where you were, Rosie said?'

Liz nodded, aware that she must seem odd and unforthcoming, but it was hard to know how to reply. Should she admit that Rosie had fibbed and that she, Liz, hadn't even known she was here? And how could she explain away the fact that she'd banned her daughter from seeing Tim out of school? It was all very awkward.

'Will you have some cake?' Debbie asked, while her visitor sat there, feeling stupid and dumbstruck. 'The icing's not set yet but I think it's best when it's warm.'

She cut two large slices, one for herself and one for Liz, and settled down on the opposite side of the table. The sleeves of her pale blue sweater were pushed up, revealing strong white arms.

'I gather you've a baby on the way.' She nibbled on a corner of cake. If she was surprised by Liz's lack of conversation, she didn't show it. 'Rosie's very excited.'

Liz took a bite herself, but the cake got stuck and she spluttered, making tears run down her cheeks.

'Lord!' said Debbie, springing up and slapping her on the back, 'Are you OK?'

Liz coughed once more, the cake dislodged and she swallowed it down, indicating that she was all right. It was only when she'd had a few sips of tea, though, that she managed to compose herself enough to speak at last.

'What is it they're doing up there?' She attempted a nonchalant smile.

Debbie gave her a funny look. 'Working on the website. It's such a great idea, isn't it?'

'Er, website?' Liz stared at her fingernails, feeling even more of a fool.

'You mean you don't know?' Debbie sounded thoroughly confused.

They were rescued by Rosie and Tim, who entered the kitchen and hovered by the cooker. Tim was staring at his feet and at the sight of her mother Rosie looked ready to throw up with nerves.

'We're doing a website for school kids with disabilities in Cornwall,' she blurted, pulling at the sleeve of her jumper. 'It's called *You're Special*, spelled U-R-Special, and it's aimed at anyone under fourteen. Mark's friend – that's Tim's brother, Mark – showed us what to do. It's got useful links and people post their problems and we get back to them. If we can't help because we don't know enough, we try to find people who can.'

Tim shuffled miserably from one foot to another. 'We wanted to h-help children like us,' he stuttered. 'Not just kids with cer-cerebral palsy or s-s- stammers.'

Debbie came to his aid. 'Mark and I monitor it very carefully, to make sure there's no nastiness. Tim and Rosie felt there was too little out there for young people, you see. There are plenty of organisations, but at times you just want to chat to someone going through the same thing. Most of the questions are about bullying, but there's also stuff about siblings or parents. One boy was even complaining about his hamster!'

Liz glanced at Rosie, who was twisting the hem of her navy

school sweater round and round a finger. Her thick fair hair was pulled back in a ponytail and wisps had escaped around her pale face. She looked thin beside the more robust Tim, and very anxious. Liz's heart melted.

'What a fantastic idea!' she said. 'I'm proud of you both.'

Rosie's relief was almost palpable and she clasped her hands against her chest.

'Do you think so? Do you really? I would have told you, only—'

'That's all right,' Liz interrupted, keen not to reveal any more than she had already. 'I'd love to see the website, but it'll have to wait. We need to get home.'

She finished her tea and cake quickly and told Rosie to fetch her things, before thanking Debbie for all she'd done.

'Maybe Tim can come to ours one evening and I'll make supper?'

Debbie smiled. 'I'm sure he'd like that, wouldn't you, love?' The boy nodded shyly. 'But there's no hurry. We enjoy having Rosie here. She knows she's welcome any time.'

Liz and Rosie were silent for a while as they drove home, watching the rain pitter-patter on the windscreen and the wipers creak from side to side. Liz guessed that her daughter was expecting fireworks, but she was in no mood for recriminations; she needed time to reflect. She'd learned something new about herself today and didn't like what she'd discovered. It was as if someone had held a mirror to her face and a mean, prejudiced person had stared back.

No doubt Tim's brother Mark had got into trouble at one stage, and Debbie herself might have gone through a bad patch. However, Liz hadn't bothered to question why, and was angry with herself for having been so quick to accept gossip as fact and condemn without evidence. What's more, she'd failed to listen to her daughter, who'd turned out to be a better judge of character than she was.

She remembered how it had been when she'd arrived in Tremarnock all those years ago, wounded after her break-up with Rosie's father. She must have seemed so shy, brittle and defensive, dodging questions about her past, eager not to give too much away. Locals might have kept their distance but, instead, they'd accepted her for what she was and taken her to their hearts, yet Liz had failed to show the same warmth and generosity of spirit. She was ashamed of herself.

Now, she understood perfectly why Rosie had felt the need to lie; in fact, Liz had pushed her into it. Rosie believed in her website, she knew it was a good idea and that Liz was wrong to ban her from seeing her friend.

'I'm sorry,' she said suddenly. 'I shouldn't have jumped to conclusions about Tim's family. Loveday only showed me a fraction of the picture. I should have looked at the whole canvas.'

'It's OK,' said Rosie, 'I know you were concerned—'

'That's no excuse.' A painful lump lodged in Liz's throat and she tried to swallow it down.

'Don't be upset.' Rosie put a hand on her knee, which only made her want to cry more. 'I shouldn't have made up that story about the play. I'm sorry too.'

'You were very convincing, I'll give you that. Maybe you should consider a career as an actress after all.'

She gave a wry smile and Rosie couldn't help smiling back.

'Tim's really nice, you'll like him, Mum.'

'I'm sure I will.'

'Can I show you the website later? I think it looks really good, quite professional.'

'I'd like that very much,' Liz replied.

Chapter Twenty

ROBERT REVEALED THE news at around nine thirty on Sunday morning when he returned from the grocery shop: 'Jesse's been released on bail.'

'What?' Liz had just sat down to catch up on RosieCraft, having sorely neglected the business this past week. Many of her orders were late and she needed to email clients to apologise. If they didn't understand, tough; they'd simply have to cancel.

The search was still under way. Andy and Sarah were up there now and Robert was planning to go along shortly, but Liz's back was aching and she needed a break. Some locals had already decided to stop due to sheer exhaustion, as well as work and other commitments; you couldn't suspend your life indefinitely.

'How do you know?' Liz asked, anxious to be sure that her husband had his facts right.

'I saw Luke. Apparently Jesse's just left the station.'

'Thank God.' Liz bent down to stroke Mitzi the cat, who was coiling round her ankles. 'I can't imagine what he must have gone through – and his mum. She must be so relieved.'

Robert made a low growling sound, like a caged animal. 'They've searched his house, his computer, his clothing, the bins, everything, and he's been told not to leave the area. Luke thinks they're convinced they've got their man, but there's not enough evidence.'

Liz shot her husband a look. 'Evidence of what? That he's a murderer? Oh, for goodness sake, Robert, Jesse's innocent, you know that as well as I do.'

Robert shook his head. 'I'm just not sure. The argument, his lies, that toy, the blood...'

Liz wasn't listening. 'Besides, why are you assuming Loveday's dead? There's no body, thank God, and I still think we'll find her. We have to believe it.'

Robert cleared his throat. 'She hasn't touched her bank account and Luke says—'

'Luke seems to know everything.'

She glared at her husband, who plonked the carton of milk and loaf of bread that he'd just bought on the kitchen table. 'What's that supposed to mean?'

The cat snaked round and round Liz's legs a few more times before settling at her feet. 'Haven't you noticed how he's always first to volunteer for things, he's always got the latest information? Don't you think it's odd?'

Robert ran a hand through his hair, making it stand on end. 'Not this again. Loveday was working for him, no wonder he feels responsible. We'd be exactly the same if one of the lads went missing from the restaurant. Or the girls. We'd do everything we could.

'I feel sorry for Luke,' he went on. 'He looks exhausted and he's on his own now. You'd think his wife would give him more support.'

Liz raised her eyebrows. 'Where's Tabitha, then?' It was the first she'd heard of it.

Robert made a face. 'Manchester, apparently. Gone to see

a friend. Left first thing this morning and taken Oscar with her. Extraordinary.'

Liz shrugged. It *was* peculiar, but she was reluctant to show any sympathy for Luke. In fact, unlike most of the village, she was more inclined to feel sorry for his wife, though she wasn't at all sure why.

She glanced at Robert and couldn't help noticing that the deep lines around his eyes and mouth had become a permanent feature. He seemed to have aged in the past few days; they all had. In fact, she could hardly believe it was only a week today that they'd discovered Loveday's note; it felt more like ten years. She wanted to reach out and touch her husband's hand, to hold him in her arms and bury her face against his warm chest, but she couldn't. He was wrong about Jesse, and she was disappointed in him for losing the faith.

'I don't blame Tabitha,' she said suddenly. 'I'm not sure I could stand being in the same room as Luke for more than five minutes, let alone live with him. I don't trust him an inch.'

She watched Robert's gentle face harden, his hazel eyes turn cold, and realised that she'd gone too far. He considered Luke a friend after all, and despite everything she should have been more careful. He was at his wits' end, just like her, a pressure cooker waiting to explode.

She opened her mouth to apologise, but he jumped in first. 'For crying out loud, Liz, I don't know what's the matter with you. Are you jealous or something, because they're richer and more glamorous than us? Because their house is bigger and they've got expensive cars? Is that it? I never had you down as a jealous person.'

Liz's mouth dropped open; it was so unfair. She would have defended herself, she would have said he surely knew her better than that. But before she could speak he'd turned on his heel and left the room, slamming the door behind him.

Jesse felt quite dazed as he stumbled up the street towards the bus stop, and he blinked several times, his eyes not yet accustomed to the light. It had been gloomy at the station and he felt as if he'd been in there far longer than seventy-two hours.

The town was usually bustling with people and cars, folk wandering in and out of shops, young mums with pushchairs chatting on the pavement, elderly men and women shuffling up the street on their way to the supermarket, bank or post office. Today, though, he saw only a handful of children loitering round the closed toyshop, and a couple of smartly dressed pensioners on their way to church, perhaps, or to see friends.

It seemed bizarre that normal life could continue when for him nothing was the same or ever would be again. As the pensioners passed by, he imagined them whispering to each other, 'That's the one, that's him!' Everyone, it seemed, had found him guilty without trial, and there was nothing he could do but clutch pitifully onto the smallest branch, waiting to crash and fall.

He was physically and mentally shot, permanently exhausted and the slightest noise made him jump. Even the skin on his hands and arms felt different, as if the merest prick would draw blood. Did the bus driver refuse to meet his gaze when he took Jesse's money? It certainly seemed so. And the woman he sat next to, with a baby on her knee, shuffled away so that there was no chance their bodies might touch. Perhaps she thought he'd contaminate her.

He alighted from the bus before the Methodist church,

thinking it was just as well that his mum lived away from the village centre, as it was less likely that he'd see anyone. As luck would have it, however, Nathan was pushing his bike up the hill towards him.

He wasn't in uniform today, but was wearing jeans and a pale blue T-shirt, no coat; he didn't seem to feel the cold like other people. There was nowhere to hide, so Jesse pretended to look at his phone, noticing out of the corner of an eye how Nathan clocked him and crossed to the other side of the road, pausing just a moment to wait for a car to pass.

Nathan had once dated Loveday and for a time relations between him and Jesse had been frosty, but they'd since made up and become friends. Jesse swallowed. Friendship didn't seem to count for much these days. Other than his mum and brother, no one seemed to believe in him, not even Robert. Alex was all right, but you could tell he wasn't sure, and Liz was very kind, but it was difficult for her because of Robert.

Nathan was almost parallel with him now, just a few yards away, and when he started whistling, fake-nonchalant, Jesse cracked. It was as if all the anger, hurt and injustice that had been bubbling for days burst to the surface, and he found himself running across the street, fists clenched, scarcely aware of what he was doing, unable to stop anyway.

'Say it to my face,' he snarled, shoving the other man roughly on the shoulder.

Nathan staggered slightly before righting himself. 'What the—?'

'Say I murdered Loveday. Go on. I know that's what you think.'

Nathan shook his head and tried to continue pushing, but Jesse blocked the way.

'Don't fuck with me. It's all right when you're in the gym,

flexing your stupid muscles, but where's your strength now, eh? Too scared to fight?'

Again, Nathan tried to proceed. 'Look I don't want—'

'Come on.' Jesse pointed to his left cheek and hopped, fists raised, from one foot to another like a boxer, 'show us what you're made of. You can tell the girls you laid one on Jesse the murderer. They'll love you for it.' He laughed nastily. 'You'll be a fucking hero.'

'What's going on?'

Jesse looked over Nathan's shoulder to see Tom walking towards them, followed by Jean. Tom was older than his wife and grey now, not as fit as he used to be. Even so, he was doing a good job of trying to look manly, his shoulders pulled back and head held high. Jean, meanwhile, in beige slacks and a green cardigan, was several steps behind, gazing on anxiously.

Jesse was fond of Tom and Jean; he'd known them all his life. They were like everyone's aunt and uncle and used to give him money for sweets. Tom had occasionally fixed his bike when he'd been a boy and Jean had come out of her house once and put a plaster on his knee when he'd fallen and grazed it.

She looked afraid and he felt ashamed and his anger melted as quickly as it had arrived. 'Sorry,' he mumbled, before scooting down the side of the church out of view. He waited, crouching by the wall and hidden by some bushes, while he heard the others talking, and didn't come out until he was certain that they'd gone. He couldn't risk bumping into anyone else so he crept, like a fugitive, across the cemetery and round the backs of houses, until he reached the safety of his mum's front door.

She and Finn were out; he hadn't rung to tell them that he'd been released, hadn't wanted to talk to anyone. He wandered from room to room, feeling the silence pressing down on him so that he could hardly breathe. He would have thumped Nathan if Tom hadn't appeared, split his lip, broken his nose – or worse. He fancied he could hear the muttering if he'd done it, from people he'd grown up with, that he'd loved and had felt so safe among – big hairy Rick, loud, cocky Tony, even sweet old Pat, recovering in hospital. 'What do you expect,' they'd have said, 'from someone like him? He's a bad sort, a wrong 'un, best keep well away until they get him under lock and key.' Would he go to jail for something he hadn't done? For all he knew, the police were simply biding their time, waiting for him to crack.

He drew the curtains in his little bedroom, climbed under the duvet and closed his eyes, praying for sleep. If he were in prison, he couldn't feel less like a free man than he did now. It seemed, to him, as if there was nowhere to run, nowhere to hide. Only the thought that Loveday might still be out there somewhere, waiting, hoping to be found, stopped him from getting up and searching the house for the means to end it right there and then.

Robert had gone out – who knew where? – and Liz had no idea what to do with herself. She could ring, of course, and apologise, but he'd said a terrible thing to her and she wasn't at all sure that she could forgive him, never mind the other way round.

She sat for a while in their sitting room, which had once seemed cosy and welcoming and now felt stark and cold. They'd spent so many hours in here, curled up in front of the open fire, when she'd truly thought that they couldn't be any happier. Yet now she wondered if that contentment had been an illusion and even as he'd stroked her hair and told her how much he loved her, ugly reality had been pushing on the door, determined to force its way in.

Tears trickled down her cheeks and splashed on to her chest before dripping on her round bump. Poor baby, she thought, running a hand over the swelling. Was he or she destined to grow up with an absent father, as Rosie had? Right now, Liz couldn't see how they could row back from this; it seemed, to her, like the end.

She felt butterfly wings beating softly in her womb, the baby stirring, and was reminded of how she'd felt when Greg had left. Somehow, heartbroken as she'd been, she'd managed to pick herself up and keep going, and if she'd done it once, she could do it again. She was a survivor and must go on, for Rosie's sake as well as for this new child cradled deep within her.

Sighing, she forced herself up and went to the downstairs cloakroom to wash her face with cold water and brush her hair. The little mirror above the basin showed a pale, blotchy woman with red-rimmed eyes, but if anyone noticed they'd think that she'd been crying about Loveday. She hesitated in the hallway for a moment after putting on her coat, thinking that she should leave Robert a note to say where she was, then she remembered, opened the door quickly and stepped into the fresh air.

It was her mother, Katharine, who'd always said that the best cure for the blues was to get out and do something. It had irritated Liz when, as a grumpy teenager, all she'd wanted was to wallow in self-indulgent gloom, but over the years she'd come to realise that it wasn't such bad advice.

She hadn't visited Pat since Loveday had vanished, and the old woman seemed delighted when her friend appeared at the door of the hospital ward, clutching a bunch of yellow roses that she'd picked up at a service station.

'Oh, my!' Pat cried, her pale, lined face lighting up in a brave smile. 'What a wonderful surprise!'

She was propped up in bed against a pile of white pillows with a pink shawl round her shoulders, her right arm in plaster almost up to the shoulder. Although Liz had seen her like this before, it was still a shock because she looked desperately frail, so unlike the doughty old woman of before.

The mobile stylist was doing her rounds – Liz had spotted her in the corridor outside – and Pat's snowy hair had been beautifully curled, but it wouldn't fool anyone. She'd lost weight, you could see, her cheeks had hollowed out and her blue eyes no longer sparkled.

As Liz drew nearer, the brave smile faded, too. 'Whatever have you done to yourself? Sit down. You look half-dead!'

Liz instantly felt her shoulders sag and the corners of her mouth start to droop. It was no good, she was a hopeless deceiver.

'I'm sorry,' she said, kissing Pat's prickly cheek as she handed her the flowers and perched beside her on the bed. The old woman took a sniff – 'Gorgeous, thank you' – before fixing Liz with a fretful stare.

'I didn't mean to bring you my worries,' Liz went on, raising her voice so that Pat could hear. 'I meant to come and cheer you up.'

'Me? I don't need cheering up,' Pat said unconvincingly. Even her voice sounded weaker. 'Everyone's been so kind. Look!' She gestured with her good arm to the table beside her, on which were arranged boxes of chocolates, a bowl of grapes, a pile of books, get-well cards and several more bunches of flowers in assorted vases. 'I've been spoiled rotten.'

'How lovely!' said Liz, opening one of the boxes. 'Would you like one?' But Pat pulled a face. 'Don't seem to have much appetite, to be honest with you. You help yourself.'

But Liz wasn't in the mood either, so she put the box away.

'I still can't believe I was that stupid,' Pat went on sadly. 'Gullible, that's the word. A silly old fool. All that money.' She shook her head and tears sprang to her eyes. 'I mean, I know it wasn't much by some people's standards, but it was a lot to me.'

Liz passed her a tissue and she blew her nose. Seeing her friend in this state made her furious. It wasn't just the broken arm, though that was bad enough, it was the fact that she'd had such a terrible fright. It wasn't fair at her age. It seemed as if all the stuffing had been knocked out of her.

'I hate those people,' Liz growled. 'They deserve to be shot.'

Pat leaned forward a little and patted Liz's hand with her own good one. 'Lord help us! Here's me going on about my problems and you must be worried sick about Loveday. Any news?'

It was typical of the old woman to think of others, even at a time like this.

'Nothing,' said Liz, fishing a tissue from the sleeve of her top and blowing her own nose. 'Everyone's pointing the finger at Jesse and the police arrested him, but I know he wouldn't touch her. I feel so sorry for him and his family, it's horrible.'

''Course he wouldn't hurt her,' Pat muttered. 'What nonsense!'

'Even Robert thinks he's guilty. I'm afraid we argued about it this morning and now we're at daggers drawn, and I don't think he'll ever speak to me again.'

'Poor lamb, and in your condition, too. I'm not surprised things are a bit tense, considering the strain you're both under. It's enough to make anyone flip their lid.'

A man came by with a tea trolley and Pat indicated that she'd like two cups. 'And two sugars for my friend here, she needs it.'

Liz took the drink gratefully, her hand trembling slightly as she put the cup to her lips, while Pat watched thoughtfully. 'What exactly was the argument about, then? What was it that made Robert lose his rag?'

Liz rested the cup and saucer on her lap and started to detail the conversation about Luke. Before she'd had a chance to finish, however, Pat shifted more violently than would have seemed possible a moment ago, almost knocking over both their drinks, and managed to heave herself a little up the bed.

'That man!' she croaked, and several people in the neighbouring beds turned to stare. 'I knew he'd have something to do with it. Why your husband doesn't listen to you instead of him I'll never know.'

Liz smiled, grateful for the solidarity, though she wished that Pat wouldn't tire herself.

'Never liked Luke,' the old woman continued hotly. 'Too smooth by half, and Loveday shouldn't have ever gone to work for him. Big mistake.'

She bobbed up and down and Liz told her to be careful, fearing that she might injure herself again.

'It's all right, Robert knows—'

'If I wasn't cooped up here I'd go round myself and give him a piece of my mind.'

She flopped back on the pillows, exhausted with the effort, then took a deep breath and said more softly, 'Your first proper ding-dong, was it?'

Liz nodded miserably.

'I thought as much. I remember when I first rowed with my Geoffrey I thought my heart would break. But when you love each other as much as we did – and as much as you two do – you get through it, and believe it or not, you come out all the stronger.'

Liz thanked Pat for the advice and was about to say goodbye, thinking that she'd done quite enough talking, when one of the nurses bustled over to announce that more visitors had arrived. 'You're quite the popular one today!'

Hovering by the door just a few metres away was Annie, in pink jogging bottoms, trainers and a grey sweatshirt, her blonde hair tied back in two plaits. Beside her stood Nathan and just behind them was a fragile-looking elderly woman, clutching on to Annie's arm.

'I've brought my gran to see you,' Annie explained, ushering the old woman towards the bed. 'I thought you'd like to meet her. She lives in Devon and the same thing happened to her – she was tricked out of her savings.'

Pat's eyes widened. 'Oh, I don't think… I wasn't expecting… Look at the state of me!'

'She's not well enough,' Hazel muttered to Annie. 'It was a nice idea but—'

Liz thought there was something peculiarly touching about the old woman who, though bent and hesitant, had taken a great deal of trouble with her appearance. Her short white hair was neatly combed and she had on just a shade too much blusher. On her top half she wore a neat, peacock-blue blazer with gold buttons, and below it a pale blue skirt and shiny white patent court shoes.

'How rude I am! Take a pew!' Pat said suddenly, and Liz was relieved that she wasn't going to shoo the visitors away immediately.

'Hazel,' the old woman said politely, stepping forward to shake Pat's good hand. 'I've had a bit of a trauma, same as you, but I'm feeling a little better now.'

Liz jumped up and Hazel glanced at Annie, who nodded at her to take the seat beside Pat's bed.

'You see...' Annie smiled '...you're not the only ones. It's happened to dozens of people.'

She turned to Liz and lowered her voice. 'Gran feels so dreadful, partly because she thinks she was stupid. She can't believe she fell for it. I've tried to tell her it's going on all over but she won't believe me. I thought if they talked to each other it might help.'

'Nice one,' Liz replied warmly. 'Better to get angry together than sit there on their own, feeling like victims. As long as they don't wear themselves out, that is.'

'We won't stay long,' Annie reassured her.

Liz left the two old women recounting the sorry details of their experiences while Nathan and Annie listened in. As she reached the exit she heard Pat cry in a surprisingly strong voice, 'The rotten scoundrel, I'd like to wring his neck!'

'Scumbag!' Hazel retorted.

'Language, ladies!' said Nathan, mock-shocked, but Liz didn't catch anything more because she was halfway down the corridor, smiling to herself and thinking that Annie's idea might just turn out to have been a very good one indeed.

Demi, that was the name of the annoying waitress. Demi, like the actress. She was lazy and arrogant, Loveday had said, but they'd kept in touch even so. Now Demi worked at some trendy bar in London. When Tabitha racked her brains some more she found that could even remember the name: Violet's, in East Sheen.

'East Sheen's not central London,' Loveday had explained over a cuppa one afternoon, 'it's on the outskirts, but you can get into Leicester Square and that quite easily. There's loads of buses and trains. She's been to some of the famous nightclubs. She's invited me to stay but I won't go. I'd like to see London, but not with her.'

She'd sounded impressed, she couldn't help it, and Tabitha had suspected that she harboured a secret admiration for Demi, however much she might try to deny it.

'You should go,' Tabitha had said. 'London's great. You'd enjoy it.'

'Nah,' Loveday had replied, a little too eagerly, 'she just wants to show off.'

Tabitha hadn't mentioned this to anyone, not Liz or Robert and certainly not the police; Luke had eyes and ears everywhere. Instead, she'd texted him on the train from Plymouth to say that she'd be staying with Molly for a few nights, because she needed to 'get away', and Molly had promised to cover for her if need be, though Tabitha hadn't said what she'd be doing.

Luke had responded immediately, furious, of course, spitting mad, ostensibly because he'd have to cancel their bookings and lay Shelley off, but Tabitha hoped he'd be so caught up in the investigation that she'd have a day or two's grace at least before his guys would come looking, and she felt reasonably safe from Carl, too. It wasn't long since Molly had seen him in Manchester after all.

Tabitha had only visited London twice in her life, once as a child when she'd been with her family to a dull religious convention, and another time with Luke. He'd taken her there for a long weekend before Oscar was born, and they'd stayed somewhere near Marble Arch and visited many of the tourist sites, including Buckingham Palace and the London Eye.

She remembered eating in fancy restaurants and seeing a

West End show. They'd either walked or hailed black cabs, so she'd never before used the underground, which she found hot, confusing, crowded and not at all convenient with a toddler in tow. Somehow or other, however, she'd managed yesterday to manoeuvre Oscar and his pushchair on to a train to Richmond, and from there it had been only a short walk to the small hotel that she'd booked in a different name in such a hurry that she'd forgotten to mention she'd have a two-year-old with her. Fortunately, it had turned out to be an ideal choice: friendly and relaxed, with a pretty garden and easy access to the shops and the river Thames.

Oscar had slept with her in the double bed last night, and they'd eaten breakfast in the restaurant this morning. He was finding it all a huge adventure. Now, as he stood at the washbasin, waiting, open-mouthed and obedient, while she cleaned his teeth, she outlined their plans for today. It was likely to be a long one and she needed to keep him sweet.

'We're going to travel on a big red bus,' she said eagerly. 'We'll sit upstairs where it's really high, and we can watch all the people and cars going by down below.'

Oscar would have spoken but there was too much tooth-paste, so he hopped up and down instead.

They left the hotel at around 11 a.m. and walked, hand in hand, to the bus stop, Tabitha pushing the empty stroller with the other arm. It was a fine day and the place was humming with noise and activity. Some workmen in fluorescent yellow jackets were standing around a hole in the road, one operating an ear-splitting drill, and he nodded as she and Oscar passed by. At the same time a cyclist in a helmet and Lycra shouted something as he swerved to avoid the safety barriers, narrowly missing a red car in the process and eliciting gasps from onlookers.

Tabitha could sense Oscar's wonder and apprehension and she felt it too, because it all seemed a world away from Tremarnock. She'd forgotten what giant, bustling cities were like and realised, with some surprise, that she rather missed the light and peace of the village, though not her husband.

She was wearing anonymous jeans, trainers and a green waterproof, and had pulled her mass of black hair back in a tight ponytail, but she wished that she'd brought sunglasses and a baseball cap, too. There again, she didn't want to look as if she had something to hide.

They had to wait about ten minutes for the bus, but the journey itself sped by because Oscar was happy gazing out of the window, pointing at the sights and making comments, and she enjoyed watching him. He was particularly taken with a fire engine that hurtled past, siren on and blue lights flashing; you didn't see many of those in Tremarnock.

'Nee-naw,' he cried, standing on her lap to get a better view, his eyes wide with amazement.

The bus jolted, he tipped forward and before Tabitha could prevent it he'd grabbed the black scarf off the lady's head in front.

She spun round, looking daggers at them both. 'You should keep him under control.'

'I'm sorry,' said Tabitha, handing the scarf back and thinking that the woman needn't be as sharp. It had been a mistake after all, and Oscar was only little. It occurred to her that folk in Cornwall would have been rather more forgiving.

On arrival, Oscar objected to being strapped in his pushchair so she had to bribe him with a packet of biscuits from their hotel room that she'd shoved in her pocket for emergencies. Her courage seemed to fail as she approached the address and spotted the sign, 'Violet's Cocktail and Wine

Bar', in round, girly letters above the door, so she crossed quickly to the other side and pretended to look in a shoe-shop window.

When at last her nerve returned she swung back round, only to realise that the lights in Violet's were off and the white door was firmly closed. Had the place shut down? Her spirits sank, until she realised that it might only be open at night and she kicked herself for not having checked on the website. Taking a deep breath, she crossed the road again and read the sign in the window that said it was open from 5 p.m. to 11.30, Tuesday to Sunday. Today was Monday. Damn.

She thought of Luke and her heart fluttered. Should she go home now, pretend that she'd been missing him and couldn't bear to be away after all? He might never find out what she'd really been up to and it was probably a wild-goose chase anyway. But the idea of Loveday, still alive, perhaps, but in grave danger kept her strong. Hopefully she, Tabitha, had covered her tracks carefully enough. She gave a deep sigh.

'Come on, Oscar, off we go, back on the big red bus.'

He didn't object; it was all still a great novelty.

As they waited at the stop, she stared back at the bar, willing it to give up its secrets, but it remained empty, mysterious and silent. There was nothing for it but to return tomorrow.

Chapter Twenty-One

IT WAS TUESDAY morning, two days since the argument. Liz and Robert had hardly spoken and it was killing her, but she didn't feel that she could apologise because her views about Luke and Jesse hadn't changed. As far as she was concerned, her husband was gravely mistaken about them both, but it seemed that he was just as convinced of his own position as she was of hers and unwilling to talk it out; they were at an impasse.

Now that all the obvious areas around Tremarnock had been checked, most of the villagers had scaled down their search, though Andy and Sarah were still out each day with the police, because doing something was better than the alternative. Robert was putting in a few hours, too, but also spending more time at the restaurant because business had to go on. He'd been obliged to hire a temporary sous-chef, now that Jesse seemed to have quit, and the new lad wasn't much good and needed a lot of supervision, which only added to the stress.

Liz knew that Robert had seen Luke because she'd bumped into Alex outside the convenience store, and he'd confirmed that Luke had eaten at A Winkle In Time last night and that he and Robert had carried on talking and drinking after the others had left.

'Poor Luke's beside himself,' Alex had said, clutching a

packet of cigarettes in one hand, a can of Coke in the other. 'I guess he needs someone to speak to. It's good he and the boss get on so well.'

Liz had felt a mixture of anger and jealousy; she missed talking to Robert herself, and missed the way that he used to pop back home between shifts because he couldn't bear to be away from her. She longed for his arms around her at night and yearned for the way things used to be.

He came down when Rosie was having breakfast and hardly looked at Liz, as if the mere sight of her caused him pain.

'Bye, darling,' he said to his stepdaughter, kissing the top of her head, 'have a good day.' As for Liz, he brushed her so lightly on the cheek with his lips that she could scarcely feel it, and the rage and injustice that was just beneath the surface bubbled more ferociously. She'd have it out with him, she'd have to, but now wasn't the right time. Rosie, Sarah and Andy were her priorities – and finding Loveday, of course. Until then, decisions about her future with Robert would have to wait.

'What's wrong with him?' Rosie huffed when he left the room and banged the front door shut. She put down her spoon and pushed away the cereal bowl. 'He's being really odd, all distant and grumpy.'

'He's just worried about Loveday,' Liz said, anxious not to give the game away. The atmosphere at home was unsettling enough, without Rosie knowing that her mother and stepfather were at daggers drawn, too.

Sarah came in, wearing a spotted dressing gown and slippers, her hair unbrushed and her face creased like a used pillowcase because she was still half-asleep.

'Hi,' she said without enthusiasm, shuffling over to fill the kettle.

'How was your night?' Liz asked, knowing even as she spoke that it was a pointless question. She'd heard Sarah and Andy talking quietly into the wee hours, rising periodically to go to the bathroom or wander downstairs to make tea. No one was sleeping well, which was hardly surprising, but it was easier to chat about the small stuff. You had to try to preserve a veneer of normality to stop yourself going mad.

'So-so,' Sarah sighed, standing by the kettle while it boiled, her back to the sink. She put her face in her hands. 'This is killing me. When's it going to end?'

Rosie scraped back her chair and sprang up. She could move remarkably swiftly when she wanted to, despite her tricky leg.

'Here, sit down,' she said, guiding her aunt to the seat that she'd just vacated and smoothing her tousled hair in the way that her mother did to her when she was upset.

Liz felt guilty. Her problems with Robert were as nothing compared with what poor Sarah was going through. Her life was suspended and would be until there was news – good or bad. Liz couldn't bear to entertain the idea that they might never know what had happened, that Loveday would end up on some missing persons register, the mystery of her disappearance never solved. Better to live in hope, convincing yourself that any minute there'd be a phone call or a tap on the door, someone arriving with the information that they'd all been waiting for.

'I'm sure we'll hear something soon,' Rosie said, as if reading her mother's thoughts. She handed Sarah a mug of tea that she'd just made, before pecking her on the cheek: 'I'll see you this evening.'

Liz followed her daughter down the hallway and helped her on with her coat.

'Is it OK if I go to Tim's again after school,' she asked, hoisting the black bag on her back, 'so we can keep up with the emails?'

'Fine, but be home by six or I'll start to panic.'

Relations between them had been so much easier since Liz had met Tim's mother and found out about the website project, and she was relieved that her daughter had something to distract her from the investigation. 'No more lies,' she'd said, when they'd discussed what had happened, and Rosie had solemnly agreed. Liz felt that she herself had learned a painful lesson and was determined to listen and trust more. She didn't want anything like that happening again.

She sat with Sarah for a while, talking quietly about ordinary matters to try to comfort her. 'I wonder when Pat'll be home. Shouldn't be long now.'

Sarah sipped her tea and nodded, but Liz could tell that she wasn't really listening; she was in her own world.

'I thought we'd have roast chicken tonight,' Liz went on. 'Andy will like that, won't he?'

Sarah looked at her vaguely, and Liz noticed how her once round face had hollowed and the skin hung loosely round her eyes and mouth, like a baggy swimsuit worn out through repeated use.

'I don't know what we're doing today,' she said. 'We haven't spoken to June yet.' June was the special liaison officer they'd been allocated, their first port of call.

'You'll want something to eat later,' Liz replied gently, 'you must keep your strength up.'

'I s'pose.' Sarah reached out and touched Liz's arm, before fixing her eyes on a puddle of milk on the table that Rosie had spilt earlier. 'Thank you.'

'Whatever for?'

'For everything you're doing for us. We're grateful, you know, having us to stay like this, putting up with us for so long...'

Liz was touched. 'Don't be daft. It's the least we can do.'

She cleared away the breakfast things while Sarah went upstairs to dress, thinking that she must make another trip to the supermarket. Though Sarah had lost her appetite, the fridge still seemed to empty extra-fast with two more people in the house, and it was important to look after the guests especially, and make sure there was plenty of food on the table.

Liz hadn't, of course, told them about her row with Robert any more than she'd mentioned it to Rosie. They'd probably take his point of view; Andy was certainly deeply suspicious of Jesse and, anyway, there was nothing to be gained from stirring things up and upsetting them further.

As she pushed the trolley round the shop, barely aware of what she was buying, she thought that her life seemed to have lost all meaning. Without Robert's love, she was merely going through the motions, making sure that Rosie, Sarah and Andy were all right, just about holding things together for their sakes and for the baby growing within her.

It seemed almost impossible to believe she and Robert had been torn apart by Luke, who'd only been in the village a matter of months, and yet it had happened. She'd thought that her marriage was indestructible, but she'd been wrong. It had collapsed at the first major disagreement, though in truth the rift had been widening for quite some time, she could see that now. Almost from the moment that Loveday had disappeared, Robert had sided with Luke against Jesse, deaf to whatever Liz tried to say in his defence. She and Robert were fundamentally different, she thought sadly, yet she'd never noticed. If he had been deaf, she must have been blind.

Tabitha and Oscar had a whole long day to kill. They'd taken their time showering and getting dressed but even after a late breakfast followed by an hour of stories it was still only 11 a.m. What to do? Her phone was turned off, it was a sunny day and she was in a part of London that she'd never visited before. She decided that they might as well try to make the most of it.

Remembering that there was a big park near the wine bar, she caught the bus with Oscar back to Violet's, dug out the map that she'd picked up at reception and took a left up the wide, winding street that seemed to go in the right general direction. The nearest park entrance was a good twenty-minute walk and she lost her way a few times, but there was no hurry and she rather enjoyed looking at the gardens and in the windows of the substantial houses on either side, trying to imagine who lived there.

There was an air of tradition, respectability and comfortable affluence about the place, she thought, and she pictured men in suits going off to work each morning, women staying at home to look after the children, wholesome family suppers, Saturday night dinner parties and summer holidays in the south of France, Italy or Spain.

An attractive, thirty-something blonde woman in jeans, trainers and a padded gilet came out of her house with two handsome red setters on leads, and she smiled at Tabitha before climbing into a sleek white Range Rover, only serving to confirm the impression. Tabitha found herself thinking that she'd like to have an easy smile like hers, a life like hers. She'd bet that above all else she felt safe.

At last they reached a set of big, black iron gates, beyond which lay a wide expanse of wild grass and trees that seemed to stretch for miles, as far as the eye could see. Oscar struggled and complained, wanting to run around, so she headed straight for a bumpy gravel footpath away from the road, let him down and in an instant he raced off like a puppy after a black and tan Dachsund that was trotting on stumpy legs behind its owner a few yards ahead.

Two women in tracksuit bottoms, trainers and T-shirts jogged past, talking breathlessly, and another on an old-fashioned, sit-up-and-beg bike trundled by with a small dog in her front basket, but no one bothered about Tabitha and Oscar. He was in heaven, climbing on tree stumps, examining woodlice, pointing at squirrels and gathering interesting sticks, until he came across a herd of fallow deer grazing in the sunshine.

'Mamma?' he cried, running to her side and hiding in the folds of her green waterproof.

She took his hand and gave it a squeeze. 'Don't worry. They're more scared of us than we are of them.'

He came out from behind her legs to admire the animals, but it wasn't until they were well behind that he left her side again to run off alone into the bushes.

After a couple of hours they were tired and hungry again, and Tabitha was grateful when a passer-by pointed her towards a café that was cabin-shaped with a sloping roof and glass sides. She and Oscar sat side by side on a wooden bench, eating soup and sandwiches that he gobbled down before falling asleep in his pushchair, while she trudged slowly back the same way that they'd come.

The sun had gone now, it was getting chilly and, wanting to be safe indoors, she wondered again if she'd been mad to attempt this journey. It was perfectly possible, after all, that Demi no longer worked at the wine bar and had left no phone number or address, or that even if she was still there, she hadn't heard a peep from Loveday. Tabitha's hunch could have been completely wrong.

Oscar woke just as they reached the bottom of the hill and turned right into the main street, lined with shops and restaurants that were still buzzing with life. He whined, wanting to be let down again, but Tabitha tried not to notice.

She wandered into various stores, pretending to admire the rails of clothes on hangers, and leafed through magazines and books in the newsagent, acting as if she was interested in buying. Then she had a cup of coffee in a café and Oscar an ice cream, all the while checking the time repeatedly on her mobile phone, wondering how the minutes could tick by so slowly.

At last, it was just after 5 p.m. and her pulse started to race as she started up the street and stared again at Violet's Cocktail and Wine Bar, noticing, now, that the door was wide open. She half hoped as she wheeled her son towards the venue once more that no one would be there after all, but she was out of luck because there was movement inside. Steeling herself, she stepped over the threshold and blinked, waiting a moment while her eyes adjusted to the different light.

Soon she could begin to make out a dark, modern, cosy interior with red walls, small, black, glass-topped tables, black benches, soft red chairs and zebra-print stools. To the left was a glossy bar and behind it an attractive young woman in a grey dress, putting out menus. At first glance anyway, she didn't seem the type to bite.

She looked up when Tabitha entered, and smiled. 'Hi! Can I help you?'

If she was surprised to see a woman with a toddler, she didn't show it. Perhaps she was grateful for company as no one else was there. Tabitha asked for two glasses of orange juice and sat down on a bench with Oscar, examining the waitress out of the corner of an eye. She was trying to remember how Loveday had described her former workmate. Good looking for sure, like this girl, but was she dark or fair, tall or short? Tabitha had no idea. When she came over with a tray, Tabitha cleared her throat and asked casually if Demi was around.

The girl put two coasters on the table and the glasses on top, plus a small bowl of nuts that Oscar reached for greedily. 'She's not in today. I think she's back tomorrow. Is she a friend of yours?'

Tabitha thought quickly. 'She used to work in the place I come from in, erm, outside London.' She didn't want to be specific.

'Cornwall?' said the girl, straightening up, the empty tray in her hand. 'She told me about it. She said it was dead quiet.'

At that moment there was a yelp. They all turned, including Oscar, and Tabitha gasped, she couldn't help it, because a strangely familiar figure in a pink coat had just walked in.

The hair was dyed blonde instead of black, and the make-up was more subtle. Perhaps she looked a little thinner, and her normally animated features were frozen in shock. But there could be no mistaking her, surely? They were the same brown eyes, snub nose, full mouth, and it was the same tough yet vulnerable demeanour.

'Tabitha!' the girl cried. 'What the hell are you doing here?'

After unloading the shopping and preparing the vegetables for supper, Liz hung about the house, twiddling her thumbs and wondering what on earth to do to take her mind off things. She was on her own and hours stretched ahead of her before Rosie, Andy or Sarah would be home. She couldn't face getting out her sewing things and tried instead to busy herself with cleaning and tidying out drawers, but her heart wasn't in it.

Finally, she could stand the solitude no longer and decided to call on Esme at her pottery studio in the next village, thinking that a friendly face might help. It was just after five now and she guessed that Esme would still be busy working on a commission, two large, matching vases and five smaller ones for a grand holiday house in St Ives. She'd left it rather late and was running out of time.

As they talked, Liz watched while her friend skilfully smoothed and squeezed the wet lump of clay into a graceful shape on the wheel.

'Have you thought of any names for the baby?' Esme asked, dipping her hands into the mucky water bowl at her side and giving them a shake before resuming her task.

'Not yet.'

'Any idea whether it's a boy or girl?'

Esme was childless herself, but had enough female friends to know that mothers-to-be liked nothing more than a 'guess the sex' chat.

'No,' Liz replied.

Esme peered at her friend over the top of the small, round glasses balanced on the end of her thin nose. Nothing much slipped her notice.

'Are you all right? You seem rather glum.'

Liz attempted a smile. 'Fine, you know, just the usual.'

She pointed to a wide, shallow bowl that was drying on the side. 'I like that one. I'd fill it with fruit and have it in the middle of the table.'

'You can tell me,' Esme persisted kindly.

Liz fixed her with burning brown eyes. 'Do *you* think Jesse's done something to Loveday? Do you think he's capable of it?'

Esme paused. 'I don't know. I don't want to believe it but…'

Liz pushed herself up to standing. She shouldn't have come; it was a big mistake. 'You, Robert, the whole village practically, except Pat. What's the matter with you? I think you've all gone mad.'

'Liz? Luke thinks—'

Liz held up a hand to stop her friend and stalked out of the studio before she could finish. She felt as if she were inhabiting a parallel universe, the only one who could see things as they really were. She'd rather live here, however, than occupy the same space as the doubters, who listened more to the opinions of someone they hardly knew than to their own hearts. Esme, too. Liz had expected better.

Tabitha gasped again, scarcely able to believe her eyes. It was what she'd hoped for, longed for, but had feared might never come to pass. Yet here she was, standing right in front of her, as real as the waitress, as real as Oscar and Tabitha herself. It was undeniably true, she wasn't hallucinating. The girl before her was most definitely Loveday.

'What are you doing here?' Loveday repeated, but there was no time to reply because in a flash Oscar shoved the table out of the way, knocking over his glass of orange juice, and ran towards his former nanny, who opened her arms and swung him high before squeezing him tight against her chest, burying her face in his soft curly hair and bursting into tears.

'He's happy,' the waitress said uncertainly, and Tabitha welled up, too. It was as if all the fear, worry and strain that she'd been holding on to surged like water from a dam, and her whole body shook with the sheer force of it.

Oscar, concerned, shouted, 'Mamma!' but she couldn't see him through her crying. It was only when Loveday sat beside her, whispering, 'It's OK, don't be upset,' and her soft, Cornish accent filtered through, that reality sank in and Tabitha perceived the truth at last in all its glorious Technicolor: Loveday wasn't dead, she hadn't been murdered. She was here, alive and well, and, whatever the reason for her flight, whatever dreadful thing had happened to make her do it, this was all that mattered.

'Thank God you're safe,' Tabitha kept saying, over and over. 'I can't believe it.' She held the girl's face between in her hands, examining her eyes, her nose, her mouth, all there and in the right places, before wrapping her arms tight around her body. She needed to feel the warmth of her living breathing presence for confirmation, to sense the beating of her heart. 'It's a dream come true.'

Oscar wormed his way between them and Loveday hugged them both back. 'I'm sorry, I didn't want to frighten you, you don't understand.' But Tabitha scarcely heard. Explanations could wait, right now she wasn't interested. Her only focus was the here and now, the fact that the nightmare scenarios she'd conjured in her brain were at an end at last.

When they'd finally calmed down enough to speak properly, Loveday whispered something to the waitress, who moved away discreetly. Tabitha hadn't even realised that she'd been standing there; she must be quite bemused.

'I'm supposed to be working but there's no customers so we've got a few minutes,' Loveday whispered urgently. 'You know you shouldn't of come… you should of left me alone.'

The waitress came back briefly to give Oscar another

drink, and Tabitha pretended not to notice while he shredded cardboard coasters and fished cubes of ice out of his juice, smearing them on the table until they turned into messy puddles.

'You have to tell me everything quickly,' she said gravely. 'You know the police are looking for you, don't you?'

Loveday nodded. 'I guessed.'

'And you're aware they think Jesse's got something to do with it?'

The younger girl's eyes widened. 'Jesse? No!'

'There's a massive search going on. They think you might have been murdered.'

Loveday lowered her eyes and chewed a fingernail. 'I've been avoiding the telly. I told Demi I don't want to know. I made her swear she wouldn't breathe a word to anyone.'

Tabitha explained briefly about the toy dragon, and how Jesse had been arrested. 'Everyone thinks he's guilty – including Luke.'

She watched Loveday carefully and at the mention of his name her left eye twitched and she swallowed nervously.

'I told the driver to stop at the top of the hill and pretended to post a letter while I threw the dragon away. It reminded me too much of home.' There was a catch in her voice. 'Luke knows perfectly well Jesse's got nothing to do with it.'

So. Tabitha took a deep breath and drew herself up. It was all the confirmation that she needed; now she knew for sure.

'What's Luke been doing?' she asked quietly, and Loveday glanced at her, frightened and mistrustful.

'You mean you don't know? You're kidding me!'

Tabitha shook her head. 'He tells me very little, but I guessed he was into something bad, something big.'

Loveday had been unable to disguise her delight at seeing

her friend again, but now the joy evaporated and she shuffled away a few inches, her eyes narrowed.

'If that's true, why didn't you stop him? Why didn't you call the police?'

Tabitha felt the blood drain from her temples, her face; she was ashamed of what she was about to admit. 'I'm afraid of Luke. I'm terrified of what he might do.'

Loveday laughed uneasily. 'You're scared of your own husband? Come on! Do you really expect me to believe that?'

'I'm married to him and I hate him.' Tabitha was startled by the venom in her own voice. 'It's a long story,' she went on, aware that she needed to convince Loveday, and there wasn't much time. 'Luke rescued me from a bad situation, a violent man who's out to get me, and I'm frightened for Oscar, too. All the while that man's around I felt I couldn't leave Luke, I couldn't say anything.' She bit her lip. 'I know it's wrong, but Oscar's my priority, don't you see? If something happened to him…' She shuddered.

'Jeez,' said Loveday, struggling to take it all in. 'You were happy enough to throw me to the dogs, though. You've ruined my life.'

Tabitha explained that she hadn't wanted Luke to employ her, or any of the villagers, come to that.

'Why would I believe you, after everything that's happened? Why would I trust anything you say?'

'It's true,' Tabitha said urgently, 'every word. I'll tell you everything, but first we need to leave here, before Luke finds us.'

Loveday glanced left and right anxiously, as if expecting him to jump from the shadows and grab her.

'I want to help you,' Tabitha went on, sensing her doubt. 'We'll go home and sort this out.'

Loveday gripped the edge of the table, ready to bolt. 'No! I'll go to prison. Luke might hurt Jesse or my family. I'd rather die.'

'Wait!' said Tabitha, grabbing her arm as she started to rise. 'I won't let that happen, I swear. Just tell me what you know.'

Loveday paused for a moment and Oscar climbed over his mother to sit on his former nanny's lap, as if sensing that she needed reassurance.

'I've missed you so much, little man,' she said, softening, and it seemed at that moment as if the last of her defences crumbled and she took a deep breath and started to recount her tale: the so-called financial services business in Plymouth; Ahmed and Sam, always on their phones in other rooms with the doors shut; the 'helpline'; the moment when she'd realised that Pat had been scammed by the very people she'd been working for.

'I thought I was doing everyone a favour, putting their money somewhere safe, but who'd believe me? No one. I've been a stupid idiot and I'll never forgive myself.'

She wrapped her arms round Oscar and rocked him to and fro as if to comfort him, whereas in reality she was the one who needed consoling.

Tabitha, who had been listening quietly, could contain herself no longer.

'He's wicked,' she said passionately, 'rotten to the core. Even I wouldn't have believed he'd steal from old folk. It's not you who's at fault, I can assure you.'

Two thirty-something men walked up to the bar and eyed Tabitha and Loveday oddly. They were casually dressed in jogging bottoms and trainers and one had a scar on his upper lip.

'Can we see the cocktail menu?' he asked the waitress. It seemed a peculiar sort of request; he looked as if he'd be more at home in the local boozer.

'I'll just have a beer,' said the other gruffly.

He tipped his head in Tabitha's direction and nudged his friend, who frowned as if to shut him up.

Tabitha's stomach lurched and she tugged Loveday's arm, hissing in her ear, 'We have to go.'

'I can't leave, I'm working.'

She pulled her arm again, more urgently this time. 'Just do as I say – please.'

The taller of the two men glanced over his shoulder again at Loveday and muttered something to his friend.

'Hurry!' said Tabitha desperately. 'Help me get Oscar in his pushchair. We need to get out of here now, before it's too late.'

'Where are we going?' Loveday asked, grabbing her coat and bag. 'I've told you I'm not—'

'Hush, don't speak. I'll fill you in on the way.'

Liz frowned. It was now around 10.30 p.m. and there was still no sign of Sarah or Andy, which was most unusual. She'd tried to get in contact but their phones were on voicemail. Rosie was in bed and Robert, of course, wouldn't be back till later, not that he'd be speaking to her anyway. She'd turned off the chicken because Rosie had eaten at Tim's and Liz certainly didn't fancy it on her own. It was all very peculiar.

She switched on the TV but couldn't concentrate, and nearly jumped out of her skin when the landline rang. She was grateful to hear Sarah's voice, but relief soon turned to puzzlement when Sarah explained that she and Andy had been summoned for a meeting with the police and would be gone overnight.

'I'll tell you more later,' Sarah said, sounding strange and abrupt. 'My phone will be off so don't try to ring.'

The house felt weird and lonely and as Liz sat on the sofa,

staring at the empty fireplace, it occurred to her that she was even more unhappy than she had been when Greg had left all those years ago. Then she'd been numb with fear and shock, wondering how she'd cope on her own, but at least any feelings that she'd once had for him had long since died. Robert, though, was a different matter, and she feared very much that, whatever he did, however far his halo slipped, she was condemned to love him till the end of time, a curse indeed.

So frightened was she by this prospect that when Rosie appeared, saying that she couldn't sleep, Liz almost fell on her, smothering her in kisses.

'Mu-um!' Rosie said, flashing her funny, gappy smile. Her hair was all over the place, her pyjamas crumpled, and Liz smiled, despite everything, thinking that she looked about seven years old.

'I'm so happy to see you, you've no idea.'

'I've only been in bed.' Rosie laughed, but, sensing that her mother needed comforting, went on, 'I love you.'

Liz made hot chocolate that they drank in front of the TV. Rosie was dreadfully wide awake and curious about Robert, realising that something was up, but Liz deflected her questions with more questions about school, Tim, the website, her friends, and managed to catch up on some of the news that she'd missed in the past few, traumatic days. They'd both be tired tomorrow, but so be it.

'Sweet dreams,' she said to Rosie when she finally tucked her in again. 'Would you like a song?'

Rosie was in an indulgent mood. 'Go on, then.'

Liz sat on the edge of her bed and sang two lullabies, watching her daughter's lips curl with pleasure and amusement.

'Another one,' she demanded when Liz finished, knowing that it would delight her, and she duly obliged.

Later, Liz had a bath and went to bed, wondering, as she always did now, where Loveday was at this precise time and what she was doing. She found it comforting to imagine the girl in some strange town, sitting on someone's sofa, legs curled beneath her, discussing what to do next. Liz could almost hear her voice, explaining in her soft Cornish accent that she needed space, that she had 'stuff to sort out', but that she'd go home soon. She seemed so real, in Liz's mind's eye, so present, that she had to be alive; it was simply a case of finding her and bringing her back.

It was in this way that Liz was able to fall asleep, only waking much later when Robert tiptoed into the room and slipped in beside her. For a moment she fancied that he was sitting up, gazing at her in the dark, poised to speak, but then he burrowed beneath the covers and turned his back.

She heard him sigh and it made her sad, but she could think of no words to narrow the gap between them, so she closed her eyes once more and prayed for oblivion.

Chapter Twenty-Two

ROBERT LEFT EARLY again the next morning and there was no news from Sarah or Andy, so Liz decided to see Pat, the only adult left in the village, it seemed, who'd retained her perspective. The old woman was on considerably better form than the last time, bossing round the nurses and insulting the lady opposite, and informed Liz that she'd been told she could leave in the next couple of days, as soon as they'd completed a risk assessment of her home and confirmed that her niece would be able to stay.

'I'm going to miss THE OLD BATTLEAXE OVER THERE,' she shouted.

Liz glanced at the fierce, fat patient opposite, whose lips pursed threateningly.

'What's that you're saying?' she said, cupping her hand round an ear.

'I SAID I'M GOING TO MISS YOU, YOU OLD FOOL!' Pat replied, 'YOU'LL HAVE TO COME AND VISIT.'

The woman grinned and blew Pat a kiss. She didn't look as scary when she smiled.

'She's not all bad,' sniffed Pat. 'Tight as a duck's arse, but I won't hold it against her.'

She straightened up a little. 'I say, that Hazel, Annie's grand-mother, she's a nice woman. Said she'd come and see me at The

Nook when I'm settled in. We're going to launch a campaign to warn pensioners about telephone scams. Someone needs to stick up for us poor old things. Felipe will help with leaflets, I'm sure.'

'Excellent idea,' said Liz, thinking, with pleasure, that Pat looked considerably less like a poor old thing today than she had the last time they'd met. She was definitely on the mend.

When she arrived back in the village and drove slowly down Humble Hill, she was surprised to see four or five police cars parked at the end of the street, their doors open. Officers in fluorescent yellow tops and blue hats were speaking into walkie-talkies, gesticulating to the crowd that had gathered on the corner of Fore Street, telling them to keep back.

Jean and Tom were outside their house, toddlers balanced on their hips, talking to Jenny, who looked as if she'd left Gull Cottage in a hurry because she wasn't wearing a jacket. Beside them, Felipe was chatting animatedly to Audrey, in her pea-green coat, and there were other villagers streaming down the hill towards them.

Liz abandoned the car and leaped out, her heart pounding.

'What's going on?' she asked two young men jogging by, before realising that it was the boys from A Winkle In Time.

'Dunno,' Alex panted. 'Something's happening at The Stables. Boss asked us to find out.'

Liz's mind started racing. The Stables? Was it something to do with Luke – or Loveday? And why so many cars and dogs? It must be serious, she thought, a knot of anxiety settling in the pit of her stomach. Had they found a body? Her head started to swim and she felt herself sway.

'Liz!' Jean cried, noticing, but her arms were full, so Audrey dashed forward to stop her from falling, but Liz pushed her gently aside.

'I'm all right, honestly.' She passed the others, rounding the bend at a wobbly trot, and almost crashed into a policewoman standing guard in front of a temporary barrier.

'Stay there, please,' the woman said firmly, forcing Liz to an abrupt halt. Glancing left and right, she could see that the barrier stretched all the way across Fore Street and more police officers were milling around behind. Liz craned her neck to try to get a proper view but it was no good, then two officers parted and, through the gap, she caught sight of a large white van, with a flashing blue light on the roof, parked outside The Stables, its doors flung wide. She stood on tiptoe to watch and within seconds two police officers emerged from the building with Alsatians on leashes.

'It's him!' someone cried behind her, and she turned to see Esme, one eye partially obscured by strands of grey hair that had escaped from her bun, and a smudge of clay on her cheek.

Swinging round again to face the van, Liz gasped, for there, between two more officers, his hands behind his back and struggling furiously, was Luke. He was wearing a crisp red and white striped shirt and tan chinos, his blond hair still slicked back neatly off his face. He could have been an off-duty merchant banker or hedge-fund manager, his smart appearance strangely at odds with the scene unfolding.

'Get your hands off me!' he roared. 'I want to speak to my solicitor!' But the policemen had him in a firm grip and they were half pulling, half pushing him towards the van. Liz caught sight of a smooth arm, a gold Rolex glinting in the sunshine, and below it a pair of thick silver handcuffs. There was momentary silence from the crowd then someone with a strong Cornish accent yelled, 'What have you done with her, you bastard?'

Luke must have heard because he turned in the direction of the noise and Liz's stomach lurched, because for a moment he seemed to stare straight at her, his blue eyes fixed on her face, but if he registered who it was you couldn't tell as his features were blank. Only his lips seemed to curl in a strange way, as if a stitch had been dropped, causing his mouth to slowly unravel.

He dragged his feet at the doors of the van, refusing to get in, but the policemen heaved him up, lowering his head as they entered, then the doors banged shut and he was gone.

The crowd was forced to move aside as the van backed up the street, reversing into Humble Hill before heading in the direction of the castle.

'What's happening?' Liz asked Rick, on her left, in a bright red sweater. 'Why have they taken him?'

'Dunno,' he replied, lurching slightly as he was jostled from behind. 'We need some answers.'

There was a general hubbub: people murmuring, dogs barking, the odd shout, a child crying.

'If he's done something to her…' said a woman whom Liz didn't recognise. She felt herself sway again.

'Where's Loveday?' someone screamed. 'Have they found her?' Liz was shocked to realise that it was her own voice. She felt her legs buckle and reached for a wall to support her, but the way was blocked with bodies and she couldn't get through. Faces, some familiar, some not, faded in and out of her vision and she cried out – 'Oh!' – sensing herself fall. Then a strong arm was circling her, a firm hand gripping under her shoulder and hoisting her up before she could hit the ground.

'It's all right, Lizzie, I'm here,' said a familiar voice. Glancing up, Liz perceived the blurred image of Robert, a deep frown cutting across his forehead like a fissure.

'I'm sorry,' she said, trying to straighten, but her limbs were like rubber and she couldn't stand on her own. The next thing she knew, he was picking her up like a baby and the crowd parted as she allowed herself to be carried, catching the faint, reassuring whiff of his soap and skin as they went.

'Does she need an ambulance?' someone asked, and she heard Robert say they were OK, they lived right here. The garden gate creaked and he wrestled a key from his pocket, taking her full weight with his other arm, before lifting her into the front room and laying her gently on the sofa.

'Loveday?' she said, her mouth dry and her brain still fuzzy. She could think of nothing else, but he didn't reply.

Quickly, he propped her head on some cushions and put a blanket over her, before perching beside her and taking her hand.

'You went completely white but the colour's starting to come back now.' He was examining her closely, like a forensic scientist. 'Thank God I was there. Do you feel any better?'

She nodded, which made her head hurt, so she closed her eyes.

'My darling,' he said, with such infinite tenderness. 'For a moment I thought…' But his voice cracked and he couldn't finish.

'What's happened to Loveday?' she asked again, more urgently this time. 'You've got to tell me.'

Robert stroked the hair off her face, still holding one hand in his. 'They've arrested Luke,' he said heavily. 'I don't know why.'

'Have they found a body?'

'Not as far as I know. Poor darling, is that why you—?'

The piercing ring of the phone made them both jump and he shot her a look. 'Shall I—?'

'Answer it,' she insisted. 'You must.'

He rose gingerly, being careful not to move her, and padded into the hall to pick up the receiver. The door was open and she pricked her ears, anxious not to miss a word.

'Hello? What? Thank God, oh, thank God.' His deep voice

seemed to echo around the house, bouncing off the walls, the furniture, the floorboards and reverberating in her skull.

Without thinking, she jumped up, throwing off the blanket, and ran to join him, forgetting that she'd almost passed out and ignoring the weakness in her legs. He was standing up straight, running a hand through his brown wavy hair, and she stared at him while he spoke, picking up as much as she could and trying to piece together the scraps of information.

'In Exeter... London, you say...? Tabitha... turned up at the station...' He was repeating some of what he'd heard, as if only by doing so would it sink in.

He didn't talk for long but it seemed like an eternity to Liz, who feared that at any moment she might spontaneously combust. When at last he hung up he turned to her with the widest smile on his face that she thought she'd ever seen, making his eyes light up and the corners crinkle.

'They've found her.' He took a step forward and pulled her to him, so that she was crushed against his body. 'She was staying in London with that girl Demi, who used to work at the restaurant. Tabitha tracked her down and took her to the local police station, then they drove them to the headquarters in Exeter. Sarah and Andy have been with them but they weren't allowed to say until now.'

'But why did she go?' Liz asked, trying to process what she'd heard. 'And how did Tabitha realise where she was?' Liz wanted to punch the air but at the same time there were so many unanswered questions and none of it seemed to make sense.

Robert rested his chin on the top of her head. 'Sarah said Luke's got some big criminal racket going on, some fraudulent scam. Loveday was helping him but she didn't realise it was illegal, then when she found out she got scared and ran. Somehow Tabitha guessed where she was and, well,

I suppose she decided to inform on her husband. The main thing is, Loveday's alive and well.' He took a deep breath. 'I can hardly believe it.'

Liz hesitated. In all the excitement she'd forgotten about their argument and his doubts about Jesse and unkind words, but now they came rushing back.

'So that means Jesse's innocent?' she said carefully, shrinking from her husband's grasp and taking a step back.

Robert nodded. 'I've made a massive mistake.'

'And Tabitha rescued Loveday, and Luke was the cause of it all?'

'It certainly seems so.' He shook his head. 'I can't believe I was taken in by him.'

She pulled a face. 'You and practically the whole of Tremarnock.'

He fixed her with steady hazel eyes. 'I said some terrible things to you.'

'You did.'

'You were right all along. I should have listened to you.'

'You should.'

I'm sorry, Lizzie,' he said in a small voice. 'I'll have to try to make it up to Jesse and...' He swallowed. 'And I don't suppose you can ever forgive me?'

He looked so sad and it was wrong to be unhappy on such a wonderful day. There'd be plenty of time to analyse they whys and wherefores in the days and weeks to come.

She took his big hands, which felt soft and strangely vulnerable, and smiled, watching the jagged lines across his brow smooth away.

'We'll have to see about that.'

It was enough, for now. He pulled her to him again and she basked in the warmth, as if she'd been lying, cold, wet and shivering, on the beach, until the bright sun emerged from behind a cloud to heat her through. She could have stayed there for ever but a sudden thought made her start and she drew back quickly.

'Quick, we must go to the school.' She turned to grab the car keys from the hall table and pass them to him. 'Will you drive? I don't think I should. We need to tell Rosie about Loveday. We'll never hear the end of it if we make her wait a moment longer.'

Of course, Rosie was far too excited to return to lessons and the head teacher allowed her to go home. She'd only miss about half an hour anyway.

'I should think you've got some celebrating to do,' the head said kindly. She, too, had joined the search in her spare time and was smiling broadly. 'I'm absolutely delighted for you all, it's the best news I've heard in a long time.'

Sarah phoned again to explain that the police had more questions and they wouldn't be home till late, so Robert dropped Liz and Rosie at Bag End and parked the car before setting off again. He'd told Alex that he wouldn't be returning to A Winkle In Time until tomorrow and if they couldn't manage they were to contact customers and close the restaurant, citing personal circumstances.

Alex, however, had assured his boss that they could cope. 'Don't worry, guv. It's under control.'

Robert wasn't looking forward to this but it had to be done – and quickly. He'd tuned in to the local radio station on the way back from collecting Rosie, and Loveday was the top story, along with the fact that Luke and nine other men, aged between 26 and 40, had been arrested at two different addresses on suspicion of fraud and money-laundering off-ences running to millions of pounds. The police had moved extraordinarily fast.

Robert guessed that Jesse would have heard by now, but he couldn't be sure. It had all happened so quickly, and the young man had been living a bit like a hermit recently, shutting himself away at his mum's and hardly speaking to a soul. He must have been under a tremendous amount of stress. There was no answer at the house and Robert hung around for a few minutes, repeatedly ringing the bell and calling through the letterbox, until an elderly woman, whom he vaguely recognised, came hurrying out of Audrey's house next door to investigate.

'I've just seen it on the telly!' she exclaimed, as if continuing a conversation she'd been having in her head. She was Audrey's mum, lived in Bude and sometimes came to stay with her daughter and help in the clothes shop. 'They've found her!' she went on, unable to hide her excitement. 'And that man from The Stables? Who'd have thought it? Audrey always said he was a slippery customer.'

Robert winced, remembering Audrey batting her eyelashes at Luke, vying with Sylvia for his attention and singing his praises like the rest of them, himself included.

'I'm looking for Jesse,' he said abruptly. 'There doesn't seem to be anyone here.'

'Poor young man,' Audrey's mum said slyly. 'Everyone muttering about him behind his back. It's shocking how folk jump to conclusions. Audrey always insisted—'

'Have you seen him?' Robert interrupted.

'You just missed him,' the old woman replied huffily. She'd clearly been hoping for more information, or at least a good gossip. 'Went off that way.' She pointed to her right. 'No idea where he was off to. Had his walking boots on. Covered in mud they were.'

She crossed her arms and made to leave, but then her eyes lit up when she spotted a neighbour on the other side of the street, opening his car door. 'I say,' she called out happily, hastening down the garden path towards him; Robert was forgotten already. 'Have you heard?'

Robert left them to it and marched in the direction that she'd indicated, hoping to catch up with Jesse. It wasn't long before he spotted a hunched figure in a grey hoodie and navy jacket on the corner of Market Square. He was walking quickly, head bowed and hugging the buildings, as if anxious not to draw attention to himself. The shop doors were open and Esme was visible through the window of the fishmonger, talking to Ryan behind the counter, but they didn't look up, and the other stores seemed quiet. Perhaps everyone was glued to the TV.

Once he was within a few paces Robert called out Jesse's name. The young man swivelled round, startled, and when he saw Robert, a look of surprise crossed his features. Instead of acknowledging his former boss, however, he simply turned away, stuck his hands in his pockets and continued his journey.

'Jesse!' Robert called again, breaking into a jog, 'I need to speak to you!'

No reply.

'Please!' Robert was alongside him now but Jesse showed no signs of slowing down.

'Loveday's safe. Have you heard? And they've arrested Luke.'

Jesse's hood was pulled up high, half obscuring his face, but Robert thought he saw a flicker of pleasure at the mention of her name. Then the look vanished and the features hardened again.

'Yeah, I know, the police rang. I'm glad she's all right,' he muttered. 'At least they'll get off my fucking back now.'

His pace quickened and Robert was finding it hard to keep up. They left Market Square and turned right down South Street in the direction of the seafront, passing Jenny and her dog outside her cottage, in a huddle with Felipe, Tom and Jean. Robert had last seen them near The Stables, watching Luke's arrest. They were no doubt still discussing the turn of events and would be for days to come. They looked up when Robert and Jesse passed and Jenny opened her mouth to speak, but Robert shook his head so she closed it again. He didn't check in the window of A Winkle In Time, hoping not to be noticed.

'Where are you going? Can I come too?' he asked Jesse as they reached the beach. Some way out to sea, three brave souls were messing around in a dinghy, but otherwise the place was deserted.

'Do what you like,' Jesse growled.

It soon became clear that he intended to take the path to Hermitage Point. Robert was wearing the wrong shoes, his brown leather lace-ups that had no tread, and he'd left his coat behind, but he wouldn't be deterred. Fortunately it wasn't cold and the winding trail that led out of the village was dry, save for a few muddy patches that he was careful to avoid.

As the way became steeper, Jesse remained several paces ahead and Robert followed behind, panting. His sweater got caught on the prickly brambles that lined the route and he pulled hard to release it, causing a hole, but he didn't stop. Further up, they overtook several wild ponies munching grass beside the track, but they weren't bothered about the two men and merely swished their tales and continued grazing.

After about fifteen minutes they reached the summit and the path widened out, the hedges disappeared and they could see miles of grey sea ahead and around them, as smooth as glass until it reached the dark rocks below and burst into seething white foam.

'I've been a bastard,' Robert shouted. His voice, though loud, was whipped away on the wind so that he wasn't sure if Jesse heard him. 'I'm sorry. You have every reason to hate me.'

They were all alone, save for a few seagulls circling above, and it crossed Robert's mind that if the younger man wished to do him harm, there was no one to stop him. Jesse still had his back turned and Robert started to explain what he knew about Loveday and why she'd left. His throat was becoming dry and hoarse but still Jesse strode ahead, giving no indication as to whether he was listening or not.

'She was scared,' Robert yelled. 'She didn't realise what she was getting herself into.'

They were scrambling up the steep slope that led to the abandoned chapel now, and he found himself slipping and sliding on the rocks, leaning forward and holding his arms out wide to try to balance, cursing his stupid footwear.

'Liz never trusted Luke,' he went on. 'I should have listened to her.'

Jesse strode into the tiny derelict stone chapel, which was nothing more than a single rectangular cell with a roof, a door and four small windows that were open to the elements. Robert followed, wondering if this was it and the young man planned to turn around again without a word and head back home. Instead, however, he stopped and stood with his back to Robert, staring out of the window at the wild, rocky coastline that snaked into the distance. Robert fancied that he could hear the young man's heart banging against his ribs, or was it his own? The damp, musty smell chased up his nostrils and the cold crept into his bones, making him shiver.

It was a bleak and desolate place at the best of times, and now was no exception.

They stayed like that for what seemed like an age, Robert scarcely daring to breathe, until all of a sudden Jesse swung round, his blue eyes moist with anger and tears.

'Liz is the only one who believed in me,' he muttered. 'Her and my mum. Everyone else gave up on me – including you.'

It was true. 'I'm ashamed of myself,' Robert replied.

'What do you expect me to do? Forget everything?' Jesse went on. 'Loveday's OK and Luke's been rumbled, so that's all right, then? Water under the bridge?' He laughed nastily and the noise echoed round the thick, dank walls. 'It was just a silly little misunderstanding? All's forgiven?'

His lips curled in a snarl and he clenched his fists, so that Robert wondered if he'd lash out; he wouldn't blame him.

'No,' Jesse continued. Was that a catch in his voice? 'It's not that fucking simple. I thought we were friends and you threw me to the wolves. I never want to see you or speak to you again.'

He tried to push past Robert and make for the door, but the older man blocked the way.

'I want to make it up to you,' he said desperately, stepping from side to side to prevent the young man slipping by. 'Please let me. At least come back to the restaurant for a while – until you finish your catering exams? Then, if you still wish to go, I'll help you find another job. Don't ruin your career.'

Jesse shook his head violently. 'That side of my life's finished, over. I'm gonna get the hell out of here. There's nothing for me in Tremarnock now.' He kicked a stone at his feet and it bounced off the wall, narrowly missing Robert's shin.

'There's your mum, and your brother, and Liz – and Love-day,' he said gently.

Jesse wiped his face with a sleeve. 'I loved that girl, I'd have done anything for her.'

'She's coming home tonight.'

'Tonight?' For a moment Jesse's face lit up before clouding over again.

'She left me, didn't she, just like that?' He snapped his fingers. 'Never told me what was going on, nothing. Dumped me in it. We're over.' He tried to push past Robert again, but his tall frame filled the doorway and he wouldn't budge.

'At least talk to her before you go,' Robert begged. 'Listen to what she has to say.'

'There's nothing to explain,' Jesse growled. 'She fell for that slimy bastard and got her fingers burned, didn't she? Maybe she'll be more careful who she mixes with in future.'

Robert felt his strength slip away, his shoulders droop. He hadn't expected for one moment that Jesse would let him off lightly, he didn't deserve it, but he'd hoped at least to open a dialogue and to be able to offer something that would help get the young man back on his feet. As it was, Jesse seemed determined to leave the village and Robert felt as if he alone was responsible for ruining the young man's life.

Sensing that he'd lost, he stepped aside to allow Jesse to pass and trailed after him down the hill. He was wondering how he'd break the news to Liz, who'd be heartbroken. He didn't know, of course, how Loveday would react, and there was still that matter of the row that she'd had with Jesse the night before she'd left to clear up, but Robert now one hundred per cent believed Jesse's version of events. What's more, Loveday's decision to flee had had nothing whatsoever to do with her boyfriend; that had been a red herring, partly engineered by Luke himself.

They didn't speak once on the return journey, but as they

reached the bottom of the path Robert decided to have one more try.

'You'll need to get some money together before you go. A deposit for a flat. I'll up your salary to make it easier for you.'

Jesse paused, as if he hadn't considered the matter of a deposit before, then resumed walking.

'I'll pay you double if you come back next week, on Tuesday when we reopen.'

Jesse stopped and swung round, his eyes blazing. 'You can't buy me off just to make yourself feel better. It doesn't work like that.'

'I'm not trying to buy you, I need you. The temporary guy's useless. He can't make crème brûlée and we had loads of complaints about the hollandaise. Alex said it looked like sick.'

Did the corners of Jesse's mouth turn up just a little?

'Think about it at least. Talk to your mum. The business is struggling and I meant what I said about the rise.'

He held his breath and watched the young man's face, hoping desperately for some indication, the slightest sign.

'Don't call me, I'll call you,' he replied.

It was around 11 p.m. when Sarah, Andy and Loveday finally arrived back at Bag End, having been driven home in a police car. Robert, Liz and Rosie were waiting up for them, though they weren't sure whether their guests would be in the mood to talk or simply ready for bed. As it was, no one, least of all Loveday, could hide their delight at being reunited and sleep was the last thing on their minds. The hugs and tears right there in the hallway went on for a long time.

It was chilly outside and Liz had lit a fire in the front room. When they finally settled on sofas and chairs, mugs of tea in hand, Andy started to explain that he'd received a call on Tuesday evening to say Loveday had been found safe and well in London. She and Tabitha had walked into a local police station and were being driven to Exeter, where Sarah and Andy were to meet them. Police had realised immediately that they had a big case on their hands, and it was important not to alert anyone else until they'd questioned the two women thoroughly, hence the need for complete secrecy. They'd all been put up in a hotel and the debriefing had started again early this morning.

'We were desperate to tell you,' Sarah said, 'only we couldn't as it might alert Luke. No one could know anything – except us, that is. I knew if I talked to you I'd let the cat out of the bag, so I turned my phone off.'

Next, it was Loveday's turn to tell her story. Sarah was beside her, an arm round her shoulders, and Liz noticed that she never let go once, as if only physical contact could convince her that her daughter really had returned and wouldn't vanish again in a puff of smoke.

When Loveday got to the moment when she'd realised that it was the phone scam that had caused Pat's accident, she started shaking uncontrollably.

'I feel so bad,' she was saying. 'Pat's going to loathe me.'

Everyone tried to persuade her that it wasn't her fault; she hadn't realised what she'd been doing and had been a victim of the scam herself. Pat would understand, they insisted, and no one would think the worse of her.

'What about Jesse?' Loveday went on, scarcely listening. 'Because of me, everyone thought he was a murderer. I didn't ever mean that to happen but it did, didn't it?' She choked. 'I love him with all my heart and now I've lost him, and it's all my stupid fault.'

Robert frowned, unsure how to relay his conversation with Jesse earlier, if you could even call it that. He explained that Jesse was understandably very upset and hurt, that he felt betrayed and had talked about moving away, but that he, Robert, still hoped to persuade him to stay.

'I'm the one who should leave, not him,' Loveday said, blowing her nose into a tissue. 'I've caused so much grief.'

'Don't you dare,' Sarah chipped in, pulling her daughter tighter. 'Don't even think about it.'

Andy, who was beside Sarah, listening carefully, patted her knee, and Loveday noticed.

'What's that about, then?' she asked, momentarily forgetting about Jesse. 'I thought you two hated each other?'

Sarah examined the fingernails on her right hand. 'Your dad's been giving me a lot of support.'

'It's not been easy,' Andy continued. 'The past week, well...' He cleared his throat. 'I think it's made us realise, hasn't it, Sar?'

He turned to Sarah, who nodded. 'It's made us realise how much you mean to us, and how much we mean to each other.'

'We're a family,' Andy added, 'and families stick together through thick and thin, don't they?'

Loveday's brown eyes opened very wide. 'So does that mean you're not getting divorced, then?'

Sarah nodded.

'Well I s'pose that's one good thing to come out of all of this. At least the house won't be a war zone any more.'

'Are you coming home, then?' Sarah asked hopefully. 'While you get yourself sorted out, I mean? I'll look after you – and your dad, of course. We'd love you to stay.'

Loveday remained silent and Andy squeezed his wife's knee again. 'Leave it for now, eh? We'll talk about it another time. She's only just come back.'

Liz got up to put another log on the fire before settling down again, tucking her feet beneath her. They'd hardly discussed Tabitha, who'd been released on police bail pending further questioning, but now Liz wanted to know exactly what role, if any, Loveday thought she'd played in the scam. When she explained that Tabitha had known very little, but that she'd admitted to being scared of her husband, Liz sighed.

'It all begins to make sense. She always seemed so frightened, poor woman. She must have been in hell.'

Andy was less sympathetic. 'She lied. She was covering up for him, wasn't she? If it wasn't for that, Loveday wouldn't have got involved.'

'And if it wasn't for her, we might never have found your daughter,' Liz reminded him. 'It must have taken a lot of courage to go to London and inform on her husband. I wonder what'll happen to her now.'

Rosie had nodded off in one of the armchairs, her head resting at an awkward angle, her lips slightly apart, and she was making snuffling noises in her sleep.

Robert yawned. 'We should go to bed.' It was well after 1 a.m.

He lifted Rosie up – she was very light – and she stirred only slightly as he carried her towards the door.

'Do you think I can go and see Jesse?' Loveday asked. 'Will he let me speak to him?'

Robert paused, wishing that he could give her the answer she wanted.

'I honestly don't know if he'll even open the door to you,' he said truthfully. 'But you have to try.'

Chapter Twenty-Three

SITTING AROUND SHELLEY'S cramped kitchen table on Saturday morning with her and her two children, Charlie and Amber, while Oscar played next door, Tabitha found herself wondering if she'd emerged from a deep sleep to discover that the life she'd thought she'd had was a dream and that this was her true family, her reality.

If Shelley had been dismayed when, three nights previously, Tabitha and Oscar had arrived on her doorstep at nearly midnight, accompanied by two police officers, she'd tried not to show it. Unable to think of a single other person to contact, Tabitha had called her from the police station and asked for a bed for a few nights. Where she and Oscar would sleep after that, and indeed far into the future, she had no idea. All she'd known was that there was no way she'd return to The Stables. That chapter of her life was finished.

Shelley had been remarkably accommodating, given that Tabitha had disappeared to London without a word, that she, Shelley, had been unceremoniously laid off work and then, to crown it all, the boss had been arrested. Her house in Callington had only two bedrooms, one for her and her husband and the other for their two children, but she'd made up a mattress for Oscar on the floor of the front room.

'I'm afraid you'll have to take the sofa,' she'd said apologetically, through bleary eyes. 'Bathroom's at the top of the stairs and help yourself to tea or coffee or anything you want.'

Tabitha had thanked her warmly, more grateful than she could say for the sight of a soft pillow and duvet, desperate to close her eyes and forget for a few short hours that any of this had ever happened.

She'd imagined that she'd sleep like a baby but, instead, she'd lain awake for hours, listening to the unfamiliar creaks and rattles of a strange house and chewing over all that had happened. Oscar was flat out, having dropped off somewhere between Exeter and Newton Abbot, and he'd barely stirred when she'd carried him inside. He'd had a peculiar and exhausting day, most of it spent in the company of a smiley female police officer who'd done her best to entertain him while Tabitha was being questioned, and by the time they'd clambered in the car, he'd been way past his best.

He'd screamed for a good ten minutes before nodding off beside Tabitha on the back seat, his body still shuddering with sobs. For the rest of the journey she'd stroked his cheek and hair, his head propped on her arm, and stared out of the window into the blackness, trying not to wonder what would become of them or dwell on the fact that, unbeknown to her son, his secure little world had well and truly crumbled.

She'd woken the following morning still tired, only to have to break the news to Shelley that she needed her to look after Oscar while she returned to the police station for further questioning.

'I'll pay you, of course,' Tabitha had said desperately, thinking she should spend while there was still cash in the bank, but Shelley had been almost offended.

'I can't pretend I don't miss my job but I don't want no

money to look after the little 'un,' she'd scoffed. 'You're in trouble and I can help and that's all there is to it.'

Tabitha's eyes had filled with tears. Shelley had always seemed so shy, nervous and uncommunicative, yet when Tabitha had really needed her, she'd shown her true worth.

'Thank you,' she'd said, praying that Oscar wouldn't kick off when he saw her leave, as she wasn't sure that she could bear it. 'I'll be back as soon as I can.'

It had been made clear to her that she was likely to be charged as an accomplice to the crime and, as such, could go to prison. It was just possible that the Crime Prosecution Service might decide not to pursue her case, given that she'd been under duress and was a key witness, but the police could offer no promises. They wanted to know not just about Henry Mount Financial Services but also about all Luke's previous Manchester dealings. They were interested in Carl, too, and had promised to check out whether or not he'd been in the Tremarnock area and look into issuing a stalking and harassment warning. This gave Tabitha small comfort, but it was something.

In any case, she was happy to divulge as many of Luke's secrets as she could; in truth, it was a relief to get them off her chest. She'd returned to Callington almost drunk with exhaustion, but with a certain strange sense of elation, too, because finally she'd come out of hiding. As frightened as she was about the future, she felt for the first time in many, many years, if ever, that she could hold her head high because she'd done the right thing at last.

She'd almost forgotten about the days of the week and months of the year; time seemed to have telescoped so that all that mattered was the here and now, getting through the next few minutes, the next half-hour, so when Shelley informed her that it was the weekend, she was quite surprised.

'The weekend? Already? Do you need me to leave?' she asked, while Shelley cracked some eggs into a bowl and put the saucepan on to heat. 'I said I'd only stay two or three nights.'

Shelley was in a faded white T-shirt and crumpled pink pyjama bottoms, her mousey hair tied back with a black plastic clip in a greasy up-do. Once Tabitha might have thought her slovenly, but now she had nothing but admiration for this kind woman who, despite losing the job that she so badly needed, had taken her in without a murmur.

'Now, what sort of question is that?' Shelley asked, spinning round, hands on hips, and giving Tabitha a reproachful look. 'Where do you think you're going to go, then?'

Tabitha had no answer.

'Don't be daft,' Shelley went on. 'I know it's a bit cramped, but you can stay as long as you like. At least the press don't know you're here. They're swarming all over Tremarnock instead, poking their noses in where they're not wanted.'

Tabitha shivered. She'd avoided newspapers and TV and could only imagine how interested reporters must be in the events unfolding. Even more reason for the inhabitants of Tremarnock to wish they'd never clapped eyes on either Luke or herself, she thought. She doubted if she'd ever dare set foot in the place again.

Charlie, who was nine, had finished his cereal and was getting bored, kicking the leg of his sister's chair.

'Stop it!' hissed twelve-year-old Amber, shoving him in the ribs.

'Can I go now?' he whined, but his mother told him to wait for the eggs. 'They won't be long.'

A strong smell of hot butter wafted from the saucepan and the kettle boiled again, filling the kitchen with steam. Shelley's husband must have put the football on TV next door because a burst of cheering erupted and Oscar appeared suddenly, alarmed by the noise, and pulled on his mother's leg, wanting to be picked up.

It was Charlie who heard the doorbell; he must have had sharper ears than the rest of them.

'I'll answer!' he cried jumping up, relieved to be released from the torture of sitting in one place.

'That'll be the postman, I s'pect,' Shelley reassured Tabitha, having noticed her start. 'It's a new one and he seems to get here quicker than the last.'

When Liz entered through a veil of heat and steam, it took Tabitha a moment or two to register who it was before her mouth dropped open. 'Oh!'

Liz addressed Shelley first. 'I hope you don't mind? I heard Tabitha was here and I thought I'd better come early to catch her.'

Shelley, who was growing accustomed to being at the epi-centre of the drama, merely nodded and fetched a mug from the shelf above the sink. 'Cuppa?'

By now, both children had given up on the idea of scrambled eggs and made a dash for the door, leaving Shelley to shrug resignedly, before lifting the spitting pan of butter off the hob. Liz pulled out a chair without being asked and sat opposite Tabitha, who instinctively shrank back, not knowing what sort of treatment she was about to receive.

'I want to thank you,' Liz said, fixing Tabitha with a pair of large, brown, earnest eyes. 'You found Loveday and brought her back to us. You were very brave.'

Liz was small and slim, much slighter than Tabitha, and she was dressed in a plain blue woollen sweater and jeans, her hair tied back in a blue spotted scrunchie. She looked delicate, fragile almost, despite the swelling that was obvious now beneath the baggy top, yet there was something powerful about her too, an inner strength that seemed to illuminate her pale features. She looked like someone you could rely on.

Tabitha felt herself shaking, and held on tight to Oscar on her lap for comfort. She hadn't expected this kindness. At most, she'd hoped that people wouldn't think quite as badly of her as before. First Shelley, now Liz. Their generosity overwhelmed her.

'I should have stopped him sooner,' she said, licking her lips that had gone dry. 'I should never have let him give Loveday that job. I didn't want her to work for him.' She shook her head. 'I should have protected her.'

Shelley was still standing by the kettle, listening in rapt silence to everything that was being said. She reached mechanically for milk and tea bags, not wishing to miss a single word, and passed a mug each to Liz and Tabitha.

'You had a lot of problems,' Liz said gently. 'Loveday told me.'

Tabitha glanced at Liz fearfully. She seemed genuine and compassionate, but could she be trusted? Tabitha had once trusted Carl, but these days she had no faith in anyone save Molly – and Loveday, perhaps.

Amber poked her head in again to ask if she could go out with her friends. She was wearing a lurid silver jacket and what looked suspiciously like lipstick and eye shadow.

Shelley frowned, as if she was about to object, then thought better of it. 'Mind you're back by dinner time, though, and I don't want you wandering round them streets, getting up to mischief.'

'We're not doing nothing wrong,' Amber whined, 'just going to the park.'

'And don't you go talking to that Puddicombe lad,' Shelley replied. 'He's bad news.' But Amber had already scarpered.

The TV was still blaring in the adjoining room and Liz wrinkled her brow.

'Shall we go out? It'll be easier to talk.'

Tabitha nodded and Shelley darted towards the exit: 'Hang on a mo while I get dressed. I'll only take a second.' She wasn't going to miss a thing.

The three women emerged into the daylight and Tabitha breathed in and out deeply, grateful for some fresh air after the closeness of Shelley's kitchen. Oscar had climbed willingly into his pushchair, keen for a change of scenery, too, and she strapped him in tightly before they set off down the narrow street, passing rows of terraced Victorian houses, some painted white, blue or yellow, others with the brick left bare, gardens bursting with spring daffodils and tulips.

'Where are we going?' Shelley asked eagerly. She was wearing a plain red sweatshirt, jeans and trainers, but Tabitha noticed that she'd dusted pale pink blusher on her cheeks and her eyes were shining. She looked younger and less careworn, almost pretty. This was probably the most fun she'd had in years.

'I don't know Callington,' Liz replied. 'Where do you suggest?'

'Main shopping street's this way,' said Shelley importantly, striding on ahead, 'and there's a nice old church. Follow me.'

Tabitha, who'd barely seen the place in daylight, found herself thinking that this had been a bad idea. What had she to say to Liz, whom she hardly knew, and how could she begin to describe what she'd been through? She wasn't even sure that she wanted to.

There was an awkward silence for a few moments until a fluffy ginger cat, sitting on a wall enjoying the morning sunshine, mewed at them and Oscar pointed excitedly.

'Miaow!' he was saying, kicking the footrest with his navy blue shoes. 'Cat! Miaow!'

Liz stopped to stroke the animal before turning to Oscar and smiling. 'Isn't he beautiful? So soft and fluffy, and he's so friendly!' Then she carefully picked the animal up, still stroking its head, and crouched down beside the small boy so that he could take a better look.

Oscar reached out, and Liz guided his pudgy hand across the cat's back. 'Gently, that's right. Don't pull his fur. He likes that, listen! He's purring.'

It was such a tender gesture and you could tell that Liz had children of her own. Tabitha was touched.

'It all started when my parents – my adoptive parents – kicked me out of home,' she said quietly. Liz glanced up and nodded encouragingly. 'I'll tell you everything, if you've got the time.'

'As long as it takes.'

Soon they reached the main street, passing by an estate agent, a tea room, a kebab house and the post office. There were plenty of people on the pavements and coming in and out of the shops, and a few paused to stare at the three women, huddled together and walking quickly, their heads bent, seemingly oblivious to what was going on around them. Some folk may have recognised Tabitha from the newspapers or TV and nudged each other, whispering, but she and her friends scarcely noticed, so intently were they talking.

Every now and again, Liz or Shelley would cry out in dismay, make a sympathetic noise or ask Tabitha to clarify something, but mostly they let her speak without interruption. Liz and Tabitha didn't even register the ancient church, which was such a feature of the old market town, or question where Shelley was leading them, and it was only when Oscar started to struggle that they realised they were heading out of the centre and up a steep main road.

'It's the country park up there,' said Shelley, pointing into the distance. 'Oscar might like it, but maybe it's too far?'

'Perhaps we should get away from the cars,' Liz said, eyeing Tabitha's son, who was protesting loudly, arms and legs flailing. 'I think he wants to walk.'

Tabitha continued her account while they crossed a housing development and skirted round a field, before arriving at a grassy recreation ground with play equipment. A young mother was pushing her daughter on a basket swing, and Oscar stood and stared, delighted, while the little girl squealed as she went high in the air shouting, 'Faster, faster!'

The three women settled on a bench, watching him all the time while Tabitha drew breath, before she described the moment when she thought she'd seen Carl in Tremarnock, lurking outside her bedroom window.

'My God, you must have been terrified,' Liz said with feeling.

'I was permanently scared, more for Oscar than myself, do you see?' She stared at the ground. 'To be honest, I've been scared all my life. I wish I'd fought back, I wish I'd been stronger.'

'You've fought back now,' said Liz. 'You've shown great courage. You should be proud of yourself.'

Oscar, bored with watching the little girl now, made for a climbing frame and she rose, followed by Liz and Shelley, helping him scramble on to the first rung where he sat for a few moments, dangling his feet and gazing at the sky.

At last, when they'd trailed after him for half an hour or so, taking it in turns to lift him up or down or stop him falling, Tabitha looked at her friends in turn and said, 'That's it, you know all there is to know about me. No more secrets.'

Her son, worn out, begged to be picked up so she swung him on to a hip and stroked his hair.

'It's him I'm worried about,' she went on sadly. 'I feel so sorry for him. He was happy in the village, he loved his dad, his home, his little life. Now who knows what'll happen to him? I might go to prison and when I come out I'll have to go into hiding, God knows where, because whatever the police say, they'll never be able to protect me.'

She kissed her son fiercely, burning a red mark on his cheek like a brand, as if it might keep him safe. 'I feel like I'm living on borrowed time and there's no one to look after him, not even Molly, because she's in Manchester and there's no way I'm sending him there.'

'Don't be silly' Liz cried, and the others looked at her, surprised. 'There's me for a start and Shelley here.' Shelley nodded, though she seemed uncertain quite what she was agreeing to.

'And there's Jean and Tom, Esme, Audrey, Jenny Lambert, Tony and Felipe. The whole of Tremarnock will want to help when they hear what you've been through. We'll protect you ourselves, if need be, with our own bare hands.'

It was so unexpected and Liz looked so small and fierce that Tabitha couldn't help smiling. 'You're unbelievably kind...'

'I'm only saying the same as everyone in the village. If you go to prison, we'll have Oscar and look after him like our own. And when you come out, there'll be a bed waiting for you and a warm welcome, and all the help you need to get back on your feet. If one of us is in trouble, we all rally round. That's just how Tremarnock is, and how it always will be.'

'Littl 'un can stay with me, no problem, as long as he doesn't mind the mattress,' Shelley chipped in, having caught up now. 'My hubby will keep an eye on him if I get another job.'

It was too much for Tabitha, whose eyes filled with tears.

'After all the terrible things I've done...' She shook her head, unable to continue, and Oscar buried his face in her chest.

'Shush,' said Liz, wrapping an arm around them both, 'don't cry. You're not alone any more.'

They were a sombre little group as they walked back to Shelley's house. Oscar had fallen asleep and, lost in their own thoughts, they spoke little, but each knew that in the past few hours something unique and powerful had happened and not one of them would ever forget what had passed between them. When they reached Shelley's house, Liz said that she had to go, but that she'd be in touch again very soon. In the meantime, she needed time to think.

'I meant what I said,' she told Tabitha, embracing the woman she'd once found so cold and hard. 'I'm going to help you.'

Tabitha smiled and thanked Liz again, but the smile quickly faded; she wanted so much to believe but all she could see ahead was a court case, prison, Oscar farmed out to some strange foster family, pain, grief and suffering.

Her son woke as they entered Shelley's house and looked around him, confused.

'Mamma?' he said, turning in his pushchair to find her. His cheeks were flushed, his eyes not yet focused. 'Mamma? Uvday? Dadda?'

Tabitha unbuckled him and held him tightly in her arms, thinking that no doctors or surgeons, no treatments, pills or potions in the world would ever be able to cure her shattered heart.

Chapter Twenty-Four

LOVEDAY FELT LIKE a celebrity as she walked through Tremarnock and, one after another, the villagers came out of shops or houses to give her a hug. Nobody blamed her for wasting their time and effort, not a single person suggested that she'd been a fool to work for Luke or believe his lies about the investigation in which he was supposedly involved. In truth, they'd almost all been bewitched by him, and had been doing some soul-searching of their own. Their delight at having her home again was almost palpable.

'Well, I never!' said Audrey, hurrying on long legs out of Seaspray Boutique, having spotted Loveday through the window. The sun was shining and she was wearing one of her own creations, a spring-like, red and white striped tunic dress with matching red tights, and showing off quite a lot of thigh. 'I never thought I'd witness this day!'

The door of Gull Cottage was open and Jenny Lambert was bent double in the hallway, fastening a shoelace. 'Have you seen Sally?' she asked without looking up as Loveday passed. 'She's gone again.' Then, when she realised who it was, 'Oh, my! Am I happy or what?'

As they stood outside the house, chatting and calling Sally's name, Rick emerged from Treasure Trove and came up the street towards them, clutching something in a white paper bag.

'For you!' he said, passing the bag to Loveday. 'Peanut-butter fudge – I know you like it.' His whiskery sideburns were more luxuriant than ever. 'Welcome home!'

When at last she could free herself, Loveday crossed into Market Square, only to bump into Felipe and Tony, leaving the bakery. They were in jeans and identical round-necked sweaters, only Felipe's was pale blue while Tony's was orange.

'Look who's here!' Tony cried. He was carrying a loaf of French bread under one arm and nibbling on a corner. 'I was wondering when we'd catch a glimpse of you. Only this morning I said to Felipe, "When's the party?" didn't I, Felipe?' He nudged his partner in the ribs.

'Eez true.' Felipe nodded gravely. 'Tony says we must have a *carnaval*.' He rolled the 'r' emphatically. 'In Rio when some-one goes missing mostly they have been murdered. Boom.' He put two fingers to his temple and staggered to the side to demonstrate.

Tony frowned. 'All right, darling, that's quite enough. Loveday hasn't been murdered, she's very much alive.' He turned to her and smiled. 'As I was saying, we should have a celebration – once you've properly settled back in, of course.'

Loveday agreed, though she was secretly thinking that this was the last thing she needed. She was enormously grateful to the villagers, but now that she'd recovered from the excite-ment of being home and seeing the family again she wanted nothing more than to try to make amends with Pat and, of course, Jesse. She wouldn't be able to rest unless and until she'd done so.

Ryan was at the counter of the fishmonger's, serving a customer. He spotted Loveday and gestured for her to wait a moment, but she pretended not to understand and gave a quick wave before scurrying by.

She decided not to take the direct route to the house, instead skirting round the back of the Methodist church, thinking that she might be less likely to meet people. The cemetery, surrounded by a low brick wall, was normally deserted, so it was a surprise when she spotted a familiar figure sitting by himself on a fallen gravestone, his blond head down, elbows resting on his knees.

She'd expected to find him at his mum's, and her heart pitter-pattered and it took all her courage to force herself not to spin round and head swiftly back in the direction from which she'd come. Bracing herself, she placed her hand on the iron latch and opened the wooden wicket gate. He seemed lost in thought and didn't hear as she padded across the long, lush, pale green grass towards him. It was only when she was within a few feet that she whispered his name – 'Jesse!' – and he turned and stared.

'What are you doing here?' There was shock on his handsome face that he tried to disguise with a frown.

Loveday took a deep breath. 'Can I sit?' She closed her eyes for a moment, thinking that it might make the rebuff easier to bear, but he said nothing and when she opened them again he was staring hard at a spot of grass beneath his feet.

'Well?'

He continued to gaze at the ground. 'I don't want to see you.'

She felt his words like a slap and inwardly reeled. 'I was scared Luke would hurt you, hurt my family if I told anyone,' she said hopelessly. 'I thought running away was the best thing.'

'You dumped me in it,' Jesse replied heavily.

Loveday, still standing, shifted from one foot to another,

thinking that this was the hardest thing she'd ever done in her life.

'I didn't know you'd been arrested. I wasn't watching TV.'

Jesse shrugged. 'Doesn't matter now anyway. You're all right, aren't you?' He was trying to sound casual, but you could hear the hurt in his voice.

The sun beat down on the back of her neck and she felt weary suddenly, a hundred years old. A brown and black butterfly flew past and landed on a straggly buddleia bush, and she wondered what had happened to the carefree girl of just a short time ago. She felt as if she was carrying the weight of the world on her shoulders.

The butterfly flew off to a clump of daisies in the corner and, in spite of his rejection, she settled on the gravestone next to him, feeling the heat seep through the seat of her trousers into her very bones. A van rattled by and a dog barked, but otherwise it was just the two of them, silent with their thoughts. She daren't touch him but was close enough to feel his presence, and for just a few precious moments she allowed herself to imagine that things were as they'd once been, that they were still in love, their futures entwined.

'I've missed you—'

'Don't!' He glared at her, his blue eyes flashing, and it reminded her of the night before she'd fled. She was the one who'd made him upset and angry and he hadn't deserved it then and didn't now.

'Can't we...?' she pleaded, but he rose abruptly and stood with his back to her.

'Jesse?'

'Look,' he said, more gently than before, 'the damage is done. You can't put us back together and there's no point trying.'

She hung her head, conscious of the tears springing in her eyes. It sounded so final, but what else could she possibly have expected? Her hands strayed to the hard stone beneath her, the patches of soft moss, and she found herself thinking it was right that they should be having this conversation here; in years to come she'd look back and consider it a good ending, if such a thing were possible, a proper burial.

But, still, she needed to do right by him, see him taken care of. 'At least go back to your job,' she begged. 'You were doing so well. Don't let me have ruined that for you, too.'

'Never!' He spun round now, his voice tight and strangled. 'They thought I'd killed you. I could see it in their faces. How d'you think that makes me feel?'

'Finish your exams,' she urged, refusing to be put off. 'Then you can go anywhere, you can be the top chef you always wanted to be. Don't let them win.'

He paused, seeming to think about it for a moment, and a shiver of hope spread through her, until his features hardened, he clenched his jaw and turned on his heels. She watched as he made for the exit, anxious to savour every last second, to fix the memory firmly enough in her mind to last a lifetime, until at last the familiar blond head disappeared from view. She wasn't sure if she'd ever see him again.

It wasn't until an elderly gentleman in a flat cap shuffled through the gate, carrying a bouquet of flowers, that she realised she must have been sitting there for hours. The sun had dropped and she trembled, feeling the absence of a coat for the first time. It was still only April after all.

'You all right, love?' the old man asked, peering at her through small, wire-rimmed glasses. He couldn't have recognised her from the TV and she didn't know him either. 'You look lonely there by yourself.'

She rose stiffly from her perch and straightened her trouser legs, which had bunched round her ankles. 'I just needed some time to myself.'

The old man nodded. 'I remember that feeling. Only when you reach my age, time to yourself is all you get.'

Without meaning to, she glanced at his bouquet, wrapped in tissue paper, and he followed her gaze.

'Tulips were her favourite, and I added rosemary from the garden for remembrance. Not that I need reminding, mind. Dead five years, my Mary, and never a day goes by when I don't think of her.'

He took off his cap and scratched his bald, pink head. 'But you wouldn't know about that. You're too young to be married.'

She wanted to tell him that, married or not, she'd met the man of her dreams – and lost him. She wanted to ask for advice, some words of comfort. Perhaps he'd make her believe that if she kept the faith, Jesse would come back to her one day, that they'd grow old together, like him and Mary. But by the time she opened her mouth the old man was heading purposefully towards a group of newish-looking gravestones in the middle of the cemetery, and the moment to speak was over.

'It makes sense for Tabitha to come here for a short while. It's too small where she is and, besides, Oscar knows Loveday. Plus, the whole community will keep an eye on her. She doesn't know anyone in Callington, other than Shelley.'

Robert was sitting on the end of the bed, listening to Liz while he pulled on his socks. It was Monday morning now, the restaurant was closed, and they'd agreed to spend the day together.

Sarah and Andy had left for Penzance an hour or two earlier. They both needed to return to work and, although they'd begged Loveday to go with them, she'd refused, insisting she had things to do and promising instead to visit soon. Naturally, Liz and Robert had insisted that she stay at Bag End instead and, when Liz had mooted the idea of welcoming Tabitha and Oscar, too, Loveday had readily agreed.

'They can take the spare room and I'll share with Rosie – that is, if she doesn't mind.'

The flat at Jack's Cottage was paid up for another two months but no one wanted Loveday to live there on her own, least of all her. She'd been round to collect a few things and had returned distraught, because it held so many memories. Liz had warned that she mustn't go again. 'I'm happy to fetch anything you've forgotten. You're welcome here for as long as you like.'

When Liz had finished speaking, Robert ran a hand through his hair. 'It's a big undertaking. I don't want you, Loveday or Rosie put in any danger, or the baby, for that matter. I'm just not sure.'

Liz went over to the window. She could still just about make out her daughter, walking in her funny lopsided way up Humble Hill towards the bus stop. The cumbersome black school bag was strapped tightly to her back so that she had to bend over, tortoise-like, and propel herself forward. Liz winced, wishing, as usual, that Rosie wasn't so stubborn and would accept a lift. Still, it was perhaps this very obstinacy that kept her going.

She vanished from view and Liz turned back to her husband, now fastening the buttons on his blue and white striped shirt.

'Here, let me do the cuffs.' He held out his wrists obediently. 'The police will install a panic alarm and we'll have a special officer as our point of contact. I want to do this for her, just until she finds a place of her own.'

Robert took his wife's hands and tugged her gently towards him, so that she lost her balance and landed on the bed beside him.

'I don't know, Lizzie.' Propped on an elbow, he leaned over and stroked the hair off her face, staring into her eyes as if searching for answers. 'I'm just not sure.'

They'd been informed by police that Luke would shortly be charged with fraud and money-laundering, and that he was facing seizure of all his assets and up to twelve years behind bars. The investigation would take months but there was already plenty of evidence, officers having searched the offices of Henry Mount Financial Services and found sucker lists of thousands of victims from all over the country.

Robert listened while Liz reminded him that, though Luke would most likely be released on court bail when the trial date was set, once free from prison he wouldn't be allowed anywhere near Tremarnock or, indeed, Cornwall. What's more, if he were to break any of his bail conditions, he'd be back in jail immediately.

'So what do you think?' she asked.

Robert tucked a strand of her hair behind an ear, still gazing at her intently. 'It's a big decision and it affects us all, not just this family but our neighbours and the rest of the village, too.'

She tipped her head on one side. 'You owe me, remember.'

He flinched, not wishing to be reminded. 'I do, but I'm thinking about your safety.'

It had just started to rain and as drops splattered against the windowpane and trickled down, making wiggly patterns on the glass as they went, she realised that, far from wanting to go out to lunch, as they'd discussed, what she desired more than anything was to stay here, with him, until Rosie returned, preferably entwined in his arms, which was her favourite place in the whole world.

'I'm not right about everything, but I'm right about a lot of things,' she wheedled with a half-smile, hoping to resolve the matter quickly. 'I thought you were going to listen to me more.'

He drew himself up to sitting. 'OK, you win. They can come.'

Then he bent down and kissed her on the lips and she closed her eyes for a moment, drinking in the sweet taste of harmony that she'd feared lost for ever. Robert, her Robert. He was back and she'd never let him go again. At that moment everything seemed just perfect, because they were as one again, and together, she thought, they could cope with whatever life threw their way.

'No more misunderstandings, Lizzie,' he whispered, echoing her thoughts. 'No more ugly quarrels. If we disagree, we'll talk it through, like now.'

They lay on the bed and she rested her head against him, listening to his steady heartbeat and feeling the rise and fall of his breath.

'I think, if it's possible, I love you even more than I did before. You're an amazing woman.'

She wasn't sure whether to laugh or cry with happiness, so she did both, and he held her tight until the trembling subsided and she was calm again, listening to the minutes tick by, the odd shout outside, the spattering rain, the occasional swish of a car as it glided through puddles, the sounds of the universe unfolding as it should.

When she finally moved, ready to rise, it seemed as if the weather was clearing at last, but then the sky blackened and another sudden roll of thunder overhead made her jump and the room shake and rattle.

Robert glanced out of the window at the rain falling in thicker, heavier sheets.

'D'you think we should ditch the going-out-to-lunch idea?'

She nodded. 'Filthy day.'

'What shall we do, then?'

'You could help me with RosieCraft. I'm terribly behind with the orders.'

'I can think of better ways to occupy our time.'

She looked at him and he was smiling mischievously. It was tempting, but… 'We can't. Loveday's downstairs.'

He jumped up and padded swiftly to the bedroom door, clicking it shut. 'She won't come in.' Then he started to unbuckle the belt on his jeans, staring at her the whole time.

'She might hear!' Liz protested, watching his every move.

'Not if we're quiet.' He looked tall and very other, more beautiful, perhaps, than she'd ever seen him.

Soon he was standing over her, manoeuvring her out of her top, her socks, her trousers.

'Robert!' she whispered, 'It's Monday morning!'

'I like Mondays.'

'Don't,' she gasped. The bra came off and he threw it unceremoniously across the room. 'You might upset the baby.'

'You should have thought of that before.'

She was going to declare that she had a long list of jobs, like washing Sarah's and Andy's sheets and calling the hospital to find out when Pat was coming home, never mind her business, which had been sorely neglected. But before she knew it his hands were all over her, his mouth on hers, and she found that she couldn't say anything more at all.

*

Two days later, Liz collected Pat from hospital and brought her home. Before they arrived, the villagers had rallied round getting things ready, and the old woman's fridge and freezer were crammed with homemade meals that she could pop straight in the oven. Jean had made several of her signature chicken pies, Barbara a variety of casseroles, while Felipe and Tony had replenished her fruit bowl and filled her cupboards with tins of soup, packets of biscuits and jars of jam and marmalade. The previous morning, Liz and Esme had spent several hours cleaning The Nook from top to bottom and putting fresh flowers in vases beside her bed and in her front room so that the whole place smelled delicious.

Now, at last, Pat was ensconced in her favourite chair in front of the electric fire, with a white shawl round her shoulders and a pink crocheted blanket over her knees. Beside her, on the little table, was a mug of tea and an open, family-sized box of luxury choccy bickies.

'You won't be able to eat the lot!' Liz laughed, picking up the cushion that had fallen on the floor and propping it behind her friend's back. She bent forward and adjusted the shawl. 'What time did you say Emily's arriving? I hope the A38's not too busy.'

Emily was to stay, as promised, for a week, and after that the villagers were to operate a rota system for another seven days so that the old woman was never alone, even at night. Thankfully, there were enough volunteers to make that possible. Pat was much improved, but the arm was still weak, and no one wanted to risk her falling over and damaging it again.

''Bout two o'clock,' Pat replied, noticing Liz glance yet again through the little window over the figurine display on the shelf. She'd thought she was being discreet.

'You can't fool me, you know,' Pat grumbled finally. 'All right I'll see her, but tell her to come quick before I change my mind.'

Relieved, Liz beckoned to Loveday, who'd been waiting anxiously outside. Soon there was a knock and the girl entered, looking for all the world as if she were about to undergo a life-threatening operation worse even than the one Pat had endured.

'It's me,' she said unnecessarily, hovering with her back to the wall and taking a piece of paper from her pocket before launching into the lengthy apology that she'd spent hours writing the night before.

Pat listened grimly, occasionally making a funny noise at the back of her throat as if something was stuck, and her mouth, thin at the best of times, seemed to shrink to a line no wider than a pencil mark.

'I told you he was a bad 'un,' she said at last, waggling a gnarled finger at the girl, 'but you wouldn't listen, would you? Oh, no! And look what happened. Stole all my savings, didn't he? The lot. Me and Geoffrey saved all our lives for that, I don't mind telling you. And I broke my arm because of it. And then to crown it all you ran away, giving your poor family the biggest fright of their lives.'

She growled like a wild beast and glared at Loveday, who stared hard at the floor, unable to meet her gaze.

'Hanging's too good for that man,' Pat went on, shaking her head. 'He should be hanged, drawn and quartered, that's what. Can't think what got into you, falling for him like that. I thought you had more sense.'

Loveday choked and Liz, who was feeling a little sorry for her, would have pointed out that others had been charmed by Luke, too, but Pat was so ferocious that she didn't dare. She'd never seen the old woman so angry; you wouldn't believe that she'd been tucked up in her hospital bed earlier, looking like a sweet old granny.

'I'm sorry,' Loveday said again miserably, sounding like a broken record. 'I was foolish, I know.'

'*Foolish?*' Pat roared. 'Downright daft, more like. You could have got yourself killed, I don't mind telling you. Men like that don't stop at nothing. You're lucky to be standing here today, having a strip torn off by me.'

There was a pause as she narrowed her eyes while Loveday shed hot tears, and Liz just stood there, feeling uncomfortable.

'Now, look here,' Pat said at last, softening a little, 'I know you didn't mean any harm, but you should have thought—'

'He seemed so nice,' wailed Loveday. 'I'll never forgive myself.'

Pat glanced at Liz, who ushered Loveday to the sofa and settled beside her, putting an arm round her shoulder because she needed it.

'It could've been worse, I suppose,' the old woman muttered. 'The money's gone but we're still here, just about in one piece.'

She cocked her head and waited for Loveday to quieten down. 'That's better. I can see you properly now. You've changed since I last saw you. You're prettier and I think...' She stroked her chin, 'Yes, that's it, I reckon you might've grown up a bit!'

Loveday peeped out of still-damp eyes to see if Pat was joking and she gave an enigmatic little smile.

'Here, let's have one of these,' she said, passing the box of biscuits from the table. 'We all need sweetening up.'

Nobody really wanted a biscuit but it seemed like the right thing to do, and while they ate, Pat filled in the silence with tales of the battleaxe in the hospital bed opposite, plus the brood of children and grandchildren who visited her.

'Right rough lot they are,' she said, sniffing. 'I'll bet not a single one earns an honest living. All scroungers, I shouldn't wonder, fiddling benefits and up to no good. You can tell just by looking at them.'

'You can't say that!' Liz protested. 'You don't know anything about them!'

'Don't need to. You can see it in their eyes. Sort of mean and shifty, if you know what I mean.'

Liz laughed, she couldn't help herself. 'Heaven help us if you judge us all on our appearances! Look at me today. I haven't even brushed my hair because I was worried I'd be late for you, and as for make-up, no chance. I look like a tramp!'

Pat eyed her up and down. 'Well, you've been better, I'll admit, and you could do with a nice neat perm like mine, but no one would take you for a criminal, your face is too honest.'

She glanced again at Loveday, who was picking nervously at the corner of a nail. 'It's all right' the old woman whispered, taking pity on her. 'Some folk are masters at disguising their true colours. You can't tell what they're like till you really get to know 'em, and by then it's too late.'

'You were right from the start about Luke, though,' Loveday said unhappily. 'Like you said, you warned me and I didn't listen.'

'In my experience, young people rarely do. We all learn from our mistakes, that's the way of the world. It's just a shame others have to get hurt in the process.'

Loveday swallowed. 'I'll pay you back,' she said in a small voice. 'Every last penny, I promise.'

Pat took a deep breath. 'We'll see about that. We can talk about it another time. Fortunately, I'm not going to starve, not with all them blooming chicken pies in the freezer. There's enough to feed the five thousand.'

There was a pause while she took a sip of tea, then she leaned forward and cleared her throat. 'Now, what I want to know is, how're we going to get that Jesse of yours back? It won't do, him avoiding us all like this and talking about going off somewhere on his own. It won't do at all.'

Loveday took a tissue from the box by Pat's elbow and blew her nose before explaining that it was hopeless, that she'd lost him, but Pat was having none of it.

'He's hurting like he's got an open wound and it's going to take time to heal.'

Loveday shook her head. 'He won't change his mind, I know it. He's absolutely determined to go away and he never wants to see me again.'

Pat harrumphed, rising up in her chair so that she looked twice the height.

'Now, don't give me that. It's your duty to put it right, after all you've done and the mess you've made. You've got to bide your time, girl. It's like my husband used to say when he went fishing, God rest his soul: patience is key. He told me amateurs fight a fish way too hard, they never stop reeling and they break it off. You mustn't allow the line to go slack, but don't pull too hard neither, then little by little you'll land your prize.'

Loveday frowned. She wasn't into fishing herself, but the analogy was clear enough.

'But how can I reel him in if he won't even look at me, let alone talk?'

Pat tapped her nose mysteriously.

'Womanly wiles,' she said, winking at her with a watery blue eye. 'How do you think I got my Geoffrey? Not by sitting around, waiting for him to come to me, that's for sure.'

Loveday looked uncertain.

'That Jesse worships the ground you walk on,' Pat went on, 'but he's had a fright and he's too proud to forgive and forget yet. But you mustn't give up, oh, no, you need to show him what he's missing. God gave women intuition and femininity and if you use 'em properly, you'll jumble the brain of any fella on earth.'

Liz decided to call in at the restaurant before going home, leaving Loveday and Pat still chatting. She wasn't at all sure that the old woman's advice made much sense, but was glad that she and Loveday had spoken at last, because the latter had been desperately worried about that first meeting.

As she passed Jenny's cottage, she was surprised to see Jesse emerge from A Winkle In Time with, she fancied, a spring in his step that had been missing for quite some time. He gave a wave when he spotted her, but didn't stop.

Her curiosity roused, she hurried inside, through the busy restaurant, to find Robert, who was in the backyard, unpacking boxes of wine and loading the bottles into his store shed.

'Why was Jesse here?' she asked and he rose quickly, with a big grin on his face. He hadn't heard her arrive.

'He's agreed to come back,' Robert explained, 'just until he's finished his catering exams.'

Liz's heart swelled with pleasure. 'That's fabulous! What made him change his mind?'

Robert shrugged. 'I kept popping round to his mum's and

dropping it into the conversation, and maybe he just needed time to think. I guess in the end he realised it was a good offer and, well, he's decided to swallow his pride – thank goodness.'

She was so delighted with the news that she almost forgot to mention her second baby scan, scheduled for next week. She'd received a letter only this morning and it was to be the day after Rosie's next MRI scan.

'Everything all right?' Robert asked, looking at her anxiously, and she nodded. 'Just routine.'

He trailed after her into the steamy kitchen, where Alex was barking orders at the temporary sous-chef, a youngish lad with angry red spots on his face and a sour expression.

'Have some melon.' Robert offered Liz a small chunk from a cut-up pile in a bowl in the corner, which she took and popped in her mouth. 'Delicious.'

As she strolled home in the early afternoon sunshine, the sweet taste of melon lingering in her mouth, she couldn't help thinking that perhaps Pat's word of advice to Loveday hadn't been so off beam after all. Maybe, just maybe, Loveday would succeed in reeling Jesse in, little by little, and that would be the most wonderful outcome of them all.

Chapter Twenty-Five

THE SCHOOLS HAD broken up for the summer, the holiday season was in full swing and the streets of Tremarnock were buzzing. After a drab June, July and August had turned out warm and sunny and the sea was alive with folk on paddle-boards, in dinghies or just swimming, while the beach was covered in sunbathers, small children and scuba divers climbing in and out of smelly rubber wetsuits.

The village seemed to have changed colour, too, now that folk were no longer wrapped up in drab coats, hats pulled down low over their foreheads to keep out the wind. The jolly bunting was up and the pinks, whites, yellows and blues of the cottages mingled with the bright tops, dresses and bathing suits of locals and visitors alike. Window boxes were bulging with pansies, geraniums and lobelia and Jean's garden, always a picture at this time of year, attracted admiring gazes from passers-by. Tom was often out there with his trowel and hedge cutters, enjoying the comments.

Everyone seemed to be in a good mood, especially Audrey, who was doing a roaring trade at Seaspray Boutique while juggling her catering business in the evenings. One particularly large family group, renting three cottages side by side, had taken full advantage of her home cooking and she'd rewarded herself with one of her own turquoise smock tops. It was clearly a favourite as she'd been spotted in it several times.

A Winkle in Time was packed every night and, much to Robert's delight, Jesse was settling in slowly. The first few weeks hadn't been easy. The others had done their best to make him welcome but he'd scarcely spoken to them, making it apparent that all was not forgiven and preferring to focus solely on work. However, it was difficult to keep himself to himself in such a busy kitchen, and gradually the icy atmosphere had thawed a little so that there were now times when he forgot to be frosty and would join in with the jokes and banter. The subject of Loveday, though, was strictly off limits. If anyone so much as mentioned her, he'd turn his back.

Of course, he and Loveday had bumped into each other; the village was too small to avoid it. But when it happened, Jesse would cross the street and look the other way, or immediately leave whichever pub he found her in. She respected his stance and didn't try to follow him, though it hurt dreadfully.

She was still living at Bag End and hadn't yet found a new job, waitressing for Robert being out of the question, of course, while Jesse was there. Tabitha, meanwhile, was now renting the ground floor of Dove Cottage, where Liz and Rosie used to live, which had now been fitted with its own panic alarm. Esme had pointed out that while Tabitha was still staying with Liz and Robert the flat was soon to be unoccupied, and they'd agreed that it seemed a good bet. It was close to them, after all, and Esme would keep a watchful eye on her neighbours down below; she knew the score.

Tabitha hadn't intended to return to the village at all, but Liz's entreaties had been so warm and persuasive that in the end she'd melted. She had nowhere else to go and knew that it was the best option for Oscar. It was only a temporary measure, however, until she could figure out something else.

As Loveday was unemployed, she was able to spend a lot of time with her former boss and Tabitha was immensely grateful for the company and the help with Oscar, although she couldn't pay anything. The Stables was empty and would eventually be sold, and the proceeds used to compensate Luke's victims, including Pat. Tabitha had nothing but the benefits she now received each week and was getting used to scrimping and saving in a way that she hadn't known for years. She'd spoken many times to Molly, who'd been shocked and relieved about the turn of events in equal measure, but so far they hadn't met.

'I want to come and see you,' Molly had begged repeatedly, but Tabitha had always refused, saying there was nowhere to stay now that The Stables had closed, and Dove Cottage was too cramped, that she and Oscar were busy this weekend or that he had a nasty cold. Molly knew they were just excuses but the truth was, Tabitha didn't feel up to an emotional reunion with her dearest friend. She thought the sight of her might just tip her over the edge when it was more important than ever that she remain strong for Oscar's sake, so she persisted in putting her off.

The really good news was the Crown Prosecution Service had decided that it wasn't in the public interest to pursue the case against her and all charges had been dropped. It was a tremendous relief but at the same time she couldn't relax because Carl was still on the loose, and she wasn't convinced that Luke's associates, the ones still knocking around, wouldn't try to harm her, too.

She stayed almost all the time in Tremarnock, only leaving the flat during daylight and visiting places where there'd be plenty of people. She felt as if she was living a half-life, but she was sure that Carl would have heard about Luke's arrest and that he'd be biding his time, waiting for the right opportunity. It was no surprise that, despite enquiries, the police had failed to find him; he was far too clever.

The biggest revelation to her had been the villagers because she'd never known that such kindness existed. As soon as they'd heard her story from Liz they'd rallied round, eager to do whatever they could. That she was still married to the man who'd done so much wrong was less important to them than the fact that she was alone, vulnerable and needed their help. She wondered, now, how she could have lived in Tremarnock for all these months and never even noticed the warmth and community spirit that surrounded her. She must have been blind.

Even Pat, who'd had such a terrible experience, seemed to have grudgingly accepted her, largely because she was the one who'd rescued Loveday, and it was in Pat's house, The Nook, that Tabitha now found herself with Oscar and his former nanny. Pat was much stronger, almost back to normal, and had been pruning the roses in her little back garden when the others called.

'It's too hot for my liking,' she complained, fanning herself with the floral apron that was tied around her waist. Her cheeks were flushed and her white hair was sticking to her forehead. 'Come in and have some lemon barley. I made up a jug this morning.'

Oscar, who was looking very cute in a pair of navy blue shorts and a bright green T-shirt, raced past the old woman into the kitchen.

'Bless him,' she said, smiling indulgently. 'Bright as a button, he is. He understands every word we say.'

He seemed to have grown up a lot in the past three months and had settled well into Dove Cottage. He liked Esme upstairs,

Loveday and her family, of course, and perhaps Pat most of all. There was no doubt that she adored children and in some ways Oscar had become a substitute for Rosie, who'd grown too old for cuddles and choccy bickies in front of Pat's favourite, slow-moving TV detective series. Oscar rarely asked for his daddy these days, which both pleased Tabitha and saddened her, but mostly she was grateful that he'd adapted so well to his new life. It could have been far worse.

It was pleasantly cool in Pat's front room and they sat sipping their cold drinks while Oscar rummaged in the old woman's sewing box, sorting through the different-coloured buttons and using the wooden darning mushroom as a sword. Loveday was full of the fact that Saturday was opening night at The Hole in the Wall pub. A new landlord had recently moved in and was promising regular live music nights, as well as quizzes, dressing-up dos and other events.

'I hope it's not going to get noisy down there,' Pat grumbled. 'Locals won't like it, and he'd better not go stealing any of Barbara's business.'

'This place could do with livening up,' Loveday sniffed.

Pat didn't hear so she had to repeat herself more loudly.

'There's nothing for young people here,' Loveday shouted. 'The Lobster Pot's full of fuddy-duddies and The Victory Inn's not as fun as it used to be.'

Pat looked doubtful. 'What's he like, this landlord, then? Does he have a wife and children?'

Loveday shook her head. 'He's quite old, in his thirties, I think. A bit of a hippy with a beard and long hair.'

Pat looked grave. 'Doesn't sound like my type. I don't like a man with a beard. I prefer clean-shaven.'

'Beards give you a rash,' Loveday agreed, 'but stubble's worse.'

They ruminated on this for a few minutes, then Loveday

asked Tabitha if she planned to attend the opening. 'We could go together.' She lowered her eyes. 'Jesse might turn up after work, but as long as I leave early it'll be OK.'

'I can't,' Tabitha said quickly.

Pat eyed her curiously. 'Why not? There'll be plenty of folk and you might enjoy yourself. Besides, I want to hear your verdict on the beardy fellow.'

'What about Oscar?' said Tabitha, and Pat leaped in immediately. 'Bring him here! I'd love to have him. One late night won't hurt him and he can always fall asleep on my sofa. It won't be the first time!'

'No, honestly,' Tabitha replied. 'I'm not in the mood for that sort of thing, I couldn't handle it.'

'Oh, go on,' Loveday pleaded. 'I don't feel sociable either but we can just have one drink. It'll be interesting to see what it's like in there now – and there might be good music.'

Tabitha hesitated. She hadn't had an evening out in months and it would be wonderful to see a live band. She'd be in no danger with so many people around and, what's more, Oscar would enjoy being with Pat and no doubt the old woman would appreciate his company, too.

'Please,' said Loveday, spying a chink in the armour. 'Liz said she'd go for a bit.'

It was a wrong call. 'Well, you'll have her for company, then, you won't need me, and there'll be lots of your other friends, too. I just can't deal with it at the moment.'

Loveday stuck out her bottom lip. 'Liz is so enormous I don't think she'll even fit through the door.'

Tabitha smiled. Her new-found friend was, indeed, as round as a barrel and the baby was due in just a few weeks.

'She told me she won't go if you don't,' Loveday wheedled. 'She'll sit at home on her own.'

'Well, we can't have that,' said Pat.

'She'll have Rosie with her,' Tabitha reasoned.

'No,' replied Loveday, 'Rosie's been invited to something at Tim's.'

Tabitha sighed, feeling herself beaten. 'All right, you win, but I'll only go for an hour. I'll pick you both up at seven.'

It was all she could do not to bolt when, on returning to Dove Cottage, Esme came clattering down the metal staircase that led from her front door, her salt-and-pepper hair flying, to announce that there was a 'special visitor'.

'She's up here,' she panted, pointing to the entrance of her flat and grinning from ear to ear. 'There was no answer from yours and she kept ringing and ringing, so I came down and there she was! She looked awfully tired and hungry so I gave her some sustenance and we've been jabbering ever since. Oh, do come up, she's been waiting ages!'

There was no escape. Tabitha's heart was in her mouth as she ascended the steps behind Oscar, who insisted on counting: 'One... two... three...' She had an idea who it might be and wasn't at all sure that if she was right, she wouldn't melt into a puddle on the floor and seep through the floorboards.

'Four... five... What next, Mamma?'

'Six,' said Tabitha absent-mindedly, watching the hem of Esme's purple, ankle-length skirt swish round the corner.

'Six... nine... ten.'

'Molly, oh!'

Tabitha's friend jumped up from the armchair and flung her arms around Tabitha's neck, at which point Tabitha burst into tears, as Molly knew she would.

'What are you...?' she blubbed into Molly's hair, vaguely

registering that it was now an unusual shade of fuchsia pink. 'I told you not…'

Molly, who was much shorter than Tabitha with big green eyes and a pale face, backed away and took both her friend's hands.

'He's dead, Tabs,' she said, eyes shining. 'Carl. He got in a fight with some drug dealer. He was smashed in the head. They took him to hospital but he never came round. He'll never trouble you again.'

Tabitha's legs gave way beneath her and she sank to the floor, her body shaking like a flame.

'Are you sure?' she whispered, searching Molly's face for confirmation and watching as her lips mouthed the words that she longed to hear.

'It's true. I swear. It was on the regional news. They had a different name for him but I recognised him immediately. It was definitely him. One hundred per cent. You're free, Tabby. You're finally free!'

Tabitha glanced around Esme's living room, seeing everything as if it was for the first time: the rich, jewel-like colours of the cushions on her wide sofa; the shimmering gold Buddha on the shelf above the TV; the strutting peacocks on the rug in front of the fireplace, their vivid blue and green feathers outrageously bright in the late-afternoon sunshine. All her senses seemed to be heightened, so that even the tinkling wind chime by the door sounded louder and sweeter. It was as if the entire planet had switched in an instant from analogue to high-definition and the intensity made her blink.

'Are you all right?' Esme asked, touching her shoulder, because she must have looked quite dazed, and Oscar eyed his mother uncertainly.

'I'm fine, honestly.' But it didn't sound like her, it seemed to come from some other woman on the floor while the real Tabitha was gazing in wonder, like Miranda, at this brave new world. 'I just can't believe it. It feels like a dream.'

Esme, ever one to prescribe a 'stiff drink' in times of stress, went off to fetch glasses, ice, tonic and the gin bottle, while Molly helped Tabitha to her feet.

'I know you said not to come but I had to tell you in person,' Molly explained, settling her friend on the sofa. 'I wanted to see your expression.' She had an improbably big mouth for a slight person, strong rectangular teeth with a space in the middle, and her wide, impish grin seemed to fill her entire face, turning her eyes into glittery slits and making you want to smile back.

Tabitha felt a surge of love and gratitude that almost took her breath away.

'You've always been there for me, Molly, always,' she choked. 'I owe you so much. I don't know how I'll ever repay you.'

Molly waved a small hand in the air. 'Ach, don't be silly.' She bent down to pick Oscar up and smother his cheeks in kisses.

'How long is it since I've seen you, little man? I've missed you.'

Oscar wasn't at all sure about this strange woman whom he hadn't met for nine months and struggled to free himself.

'He's forgotten me!' Molly wailed when she could no longer keep him still and had to set him down.

'Such a lot's happened to him recently, he's just confused,' Tabitha apologised as he scrambled on her knee. 'You know, it still hasn't sunk in, this news, it's going to take a while. I keep thinking you're an illusion and any minute now I'm going to wake up!'

Molly laughed. 'I'm real all right. Here, let's get this down you.'

She passed Tabitha the large gin and tonic that Esme had poured, before taking one for herself.

'Chin-chin!' Esme cried, raising her own glass high in the air. 'I'm not sure whether to laugh or cry, to be frank.' She took a sip of her drink then dabbed the corner of an eye with a finger. 'You've been through so much. Let's toast the start of a whole new chapter.'

'Hear, hear!' Molly took a slurp and shivered slightly. 'Ooh that's strong!'

'It seems awful to be celebrating someone's death,' Tabitha commented, poking down a slice of lemon.

'Normally I'd agree, but not in his case. Carl was a monster. The world's a better place now he's gone.'

Oscar went to examine one of Esme's picture books on the shelf beneath her window. She had a large collection of colourful children's stories and fairy-tales and often drew inspiration from them for her ceramic designs.

'How long are you staying?' Tabitha asked Molly, who had taken off her sandals, reached for one of Esme's cushions and was sitting cross-legged on the floor. She seemed very much at home.

'I've got the whole week off work.' She looked very pleased with herself. 'I'm going to help you pack.'

'Pack?' Tabitha's eyes opened wide. 'What do you mean?' She was still busy processing the information about Carl.

'Home with me, of course. You and Oscar can take my bed and Dom and I will sleep in the sitting room.' Dom was Molly's on-off boyfriend. 'Don't worry, he's cool about it. In fact, it was his suggestion. I'd have given you the airbed.' She winked.

'But what about—?'

Molly read her mind. 'I already spoke to the liaison officer here – you told me the name, remember? Luke's in Norwich and they can extend his no-go zone to include the whole of Manchester. We'll get a panic alarm fitted in my flat, but I honestly don't think you'll be in any danger, not now you've given your statement. The guys that haven't been caught yet are petrified it's their turn next. The last thing they want is trouble. They'll be lying low, they've probably even left the country.'

Tabitha was silent for a moment, wondering what to say.

'You can come back, Tabs,' Molly went on, 'to Manchester where you belong. You hate this place...' She glanced at Esme and shrugged. 'I'm sorry but it's true. We'll find you a little flat somewhere eventually, and Oscar can make local friends before he starts school.'

She clapped her hands, so taken was she with her own plan. 'And you and I can go clubbing together and to restaurants without constantly having to look over our shoulders. You could even re-join the band if you want to. We need a kick up the arse, we're going nowhere fast at the moment.

'It'll be a whole new life, Tabby. No more wind-swept beaches and...' she gazed around for inspiration and her eyes alighted on Esme's collection of vintage teapots on a shelf by the fireplace '...cream teas.' She wrinkled her nose. 'And Oscar will speak proper Mancunian, not all this ooh-arr lark.'

'I like the accents here,' Tabitha said, without thinking.

'Nothing wrong with a Cornish burr,' Esme agreed. 'They still use some of the old words, you know. It's a most ancient and fascinating language.'

Oscar pointed at a picture he was examining and made a snorting noise. 'Pig,' he said proudly.

Tabitha scarcely registered. 'When do we leave?' She was gazing into her glass, which was still half-full.

'As soon as possible. You don't need to worry about money. I can tide you over until you get everything sorted. I guess you won't be able to reclaim the rent on the flat here, but it doesn't matter because staying with me won't cost you anything.'

'I'll pay you back when I get a job,' Tabitha replied in a small voice.

She placed her drink on the floor beside her and stared into space. She was thinking about Loveday, Liz and Robert, Esme, Pat, Shelley and all the others who'd taken her to their hearts since Luke had been arrested. She was remembering how only this morning she and Loveday had sat on one of the benches by the beach, Oscar between them, eating ice creams and watching the children race in and out of the ocean.

When they'd finished, Oscar had insisted on venturing onto the beach himself. They'd had their bathing suits on under their clothes but it hadn't been as warm by the water's edge. Even so, they'd stripped off and waded in, hand in hand, squealing as the icy waves had risen up their knees, their thighs, their waists, until at last the torture had become unbearable and they'd plunged in, laughing as Oscar's expression had turned from shock to dismay and, finally, delight. She was going to miss all that.

'I guess I never really fitted in here,' she said quietly. 'I'm a city girl through and through. I like the hustle and bustle, the smoke and traffic, the crowds, the cinemas, busyness. I'd hardly even seen a field of cows before I came to Tremarnock, and I certainly never popped in and out of people's houses, or knew what my neighbours were up to. It's just not what happens in a town, you're more anonymous.'

She was aware of Esme, peering at her down her long nose. 'You don't have to go,' she said softly.

Molly jumped up. 'Come on!' She was wearing a short

strappy sundress in ice-cream colours that went rather well with her pink hair. 'Let's do a tour of the village, the packing can wait till tomorrow. Then you can show me where I'm spending the night. The sofa will do, I'm not fussy. After that I'm in your hands. How about fish and chips for tea?' She frowned. 'That is, if you have a fish and chip shop. It doesn't look like there's much around.'

'We have a very good one as a matter of fact,' Esme said rather sharply, 'and an excellent restaurant, too.'

But Molly was preoccupied with putting on her sandals and didn't seem to hear.

Chapter Twenty-Six

ROBERT HAD TAKEN Rosie to Tim's house at around four, leaving Liz plenty of time to shower and get dressed. It was Tim's mother's birthday and she was having a bit of a party, to which Rosie had been invited.

She'd just received welcome news about her most recent scan, which showed that the sliver of brain tumour that doctors had been unable to remove was still dormant. Furthermore, the website that she and Tim set up had received some publicity in the local press, meaning that they'd acquired a certain celebrity status in school, to which they were still adjusting.

Of course, Loveday teased Rosie about the relationship, while Liz made delicate enquiries, but Rosie insisted that she and Tim were classmates, nothing more, and Liz was inclined to believe her. They were only thirteen and had originally been brought together more through mutual suffering than anything else, although the fact that they got on so well and their bond had persisted would seem to suggest that their feelings, subconscious or otherwise, might go somewhat deeper than mere friendship. Liz just hoped that neither would be hurt; in her book, they were far too young to be dating.

She stood in front of her open wardrobe and eyed the garments inside suspiciously. She had only two pairs of maternity trousers and a few loose tops that she was heartily sick of. She felt well in herself, blooming, everyone said, but the baby was now so low in her abdomen that she needed constant trips to the loo and sometimes felt as if she might burst like an overripe tomato. All in all, it was about time for this child to make its appearance but, then, they came when they were ready and not when you wanted them to.

She pulled out the black trousers and a turquoise, V-neck tunic that she hadn't worn for, ooh, three days. Better than the pink one that she virtually lived in. Once she'd added one of her own, diamanté hair clips and put on some sparkly earrings and a matching necklace, she felt more glamorous and padded downstairs in bare feet to wait for the others.

Tabitha arrived with Molly while Loveday was still dressing. Both women looked young and stylish, though they could hardly have been more different. Tabitha was wearing dark trousers, trainers and a sparkly gold top, her black curly hair fanning out round her face like a dusky aura, while the petite, pink-haired Molly was in a denim mini-skirt, white camisole and sandals, with rather startling, bright blue mascara on her lashes. They certainly were an eye-catching pair.

Liz had met Molly the day before, when Tabitha had popped in to introduce her, and had taken to her immediately. She'd been dismayed, however, to hear about the Manchester move.

'Are you sure it's what you want?' she'd asked Tabitha, scanning her face for reassurance. 'I mean, you must do what's right for you and Oscar, of course, but, ooh! We'll miss you!'

'It's where she belongs,' Molly had said quickly, linking arms with her friend who had been beside her on the sofa. 'She never wanted to leave Manchester in the first place, remember, it was all Luke's idea. He never gave her a choice.'

'Of course,' Liz had agreed, but had that been a twitch in the corner of Tabitha's mouth, and why had her eyes been moist? Liz had decided that she must have been imagining it. After all, Tabitha and Molly had known each other for ever and there was no doubt that Molly had her friend's best interests at heart.

Liz pulled a face and shifted in the armchair, trying to find a comfortable position. It wasn't easy with a bump that size.

'Are you OK?' asked Tabitha.

'Yes, but I feel like such an elephant. I can't believe I'll ever be normal again.'

Loveday appeared and embraced the visitors, and Liz was pleased to note that she looked more cheerful than of late. She'd made a real effort and was wearing black skinny jeans, a low-cut purple vest top and purple platform shoes. With her heavily kohl-rimmed eyes, her hair, now dyed black again, growing fast and scooped up in a stubby side ponytail, and her giant, silver-hooped earrings, it was almost the old Loveday, not the sad, washed-out girl that she'd been recently.

'Let's go!' she declared, fiddling with the waistband of her trousers, which were awfully tight. She grinned. 'It'll take Liz half an hour to waddle there. Hope the baby doesn't come on the way 'cos I'm dead squeamish.'

Tabitha must have felt strange walking past The Stables and turned her head in the other direction.

'Don't think about it,' Molly whispered, giving her a hug, 'it's all over now.'

The door of the pub, once a haven for smugglers, was so low that anyone over about five feet six inches tall had to stoop to get in. Loveday almost tripped over the raised step but, fortunately, Tabitha managed to catch her.

'That could have been a dramatic entrance. You'd better be careful in those shoes.'

It was dark inside, hot and crowded already, and at first

glance there was nowhere to sit, but Molly spotted a tanned young woman in a lurid, tie-dye T-shirt dragging a chair over to where her friends were standing.

'I'm sorry, I need that,' Molly said, grabbing the chair. She might be small but she was ferocious when she wanted to be and Liz, embarrassed, pretended not to notice.

'Hey!' The woman scowled, trying to yank the chair back, but Molly was too quick.

'There's a pregnant woman. Don't you have any manners?'

Duly chastised, the woman slunk away wordlessly.

Liz insisted on going up to the bar with Tabitha and Molly, while Loveday guarded the precious chair. Annie and another young woman were serving drinks.

'I'm paying!' Liz declared, refusing to take no for an answer. 'This might be the last round I buy for a while!'

'I thought you were a fitness trainer?' Tabitha asked Annie, while she poured Liz's orange juice. 'Don't you do classes at the Methodist church?'

Annie, who was wearing the same red T-shirt as the other bartender, fetched a bottle of Chardonnay from the fridge and unscrewed the lid. 'I am, but I need the extra money. I'm saving up for a holiday. Nathan and I want to go to India. Danny said I could just do a couple of nights a week here, which is ideal.'

Liz was about to ask who Danny was when a tall man arrived, with long fair hair tied back in a ponytail and a neatly trimmed beard, carrying a bottle of Plymouth Gin that he proceeded to attach to the optic rack behind him.

Molly took one of the glasses of wine back to Loveday, while Liz and Tabitha waited for the other drinks, watching a gaggle of noisy young people arrive with guitars and a fiddle. The man with the beard turned and waved.

'Hi!' he called loudly, as they made for the room at the back. 'Be with you in a minute!'

He was lean, lightly tanned and muscular, with an intelligent, slightly weather-beaten face, as if he were often outdoors. He was wearing a red T-shirt like the girls, and low-slung jeans held up with a wide, brown leather belt. Liz couldn't help thinking that he was rather dreamy.

When he noticed the women standing there, he held out a hand. 'I'm Danny. I've just taken over this place. Are you local or just visiting?'

Liz told him that she lived round the corner and waited for Tabitha to explain her own situation.

'I'm local, um, well sort of…'

She was blushing! Liz was certain of it, and she stifled a smile.

Molly returned and put an arm round Tabitha's shoulders, grinning. 'This is my partner in crime. We used to be in a band together.'

'Did you?' Danny crossed his arms, tilting his head to one side. 'What sort of music?'

'Folk rock,' said Tabitha, shuffling uncomfortably, 'but it was a long time ago. We were just kids, really.'

Danny gave her a quizzical look. 'You should think about re-forming. Let me know if you do. I'm on the lookout for good bands. I want to be a showcase for local talent.'

Molly ran a hand through her pink hair, making the silver bangles on her slim arm tinkle. 'The group's still going actually – just. I'm determined to persuade her to join us again, she's got a great voice. There'll be no excuse when she's back in Manchester.'

'Manchester?' He raised his eyebrows and fixed on Tabitha. 'You're moving?'

Tabitha pretended to fiddle with the clasp of her silver necklace, as if it had come loose, and Molly answered for her.

'In a week,' she said cheerfully. 'I've been helping her pack.'

'That's a shame.'

They were interrupted by a loud voice coming over the microphone next door, signalling that the music was about to start.

'They're from Tavistock,' Danny shouted, as someone struck up on the acoustic guitar. 'I think they sound great.'

The women fought their way back through the crowds to Loveday, who'd been joined by Tony, Felipe, Rick, and Esme, in a rather fetching purple turban with a sparkly brooch pinned to the front, wisps of grey hair snaking artfully out from underneath.

'Where's his girlfriend?' Liz whispered to Esme, thinking that she hadn't seen Sylvia for a while, and Esme shook her head.

'Ditched him for an estate agent with a BMW soon after Luke Mallon's arrest, but Rick had already decided that she wasn't his type. Too vulgar by half.' She patted her turban in a self-satisfied sort of way.

It occurred to Liz that the pair were standing very close and she couldn't help noticing that Rick's hand was resting lightly on Esme's bottom. To Liz's knowledge, she'd never had a boyfriend; she'd never seemed much interested. She didn't seem to mind the attention now, though.

Loveday sidled off when Liz sat down, having spotted Nathan, Ryan and various other friends. Audrey poked her head in, stuck her fingers in her ears and vanished immediately, appalled by the din. It was so loud that there was no point trying to talk, so the rest sipped their drinks and listened to the words of the deep-voiced vocalist doing an Ed Sheeran number.

'You all right?' Tabitha mouthed, and Liz gave a thumbs-up.

In truth, though, she was feeling uneasy. A strange niggling had started up in her abdomen, a tightness like a little ball.

It wasn't exactly painful but it put her on edge, she couldn't relax, and the baby was pressing down heavily, making her want to go to the loo yet again. She shifted slightly to see if it made a difference and wondered if she should leave, but there were so many people and the effort seemed too great. Better to wait, she decided, until the others were ready to go and could walk her home.

The band played for fifteen or twenty minutes before taking a break, at which point Molly went back to the bar with Felipe. She was clearly enjoying herself immensely and Tabitha, too, seemed in no hurry to leave, despite having insisted earlier that she'd only stay for one drink. Danny had joined her, they were deep in conversation and Liz didn't want to disturb them. It was good to see her friend laughing and smiling and she found herself wondering if this was what she'd once been like, before she'd met Luke or Carl. She looked wise and beautiful, with so much to give the world.

'How're you doing, Liz?'

The voice was familiar and she turned, surprised, to find Jesse crouching beside her; as far as she knew, he rarely went to village events these days and, besides, she'd imagined that he'd be working.

'Day off,' he explained, before she could ask. 'One Saturday in four.'

He looked terribly handsome, with a golden brown tan, his hair bleached almost white from the summer sun. He was wearing a white T-shirt with black lettering on the front, and he leaned over and kissed her cheek.

'It's great to see you here,' she said, meaning it, and she was pleased when Jean and Tom made a point of coming to speak to him.

'Bit noisy,' Jean complained. She was wearing a bright red top that almost matched the colour of her cheeks. Tom poked her in the ribs. 'What do you expect, woman? It's live music night.'

Liz felt another twinge, stronger this time, like a tugging in the gut. She was about to ask Jesse if he'd mind escorting her home when the music started up again and it was impossible to hear a thing, so she closed her eyes and lost herself in the lyrics of Bruno Mars's 'When I Was Your Man'.

When she opened them again, she noticed Loveday cross the throng, heading towards the entrance of the room next door, presumably to get a better view of the band. She was taller than usual and strikingly attractive in her tight top and high heels, walking tentatively, as if scared of falling over, clutching her drink in one hand while she used the other to nudge people aside.

Liz rose herself to have a stretch and at that moment Jesse stood up too, and Liz felt his body stiffen when he clocked his former girlfriend just a few metres away. Loveday spotted him also and stopped dead, as if unable to work out the quickest escape route, before raising a hand and pointing with the other at her chest.

'I'll go,' she mouthed, clearly meaning for Jesse to stay and enjoy the evening, but he shook his head and stepped towards her, elbowing people aside as he went.

Liz held her breath, praying that he wouldn't make a scene, because it was no one's fault. Loveday had deliberately arrived early in order not to bump into him after the restaurant closed; she hadn't known that it was his day off. Her face seemed to crumple, until he put a hand on her arm and guided her towards the bar, and Liz looked away quickly, fearing that she might jinx them.

She sat down again, only to feel a stabbing in her lower back that made her gasp. She wished that she could summon

Tabitha, but she was at the bar, too, with Danny, who'd resumed his post, and Molly and Felipe were nowhere to be seen. Tony, meanwhile, was in a huddle with Rick and Esme, and Jean and Tom had taken up with a couple whom she didn't recognise. Tom was laughing a little too loudly, unaware, it seemed, of the fierce looks that his wife was shooting periodically in his direction.

The music was getting louder and Liz felt quite sick. Deciding that she could wait no longer, she rose carefully and started to stumble towards the door, aware only that the tightening in her lower tummy was becoming stronger and less able to bear.

'I have to get out,' she gasped, shoving through the crowds who seemed not to notice her distress, and she gripped the doorframe for support as she staggered into the cool night air.

Unable to think properly and conscious only of the need to get home, she started to zig-zag up the street, stopping every now and then to lean against the wall and catch her breath and cursing herself for having forgotten her mobile. Her progress was painfully slow and she only managed a few paces before she felt another strong contraction, and knew for certain that she was in labour. She wasn't due for nearly three weeks but, still, the doctor had warned that she might have got her dates wrong and shouldn't be surprised if it came early.

She tried to breathe deeply, her body bent double, head bowed, and told herself not to panic. As soon as the contraction subsided, she'd crawl up South Street on all fours, if necessary, and call Robert.

There was a hollow groan, like that of a wounded animal, and she realised that it was coming from her.

'Liz? Oh, bloody hell, I think she's having the baby.'

Tabitha's voice cut through the pain and Liz felt a wave of relief. Thank God she was no longer alone.

'Someone, help! There's a woman in labour!' It was Molly this time.

Liz felt strong shoulders beneath her arms, propping her up, and allowed herself to be carried up the road. Meanwhile, Jesse was now beside them too.

'I'll fetch Robert,' he barked. 'Loveday, ring the ambulance – now!'

'You've got to come quick,' the girl screamed down the phone, sounding excited and terrified in equal measure. Liz could only half see her out of the corner of an eye, still wearing the purple platform shoes.

Now that she had some assistance, she could concentrate better on her breathing. Keep calm, she was telling herself, your body will do the rest. They were almost at Bag End, not far to go...

Another violent contraction made her howl. So soon? She was sure they hadn't come that quickly last time. She wanted Robert desperately and cried his name.

'He'll be here any second,' Tabitha whispered, struggling up the front path with her. 'The ambulance is on its way.'

'How long will it take?' It was Felipe speaking. Where had he come from? Liz didn't hear the reply, because her body was in the grip of a force beyond her control and nothing could stop it now.

'Oh, my God! My God, put me down, I have to push!'

'Where are the keys?' Tony this time.

Loveday must have found hers because the door burst open and they all helped Liz into the front room, where she crouched on hands and knees, panting. She was aware of a lot of activity – sheets and towels being fetched and laid down, a plastic bowl from the kitchen, gentle but firm hands helping her off with her clothes.

'Liz, darling!' The sound of Robert's voice made the tears rush to her eyes and he crouched down and took her damp face in his hands and kissed her forehead.

'I think it's coming,' she gasped. 'Where's the ambulance?'

Someone passed him the phone and he started talking to the operator, moving round to her other end to get a proper look.

'Yes, I can see it... black hair...' he muttered, before shouting up to her, 'Pant, one, two, three, blow... Keep going, my love, you've got to try and slow it down.'

'I can't! Where's the ambulance?' she cried again.

'I don't think they'll be here in time. We're going to have to deliver it ourselves.'

Liz, frightened, started to protest, 'No!' But the desire to push was overwhelming.

She could hear him taking instructions while Tony wiped her brow with a damp flannel, whispering gently, 'You're doing great, you're going to be fine...'

Jesse, who must have followed Robert in, moved quietly around the room, switching on table lamps and turning off the garish overhead light, so that they were in comforting shadows.

'I can see the head!' Robert shouted suddenly. Then, to the operator, 'No, the cord's out of the way. It looks OK.'

'Easy now,' said Felipe, who was down at Robert's end. 'Let the nature take its course. Eez good.'

'Sweetie, I don't think—' Tony started to say, but Felipe interrupted.

'I have delivered many baby cows in my native country. I know what I am doing but with them the feet come first, then the nose.'

Tony, for once lost for words, clamped his mouth shut.

Tabitha was now kneeling on one side, Loveday and Molly on the other.

Keep going, Lizzie,' Robert hollered, 'you're doing brilliantly!' and to the operator, 'yes, the shoulders are out... The rest is coming... It's slippery...'

Liz gave a long, low groan and pushed with all her might, feeling as if the entire contents of her insides were spilling on to the sheet beneath her.

'Oh!' Robert's bloodcurdling yell brought her to her senses.

'Is it all right?' she asked, frozen with panic. Nothing else mattered, just this one crucial fact.

She could hear him gabbling, 'Yes it's breathing... Pinkish...' Then there was a high-pitched, unmistakable cry, the most wonderful sound that Liz thought she'd ever heard, and Robert's responding laugh was like a stream gurgling over mossy pebbles: 'It's a little girl!'

The next thing she knew was that gentle hands were turning her on her back, propping her head against a pillow, then her husband placed the warm, waxy, slithering body of their new baby daughter on her chest, close to her heart.

'You've done it, Lizzie!' he said, squatting beside her and stroking her damp hair, her cheek, before wrapping her and her baby in a soft blanket. His eyes were sparkling like jewels. 'We have a beautiful baby girl!'

At that moment, Liz felt as if all her life she'd been waiting for this moment; if she were to die now, she wouldn't be short-changed, because she'd completed the task that she was always meant to, she'd fulfilled her destiny and brought forth not one but two beautiful girls, and she couldn't imagine ever being happier or feeling more truly blessed.

'You clever, clever girl,' Robert said, kissing first her head, then their daughter's, and tears of wonder and gladness trickled down her cheeks, which Tabitha wiped away with the soft edge of a towel.

In the months to come, Liz would tell people that she could scarcely remember what happened in the next half-hour or so after that. She knew that the paramedics arrived and checked her and the baby over, that she delivered the placenta, they pronounced everything well and then, eventually, left, but their names and what they looked like were a complete blur.

Following their departure, though, her recollections became less vague. She could still picture Tabitha, Molly and Loveday fussing round her, lighting the fire, fetching more pillows for her head and handing her a cup of sweet tea while they chatted in low, happy voices with Robert, Tony, Felipe and Jesse. 'God, I was worried... Never imagined I'd deliver a baby... We were a good team... Baby cows eez more easy, I think... She's gorgeous!'

The birth wasn't exactly as Liz had planned but, looking back, she had to admit that there was something rather wonderful about the way it turned out. She was at home, after all, in her favourite room, surrounded by friends and family and the man she loved, who'd risen to the challenge and proved utterly heroic in an emergency. She thought he was a complete star.

And despite her hazy, milky, post-birth memory, there was another thing that she'd have no trouble bringing to mind. She was still settled by the fire, the baby suckling contentedly at her breast. Robert had been to fetch Rosie from Tim's house, and Tabitha, Molly, Loveday, Tony, Felipe and Jesse were on the point of leaving. No one had bothered to check the time but it must have been at least 3 a.m., later perhaps, because the night sky had just started to turn from black to inky grey.

'What are you going to call her?' Tabitha asked suddenly. 'You haven't mentioned a name.'

Robert, who had collapsed on the sofa looking white and exhausted, scratched his head. 'We're not sure yet. We haven't been able to agree on anything.'

Liz was about to throw a few suggestions into the ring when Tabitha made a strange noise, and they all turned to look.

'I can't leave Tremarnock, Molly,' she blurted.

Everyone was startled, because it had come from nowhere.

'But...' Molly protested, before letting out a long sigh. 'I feared you might say that.' She peered at her friend through bright blue lashes. 'Can you be persuaded?'

Tabitha shook her head firmly. 'I've made up my mind. This is my home now.'

There was a pause while everyone digested the news, then Rosie, who'd been on the floor beside her mother, suddenly cleared her throat and rose, pulling back her shoulders and puffing out her chest.

'Lowenna,' she declared. 'That's what we should call her.'

Liz raised her eyebrows. 'Lowenna? I've never heard it before. I rather like it.'

'It's Cornish,' Rosie informed her. 'It means joy.'

Liz glanced at Robert, and then the others in turn. 'What do you reckon? The delivery was a joint effort. Let's have a democratic vote.'

'It's pretty,' said Tabitha and Molly in unison, and the rest muttered their approval, all apart from Robert.

'What's your view?' Loveday asked him. 'You haven't said anything yet?'

'Lowenna...' He grinned at last, rolling the name round on his tongue. 'I think it's perfect. A Cornish maid, made in Cornwall.'

He gazed first at his wife, then at Rosie, then at his new baby daughter, and his love seemed to wrap around all three, binding them together like ivy round a tree.

'Lowenna it is,' they chorused.

Acknowledgments

I HAD A great deal of help in the writing of this novel from Inspector John Shuttleworth from Devon and Cornwall Police, who patiently answered my questions about fraud investigations and gave me invaluable advice. Any errors regarding police procedure are entirely my own.

Huge thanks, also, to Sarah and Dylan McLees Taylor, from Westcroft Guesthouse in Kingsand, Cornwall, whose gorgeous rooms I cannot recommend highly enough, and to Dawn Leopold, manager of the Devonport Inn, Kingsand, who serves the best mussels I have ever tasted. Patricia Crowley, from the Hermes Hotel, Kingston upon Thames, kindly told me much about the ups and downs of running a bed and breakfast establishment.

I couldn't haven written this book without the support of my husband, Kevin, our children, Georgia, Harry and Freddie, and my sister, Sarah Arikian, the most widely read woman I know.

Last but not least, thanks as always to my wonderful agent, Heather Holden-Brown, my fantastic editor, Rosie de Courcy, and all at Head of Zeus for their brilliant expertise and unstinting support.

Emma Burstall

'Burstall is a great writer'
Daily Mail

Tremarnock
Summer

Chapter One

'IT'S FOR YOU.'

Bramble frowned. Her step-mother, Cassie, was bent double over the doormat, her not insubstantial backside blocking the hallway. Bramble was late, as usual, and she didn't like letters. They were usually bills, after all – mobile phone, credit card, store card. The only post she looked forward to was the clothes catalogues that regularly plopped through the letterbox with enticing discounts not to be ignored.

When Cassie rose, Bramble grabbed the letter, preparing to stuff it in her bag and read it on the bus on the way to work. Or this evening – or tomorrow, even...

'I wonder what it is.'

Something in Cassie's tone piqued Bramble's interest and she paused to cast an eye over the white envelope. It was thick and expensive looking, with her name, Miss Bramble Challoner, and her address handwritten in black ink. Whoever penned it might have had calligraphy lessons, because the script was so neat and even. There was no stamp, just a blue mark saying 'Delivered by Royal Mail' and 'Postage Paid'. No clue then, but it didn't seem like a bill; it was too *personal*.

'Looks official,' Cassie commented unnecessarily, and Bramble felt a prickle of irritation.

'Yeah, well, it can wait till later.'

Cassie's face fell. Fifty-four years old and she still acted like a little girl sometimes, unable to disguise her feelings.

Bramble, softening, kissed her on the cheek and Cassie reluctantly moved aside as she headed for the exit.

'I'm staying at Matt's tonight. I'll give you a call, OK?'

'Don't forget your Dad's birthday tomorrow!'

But Bramble was already halfway up the garden path, wobbling in her new high heels across the uneven tiles. If she didn't get a move on, she'd miss the 8.23.a.m. and then there'd be fireworks.

*

THE BUS WAS packed, as usual, and she hung on to the metal rail as it lurched to and fro, cursing silently when the phone buzzed in her cavernous bag because she'd have to rootle inside, which wouldn't be easy with only one free hand.

It was Matt, wanting to discuss arrangements for the evening.

'It's the Premier League title decider,' he wheedled, 'can't we catch your film another time?'

'No,' said Bramble firmly. 'It's had great reviews.'

More and more, she was finding that nights at his place did her head in, especially if there was football on. In fact there always seemed to be some big match or other: rugby, football, cricket, snooker, darts, even. When it came to sport, you name it, he'd watch it all evening if she'd let him.

'I'll take Katie instead,' she warned, knowing that would shut him up. He wasn't that keen on going out but he was even less keen if she went out with someone else; he said he missed her.

His idea of bliss on earth was snuggling up on the sofa, one arm around her waist, the other clutching a can of lager, a bowl of popcorn balanced on their laps and the telly up full blast.

'What more could a man want?' he'd sigh contentedly above the din.

She had no right to complain, had she? Matt was handsome, loyal, solvent and he loved her. Lots of girls would give their eyeteeth to be in her position. She ought to be grateful.

It wasn't until much later, when she was on her lunch break, that she remembered the letter and pulled it out of her bag while Katie went to the loo. They'd managed to find a seat in their favourite café, that served filled jacket potatoes as well as sandwiches and salads, all at a very reasonable price, and Bramble was willing Katie to get a move on so that they could return to their favourite subject: the boss, Judy. In a way it was just as well that she was such a cow because slagging her off helped while away the monotonous hours.

The café was hot and crowded and the windows, that looked out on to the busy high street, were clouded with steam. It was a beautiful sunny summer's day and they were missing it. They should have bought sandwiches and gone to the municipal park to top up their tans.

Bramble ripped open the envelope and pulled out the letter, noticing the name and address on the right-hand side: 'Slater Brown Solicitors, Caxton Street, Westminster, London, SW1.'

Intrigued, she read on…

Dear Miss Challoner,

I regret to inform you that your grandfather, Arthur George Penrose, Lord Penrose, died on 10th June. On behalf of the firm, I would like to offer my condolences for your loss…

She stopped for a moment. It seemed so strange to see the word 'grandfather', for she'd never met him and the little that she'd heard about him had been distinctly unfavourable. Why, she wondered, would they bother telling her? Lord Penrose hadn't exactly taken an interest in her or his daughter Mary, Bramble's mother. In any case, Bramble didn't consider Mary to be her real mum. That was Cassie, who'd brought her up since she was two years old.

Her eyes scanned down further.

Lord Penrose left a will dated 1 June 2010, under the terms of which myself and my partner in this firm, Henry Brown, were appointed as the executors and you are the sole residual beneficiary. This means that you inherit the entire estate after the payment of the costs of the estate administration, any debts and inheritance tax.

Lord Penrose's estate comprises the land, building and out-buildings of Polgarry Manor, Tremarnock, as well as its contents, and a sum of cash to the value of £670,000. One of our first tasks is to arrange for the assets in the estate to be valued so that we can work out the inheritance tax liability and how this might be settled. Once we have clear indication of what this is, we will write to you again.

If you would like to meet to discuss the estate in more detail, and indeed perhaps visit the manor, please let me know so that this can be arranged.

Yours, etc.

Bramble was so surprised that she had to re-read the letter several times to make sure that she wasn't imagining it. Perhaps it was a prank and she was secretly being filmed for a TV show. She glanced around furtively, half expecting a camera crew to leap out from under the table or behind the café counter, but no one came.

She stared at the half eaten jacket potato on her plate and tried to collect her thoughts. Polgarry Manor? It sounded so grand. And £670,000 was an absolute fortune. The figure swam in front of her making her dizzy.

'You all right?' Katie asked when she returned. 'You look like you've seen a ghost.'

Bramble slid the letter across the table and Katie sat down to read, her brown eyes growing wider by the second.

'Blimey!' she said at last, pushing back her chair so sharply that it tipped up, almost causing her to topple onto the customer behind, who spun around, scowling.

Preview

'Sorr-ee,' said Katie, with an indifferent shrug then, turning back to Bramble, 'A manor house? Cool! And all that dosh! You're gonna be rich!'

But Bramble could only manage half a smile.

'I'm scared,' she whispered. 'I feel all weird and sort of... like I'm looking down on myself from up there somewhere.' She pointed to the ceiling. 'I can't believe this is happening.'

Katie squeezed her arm. 'Don't worry, I'd be freaking out too. Polgarry Manor?' She said the name slowly, as if testing it on her lips. 'It sounds sort of romantic – and a bit spooky, don't you think? I wonder what it's like.'

Bramble nodded, scarcely able to focus, and Katie peered at her through her dense, dark fringe.

'By the way, why have you never told me about Lord Penrose? You've kept that under your hat.'

'I never met him,' Bramble explained. 'He was an oddball, eccentric. He lived alone and had nothing to do with my mother after she was born, he completely disowned her. There didn't seem any point telling you. He's never been part of my life.'

Katie took a sip of Diet Coke.

'Maybe he regretted being so mean to your mum,' she said at last. 'Maybe this is his way of saying sorry. Anyway, who cares if the miserable old git's left the lot to you?'

Bramble was about to tell her off for being disrespectful to the dead, but she didn't get the chance.

'I can picture you as Lady Muck, bossing round the servants,' her friend added with a mischievous grin. 'And by the way, where the fuck's Tremarnock?'

Preview

THE AFTERNOON SEEMED interminable, and there was no opportunity to make a phone call, not with Judy breathing down her neck. Bramble didn't want to tell her about the letter, didn't want her to know, just in case it was all a wind-up and then her boss would have a field day; she'd laugh in Bramble's face.

At about half three, when she could stand it no longer, she told Judy that she was feeling unwell.

'What's the matter?' the other woman said, narrowing her eyes, 'you were perfectly all right earlier.'

'I feel shivery. I think I'm going to throw up,' Bramble replied, burping several times; it was a skill that she'd perfected at school and it had come in very handy down the years.

Alarmed, Judy said that she'd better go home immediately.

'Don't you dare vomit on the carpet.'

Relieved, Bramble grabbed her things and hurried from the office, nodding almost imperceptibly to Katie on the end of the row of desks as she left. Katie knew the score. She was familiar with the burping trick, though she herself generally favoured the toothpaste in the eye routine. Done properly, it looked remarkably like conjunctivitis which, as everyone knew, was highly contagious.

*

BRAMBLE CAUGHT THE bus to Matt's and let herself in with her own key. It was a small flat, consisting of three rooms, just around the corner from the out-of-town industrial estate. He rented it off an older guy called Joe, who had his own carpet fitting business. Joe must have done all right because he owned several properties in the 1960s block and drove an Audi convertible, which he'd park ostentatiously in front of the main entrance, half on the pavement, half off, when he came to check on his tenants.

When Matt first took possession, he and Bramble had thought the flat a palace, but it had soon started to feel cramped with all his clobber and a fair amount of hers, too. He'd begged her to move in with him but she'd resisted.

'I'm not ready for the commitment,' she'd insisted. 'It's too soon.'

'You're twenty-five and we've been together nearly ten years,' he'd replied grumpily, 'how long do you need?'

So she'd tried a new tack, reasoning that it made more sense for her to stay at her parents' while she helped save up for a deposit to buy somewhere of their own. This had temporarily mollified him, the only problem being that her plan wasn't working too well. Thriftiness wasn't her forte and the more money she had, the more she seemed to spend. Just as well he didn't get to see her credit card bills; he'd be appalled.

She plonked down on the squishy black sofa on one side of the living room and took the phone from her bag. Matt wouldn't be home till after six and she wanted to speak to her dad first.

'Can you talk?' she asked, when she heard his gruff, reassuring voice. She needed comforting right now because she was all at sixes and sevens. 'Are you alone?'

Bill was a cab driver and always answered when she rang, but she didn't want any of his customers overhearing.

'Just dropped someone off. On my way to Surbiton now. What's up, sugarplum?'

He had a host of silly nicknames for her: honeybun, lamb chop, hoppity. Where did *that* come from?

He listened quietly while she told him about the letter, and when she'd finished, he let out a long sigh. 'Well blow me! Never thought I'd hear that old bugger's name again.'

She wasn't entirely surprised. From the little that her dad had told her about Lord Penrose, it was clear that he loathed the man. Way back in the Seventies, the story went, Bramble's grandmother, Alice, had visited the Earl at his manor with her parents when she was about seventeen and he was considerably older. He'd taken advantage of Alice's youth and naïvety and when the poor girl had found out that she was pregnant, he'd turned his back. Despite her parents' entreaties, she'd refused to have the child adopted and Bramble's mother, Mary, had grown up with Alice in the suffocating, joyless Oxfordshire house of Alice's parents, forever made to feel ashamed of her very existence.

The moment she was old enough, she'd escaped to London and found herself a job and a place to live. Soon she'd met Bill, Bramble's dad, who'd been dazzled by her beauty, wit and upper-class otherness.

'Never seen anyone like her before in my life,' he told Bramble wistfully whenever she asked about her real mum. 'She was like something out of a fairytale.'

Kind, funny, down-to-earth Bill must have seemed like

a breath of fresh air after the chilly isolation of Mary's upbringing, but sadly the marriage hadn't been a success. Bramble never heard Bill say a bad word about his first wife, but she could imagine that he'd had no idea what to do with the bewitching but highly damaged young woman he'd fallen in love with, no idea how to reach out to her.

'It was her nerves,' he used to say sadly when Bramble probed. 'She suffered dreadfully from 'em. Couldn't find peace, except in the bottle, and no good ever came of that.'

It must have been torture, watching his young wife drowning her sorrows in alcohol, while he struggled to raise their small daughter and earn enough to keep a roof over their heads. Mary's family wanted nothing more to do with her. He said he tried everything: throwing out the drink, hiding Mary's purse, even locking her in the house, but she was devious. One night she'd slipped out to join her boozing friends, fallen over the bannisters at a party and suffered catastrophic injuries. She'd never regained consciousness and had died the following day.

Bill had been heartbroken and said if it hadn't been for Bramble, he might have chosen to end it all himself. They'd struggled on for a year on their own then, thank goodness, Cassie had joined the office of the taxi firm where he worked.

'Fell in love with him the moment I set eyes on him,' she was wont to repeat to Bramble from time to time. 'It was that little boy lost look. Melted my heart, it did. And then when I met you, with your pigtails and your cheeky smile, well, that was me sold.'

Preview

Bramble could hear the noise of cars in the background, the odd hoot. It was still warm out and her dad probably had his window down. When she asked for advice, she could often guess more or less what he was going to say before he uttered a single word, but she wasn't prepared for what came next.

'We'll get that old place straight on the market. It's gone to rack and ruin, by all accounts. The sooner it's off your hands the better.'

Bramble felt a stab of disappointment and wondered why, until it dawned on her that she'd already been mentally wafting around the property, running her hands through the floor to ceiling drapes, testing out the quaint old chairs and silver cutlery, trying out the dusty beds for size.

'Do you think it's true?' she asked. 'I mean, the letter could be a hoax?'

Her father growled, a low sound like a bated bear.

'It's legit all right, you mark my words. Just the sort of thing that man would do, spring a surprise like this to throw everyone into a flat spin. Evil, that's what he was. Malevolent.'

Bramble swallowed. She trusted her dad over anyone, he always had her best interests at heart, but right now she couldn't see his point of view.

'Shouldn't we at least go and visit the place? I mean, it's not every day you inherit a manor. We might even want to do it up and live there!'

Her father snorted. 'Not on your life. You take the money and run, my girl. Buy yourself a nice new house round here, one of them detached ones on Gloucester Road, maybe, with a car port and a decent bit of garden. Enough bedrooms so you and Matt can start a family when you're ready. After you're married, I mean,' he added hastily.

'Put the rest in the bank for a rainy day and don't tell no one, *no one...*' he repeated fiercely. 'You don't want to be one of them daft types who comes into some money and goes, "Wahay", and blows it all on foreign holidays for Uncle Tom Cobley and all. I don't know what that manor's worth, not a lot is my guess, but the cash'll go soon enough if you're not careful. You should be canny. Spend just what you need and not a penny more.'

He paused. 'We'll call that lawyer fella in the morning and tell him what we've decided. There'll be someone wants a gloomy old pile in the middle of nowhere but not us, for sure. The sooner it's sold, the happier I'll be. That man caused nothing but trouble while he was breathing. I'm not having him casting a shadow over my girl now he's turned up his toes.'

When he'd rung off, Bramble leaned back and closed her eyes. For a few short hours she'd almost allowed herself to feel excited, to think that something was actually *happening* at last. She gave her herself a shake. She was coming into money, for goodness' sake, rather a lot, in fact, more than she'd ever dreamed of. As her dad said, she and Matt could get married, buy a really nice house round here and settle down. What more could she wish for?

She found herself googling three and four bed houses for sale in the area on Matt's tablet and gazing at an array of master bedrooms, en-suite bathrooms, utility rooms. Cassie would kill for one of those. She said she'd always hated having to do the ironing in the front room.

She was still eyeing up properties when Matt walked in, jangling his keys in one hand, the jacket of the pale blue suit, that they'd bought together at the designer outlet, slung over his shoulder. Matt was of medium height and solidly built, 'dependable,' Katie used to say, with a small nose, soft grey eyes and fair hair that was just beginning to recede at the sides. He was the general manager of a nearby gym, but he wasn't all that keen on using the facilities himself; he said he was more of an armchair athlete.

'Hello gorgeous,' he said, strolling over to the sofa and giving Bramble a kiss. The sleeves of his white shirt were rolled up and the collar was undone – no tie. 'Good day?'

He hadn't even time to take off his suit or grab a glass of water before she was telling him all about the letter that she produced from the bag beside her and thrust into his hands.

'My dad says I should sell the manor immediately, not even go and visit,' she said, watching impatiently while he sat down beside her to read. 'What do you think?'

Bramble and Matt had attended the same comprehensive school and had been going out together since Year Ten. He seemed to take an age to get to the bottom of the letter and when he'd finished, he scratched his head slowly and stroked his chin.

'Your dad's right,' he said at last. 'What would we want with an old ruin anyway? Even if we had enough money to do it up, I can't think of anything worse than living in some drafty hall, miles from anywhere, with hundreds of empty rooms, creaking floorboards and creepy corridors. Ugh.' He shuddered. 'There's probably loads of spiders, too.' He hated spiders.

Bramble tipped her head to one side and a strand of bleached blonde hair fell across her face. She stuck out her bottom lip and puffed it away, only for it to settle back in the same position.

'It might not be creepy, it might be amazing,' she persisted. 'We should take a look, don't you think?'

Matt rubbed his palms up and down his sturdy thighs. Bramble had always liked his thighs; they made her feel safe.

'Why would we want to leave here? We've got everything we need.'

She thought of the familiar suburban streets that she'd tramped up and down since she was old enough to walk, the high street stores that she knew like the back of her hand, the cinema, the trains that could whiz you to London's Waterloo in thirty-six minutes on a really good day, the doctor's and the bowling alley. It's true, they didn't want for anything. Yet…

She stared at him with wide open eyes and at that moment, it was as if the heavens parted and a bolt of lightning flashed through the ceiling into the little sitting room, landing on the dark grey carpet right in front of her nose.

'Stop being an old stick-in-the-mud!' she cried. 'Where's your sense of adventure? Don't you see? This could be just what we've been waiting for!'